P9-BYX-258

The

Ghost

of Greenwich

Village

Wells Memorial Library
P.O. Box 57
Upper Jay, NY 12987

The
Ghost
of Greenwich
Village

A Novel

Lorna Graham

BALLANTINE BOOKS TRADE PAPERBACKS
NEW YORK

The Ghost of Greenwich Village is a work of fiction. Names, characters, places, and incidents are the products of the author's imagination or are used fictitiously. Any resemblance to actual events, locales, or persons, living or dead, is entirely coincidental.

A Ballantine Books Trade Paperback Original

Copyright © 2011 by Lorna Graham

All rights reserved.

Published in the United States by Ballantine Books, an imprint of The Random House Publishing Group, a division of Random House, Inc., New York.

BALLANTINE and colophon are registered trademarks of Random House, Inc.

Library of Congress Cataloging-in-Publication Data
Graham, Lorna.
    The ghost of Greenwich Village : a novel / Lorna Graham.
        p. cm.
    ISBN 978-0-345-52621-2
    eBook ISBN 978-0-345-52622-9
    1. Young women—New York (State)—New York—Fiction.
2. Haunted places—Fiction. 3. Beat generation—Fiction.
4. Family secrets—Fiction. 5. Greenwich Village (New York,
N.Y.)—Fiction. I. Title.
    PS3607.R344G46 2011
    813'.6—dc22

                                                    2010048260

Printed in the United States of America

www.ballantinebooks.com

9 8 7 6 5 4 3 2 1

Book design by Caroline Cunningham

For Charley, across the table

And for my mother

There is really one city for everyone
just as there is one major love.

—DAWN POWELL, AMERICAN WRITER

The
Ghost
of Greenwich
Village

Chapter 1

Eve pressed hard against her temples and he responded by shifting a little. The pain abated for a moment, then parked itself behind her left eye. She squinted, sipped the last of the tea that had failed to calm her nerves, and set the chipped china bowl in the sink. Today of all days, she wished Donald would just get out.

"I heard that," he said, with a little buzz behind one ear. "I'm not going anyplace. And don't try to change the subject. We were talking about this 'interview' of yours and why you won't tell me whom it's with."

"Not now. I'm going to be late," said Eve. Retying her kimono around her waist, she hurried down the narrow hallway of her apartment and into her bedroom, where she pulled open the French doors of her closet and reached for the dangling chain of the overhead light. She surveyed the racks, determined to find something elegant, professional, and, most of all, lucky.

"You wouldn't need a lucky dress if you didn't pursue these nonsensical jobs," said Donald. "What was the last one? Party planner? Never heard of such a thing. Who plans a party? A guitar and a couple of blotters—there's your party. And before that?" He considered. "Selling videogames to teenagers, was it? What exactly *are* videogames?"

"Quiet," said Eve, running her palms over the rows of vintage tweed, tulle, silk, and suede that she'd inherited from her mother, Penelope. Once she'd grown into them, she hadn't had to have even one thing altered. The bounty included structured skirt suits and dainty blouses, pert kitten heels and flowing silk scarves. Her eyes fell on a peacock blue sheath by Pauline Trigère, a favorite of her mother's, and she held it up with a critical eye.

"Why on earth can't you do what I used to do?" asked Donald. "Sweep floors, wash dishes, wait tables. Sweat of your brow! Good, honest work. The kind the creative class has been doing for centuries. And think of all the time it would allow you for taking down my stories."

"For the hundredth time, Donald, this isn't the fifties," said Eve impatiently. "No one can wash dishes and afford to live in Greenwich Village anymore." She dabbed at a spot on the sheath's tulip skirt with a wet washcloth. "It's one of the most expensive neighborhoods in the city, full of bankers and lawyers. Remember? You've had them as tenants, you told me."

"What kind of job is it, then?" Donald pressed.

Eve knew that telling the truth would set him off completely, so she busied herself with the choice between skimmers and spectator pumps—a sure way to throw him off the scent.

"The cream ones with the black trim, definitely," said Donald dryly. "Fine. Don't tell me. I don't care. What we need to talk about is our next story, the one about the rubber glove that eats Manhattan. I believe I've found the beginning. The secret is to start in the middle."

Eve threw back her head and looked at the ceiling. "First of all, it's not 'our' story, it's yours. And second, I couldn't possibly take dictation now, if that's what you're hinting at. I need to focus." Usually, Eve didn't mind listening to Donald. In fact, she liked to think she was a good listener in general. But she would have preferred having the choice of when to listen and to whom.

The pain took real root now, spreading wide and deep. She needed aspirin. Not that it would help. There were so many pills on the market for so many different afflictions: muscle aches, allergies, depression. What they really needed to make was one for hauntings. "For the painful symptoms caused by the spirit of a dead man playing hopscotch across your brain synapses while complaining you won't take down his 'Pulitzer Prize–worthy' short stories," the label could say. She'd snap up a truckload.

"My, there seems no way around your peevishness today," said Donald. "But grant me a minute. This is the story I was in the middle of when I, you know, *left*." Donald never liked to admit outright that he had died, usually preferring to employ any of a half-dozen euphemisms. "And recently I realized how to get past my stumbling block. It's about this mitten that wants to be a glove. . . ." He began to prattle in earnest now, like sandpaper on the cerebellum.

Eve groaned and flung herself on her bed. The worst thing by far about being haunted was that you couldn't tell anyone about it. Well, you could if you came from one of those dramatic Southern families. Or if you were a child. But there were no ghosts among the upwardly mobile in Manhattan. Really, what would one say? "I've got six hundred square feet in an 1845 townhouse, complete with crown moldings, a fireplace—and a dead writer demanding I help him finish his life's work"?

"Are you paying any attention whatsoever?" asked Donald.

"Soon I'll have my own writing to worry about," she said. It slipped out before she could stop it, but Eve couldn't help but enjoy how the whirring in her head came to an abrupt halt as he took this in.

"What are you talking about?"

"My interview. It's for a writing job. I'm going to be a writer, too." Saying this proved immensely satisfying for some reason. "What do you think about that?"

A few moments of ominous silence followed. "There is no such thing as a 'writing job,' " Donald intoned with ostentatious gravity, a sure sign he was about to embark upon a rant. Eve put her head under a large, lace-edged pillow as he continued. "Writing is not a nine-to-five thing. It is not a way to pay rent. You either are a writer or you aren't. You either inhabit the craft or you don't. You either challenge the métier or wither. You either—"

"It's a *television* writing job," she said importantly.

"Television! *That* Pandora's box?" Instantly, Eve regretted telling him anything at all. "That which would steal our waking hours, hypnotize us with its propaganda and corporate double-speak, and drain us of our humanity? You would be a cog in that evil machine, a worker bee servicing the fat queen of mediocrity, a jabbering messenger of commercial colonization? Absolutely not—out of the question."

"As a ghost unable to muster physical form, I hardly see that you're in a position to stop me," said Eve, pulling the pillow away so she could breathe. "And anyway, if I don't land this job, we're both in trouble. I don't have next month's rent. Nothing near it. I'll be out and your stories will never see the printed page, understand? I'll have to go back home."

Her intention was to rattle Donald, but it was she who shuddered as the words came out of her mouth. She'd never really had to manage money before, and looking at her checkbook last night, she realized with horror that after only six weeks in the city, her bank account had plummeted to less than four hundred dollars. She would need several times that in the next couple of weeks for Mr. De Fief, the kind of landlord who sent burly young men around to collect the rent of any tenant who was late, as a "courtesy."

The idea of going back home was too painful to think about. She couldn't leave New York. Not yet.

She bent to open the bedroom window to air the place out now that it had stopped raining. The moisture had caused the peeling old wood to swell, and it took several good yanks to move the sash even a few inches. Eve slipped into the Trigère, enjoying the silk's structured yet soft embrace, and checked her reflection in the full-length mirror that hung by a ribbon on the back of the closet door. Her ink black bob hugged her head in becoming fashion, though shadows of worry purpled the skin beneath her large hazel eyes.

If she'd had any idea the night she decided to move to New York that soon she'd not only find a reasonably priced apartment in the Village—which everyone said was impossible—but share it with a ghost of a local writer, she would have clapped her hands with joy. She'd have reveled in elaborate fantasies of chatting cozily with Henry James, glowing softly white, complete with waistcoat and walking stick, the two of them discussing point of view in literature and French food. Or communing with Edith Wharton, who would float above the floor in a feathered hat and bustle, using her famed decorating skills to advise Eve on where to hang her nascent collection of gallery posters. Or playing poker and cracking wise with Mark Twain, his cards hovering over the table.

But no such luck. Eve had wound up with Donald Bellows, the Beatnik from Hell.

He possessed neither the others' fame nor comportment. He was insecure, irascible, and bitter about dying before completing his "crowning collection" of avant-garde stories. And he didn't even have the good grace to appear! There was no apparition hanging in the air above her bed, no doors slamming in the night, no *"Mwaaaaaaaaaaa"* coming from the dumbwaiter. All of that would have been fine, fun even; it would have lent her thoroughly modern life a sense of old-fashioned romance. But this voice inside her head, with its fizzing and churlishness? Hardly romantic.

Which was fitting because Donald himself wasn't romantic. He came from an era, he informed her, when women turned their backs on marriage and its attendant obsession with household appliances, embracing instead the life of the mind. They certainly didn't expect chivalry. And to him, chivalry extended to anything resembling politesse. There was no need for such pretense, he claimed, not among thinking people.

Eve turned to her jewelry box and mulled over her mother's collection of rhinestone earrings, holding up an outsized pair she'd first clipped to her ears when she was six. She'd always remembered the moment because when she turned from the vanity to face Penelope, her mother had looked up from her book and burst into delighted laughter, a sound rarely heard in their house.

Penelope. She, and the mystery at the heart of her life, were a big part of why Eve was here. And was determined to stay. But it was a tight calculus she was up against. No temp work would pay enough to cover the rent of even this "affordable" Village apartment, which was exorbitant by the standards of any other place. And then there were the light and phone bills. And food. Takeout was ridiculously expensive, so much so that Eve was making two meals out of every one she ordered, supplementing with cereal when she was particularly hungry. People complained about living "paycheck to paycheck." She would kill for that. She needed a real job and soon.

Eve shook her head as if to dislodge her fears. She wasn't going to be forced out. No way.

"Well, well," said Donald. "We certainly don't want you going back to the Ohio *suburbs*. Perhaps I can be of some assistance for this interview. So, tell me. What is this evil enterprise of a job?"

This was an awkward question. The truth was, Eve didn't know. She had no idea what being a writer at *Smell the Coffee*, the nation's number two morning show, actually entailed. What was there to write at a news program? She'd never watched much television and didn't even have one in her apartment. But her impression of people who delivered the news was that they just . . . talked.

Even Vadis didn't really seem to know what the job involved, and she was the one who'd set up the interview. Vadis Morales was a college friend with whom Eve had reconnected at a dinner honoring the opening of a fellow alumna's off-Broadway play. Now in their thirties, nearly all the women present that night had met with rather astonishing levels of professional success. Vadis herself owned her own Manhattan PR firm and seemed to know everyone on the island, including *Smell the Coffee*'s managing editor. She'd taken to calling Eve her first *pro bono* project and, over drinks, had assured Eve that the television job would be both easy and fabulous, a gig where you "read magazines, talk about the articles with your boss, and then go to lunch." Vadis said all this breezily but Eve sensed her friend was running out of patience with her. True, Eve had lost the first two jobs Vadis had set her up with, but to be fair, party planning and videogame sales had been wildly inappropriate matches.

"Well, let's start with what we do know," said Donald. "We know you've shown some promise as a writer, yes? All those contests you won." There had only been one contest, years ago, but Eve didn't want to dwell on that. "Though they won't actually expect you to write something *today*, I hope? We'll have a lot of work to do first."

"I appreciate that vote of confidence," said Eve. "No, I won't be writing today. This is just an interview." Which was bad enough, though, because Eve had never been on a job interview in her life. Thanks to her father, she hadn't had to.

She settled on a pair of faceted jet earrings and a cameo necklace, lamenting that New York hadn't turned out to be the easiest place to take the reins of one's fate for the first time. It was complicated, fraught, and fast; vital decisions seemed to be made and fortunes won or lost in the time it took for a yellow cab to peel away from the curb.

"You need to start thinking optimistically," said Donald. "You'll have a chance at this job, but only if you're sure of yourself," he said. "Conviction is the lifeblood of this city, whatever people tell you about money."

"Great," said Eve, slipping into a pair of slingbacks. She

yanked the string of the closet light so hard that it came away in her hand. She sank back down on the bed, a sudden attack of nerves robbing her of her vigor.

"Sarcasm and defeat hardly become you, my dear," Donald advised. "Try this for your interview. Picture how a confident person moves and adopt that posture, even if it's a complete ruse. Your back is straight, your handshake firm, your voice even."

This didn't seem particularly profound. And she'd really have to work on the voice part. Since Eve had arrived in New York, hers had almost gone hoarse from lack of use. She guessed she uttered fewer than fifty words a day, most of them to Hyo behind the counter of the deli, who raised his sparse eyebrows at her request for a "horseshoe sandwich," a favorite from home, and Mrs. Swan, her retired neighbor next door. Though anytime she was tempted to bemoan her solitude, Eve spared a thought for Donald and how lonely he must have been during the thirty-five years before she moved in.

Eve was touched that he was making an effort. She sat up straight, lifting her chin slightly. "All right."

"Second: Convince yourself that you belong. This is your city and this job is yours for the taking. Can you manage that?"

Eve exhaled. "I can try."

And she would. For both of them. Without her, Donald would never finish his story collection; that was clear. He'd tried with most of the previous occupants of Apartment 7, who either couldn't hear him or who packed their bags the moment they did. (Which explained why the place had been both available and "a deal" when Eve came along.)

What wasn't clear was whether Donald could write. Eve had minored in English, had studied reams of literature, and still she didn't know. So far, from the bit of dictation she'd taken, she didn't care for his quirky style. He wrote about everyday objects that seemed to represent other things or ideas, but what those were was never clear. His work came across as sophomoric and unnecessarily opaque. Perhaps the best thing for Donald would be to get over his childhood dreams of being a famous author—accept that he just hadn't had what it took. Move on.

On the other hand, maybe she just didn't understand his approach. The question nagged at her: What if he was actually brilliant? What if only his premature death, back in the seventies at just forty-three, had prevented him from advancing the short story to a new level and attaining worldwide fame? What if Donald belonged on the same shelves as the great New York authors, the ones whom her mother had so tenderly taught her to love at such an early age? Eve would never forgive herself if he did and she hadn't helped put him there.

And then there was the little matter of money. Donald assured her his stories would be worth more than she could spend in a lifetime. Hubristic, yes, but what if it was true?

She looked at her watch, startled by the time. Donald always ate more of it than she realized. She was in real danger of being late now, and in this town they got very huffy if you were late. She'd found that out the hard way, when she turned up four minutes past nine on the first day of the party job and nearly wasn't allowed in "as a matter of principle." She hurried into the living room, where she gathered up her coat, which was draped over one of the black leather and chrome bar stools. She retrieved her bag from the love seat and tucked it under her arm.

"Here goes nothing," she said, swinging open the front door.

"Wait," said Donald. "One more thing."

"Yes?" said Eve, stepping back inside in case Mrs. Swan entered the hallway and thought she was talking to herself again.

"If all else fails, look this interviewer in the eye and picture him—"

"Her."

"All right. Picture her—"

"Don't tell me. In her underwear?"

"I was hardly going to offer something so prosaic."

"What then?"

"Picture her as a child."

"A child?" Eve shook her head. "Why?"

"Because that's who everybody is, inside."

"Right," she said. "Well . . . thanks." She stepped onto the landing and closed the door behind her. She was off to take on the children of New York, and soon—if she got this job and kept this apartment—she'd be one of them.

As she made her way down the stairs, she felt Donald's presence growing weaker and weaker inside her, before it disappeared neatly and quietly, like water swirling down a drain.

Chapter 2

The hunched, sloe-eyed girl behind the front desk put down the phone. "Have a seat," she said. "It'll be a couple." She turned back to a list of some kind, which she attacked with a red pen.

Eve nodded, tucked her hair behind her ears, and tried to make her breathing normal after running the three blocks from the subway. Beyond the desk, the office natives slid by on their errands and drummed on their keyboards, clad in clingy black and self-assurance. After about forty minutes, a young woman so slender that the loops of blond hair piled atop her head made her look like a dandelion, strode into the waiting area.

"Let's go," she said, beckoning with fingers flapping against her palm. Eve sprang to her feet and followed the girl through large glass doors and a warren of cubicles and filing cabinets to their destination, a large, glass-fronted office belonging to Orla Knock, Managing Editor. The office lights were off, but the computer screen was emitting a dull glow from the far side of the room. The young woman sat down at an overflowing desk and nodded toward a seat, which Eve took.

"So. I'm Tanya, Orla Knock's assistant. Unfortunately, Orla had to leave for the day. She sends her apologies."

Eve felt a mix of disappointment and relief. She needed the
job but her attack of nerves began to dissipate nicely the moment
she realized the interview was off. "That's completely fine. These
things happen." She asked, reaching into her purse for her ap-
pointment book, "Shall I come back another time?"

"Actually, no. We need you to write a segment for tomorrow's
show."

Eve's hand fell out of her bag, hanging limply at her side. "Excuse me?"

"We're, um, unexpectedly short-staffed today and could really
use a pair of hands. Orla says you were referred to her as having
lots of experience."

Eve thought of her résumé with the rather large font and
wished Vadis hadn't oversold her. Again. She'd told the event-
planning director that all Eve needed was a phone and two hours
to pull together a corporate investor dinner for fifteen, and she'd
claimed to the advertising executive that Eve was bursting with
ideas about integrating videogame images into high school text-
books. Eve had lasted less than two weeks in each job.

"Well . . ." she began.

"Yes?" asked Tanya. Eve looked for the child within but saw
only probing green eyes and a sharp little crease in the brow between them.

"Well—yes. *Yes.* I have experience. Tons."

"And you watch the show?"

Eve lowered her chin in a half-nod.

"It's our hosts that you'll be writing for. Hap McCutcheon
and, of course, *Bliss Jones.*" She said this name with particular
emphasis. "So here's the deal," she continued. "Our celebrity
chef, Zorin, is doing bouillabaisse—just a little four-minute
demo at 8:36, after the weather—and we need you to write the
intro and block out the segment. Hap's handling this one. He's
not great at prop spots, so you'll have to be extra careful. Put
each and every step in his script along with the necessary graph-

ics so he can follow along with Zorin. You'll also have to go down to the studio and, since the food producer is out sick, put together a sample pot of the finished product so that everyone can taste it in the morning. Better do that first—someone said it needs to simmer a long time. The instructions were sent over by Zorin's people; they're on the kitchen counter. Oh, and for the intro, don't be too clever. Hap hates puns, alliteration, and cute turns of phrase. Questions?"

Eve remembered her mother once telling her that in New York, one minute you were on the sidewalk, the next, through the looking glass. She'd made this sound fun. But graphics? Intro? Prop spot? This did not sound fun.

Tanya widened her eyes and gave her head a little shake. "Hello?"

"No questions," said Eve.

"Then you should be on your way down to the studio. It's on the ground level, back of the building. Our director will be around somewhere. She'll show you where everything is. And when you're done with the cooking, come back up here and I'll find you a desk and get you set up on the computer. The system's a bit tricky, but since I assume you're familiar with NewsPro you should get the hang of it quickly."

Vadis's claim that the *Smell the Coffee* job was most likely a "glam gig," where you read articles and went out to lunch, now appeared to be well wide of the mark.

Tanya turned to a stack of papers on her desk. If there had been a time for Eve to mention that she knew nothing about software or television or exotic cooking, it had clearly passed. She stood. "Sounds good. Thank you."

"Don't thank anybody yet. This is just a tryout."

In the elevator, as the numbers ticked down toward the ground floor, Eve wondered how complicated bouillabaisse might be. She'd broiled plenty of steaks and chickens for her father in the years since her mother died. She'd never enjoyed it much, but if she hadn't cooked for him, he'd have subsisted on the nutrients in canned stew and Arnold Palmer iced tea.

The doors opened and a guard swept his eyes over the temporary ID badge clipped to her lapel and raised an eyebrow. When she explained she was looking for the studio, he directed her leftward and down a scuffed linoleum-floored hallway. As she reached for the double doors at the end, they were pushed open from the inside. Two stocky men in black T-shirts and headsets stopped when they saw her.

"Help you?" the taller one asked.

"I'm supposed to be working on a, um, prop spot? In the studio."

"You're in the right place. Go on in," said the first one.

After going through another set of double doors, she found herself in a cavernous, dark blue space roughly the size of an airplane hangar and cold as an igloo. She moved through the silence, feeling as if she were treading a lunar landscape. Above her, not stars, but a thousand lights of every different color, hanging from the ceiling. In various directions, tiny solar systems hugged their orbits: here a living room set, there an assortment of gym equipment, here the tiny tables and chairs of a children's playroom, there the counter and appliances of a kitchen. Eve strolled through the parallel universe, finding that its objects bore only a passing similarity to what they appeared to be. "Wood" floors were laminate painted to look like oak, "marble" was plastic, and walls that appeared solid could be knocked over with a breath.

The bookshelves were lined with a beautiful set of classics like *The Collected Shakespeare, Adventures of Huckleberry Finn,* and *Moby-Dick*. She reached for the Shakespeare, thinking she'd center herself with a sonnet or two, but the binding came away in her hand, revealing nothing more than a book-sized cardboard box.

She approached the gleaming kitchen, its counter big as a bus.

"Hey there. Where's Kevin?"

Eve turned to find an extremely tall, ebony-skinned woman

with cornrows halfway down her back and white teeth as perfect as subway tiles. "Who?"

"One of the writers. I thought he was doing this soup mess."

"I don't know. I just got here and Tanya sent me down."

"Oh, well. Hey. Welcome, then. What's your name?"

"Eve Weldon."

"I'm Lark Carmichael. Director. I'd shake your hand but I have a wicked cold," she said, dabbing at her nose with a tissue. "All the stuff is laid out for you. It shouldn't be too bad. As long as it looks good, that's all that matters. When Zorin's done pretending to cook it tomorrow, Bliss and Hap will pretend to taste it and pretend to love it. I'd help you, but I probably shouldn't handle food right now." She sneezed twice and turned to go.

"No problem. Nice to meet you," said Eve, sorry to lose her fellow space traveler so soon. She ran her eyes across the staggering array of ingredients on the counter: a dozen lobster tails, slabs of red snapper, halibut, and sea bass, and piles of shrimp, crab legs, mussels, oysters, and clams. The recipe said the entire lot was to be cleaned, cracked, de-boned, de-shelled, and de-veined. *De-lightful.*

She leaned in close, poked a finger at a set of glistening silver scales, and wrinkled her nose at the smell of raw seafood. She tried breathing through her mouth, but there were other hindrances. The cold slime of the flesh turned her fingers to ice, and the tiny bones hidden deep within put up fierce resistance to separation, driving her nearly mad with frustration. Gradually, she got used to the odor, though the halibut seemed particularly malevolent. Well, raw fish wasn't exactly known for its pleasant aroma. She briefly considered finding Lark to ask her opinion, then decided against it. If Eve had learned anything during her two forays into the New York City job market, it was that nobody wanted to hear your questions or your problems. They expected you to get on with things. Figure it out.

When she was finished, she washed her hands and bent over the directions. "Heat oil in large pot." The pot came up to her neck, but after finding a crate to stand on, this was doable. "Add garlic, onion, leeks, and bay leaf and cook until onion is tender but not browned." Check. Now, this actually smelled quite lovely, she thought, inhaling the woody steam. She was really cooking now, cooking on the moon. "Add tomatoes, fish stock, wine, fennel, saffron, salt, pepper, and parsley." Check. Check. "Bring to boil. Reduce heat and simmer five minutes. Add lobster, snapper, sea bass, and halibut and cook ten minutes. Add shellfish to pot and cook five more minutes or until shells open." Not difficult, but a little disconcerting to watch the mussels spring apart, as if expressing their horror at this ghastly turn of events with a unified silent scream.

All right now. It looked fine. Good, even. The deep red-brown broth, glistening with flecks of oil, offered up its treasures in a most inviting way. Even the halibut's nasty smell had subsided. Now she only had to "write up the segment." With no alliteration, puns, or "clever" turns of phrase, of course.

. . .

Tanya led Eve through the vast open-plan room and down a hall on the far side. They made a right turn, then a left, and then another right. They walked a good minute before going around two more bends, where they were confronted by a locked door. This Tanya opened by punching a code onto a small panel. On the other side lay another long, extremely narrow hallway. At the very end, they came to a windowless office that seemed cut off from the rest of the world. A space capsule for one. The room was a study in corporate cheerlessness: gray walls, gray carpeting, gunmetal shelving. Eve sat down while Tanya silently logged her onto the computer with a few keystrokes. As she turned to leave, Eve looked at the screen's blank page, which was divided in half vertically by a long black line and looked quite unlike anything she'd ever seen before.

"Excuse me . . . ?" Tanya turned around. Eve didn't want to admit she had no idea what to do, but this represented more daunting a challenge than some odorous fish. "Could you maybe just get me started?"

"What do you mean?"

"What exactly am I supposed to do?"

"Didn't you just make the bouillabaisse?" asked Tanya. Eve nodded. "So now, hello, just write the segment."

"Sure," said Eve, improvising. "But you know, each TV station has its own style. I just wanted to know how you do things here."

Tanya plunked her hands on her hips. "Um, not really, no. Television scripts look pretty much the same everywhere. And this isn't a 'TV station,' you realize that, right? It's a network. Jeez." She headed off down the hall. Eve stared at the strange screen, willing it to make sense. It glared back, brazen. "Okay, look." Tanya reappeared in the doorway. "The head writer's next door. His name's Mark. Maybe he can help you." As quickly as she'd materialized, she was gone again.

Eve ventured into the hall. She could hear the man in the next office talking sternly on the phone.

"Look, Steve, you sound like crap but we really need you in today. Orla Knock had some kind of meeting, so I'm editing. And guess what? Before she left, she canned Kevin." There was a pause. "No, I'm not joking. Apparently I'm now responsible for helping some new freelancer through the drill and then I'm supposed to report to Orla on how she does. So that's an extra hour out of my day. We're spread way too thin and all we need is more grief from Giles about this department. So really, buddy, get your ass in here. Thanks." He hung up.

Eve knocked and pushed the door open. "Uh—hello, are you Mark?" she said. "Sorry to bother you, but I'm about to write a—um, segment—and I'm ready to go and everything, but . . ." Mark shuffled through some newspapers on his desk and seemed intent on ignoring her. "I was wondering if you could just give me a push?"

Finally, he looked up. He was close to forty, she guessed, with a long, lean frame, pronounced bones in his face, and long dark lashes. He stared a moment before speaking, seemingly thrown, as if her appearance did not match what he'd been expecting.

"So you're Kevin's replacement," he said. "I couldn't believe they found someone so fast." He wiped the back of his hand across his forehead. "That's the thing about the networks, man. They can abuse you any way they want because people are literally lined up to take your place."

"I wouldn't say I was 'lined up.' And anyway, Tanya was quick to let me know this is just a tryout."

"Well, that's the way it works around here. Unless you come over from the *Today* show or *GMA*. You didn't, did you?"

"No."

"So." He pulled a piece of paper off a stack. "By my calculations, you must be bouillabaisse. I knew when I saw Kevin's name down for that one he was going to have a fit. I didn't have a clue he'd actually make a stink with Orla, though. Let's go back to your computer and see what's what." He brushed past her and they went back to her office. "So, where have you worked?" he asked, sitting down at her desk. She said nothing. "Damn, this thing's slow." He hit the side of the monitor with the flat of his hand. "Which news software are you familiar with?"

Eve couldn't look him in the eye, so she settled for his nose. "I can't remember what it was called."

"But you've written news scripts before, right?"

Eve wrapped her arms around her waist.

He pushed back from the desk. "You've got to be kidding. What, you just walked in off the street and said, 'Hi, I'd like a job in TV'?"

"Hardly—"

"May I assume you're a print journalist, then?"

"I was published in my college paper."

"This just gets better and better. You had a byline? A column?"

Did he really need to be this disagreeable? "It was an excerpt of a paper I wrote."

"*Fabulous*. About what?"

"An examination of Toulouse-Lautrec's influence on Modigliani. It won second place in a southern Ohio college essay contest." Eve tried to infuse this line with a sense of relevance.

He kicked the desk. "Christ, are you for real?"

Eve looked for the little boy inside her interrogator, but once again, it was only a tetchy adult who glared back at her. A clock on the wall ticked the seconds. She saw it all slipping away—the job, the apartment, everything. "Look, a friend set up this meeting with Orla Knock. That's how I got in. But I'm here now and you need help," she said quietly but firmly. "Can we just see how it goes? I really can write."

He sighed. "This is nuts," he said. He looked at his watch and mumbled something. "Fine, whatever. Can't *wait* to see what you can do. I'm setting up the page. Here, on the right, is where you'll write what Hap says to introduce the segment. That's called the 'intro.'"

"So let me get this straight," she said after watching him work for a few moments. "I write what this man is going to say?"

"Um, yeah. Everything you hear a network anchor say was written by a union writer, except when they ad-lib, which is usually an unmitigated disaster. Sometimes they rewrite what we write, but they almost never start from scratch."

"So we're . . . their voices?"

"I suppose, but for God's sake never say that again." He pointed to the screen. "Now, see here? At the bottom? The computer will tell you how long your copy runs when spoken. If the rundown—that's this sheet that has the whole show on it—says your intro should be twenty seconds, write twenty seconds. Exactly. No more, no less."

"Does it have to be exact-exact?" she asked. "Isn't the show two hours long or something?" She didn't want to trigger any more animosity with her questions, but curiosity got the better of her.

"You're a walking faux pas machine." He closed his eyes and shook his head again. "Timing a live show is unbelievably complicated. First of all, there are, like, a thousand elements: the segments, the commercials, the bumpers, the teases, the 'hello' pages." Eve wished she had a pen to take notes. "Plus, twice an hour, the computer takes the network off the air and goes to the local news and weather cut-in. If the anchor's still blabbing away because you wrote too much, or put in too many questions for him to ask, it looks really ugly having him disappear from the screen mid-sentence. On the other hand, if you write too little, and leave the host with nothing to say and time to fill, let's just say don't bother coming into work ever again."

"I see," said Eve. *Who would want this job?* "And how am I supposed to come up with precisely twenty seconds about bouillabaisse?" she asked. "Could I ask Hap McCutcheon what he'd like to say?"

"You're elevating my blood pressure," said Mark distractedly as he tapped on the keyboard. "No, you cannot ask Hap or Bliss what they want to say. You'll probably never even meet them. They work mornings; we work nights. I've been here four years and I'm sure neither of them could pick me out of a police lineup."

This was starting to sound like a very strange arrangement, writing for people you didn't know. Rather like choosing an outfit for someone you'd never seen. But Eve had to admit this Mark was slightly more obliging than her two previous New York bosses, and she decided she ought to be grateful. "Got it," she said.

"It's *your* job to figure out how to interest the American people in some foreign soup with a hard-to-pronounce name. At eight-thirty in the morning. No one else's."

"Okay."

"So—go to it." He stood up and motioned for her to take the chair behind the desk.

Eve took her seat, thinking hard about bouillabaisse. *Bouillabaisse. Bouillabaisse.* "Well," she began. "I guess the name itself is appealing."

"Because?" he said, looking at his watch again.

"It sounds glamorous. It makes me think of sophisticated French people sitting around in striped T-shirts and neck scarves on the shores of the Mediterranean." She'd been there as a child during a family trip to France. Her mind strayed further as the reverie took hold. "They're under the stars, drinking red wine. They're laughing—at a political joke. Or a Jerry Lewis reference maybe. And they're eating this wonderful bouillabaisse, big steaming bowls of fish and fragrance." She opened her eyes.

He nodded a little impatiently. "Okay. But now imagine you're a mother of four in Indianapolis."

"Why?"

"She's our target audience. You have to make her obsessed with making this soup. And to her, that fantasy sounds intimidating. These French political joke makers are so urbane and this bouillabaisse sounds pretty complicated."

Eve jumped in. "Oh, but it's not. I just made it, down in the studio. All by myself. I mean, it took a while because I was making a large amount. But for a normal dinner party, I think it'd be pretty easy."

"All right," he said. "Take those two ideas and put them together. Most intros are a combination of two contrasting ideas. See what you come up with. Make it conversational and of course mention Zorin at the end. Show me when you're done."

Just then, Tanya popped her head in, looking irritated. "Hey, it's time for your pre-interview with Senator Farnsworth. You're not at your desk and his aide is giving me all kinds of grief."

"ShitShitShit. Okay." For an instant, his commanding demeanor seemed to slip. He threw a glance at Eve and left.

A senator on the phone? Great Scott. Eve was relieved to have only soup on her plate, or in her bowl, as it were. She perched her fingers on the keyboard but all the ideas she'd had evaporated. Striped shirts? Beaches? What had she been thinking? Either her attention span had shrunk to nil or Donald had messed with her brain's wiring somehow. Or maybe this job—writing a handful of very specifically tailored sentences—was just too difficult.

She thought of her job back home. The paralegal work she did for her father, Gin—taking notes during depositions, summarizing documents, and preparing reports—came easily. It always had. Only lately had that effortlessness begun to feel constraining. But it had been weeks and weeks since she'd done even that, and she was feeling rusty.

Her fingers hovered above the keys. Donald rarely seemed to have a problem getting started. What was it he said about writer's block? Ignore it. Write your way round it.

She began to type, slowly at first, before picking up steam as her dormant skills roused themselves. She looked down at the computer timer: Her first attempt had yielded four minutes of copy. She began to play with the words—adding, subtracting, and changing their order as if stringing them on the add-a-pearl necklace she had when she was twelve. But no matter how much she reworked it, she kept winding up with twenty-two seconds. She had to lose three words, but which ones? "Rich and delectable"? Or "hearty yet elegant"? It was a linguistic *Sophie's Choice*. Half an hour later, she printed her best effort.

(HAP:)

BOUILLABAISSE. THE VERY NAME
CONJURES UP SUMMERS ON THE
MEDITERRANEAN, AND THE RICH
FLAVORS OF ITS SEAFOOD. IT'S
DELICIOUS AND EXOTIC—THE

PERFECT DISH TO SERVE FRIENDS
AT YOUR NEXT DINNER PARTY . . .
IF ONLY IT WEREN'T SO DIFFICULT
TO MAKE. WELL, GUESS WHAT? IT'S
NOT. IN FACT, YOU CAN THROW IT
TOGETHER IN LESS THAN AN
HOUR, AND EVEN HAVE TIME LEFT
OVER TO TOSS A SALAD BEFORE
YOUR GUESTS ARRIVE.
IIERE TO SHOW US JUST HOW EASY
IT IS IS CHEF ZORIN.

Eve went out into the hallway. The other office doors were now open, and she could hear the low sounds of conversations and typing. Before knocking on Mark's door, she overheard what appeared to be the last of his discussion with the senator.

"I can't promise you that Bliss will ask you that exact question, sir." Pause. "Yes, I realize that, but as you know from your previous appearances on *Smell the Coffee,* she tends to do her own thing." Another pause. "I understand you want to discuss your wife's new charity, and I will include a question about that, but it's impossible to guarantee—" A few moments of silence followed before he said a polite "Thank you" and hung up. Eve knocked lightly and pushed the door open.

"That was fast," said Mark. He waved her into a chair. Silently, he took the page from her and ran his eyes over it, frowning slightly in concentration as he did so. "This isn't awful." He raised his eyebrows. "I think we can work with it."

Eve took the first real breath since she'd arrived.

"Now let's go through the rest." Mark showed her how to convert Zorin's recipe into a script so that Hap could follow along. They put the list of ingredients on the left side of the page, and on the right side, questions for Hap to ask, like "That smells great. What goes in next?" and "Can you substitute pike for red snapper?" and "Will you think I'm a wimp if I tell you I don't like cayenne?"

When they were done, he leaned back in his chair. "All right, Toulouse-Lautrec. You just eked out a segment."

"I couldn't have done it without you," she said.

"True. But listen, next time, you'll have to come up with all the interview questions on your own, okay? That's part of the job."

Eve nodded. "You think there'll be a next time?"

"Well, it's up to Orla, of course. And she's hard to predict. She can be really tough—she fired someone just today, for God's sake. But she can be surprisingly supportive if you press the right button. Though if she gets a chance to read your résumé and realizes you're not a newsperson . . ." Thankfully, Mark abandoned this train of thought. "But look, we do lots of non-news stuff around here. And you did a decent job with the writing, so it should be fine. I'm a bit surprised by your aptitude, actually. I'll talk to Orla tomorrow after the show and we'll go from there."

"Thank you," said Eve.

"One piece of advice. If you do wind up coming aboard, make sure to watch the show *every* morning."

"Are you kidding?" Eve said. "I can't wait to hear my words on national television." As she said this, she realized it was true. What an incredible experience it must be. Even Donald couldn't say he knew what that was like.

A small laugh bubbled up in Mark as if she had just said something childish. "I guess. But the real reason is so you'll know which way to come into work."

"Subway versus taxi?"

"Elevator versus stairs. If your segment went well, you can come up in the elevator and walk in the front way." Eve didn't want to hear the corollary. "But if it goes badly—whether it's Bliss's fault, Hap's fault, Lark's fault, Zorin's fault, or even God's fault—do not take the elevator. Come up the fire stairs, check the halls for anyone even remotely resembling one of the senior-level producers, make for your office and keep your head down."

"Okay." It sounded like a war zone.

"Hey, like I said, you should be fine. Now go on home." He stood up and offered his hand, squinting at her temporary ID. "I didn't get your name. Does that say . . . *Eventual?*"

"Everyone calls me Eve," she said.

"Ah. Pretty." The way he looked at her, she couldn't quite tell if he was talking about her appearance or her name. "Anyway, sorry about before. I didn't mean to be rude. It's just sort of stressful around here, and the writers . . ."

"That's okay."

"Guess we'll be seeing you soon." Finally, there was a small smile and Eve realized that on closer inspection, Mark was more handsome than she'd realized.

Chapter 3

Taxis clustered along Seventh Avenue like bouquets of yellow tulips, and Eve plucked the closest. She hummed as she looked out the window at the enchanted Manhattan she'd come to know in the last few weeks, a Narnian landscape of strange, wild creatures. There were no trolls exactly, but there was the lumbering, grunting super of her townhouse who enforced recycling rules with shocking ferocity. Down on Wall Street, executives with the bodies of men and the heads of bulls bellowed their deals on street corners, while the streets played home to bike messengers who whizzed by like sprites, barely missing pedestrians and dancing off, laughing at the mayhem in their wake.

The fare came to $6.35. Flushed with triumph, Eve handed the driver a ten and told him to keep the change as she hopped out onto the slate sidewalk of Perry Street, enjoying, as always, the sight of her slightly shabby townhouse with its wrought-iron gate and steep stoop.

It was after eight in the evening and she was starving. She contemplated sushi to celebrate her good fortune, but instead resigned herself to getting upstairs. She wanted to tell Donald everything that had happened. And she had some leftover moo shu shrimp in the fridge. As she made her way up the burgundy-carpeted stairs and past the coffin corners decorated with bud vases, each holding a single silk rose, she heard the faint sound of whining. The higher she climbed, the louder it grew. On the top floor, her neighbor's door stood open.

"Mrs. Swan? Are you all right?" She heard the old woman's customary heavy-footed walk and then she appeared, clad in a tie-dyed T-shirt, long denim skirt, and clogs, her flowing gray hair submitting halfheartedly to the confines of a topknot. She leaned heavily on her cane.

"Thank goodness you're back." Her heavy-lidded blue eyes searched Eve's. "You're usually home and I've been trying to . . . anyway, how are you, dear?"

"I'm extremely well. What's the trouble?"

"It's this little thing here." Mrs. Swan stepped aside, revealing a pointy-nosed puppy covered in speckled fur of black, white, and brown shivering behind her in the doorway. The dog continued to whimper for a moment, made a hiccupping noise, and fell silent.

"Whose is it?"

"You know the boys downstairs? The ones who always leave hockey sticks in the hallway?" Eve knew them. Four hulking twenty-somethings whose music pumped out from behind their front door in waves and for whom the hall served as a locker room. She still had a bruise on her knee from tripping over their equipment. "Apparently, they were late with the rent. Only three or four days, but that was enough for De Fief. He didn't even send a letter first this time."

"Really?"

Mrs. Swan took a few steps into the hallway and peered over the railing. "He's famous for harassing tenants," she said in a low voice. "If he decides he wants you out, it can get pretty nasty."

"What does he do?"

"We've seen it all. Cutting off the heat, threatening phone

calls in the middle of the night. The works. With the boys, he had some thugs 'escort' them out with about fifteen minutes' notice."

"He can do that?" asked Eve.

"Apparently he can," said Mrs. Swan, shaking her head. Eve glanced down at the dog, and Mrs. Swan remembered what they were talking about. "Anyway, all of a sudden there's a pounding on my door and one of them is standing outside with the dog and a bag of food, saying they have to vacate, they have no idea where they're going and are probably going to have to split up and can I please take the puppy. He seemed absolutely desperate, so what could I do?" The pup peeked out from behind Mrs. Swan's knee.

"Poor thing. It can't be more than what? Two months old?"

"Well, I really don't know much about dogs. I've asked everyone else in the building if they could take her, and so far, nada. I can't because my hip surgery's finally come through."

"Congratulations!" Eve gave Mrs. Swan a quick hug. The old woman had been waiting for months.

"Thank you. The thing is, I'll be in the hospital for a week and then I'll be staying with my daughter in New Jersey for several months, maybe longer. You can probably see where this is going. I thought you might know someone who—"

"I can take her." The words were out of Eve's mouth before she could think.

"Could you? I know it's a lot to ask, but you're home quite a bit. . . ."

Eve decided not to disclose her new status as New York career woman. She knelt down to get a better look at the dog.

"What's the matter, sweetie? You shy?" The dog shrank back. "What's her name?" Eve asked Mrs. Swan.

"No one knows. Guess it'll be up to you."

Eve liked dogs. She hadn't had one growing up because of her mother's allergies, but her parents had run with a rather horsey set, and since horsey sets inevitably comprised dog people, many a long afternoon at the Watsons' or Giffords' had been passed in the pleasant company of a retriever, beagle, or spaniel. Plus it was spring now and it would be most pleasant to stroll the Village with a well-behaved dog at her heel. Wasn't it a tenet of city life that dogs brought people together?

"What do you think, fuzzball? Want to come next door?" Eve snuck a hand under the dog's belly and picked her up gently. The pup struggled, her little legs flailing wildly.

Mrs. Swan pulled out a shopping bag filled with dog food, toys, and a leash. "From the boys' apartment."

"Thanks," said Eve, looping the bag over her wrist.

"I should warn you, she's a bit stressed. Howling like a banshee. Post-traumatic stress maybe."

Eve slid her three keys into their appointed locks and opened her door a crack. "She seems okay now. I'm sure it'll be fine. . . ." She felt a claw nick the underside of her chin. As she set the dog on the floor of her apartment, Mrs. Swan lumbered forward.

"Let me come in with you. It might help her transition—"

"Actually, it's not a good time." Eve felt her heart race. She'd long dreaded the moment when someone would ask to visit. Donald would no doubt pull something and send the person running for the hills. Or for their nightmare landlord. Luckily, New Yorkers seemed content to live mere feet from each other for decades without setting foot in one another's homes. "I'm having a plumbing problem. There's water on the floor and—"

Mrs. Swan's eyes flew open wide. "We have to call Vladimir immediately! He'll come in the evening if it's an emergency. Flooding is dangerous; it can weaken the whole building." To Eve's horror, Mrs. Swan began to push past her. Just as unbelievably, Eve found herself stepping in to block the old woman's path. Their thin arms were actually pressed against one another and they looked into each other's face, eyes widened with mutual incredulity.

"No!" said Eve. "I mean I've cleaned up the water. Everything's fine now. It actually wasn't a leak. I just spilled a pot of water, that's all. But it's all cleaned up. The problem is, I'm expecting a call. Transatlantic." The puppy, apparently distressed at the commotion, began to whine again. "Shhh. It's going to be okay," Eve soothed. "Don't you worry, Mrs. Swan. I'll take good care of her. But I do have that call now."

Eve stepped inside and pushed the door shut with deliberate force, hearing Mrs. Swan stumble backwards. She surely thought Eve had gone insane, but, thanks to Donald, who might just find popping into the old woman's head a refreshing change of pace from Eve's—likely scaring her into an early grave—there was nothing to be done about it.

Eve tried to carry the puppy down the hall, but the little thing jerked and kicked as if suffering an epileptic fit. Hot breath assaulted Eve's face and scratches multiplied along her arms. "Stop it now, honey." She put the dog down and crossed the noisy, complaining floorboards to the galley kitchen, where she retrieved her china bowl from earlier and filled it with cold water.

"Come here. Have something to drink." The dog began to whine again. "Well, I'm certainly going to." Hands shaking, Eve fixed herself a highball of bourbon and soda at her tiny art deco bar by the window that overlooked the courtyard. Shaped like a half-moon and covered in somewhat dulled black lacquer, it had been the only piece of furniture in the apartment when she moved in, and it was, except for the bed, still the one she used with the most regularity.

The bitterness and fizz of the drink were wonderful. "Donald?" Eve murmured his name but received no answer. He was "out" and there was no way of knowing when he was coming back. He wasn't always able to control his status. He came and went, staying for minutes or hours, with little rhyme or reason, and this had made their initial introduction more than a little alarming. A couple of weeks after she'd moved in, she started hearing a faint voice in her head. It wasn't her voice—that was for sure. It had a different cadence; it employed a different vocabulary. She had never in her life used words like "exfluncticate" or "slumgullion."

Usually the voice went away after a few moments and she half thought she'd imagined it. Then one day, as she sprinkled hot sauce on some enchiladas, a violent itch sprang up on the right side of her head. She dug her short red-polished nails into the skin and scratched hard, but the tickle was so deep she couldn't get anywhere near it. She scraped and scraped. Nothing. It was intolerable. Then the words came, from the exact place from which the itch had sprung. She heard them, but strangely: from the inside out, instead of the outside in. They came on strong, then faded, like a radio station flirting with the tuner. *EEEE-wshhhhhh. EEEE-wshhhhhh.* Some static, then a man's somewhat metallic speech: "Must protest the homogenization—" More static. "Subjectivity brought about by—" Then some words she couldn't make out, and finally, "—MEDIA SATURATION AND POP PSYCHOLOGY!"

"Ohhhhhh!" Eve screamed and jumped violently, shaking a plume of sauce high in the air. A drop landed in her left eye; the burning was excruciating. She felt her way to the bathroom, where she rinsed her eyes. In the bedroom, she sat down at her vanity table. She moved her eyes all the way around in their sockets, working them steadily into each corner, trying to look back into her head. But her eyes, perhaps flummoxed at being called upon to monitor the very brain that operated them, reported nothing more than blurry darkness.

She must be insane. Schizophrenic. She broke out in a cold sweat.

"Relax." The voice was coming in clearly but gently now. "There's nothing wrong with you."

"Who . . . what . . . are you?"

"No need to yell. No need to speak, even. I can hear your thoughts and they're much more interesting than your words.

I've been listening to them for days now. Finally, I got you to hear mine. I'm just sorry it was one of my rants. Really, they're quite rare." The voice paused and there was an apologetic little chuckle. "Look, dear. I realize this is a bit of a shock. Why don't you take a few deep breaths and I'll introduce myself properly?" Feeling a bit silly, Eve closed her eyes and breathed deeply several times. After a few moments of silence, he began again. "Eventual Weldon," he said with a flourish, "I am Donald Bellows." He said it with the pride of a three-star chef pulling a metal dome off a signature dish. He paused, waiting for a response. "Ring a bell?"

"Honestly, no. Should it?"

With a sigh like a breeze inside her mind, he began his story. His words were like tiny toes, skipping from nerve cell to nerve cell in her brain, sometimes tickling, sometimes pinching slightly and making her squint. Donald explained that he was a writer who'd lived in the Village on and off from the fifties to the seventies. In Eve's very rooms, he'd penned some of his most meaningful work. He drew a picture in her head of himself at his rolltop desk, which sat where her bar resided now, listening to the same London plane tree pulling its bony fingers across the window.

As he spoke, something dawned on Eve. Her mother had lived in the Village in the sixties. Maybe she and Donald had known each other.

"I don't remember anyone by that name," he said in answer to her unspoken question. "I'm sorry."

Donald's description of his life as an artist went on for a good hour more, but it was rambling and far from complete. So, a few days later, overcome with uncertainty as to whether this was a real person or if she had dreamed the whole thing, Eve had gone to the Jefferson Market library. It wasn't her first visit to the turreted red-brick building with its dramatic cupola that looked like a small castle on Sixth Avenue. Since she'd moved to New

York, she'd prowled its racks a number of times. The library boasted several shelves on local lore, and Eve devoured the books, hoping, even though she knew it was ridiculous, to find something about her mother.

Penelope had died when Eve was just eight, and even though it wasn't true, it often felt to Eve at that young age as though everyone had forgotten Penelope quite quickly, her clothes packed away almost instantly by a couple of her churlish cousins and her beautiful name rarely uttered in the house. But though Eve had lost her mother before she was old enough to really know her, there was one thing that she understood: Penelope had been truly happy only once in her life—long before Eve was born, during the two years that she'd lived in Greenwich Village. During that time, she'd known many writers, and Eve thought maybe, just maybe, one of them had put her in a story or memoir. Eve would be grateful for any scrap, any glimpse of her mother during those times. So far, though, she'd found nothing.

But on this day, it was all about Donald. She made her way through the aisles, so much like those at the libraries she'd grown up with: airy, dignified, gracious in repose. At last she found a dusty volume entitled *Mid-Century Writers East of the Hudson and West of Sixth Avenue,* which contained one relevant passage.

Donald Bellows of Perry Street, 1932–1976, is counted among the West Village writers, postwar, sub-Beat-generation division.

Eve smiled. This explained some of Donald's amusing hipster expressions, like "daddy-o" and "strictly dullsville."

Unlike many of his contemporaries, Bellows never became a household name. Flat feet kept him out of combat, but during the Korean War he was briefly tasked by the military with creating propagandist fiction to "sell" the conflict to war-weary, post-WW2 America. The bulk of his career is believed to be a reaction to that straitjacket assignment in that he declared he would never again write with restrictions. In the fifties, Bellows existed on the fringe of the Beat crowd. When the Beats went west (to San Francisco), he went east—to Europe. Though he enjoyed a minor, almost-cult-type success among a handful of members of the avant-garde while living, he was never taken to the breast of a large readership, and it's not clear whether he inspired any acolytes who sought to push forward with his ideas. Bellows is, however, credited with attempting a potentially exciting, subversive form of fiction in which everyday objects become symbols, which play a part in seemingly simple narratives with deceptively nuanced meanings. They are also noted for containing little emotion and requiring a great deal of patience on the part of the reader. However, in his lifetime, this unique style remained more of a germ without developing into an established genre, and its value was never determined.

The next time they spoke, Donald explained to Eve that his greatest regret was "disappearing" before completing a particular collection of short stories that he felt was sure to seal his reputation.

"How—how *did* you . . . you know . . . ?" she asked.

"Brain hemorrhage. At least I think so. On a wonderful spring day, too. I'd just had eggs and toast at La Bonbonniere on Hudson—is it still there?—and I'd come home feeling the world was ripe with promise. I was ready to dive into some new stories, and maybe make some changes in my life." He trailed off here but his tone suggested this was not a tangent to be pursued. "Anyway. I came home and went into the bedroom. I felt a splitting pain in my head and suddenly my teeth were in the floor. For a moment, I saw the world through a keyhole. Then someone covered the keyhole."

"Where are you buried?"

"I don't know."

"Why not?"

"I hadn't made any arrangements. And I didn't have any family. At least none that I was speaking to." He paused thoughtfully. "Maybe that's why I'm here. My spirit, or energy or whatever it is, doesn't know where to go."

After a few moments of respectful silence, Eve raised the question that had just occurred to her. "You passed in 1976, you said?"

"Yes," said Donald. "Were we alive at the same time?"

"Barely. I was born in '74."

"I suppose if we'd met back then, we wouldn't have had much to say to one another."

Eve smiled, grateful he'd lightened the mood.

Donald continued with his tale. He was gone, but not *gone*. While incapable of a physical presence, in a small measure of consolation, and only after what he imagined were years of practice, he'd found that his current state, which was best likened to a rhythm of energy, could be made to move in sequence with brainwaves. This made possible a kind of rudimentary communication with any person, as long as he or she stood within his four walls, presumably where his force was most concentrated. But it wasn't always easy.

"I tell you, most psyches are frenzied thickets. The young CPAs and stockbrokers who've lived here—they're the worst. Their brains process tax returns and balance sheets in their sleep. I couldn't even *begin* to scale their retaining walls of useless information."

With Eve, it hadn't been exactly easy either, he'd said. Her mind was open and pliant but too full of other writers and artists. But though he'd been prepared to loathe her as much as his previous tenants, he had admitted that he'd come to enjoy her company. She might be young; she might be silly. She might have gone an entire college career without reading him. But her whimsical outlook and habit of anthropomorphizing everything around her reminded him of his early writing, her way of turning things upside down and inside out played to his ideas of deconstructing language, and her stream of consciousness (which was all he was privy to, for he could not mine her memories unless she called them up) was quite amusing. She'd helped him pass quite a few lonely nights since she'd arrived on the scene, and he found himself thankful. Not to mention that she was the instrument through which his legacy could finally be cemented.

In their time together, Eve had found something to appreciate in Donald, too. Namely companionship. Despite coming from a large family, she was essentially a solitary person; her childhood home had rarely been a place of comfort. With three siblings, she might have been lost in the shuffle anyway, but she also had the misfortune of being born thoughtful in a house of bluster. Bill, Bryce, and Baines had dominated their Victorian with races and belches, toys stuffed down toilets, and pranks like slugs inside her school shoes. There was no real bullying, but neither was there much intervention on the part of their parents. They tended to treat the children rather like charges at a small summer camp: As long as everyone was up and dressed in the morning and had bathed and said their prayers before bed, all was well.

This hands-off approach was born largely from their father, Gin, being a workaholic, and the fact that their mother's life seemed to take place mostly in her head. Penelope wasn't sad, exactly, more like withdrawn. While she wore the "lady of the house" mantle well, she always seemed to be somewhere else, as if watching an unseen movie. She performed the regal chores of a woman of leisure: tending orchids, restoring antiques, and rearranging furniture, all the while singing scraps of songs and uttering words from some long-ago, or perhaps imaginary, conversation.

Mostly, though, you'd find her in her room, reading her New

York stories: *Breakfast at Tiffany's* by Truman Capote, *Here Is New York* by E. B. White, Edith Wharton's *Age of Innocence*, and, her favorites, the many books by Dawn Powell. Under the rose-print canopy of her bed, she whiled away the hours with books spread around her like friends at a ladies' lunch. On weekends, Gin would usually have the boys out hunting or camping, while Eve was left with Penelope. When she was very young, Eve would sit on the floor next to her mother's bed, acting out stories with her dolls. As she grew older, books became her companions, too, and she leaned against the bedpost absorbed in the tales of Enid Blyton or C. S. Lewis. Eventually, she worked her way up to Laura Ingalls Wilder and up onto the bed itself, where she lay reading, looking up every few pages at the curve of her mother's slender back.

Sometimes Eve felt a stab of pain that if ghosts existed, why couldn't it be her mother who came to her? But she and Donald had settled into a mostly harmonious rapport. Like many twosomes, they enjoyed a remarkable knack for maintaining equilibrium. When one despaired, say, over being dead, the other extolled the silver lining of not having to put up with telemarketers. And when the other grew angry about street noise, for instance, the first might gently remind about the pleasures afforded by being able to stroll a museum.

They came up with a system of rituals and boundaries. Donald never eavesdropped on Eve's telephone conversations; she picked up a tattered book of his early essays at the Strand. He stifled complaint when she pulled out the odd mystery; she agreed to take dictation of his unfinished works. They were something like an old married couple, without the fights over sex and money.

There were, however, a couple of problems with their arrangement. Anything she wanted to keep private, Eve could think about only when she was out of the apartment. When she found herself unable to stop mulling something delicate while at home, she'd pick up a book or magazine and read it aloud, silencing her inner monologue. Living this way was a bit like keeping two overlarge pancakes separated on a grill, and it didn't always work. The whole situation would have exhausted her utterly except that Donald spent so much time "away." Perhaps he slept or perhaps he traveled, but either way he was "gone" much of the time.

Another snag was that Eve could never invite anyone over. Not that she'd had occasion to yet. But her dearest wish was to have a gang of New York friends, like her mother had. And when she finally did, well, she could hardly host a cocktail party or dinner. If she explained about Donald, her guests would think she was crazy. If they actually "met" him, they'd call the police or an exorcist or something. As long as she lived in this apartment, Eve knew, she would be in some sense isolated from the city she had come so far to be part of. But until she had a good bit more money saved up, she wouldn't be able to move out.

"*What is that?!*" Donald yelled suddenly. Startled, Eve almost fell off her bar stool. Her drink swirled dangerously close to the edge of the glass.

"What's what?" she asked, her heart beating fast.

"The thing you've brought into this apartment."

For a moment, Eve had no idea what he was talking about. Then she remembered. "You mean the puppy?" She looked around but the dog was hiding.

" 'You mean the puppy?' " Donald repeated, his tone dripping with mockery. "I mean whatever thing it is that's introduced another set of—albeit rudimentary—brainwaves to this space. They've completely thrown me off. I've had a killer time getting through."

"I'm sorry. I had no idea she'd present a problem." Eve explained about the hockey boys and their untimely exit. "She needs a home. Please don't be difficult about this." Donald paused, and Eve thought her bid for sympathy had worked.

"It's not enough that I departed the world at a young

age. . . ." He began what promised to be a classic tirade, which would inevitably include references to rejections from various literary magazines and non-wins of prizes. Several minutes later he concluded, ". . . but then I opened my home to you as well. And now this."

Eve wanted to remind him that it was a real estate broker who'd "opened his home," and that without her, he'd never finish his stupid stories. But she was feeling generous after her successful afternoon, so she opted for conciliation. "No doubt about it, you've faced more than your share of injustices. So why don't we do a little dictation now? About 'The Handbag That Swallowed Midtown' or whatever."

"I am not fooled. And I am not mollified. But luckily for you, I am eager to get back to my work." Donald's narcissism made him an easy mark for a gambit like this. "We'll get back to the mutt later. But for now, let me prepare myself and we'll begin." Several moments of silence followed, during which Eve found the notepad she'd been using for their work. She placed it on the bar and waited. Finally, he began. "The glove was thick and snappy, like a surgeon's. It stretched and loomed, high above Gotham. . . ."

As she scribbled, Eve wondered if the story was as odd as it appeared or whether she was taking it down wrong. The words on the page looked at each other as if even they knew they didn't belong together. She was just about to interrupt when the puppy made a noise. The sound began in the back of her throat, a low, pained murmur. Eve stiffened.

Donald, of course, was unaware of anything but his own brilliance. ". . . The glove's fingers are bulbous, dangling ominously above the Chrysler Building. . . ."

"Hang on a moment—"

The dog's mewling grew more pained and intense. Eve knelt down on the floor, trying to tune out Donald and soothe her.

"I know, I know, you're in a new place and it's scary. . . ."

". . . The citizens of New York look up to the sky, wondering if the glove came from Bloomingdale's. . . ."

"Donald, please. Give me a moment."

Eve reached out to pet the dog but she leapt away, hitting her head on the coffee table. Her yelp filled the room. *"Arauuu!"*

"Oh, sweetheart. Let me see what's wrong—"

"—The glove is expanding, as though someone is blowing into it. Now it covers Central Park, now the Upper West Side—"

"Shhhh."

As Eve reached out again, the dog threw her neck back like a coyote under a full moon. There was a dramatic pause before she let out a heartbreaking yowl. Perhaps it was a delayed reaction to losing the only family she'd ever known, if four sloppy, thoughtless boys counted as family.

"Arauuuuuuuuuuuu. Arauuuuuuuuuuuu."

"Quiet, doggy, now—"

"—The glove is beginning to block out the sun, shadows fall darkly on the island—"

"—Donald—"

"Arauuuuuuuuuuu."

"—Everyone is running for a taxi—"

"Arauuuuuuuuuuuuuuuuuuuuu."

"—But the taxis have all turned red—"

"Arauuuuuuuuuuuuuuuuuuuuuuuuuuuuuuu."

"—Red, the color of death—"

Eve sat down heavily on the floor, covering her face with her hands. There was absolutely nothing, she decided, as wretched as the particular loneliness wrought by the wrong sort of full house.

Chapter 4

The little pearl-faced clock on the nightstand read five-thirty in the morning. There was just an hour and a half until *Smell the Coffee*. Eve's arm itched; something was tickling it. She opened one eye and saw the dog, curled up next to her in a tight ball, her breathing deep and rhythmic. How had the tiny pup even gotten up onto the bed? Surely it was too high. Yet here she was, sleeping deeply, presumably exhausted from her fit the previous evening. Eve looked at the dog's trusting chin resting on her forearm and felt a tug of affection. She disengaged herself carefully and stumbled toward the kitchen to make coffee. Cup in hand, she gazed out the window at the buildings across the courtyard. The light was just starting to come up, a thin sapphire front pushing away the blackness across the east.

It was funny that Eve should be getting up at dawn; when Penelope had lived in New York, as she'd dreamily confided to Eve, she'd never come home before it. The city of her youth had been a place of literary salons and poetry readings, cigarettes and jazz. She and her friends would hop from the Café Carlyle to the Stork Club, then down to the Village, to someone's loft or basement, during long nights fueled by liquor, intrigue, and repartee, returning home only when the first rays of sun hit the slate sidewalks. The night simply hadn't been long enough to contain their revelry.

These images danced in Eve's mind as she hunted through the dim kitchen for something to nibble, but the breadbox and pantry shelves were empty. Quite a contrast to the bright *Smell the Coffee* studio with its bouillabaisse bounty.

"Bouillabaisse? What an odd thing to ponder." Donald's salutation was like a stone thrown in her pool, sending a series of ripples outward, fragmenting her daydream.

"I made bouillabaisse yesterday. A giant pot of it. Mussels, fish, everything. You should have seen me."

"You've taken up cooking?" heaved Donald with a sniff. "Girls in my day would have killed anyone who tried to stick *them* in the kitchen. It is the lowest kind of women's work. Putting your mind on hold to feed the stomachs of the patriarchy, offering sustenance to others while your soul starves—"

"I was only cooking because it was part of my interview. The food person was out. The real point is, I wrote my first television script and, in case you're wondering, it went quite well."

"I see," he said. "How nice that *your* writing career is taking off."

At six forty-five, Eve held up the leash. "Ready for a walk?" The dog stirred, blinking. Eve hooked the leash to her collar. Together, they crept softly down the stairs to avoid waking Mrs. Swan and the other neighbors and outside into the cool, hushed morning. They walked several blocks, Eve scanning the buildings, wondering, as always, if any of them might have been Penelope's. She'd never mentioned where her apartment was, nor had any of her old papers contained the address. It seemed she'd thrown almost everything out from her old life. But each time Eve passed a townhouse or tenement, she tried to picture her mother there, looking out a window or sitting on the stoop, as the locals so loved to do.

Before long, the moment that Eve had been dreading came: the dog's sudden pull out to the curb and ominous squat. Sure enough, contractions began, and suddenly, there it was in all its reeking banality. Eve had thought raw fish was bad. But there was absolutely no doubt about what she had to do: Dog owners who didn't clean up after their charges were considered the lowest of the low around here.

"You've done your job. Now I must do mine," Eve said to the dog as she fished out one of the crinkled plastic bags Mrs. Swan had provided. She squatted down next to the blight, holding her breath. She looked up at the sky and began to tap the ground with a bag-enclosed hand, hoping to find her target without having to actually look at it. A couple of punky girls in heavy black eyeliner, who looked like they'd been out all night, walked by arm in arm, giggling at her. After several attempts, Eve's fingers went from the unforgiving hardness of concrete to the sickening yield she sought. With a clawing motion, she picked up the mound and, still holding her breath, sprinted like an Olympian to the nearest trashcan, the dog struggling to keep up on her short legs.

At six minutes before seven, she placed the puppy carefully in an old leather tote and pushed open the door of the diner. She saw Vadis's hand go up from a nearby table.

"Hey." The combination of Vadis's olive skin and wide-set pale eyes—gifts from her Colombian father and Swedish mother, respectively—made her stand out even in New York's diverse population and drew admiring glances from a couple of nearby diners.

Eve half leaned in for a cheek kiss, but when Vadis made no move, she pulled back. "Thanks for coming all the way downtown," she said. "I could have come up to you." She sat down, gingerly placing the bag on the floor next to her chair.

"Nah, it's cool. I have a meeting in Soho at nine-thirty," said Vadis. She went back to scrolling through her BlackBerry's reams of contacts. No doubt about it, she was part of this town. Vadis was a real New Yorker. And she was the one who'd insisted that Eve could be—and should be—one, too.

It all started almost three months previously at the reunion of the Ambrose Aesthettes, the club for art history majors at Ambrose College. The college dedicated to creating "the women leaders of tomorrow" lay just outside Columbus, but the girls had gathered in New York to attend the opening of Inez Montoya's play, *Recognition*. Over dinner afterward in the theater district, the other alumnae shared their own stories of triumph: Several ran their own businesses, one had won a genius grant, another had adopted a pair of Mayan twins, and still another had just celebrated her marriage to a minor member of the English aristocracy.

Eve couldn't bear to admit she worked for her father—and lived in a condo several doors down from his amid the electric green hills of Rolling Links, a golfing community just outside of Greenwich, Ohio. It was every bit as claustrophobic as it sounded. More so, because most of her relationships were with the sons of Gin's law partners and golfing buddies, a singularly privileged and feckless set. Especially her most recent boyfriend, Ryan, who ran his father's company, which involved selling drainage systems to farmers, and who'd lately taken up the topic of marriage.

But Eve had been so deep inside this life for so long, she had no idea that when she surfaced, when she finally had occasion to pop her head out of her little gopher hole, her contemporaries would be so far down the road.

After dinner, Vadis asked if anyone wanted to meet her friends for a nightcap in the Village. Eve, more than ready to drown her sorrows, was the only one who wanted to go. They made their way through a deserted brick courtyard surrounded by weathered tenements to a door in the back. Vadis wrapped her hand around the doorknob and gave it a twist. Eve wondered what on earth was going on; it looked like they were about to barge into someone's private home. But when the door opened, out floated the sounds of a rollicking bar.

"Former speakeasy," said Vadis over the music. "No sign."

They claimed a back booth. The sepia walls around them seemed to hold the smoke and secrets of a century, while the names carved into the battered tables hummed with the spirit of countless departed drinkers. A sudden wave of déjà vu made the hairs on Eve's forearms rise. She'd never been to New York before, let alone this bar, so why did it feel so familiar?

"You missed your turn back at the restaurant. To tell everyone what you've been up to," said Vadis, sipping her wine. "Though I get the feeling that was no accident."

You never could get anything past Vadis. Eve was tempted to make something up, something about writing a novel or designing clothes, but she decided to come clean. She took a long pull of bourbon and told her friend about living between sand traps on the fairway and working for Gin.

"And now he's upping the ante," said Eve. "He wants me to go to law school, and as long as I agree to work for him for five years, he'll even pay for it."

"Are you going to take him up on it?" Vadis asked.

"I guess. I mean, I've dug myself in a bit of a trench. After twelve years of paralegal, what else am I really cut out for? Plus, it's not like there are a lot of options in Greenwich."

Vadis signaled to the waitress for another round of drinks. Then she touched Eve on the arm in a way that indicated she was about to say something important. "Just say no to law school."

"And yes to . . . ?"

"I dunno. Moving here maybe?"

"What?" said Eve.

"There's no better place than New York for starting over."

"What would I do? Where would I live?"

"Do a *job*. Live in an *a-part-ment*." She strung out the last word as if talking to a child. "Not that hard, you know. Thousands of people do it every day." She shrugged out of her leather jacket. "I could help you. You could be my project."

Eve was about to probe this idea further when Vadis's friends descended on them: three young men with intricate facial hair and tiny round eyeglasses and two women in long bohemian scarves and ruched suede boots. They piled into the booth and Eve listened with curiosity and not a little envy to their clever banter, peppered with references to politics and books and *The New York Times,* most of which she didn't understand. Their world seemed wide, their prospects vast. Everyone burst into laughter at a joke told by the young man sitting next to Eve.

And something clicked inside her. The courtyard, the unmarked door, the tables with the initials. "Is this place called Chumley's?" she asked suddenly.

"Yep," confirmed everyone, helping themselves to another round of beers from a tray going around the table.

Eve hugged herself, looking around the room as the story came back to her.

Her mother had celebrated a birthday here. Penelope had lovingly recounted an evening at a place called Chumley's—a so-called "secret bar"—with a big gang of her friends. She'd met most of them through her job as a reader for a literary agent in Midtown. Carol and Robert were also readers, the three of them becoming fast friends over the enormous piles of manuscripts that dotted the office. Most of her other pals were writers, editors, or artists. They had become the family that she'd longed for growing up in their clammy little corner of Ohio, she'd told Eve. They'd made her feel part of something larger, of the world itself, of her very times.

As Eve studied the animated faces around her, she wondered if she could be happy in New York, too. Maybe Vadis was right. How hard could it be to live here? It was just a spot on a map like any other. One that held not just Chumley's, but all the other places her mother had spoken of with their wonderful names, like the Gaslight, the Cedar Tavern, and the San Remo. Forty years had passed, but maybe Eve could uncover a bit of the magic Penelope had once known.

When she got back to Ohio, she sat her father down and informed him that as soon as she could put her affairs in order (which would include simultaneously breaking up with Ryan and fixing him up with her friend Corrine), she'd be moving to New York.

Today, after the show, she'd call Gin to tell him he could forget his misgivings, that it had all been worth it; she'd landed a job at *Smell the Coffee*.

The bag wobbled and Vadis jerked her chin back. "What the hell is in there?"

"A dog," said Eve, in a low voice.

"Why not let it out?"

"Are dogs allowed in here?"

"It's okay. I know the owner."

Eve lifted the puppy out and set her on the floor. She blinked up at them. "Voilà."

"So cute!" Vadis, in suit and heels, got down on her knees and rubbed the dog behind her ears. "I wish I could have one but who has time for a pet? What's her name?"

"Doesn't have one yet. I just got her."

"Aww." The dog, amiable, and seemingly well recovered from the previous day's drama, licked Vadis on the knuckle. "There'll be some bacon in it for you later," Vadis said, standing and brushing off her knees. "So—check it out." She pointed at a television hanging on the wall. "I told them all about your big moment and got them to put on Channel 6 instead of *Squawk Box*."

"Thanks," Eve said, tying the leash to her chair. They looked at their menus for several moments before she spoke again. "So, how do you know Orla Knock? You never said."

"Concert at Chelsea Piers. I was trolling for new clients." Vadis leaned forward. "Corporate PR stuff pays well but it's boring. So I've decided to go after musicians. So far I've only signed one band, but I'm going to knock them into the stratosphere."

Vadis had always been hard-charging. She'd won the Aesthette's presidency junior year over one or two seniors chiefly due to bravado and a breezy comfort with sizing up club members and telling them what to do. It was as though she saw those around her as pieces in a chess game, but she had an uncanny way of making people want to please her, which seemed to keep the other girls from taking offense.

The waiter poured some coffee and took their orders.

"What's the name of your band?" asked Eve.

"Spoilt Picnic. They're rap/folk, totally modern. I'm trying to get Orla to put them on *Smell the Coffee,* to promote their debut CD. She's stalling, though. Says she's not sure they're ready for national TV. So I'm taking them on tour around the Northeast and hopefully, when we get back, she'll decide it's go time." Vadis raised her cup in a toast. "Plus thanks to you I'm going to have another in at the show, right?"

"Right." Eve toasted back, trying to quell her distress that her only friend in town was going on an extended trip. Eve would be completely alone in New York. Though with her new job, she was about to gain a whole bunch of colleagues.

"So, what is the job, anyway? Pretty much what I said?" Vadis asked.

Eve explained about bouillabaisse and senators and scripts with a line down the middle and writing exactly twenty seconds, enjoying the surprise spreading over Vadis's face.

"Damn." Vadis gave a low whistle. "Still, writing for Bliss Jones will probably open a lot of doors."

"You think?" asked Eve.

"Um, yeah, she's, like, a major deal." Vadis reached for a mini muffin in the basket that had arrived, then continued. "You really don't know?" Eve shook her head. "First off, she's the only person alive who's been a Miss America runner-up and a Rhodes scholar. She's interviewed practically every world leader and parachuted into war zones. She's supposed to be the highest-paid journalist on television and her Q score is higher than Santa's."

Eve wanted to ask what a Q score was but Vadis had already moved on.

"And Hap McCutcheon is hot. He was a baseball player in the eighties. Can't remember what team. At some point he got hurt and became a commentator. Then he snagged an interview with Castro during a secret trip to check out emerging players in Cuba or something. I think that's how he wound up in news."

Eve reached for a muffin but put it down before taking a bite. War zones. Castro. These were the people she'd be writing for.

"Hey, it's starting," said Vadis, looking at the TV hanging on the wall over Eve's shoulder. "When's your thing on again?"

"Not for a while. Eight-thirty-something."

The food arrived but Eve's eggs grew cold while she gazed at the television. So this was *Smell the Coffee*. The two anchors introduced themselves from behind a sleek blue desk. Bliss Jones was a vision in a glossy blond bob, with purply-blue eyes and the best kind of nose, the kind that didn't interfere with the rest of your face. Hap McCutcheon sported cinnamon hair and a comforting, dad-standing-over-the-barbecue smile.

After a short newscast hosted by a no-nonsense brunette named Sandy Horowitz, which featured videotape of various world conflicts, forest fires, and squirrels on water skis, the show segued into a series of discussions about politics (with an animated-looking Senator Farnsworth, who never did get to bring up his wife's aid organization), classroom size, and a drug recall in which Bliss and Hap led participants who gestured wildly at each other.

The dog nuzzled Eve's calf and she fed her a piece of toast. At exactly eight o'clock, Bliss's voice sounded urgent as she introduced the next segment. "—New information just coming in at this hour on an ongoing crime spree here in New York City. It involves a mugger holding up his victims at knifepoint while wearing, very often, women's clothing—and always sporting high-heeled shoes. So far, four victims, one seriously wounded. Here with the latest on the attacks is Police Chief Sebastian Pell. Chief

Pell, thank you for joining us. Please start, if you would, by telling us what we know about the man they're calling the Stiletto?"

The police chief was barrel-chested and the bristle of his salt-and-pepper crew cut made Eve want to pass her palm over it.

"Well, Bliss, thank you for having me this morning. This is one perplexing case. You have no idea the manpower we've had to put on this." He went on for a good thirty seconds, saying, if you listened carefully, precisely nothing.

"Be that as it may," said Bliss, sounding irritated, "what our viewers want to know is, who is this madman? And why can't you find him?"

The chief cleared his throat and began again, this time soberly detailing the most recent attack and explaining that the victim had arrived at the hospital overnight, slashed in the stomach. Thankfully, she was expected to recover. "The Stiletto is a dangerous, disturbed man," Pell continued. "His MO is unlike any we've seen. . . ."

When the interview was over, Vadis began making notes on what looked like a contract, while Eve sipped her coffee. The next time she looked up at the television, the hosts were donning boxing gloves for a workout segment. After that it was gardening overalls and straw hats to dig in an on-set garden, and then crash helmets for a spin in some bumper cars. Finally, there was Bliss Jones saying, "Coming up a little later, why your socks could be killing you. But first, the exotic flavors of southern France, right here at home. When *Smell the Coffee* continues."

"This is it," announced Vadis, lifting her voice to address the surrounding tables. "After this commercial, my friend here's going to become a television legend. She wrote everything Hap McCutcheon's about to say. And she made the soup they're about to eat, too." A couple of other diners looked up from their breakfasts to offer polite smiles. The dog put her front paws on Eve's knees and yawned deeply. Eve thought she'd heard somewhere that dogs yawned when they were nervous.

A commercial for bug repellent faded from the screen and Hap appeared in a long white apron. Eve sucked in her breath. This was it. She closed her eyes and imagined flying over the breakfast tables of America as each family heard the word "bouillabaisse" and realized that *that* was what was missing from their lives. They'd put down their coffee cups and maple syrup, hypnotized by her words, enthralled by her images, and believe that they, too, deserved a hearty fish soup at the end of a long hard day.

Hap stood next to a portly man in a crisp white chef's outfit with a giant *Z* over the left breast and a billowy hat. In front of them, the same panoply of ingredients Eve had used, and the big steaming cauldron she'd prepared yesterday. Her heart was beating like a hummingbird's wings as Hap opened his mouth in slow motion and began to speak:

> **(HAP:)**
> BOO—BOOL—BOOEEE—BOO-EL-
> BASE. BOOL-BASE. OH HECK,
> GIMME CAMPBELL'S ANYTIME. AT
> LEAST I CAN SAY IT.

Eve grimaced.

> BOO-YAH-BASE. *WHEW*. OKAY. THE
> VERY NAME CONJURES UP
> SUMMERS ON THE
> MEDITERRANEAN, AND THE RICH
> FLAVORS OF ITS SEAFOOD.

Her mouth found the words along with Hap.

> IT'S DELICIOUS AND EXOTIC—THE
> PERFECT DISH TO SERVE FRIENDS

AT YOUR NEXT DINNER PARTY . . .
IF ONLY IT WEREN'T SO DIFFICULT
TO MAKE. WELL, GUESS WHAT? IT'S
NOT.

He said it all with such sincerity he could have been a world-class bouillabaisse expert. The words sounded exactly as they had in her head. Everyone in the restaurant fell silent, clearly awestruck.

IN FACT, YOU CAN THROW IT
TOGETHER IN LESS THAN AN
HOUR, AND EVEN HAVE TIME LEFT
OVER TO TOSS A SALAD BEFORE
YOUR GUESTS ARRIVE.
HERE TO SHOW US JUST HOW EASY
IT IS, CHEF ZORIN.

Vadis gave Eve a thumbs-up.

Chef Zorin playfully slapped a dish towel at Hap. "Ees bouillabaisse. BOO-YAH-BASE-UH. Hap, you seely-beely. I show you how make."

Zorin began putting the ingredients together. He sautéed an onion before adding the shrimp and the halibut. Then came Hap's first question, just as she had scripted it: "Can I leave out the red pepper flakes if I want?" Zorin assured him this was entirely possible. On they went until the chef announced with flair, "And here we have the feenished product, already seemering on the stove! Time to taste." Eve watched as Zorin dipped his ladle into her pot. He lifted out a series of steaming bowlfuls and handed one to Hap and another to Bliss, who entered the frame with an expression that said she couldn't believe her luck at finding fish soup in the studio at 8:42 in the morning.

In unison, they dunked their spoons, then lifted them into the air. "One. Two. Three," Hap called out. Spoons disappeared into mouths, accompanied by appreciative murmurs.

"Delicious, Zorin, as always," said Hap, although he sounded slightly less convincing than in the intro. "Stay with us everyone. *Smell the Coffee* continues."

Eve nearly floated off her chair. She wanted to dance around the room. Vadis leaned over and patted her hand. "Right on," she said. Then she looked around. "Everybody, huh? What about my friend?" A man at the next table raised his coffee cup and somebody put their hands together in a single, tiny thunderclap of approval.

Vadis went outside to make a call and Eve picked up the dog and held her tightly, savoring the earthy, sweet smell of her fine fur. After the commercial break ended, she looked up to see Bliss Jones leading into another segment.

". . . deadly new strain of bacteria, showing up in laundry hampers across America. Joining us now is our medical editor, Dr. Frank Gibbons. Frank, who needs to be worried about this?"

The doctor crossed one leg over the other and began his answer. "Well, Bliss, it's complicated. You see . . ." He spoke for a few moments, then cut himself off. "You all right?"

The screen cut to Bliss, hunched over, with one hand on her sweating forehead, the other on her abdomen. Her delicately painted face had become a tangle of pain and confusion. "I'm sorry, I just—I just don't feel well. It's come over me all of a sudden. I don't know what's wrong. L-L-Lark, would you take us to commercial, please?" She lifted her head and somehow produced a glorious smile. "Stay with us everyone . . . *Smell the Coffee* continues."

A chill gathered around Eve's neck. Several people glanced in her direction. She squirmed in her seat, waiting for the commercial break to end. Finally, Sandy Horowitz came back on, just as Vadis arrived back at the table. Sandy announced that Bliss would be unable to finish the program. It seemed to be a mild case of tummy trouble, but Dr. Gibbons was seeing to her and she was expected to be "just fine." The rest of the broadcast would be filled by a taped interview Bliss had done with Colm Lowry, author of *Mothers and Daughters: The Healthy Spleen Connection.*

Icy pricks of sweat sprouted on Eve's upper lip. What had happened? As Vadis looked at her with alarm, she went over all the steps she'd taken. She'd followed the recipe exactly. Except . . . that odor. Hadn't it been a bit worse than seafood was supposed to smell? Especially that spiteful halibut. Could it have gone bad? And if it had, how could she not have known? Then, with a shudder, she realized she had at least suspected it. She'd just chosen to tuck her misgivings behind her dreams of success, like the driver who sees, but doesn't see, the oil light come on.

"Please tell me this has nothing to do with you," said Vadis in a low whisper.

"Well, I—"

"Because I went out on a limb with Orla Knock. You were desperate and I told her you were great. So please—tell me it was nothing you did."

Eve wished she could but no words would come out of her mouth.

• • •

She stood at her bar and poured a second highball. Booze at ten in the morning; things were going really well.

"Highball, highball, highball," she mumbled. Why was a drink called that? Probably because it was fun to say. "Highball, highball, highball." She said it again like a mantra, the dog cocking her head each time.

"You like that? Highball?" The dog stared intently. "That's no name for a dog, silly." Then again, thought Eve, her chin on the bar, "Eventual"—her mother's capricious way of welcoming a girl after a pair of rambunctious boys—was a pretty odd name for a girl. She held out her hand. "Highball?" The dog touched her baby-pink tongue to Eve's skin. "Your gesture shall be read as assent. 'Highball' it is."

"You're naming that fleabag?" asked Donald.

"You startled me."

"You didn't answer my question."

"Yes, I am," said Eve. "I'm naming the fleabag!" This set her off into a wave of silent giggles.

"Are you drunk, young lady? What time is it?"

"It's poetic license to drink before noon. I'm a writer now, remember? And this is what writers do." Was she still speaking aloud or was she simply thinking? Not that it mattered with Donald but the bourbon made it difficult to tell.

"Ah, yes. The television job." He said the word "television" like a gourmand might say "spray-on cheese." "I take it the bouillabaisse was a success?"

"Oh yes. I am the queen of soup. And of language. I'm a writer who can do no wrong. Right, Highball?"

"Tell the truth," said Donald. She took another sip instead. "How come I'm seeing a memory of an overpainted blond woman on a TV screen looking ill? And a Negro woman, looking as if she'd like to wring your little neck?"

Eve tried to banish these pictures from her mind, but they kept replaying as if on a loop. "You be quiet," she said to Donald. "It's none of your concern. By the way, my friend is *Latina*, not black." She grabbed the leash. "And FYI? No one says 'Negro' anymore!"

As she slammed the door she heard Donald griping in confusion, "What in the heck is *eff why eye*?"

. . .

Eve and Highball wandered down Bleecker Street, the city seeming to her like a giant clique, impenetrable. She was never going to find a way in. She looked hard at each person she passed, every store merchant, every police officer, every deliveryman. What was the damn secret?

At 190 Bleecker, she stopped. It was just a hole-in-the-wall takeout place, but a plaque near the door caught her eye. It noted that an apartment in the building had been home to Gregory Corso, one of the most famous of the Beat poets. Eve had read some of his work at the library recently, but what she remembered now was that he'd suffered a run of bad luck second to none. Abandoned by his mother, he'd spent years in foster homes, was dispatched to New York's most fearsome jail at thirteen, and after that lived on the streets.

Then he met Allen Ginsberg at a Village bar and everything changed.

They turned north and soon arrived at Washington Square Park. At the far end lay a cordoned-off area called a "dog run," where it appeared dogs were permitted to go leashless. Eve closed the metal gate behind them, then plunked down on a peeling wooden bench. She unhooked the dog, wishing she didn't have quite so much liquor coursing through her. It was a foolish way to deal with disaster, she knew it. Her eyes swept over the green peacefulness of the park, gathered contentedly under its bone white arch, a miniature version of Paris's Arc de Triomphe. She leaned back, wishing she were in Paris for real.

Around her, it was knee-high chaos: thirty or so dogs engaged in what appeared for all the world to be a canine cocktail party. She shaded her eyes from the sun and surveyed the array: boxers, jowls flying like banners as their powerful legs propelled them around in short bursts; German shepherds with their sloping backs that made it look like they were forever sneaking up on people; dachshunds like fur-covered bullets; corgis, barrel-chested and nippy; and several pugs, plush gargoyles with madly twirling pigs' tails.

There was one dog that remained apart from the hubbub, the surly guest at the party. He was dramatic in appearance: about the size of a small Labrador but with blindingly white short fur, ice blue eyes, and a head like an anvil. He planted himself in a corner, his eyes following the squirrels in the trees.

A collie-basset mix sniffed Highball eagerly before running off, and Highball gave chase. As Eve's eyes followed her, she wondered how bad law school could be. It would be nice to make her father happy. He'd been stunned and confused when she announced she was pulling up stakes for the Big Apple after what was supposed to be a long weekend with some school chums. And yet there had been a tinge of resignation in his tone when she told him. Almost as if he'd known this day was coming.

Just as Eve realized she couldn't see Highball anywhere, a snarl erupted from the run's general cacophony and Eve's eyes flew toward the sound. About a dozen dogs had become part of what looked like a solid mass of writhing fur. Other dog owners darted over, shouting and gesturing.

In a breath, Eve was beside them. She caught sight of Highball's speckled fur deep within the mass and stepped in, her legs battered so fiercely by hurtling dogs that she immediately fell, landing heavily on the gravel. Attempting to stand, she batted away the pummeling noses and tails and felt a pain shoot through her wrist. Suddenly the sea parted, revealing Highball in the grip of the white dog. Its teeth were buried deep in her neck, rich red-brown blood dripping from the wound.

Everything fell away, leaving only the pulsating sound of screaming, muffled and distant. Eve's fingers found the place where the white dog's teeth met Highball's skin. She pulled with all her strength but they'd taken root like redwoods. With Highball starting to go limp, Eve flew to the rear flank. Blurrily, she heard the shouts: *Get outta there! You don't know what you're doing!* Eve wrapped her fingers around the white dog's ankles and pulled. Nothing happened. She pulled again, harder. Still nothing. Why wasn't anyone helping? She pushed her heels into the ground, closed her eyes, and put every ounce of her muscle into another tug. The dog released its grip with a cry of fury, and Eve let go, falling backward. Two men rushed forward to grab the white dog as if it were what they'd been meaning to do all along. A third clapped her on the back. *Damn,* she heard from somewhere. The world began to come back and the faces of the onlookers came into focus.

Then her eyes fell on Highball, who lay pressed into the ground, eyelids fluttering, chest moving faintly.

· · ·

The vet, young and shiny-skinned, said Highball was extremely lucky. Her jugular had been missed by less than an inch, the thick ruff at her throat having likely confused her attacker. He told Eve it would take a few stitches, a couple of shots, and bed rest to restore Highball's health, but in the meantime, hadn't she better get herself to the ER?

· · ·

That evening, Eve looked down at the four stitches they'd given her at St. Vincent's—the same number as Highball had received—on the pale inside of her left arm. Precise and lovely, they looked like those on the hem of her mother's eggshell Chanel jacket. Unlike the Chanel stitches, though, they vibrated with pain, biting their way across the skin. She leaned over, blowing on them quietly to keep from waking Highball, who lay splayed next to her on the bed.

"What's happened?" Donald's tone was tender.

"Nothing," she said, wincing.

"You're hurt," he replied. "I can feel it. Tell me." Haltingly, Eve recounted the dog-run drama, but it came out in a painkiller-sodden jumble. At the end, she moaned, spent all over again. "I wish I could help," said Donald. "But so far I'm utterly incapable of anything but continuing with my contributions to literature."

"So far? What else have you been trying to do?" Despite her pain, Eve was curious.

"I've been attempting to marshal a measure of physical skill since before we met. Hopeless at the moment, but one day I may surprise you."

"Really . . ." murmured Eve. "And just what might you do?"

"What would you like?"

"Hmmm," said Eve, rolling over. "How about you pour me a bourbon?"

"You're still juiced from your last bender and you're trying to line up your next drink?" Donald chastised. "In any case, I'm a million miles from such a stunt."

"Well, that shouldn't stop you from trying. I'm a million miles from landing a job and that's not going to stop me." And it wouldn't, she decided. She would not, not, not go to law school.

"All right, my little scamp. One day I will pour you a bourbon. But for now, why don't you try to get some sleep?"

. . .

When she awoke, shadows had stretched across the room like a net and Highball was curled in the crook of her arm, snoring in little wisps. The phone was ringing.

"Hello?" Eve whispered.

"Eve Weldon, please."

"Speaking," she coughed, trying to sit up and get her bearings. She looked at the clock. It was after six in the evening.

"It's Mark."

"Mark . . ."

"Mark—*Smell the Coffee* Mark. Remember? Bouillabaisse?"

"Oh, of course. I'm sorry. I'm a bit . . ." She shook her head. "I'm fine. Sorry. How are you?"

"How am I? Are you kidding?"

"Oh, right." The morning's events returned.

"You saw the broadcast?"

"Yes." Eve gathered her knees up under her chin. "I don't know what to say. I should have called. I was horrified. Is—is everyone okay?" She swallowed. "Is Bliss Jones all right?" Her voice had dropped so even she could barely hear it.

"She's fine—now. So is the person from the studio audience who got sick." He covered the phone and had a few terse words with someone. Then he came back. "But they had a couple of uncomfortable hours. They eventually realized that each of them had gotten a piece of the halibut, which was bad. Thank God no one else did. Didn't you notice something was wrong with it?"

"It did smell funny, but I thought, well, fish smells funny, doesn't it? And you all seemed really busy and I didn't want to trouble anybody."

Mark exhaled loudly. "Look, in the journalism business you *have* to trouble people. Trouble them to answer your questions, trouble them to tell you the truth. If you don't, you put wrong information on the air. A network can get sued for doing that."

She had been hanging on every word, but now it occurred to Eve that this conversation might be sliding into a very bad place. "Are you—are you telling me all this because they're suing me?" she breathed. "Over the soup?"

"No, Eve, I'm telling you all this because, unbelievable as it sounds, I'm giving you another shot."

Chapter 5

The following Monday, Eve gazed into the mirror, turning this way and that in a navy fifties pinstripe skirt suit with three-quarter sleeves. Though perhaps this was overdoing it. The rest of the *Smell the Coffee* staff's attire, from what she'd glimpsed, was comprised of suits or button-down-and-slacks ensembles. Those she'd spotted along writers' row seemed inclined toward jeans and baggy sweaters, looking as though they'd been beamed in from a smoky bar in the East Village where only minutes ago they'd been stabbing cigarettes into the air and making impassioned points about existentialism. Eve thought briefly about trying to adopt this costume, but she'd been waiting since she was a teenager to wear her mother's vintage. Doing so in the Midwest, land of shirtdresses and khakis, would have made her feel too conspicuous.

She disembarked the subway at Thirty-fourth Street, still amazed at how different Midtown was from the Village. In the Village, locals meandered, strolled, ambled at best. Here everyone marched smartly in military precision, as if taking orders from some unseen general. *You there! Knees up! Look alive! And you! Watch the hot dog vendor. Keep up, you in the purple sweater. All together now: Around the tourists! Around the tourists!*

The gleaming, forum-like entrance to the network loomed. Enormous double doors swung open and Eve stepped inside the glistening marble foyer. A series of full-length color portraits of the network's anchors and correspondents hung from the two-story ceiling. The men all wore gray or blue blazers, the women red or yellow. The men folded their arms across their chests like aging white rap stars; the women clasped their hands behind their backs in the manner of Degas ballerinas. Bliss Jones's banner hung in the center, slightly in front of the others'. Blinding teeth and reassurance radiated from the gently fluttering canvas.

Eve showed her ID to the guard and, after tiptoeing her way up five flights of cigarette-butt-strewn back stairs, found her way to Mark's office. The door was open, and as she walked in, several people simultaneously swiveled in her direction and stopped talking.

"Ah," said Mark, waving her in. "Well, here we go. Everyone, this is Eve. Eve, these are the writers." They looked at her with frank curiosity as Mark introduced them, one by one. First came Archie Meyers, graying, scruffy, and somewhat distracted, who appeared to come with a copy of *The New York Times* surgically attached under his arm. He'd worked at the show for fifteen years and his expertise was politics; he'd interviewed each of the last three presidents (or at least their top aides). Next came Quirine Veselier. She was French, though she'd lived in the U.S. for fifteen years. She still had a bit of an accent and was darkly gamine in a simple but perfectly cut dove gray blouse and wide-legged trousers. She handled most of the segments on social issues and the environment, about which she maintained Americans were "frighteningly ignorant." To her left stood blond, green-eyed Steve Andrews, who had the look of a college quarterback crossed with a down pillow. He handled sports segments and anything to do with cars or power tools. Last to be introduced was Russell Washington, his pate black and glossy as an eight ball. He held himself with great dignity but possessed a twitchy mouth that looked capable of unleashing a wicked string of bons mots. He and Mark had no journalistic "niche"; they handled, as needed, any topic that came up.

The team of office-chair superheroes, each armed with his or her unique skill, made for an impressive tableau. Eve imagined brilliantly colored capes blowing from behind their shoulder blades, to go with the glimmer in their eyes that said, "Don't you worry. We've got it covered." Everyone made polite small talk for a few minutes, but much to Eve's relief, no one mentioned the bouillabaisse.

"Where's Cassandra?" asked Mark.

"Late again," said Quirine, rolling her eyes. "Perhaps she had an audition."

"Okay, guys. Back to the salt mines," said Mark. As the gang filed out, he asked Eve to sit. "So. You took the back stairs?" She nodded. "Glad you know how to follow directions. So, first up, HR has given me some paperwork for you to fill out and—"

There was some noise in the hallway. The door swung open and a woman appeared. She was in her late fifties, Eve thought, with highly styled dark hair with a shock of steel at each temple and red-framed glasses. She seemed to be finishing up a conversation with the other writers.

". . . up to you to hold down the fort in my absence, everyone. I know you're up to it."

She stepped inside and closed the door behind her and took a step toward Mark. "Just wanted to make the rounds before I leave for the retreat. There's talk of some of us going out to L.A. afterward, so I may be away longer than we discussed. I'll let you know from the road. I have some notes about May sweeps to give you, too."

Mark rose from his seat. "I, um, thought you were already gone." He accepted the papers she handed him, shuffling through them slowly as if stalling. "But these are great. Thank you."

The woman swept her eyes over Eve. "Who's your friend?"

Mark cleared his throat. "This is Eve Weldon. Eve, this is Orla
Knock." Eve started to stand up as well but the woman's eyes
snapped back to Mark's face and Eve sank back down.

"I thought we talked about this," said Orla.

"I know we did. But I tried Samantha Peters and Michael
Kramer like you asked and they're both doing vacation relief at
CNN. Their schedules may free up in a couple of weeks, though.
I'll keep checking in with them."

"There has to be somebody else."

It was humiliating to be discussed like this, her future being
bandied about like a fuzzy green tennis ball, but Eve couldn't
think what she could possibly add to this conversation.

"There isn't," said Mark. "Not on such short notice anyway.
Plus, I was thinking. If we don't bring Eve back, isn't it tantamount to admitting that it was the writing department's fault,
when really the blame should fall on Katrine for not coming in
and not getting a replacement? The producer is responsible for
the props, not the writer."

"This is the case you'll make if anyone asks?" Orla lowered
her glasses down her nose and looked hard at Mark.

"I already spoke to Franka and she agreed. I'm sorry, like I
said, I thought you were gone or I would have cleared it with you
first."

"Fine. But this is on your head, Mark. You're taking total re-
sponsibility for—Eve, was it?—and her work, you understand? I
don't want any calls from Giles while I'm holding hands with
other managers and chanting Eastern self-help phrases."

Mark swallowed. "I understand. Eve will be my responsibil-
ity. Totally."

Orla's cellphone went off. She frowned down at it. "I have to
take this. Good luck, one and all." She nodded briefly at no one
in particular and was gone.

"Shit." Mark closed his eyes and pressed his palms to his temples.

"You okay?"

"No. Yeah. Fuck."

"Can I do anything?"

"Well, if it's not obvious, you need to do a good job today. Really good. She'll be watching the show tomorrow from wherever she is with an eagle eye and her finger poised over the speed-dial button." Eve chewed a fingernail, chagrined to find the stakes of the day exponentially heightened. "I guess you get the picture," continued Mark. "As you can probably tell, Orla wanted to nix you outright. But the food producer really was to blame, ultimately. So now she's been fired."

Eve stared at him, deeply uncomfortable.

"Yeah, well, it's dog-eat-dog around here and our department can't afford to go down another head. If we do the show with six writers for even just a few days, they'll wonder why we can't do it that way forever." Mark took a sip from his water bottle. "Look, aside from making Bliss Jones vomit, you did all right. And it seemed like a waste that I showed you how to do everything only to cut you loose. You learn pretty fast. So what I figure is, we go from here, and by the time Orla gets back, you'll have some decent segments behind you." He handed her the HR papers. "Okay, they're going to set up a computer account and a phone line for you today, and though I doubt it, it's possible that people may be calling you for a quote."

Now, this was exciting. Not only was she going to be a member of a bona fide news organization, she was going to be *in* the news. "Really?" she asked, trying not to let her voice betray her excitement. "They'll want to know about me? Like for a story about 'new faces in the news' or something?"

Mark looked incredulous. "Have you ever seen a piece like that anywhere? Think before you answer."

"Well, not per se . . ."

"But you do read the papers."

"Of course."

"Which ones?"

"Well, let's see." Her mind raced. What had she seen on the stands? "You know, I enjoy *The Observer* and . . ." She trailed off.

"No, not the pink paper with the drawings. Real newspapers: the *Times, The Washington Post, The Wall Street Journal,* the *Daily News, Newsday?*"

She said nothing.

"So why are you here?"

Eve thought of Highball and Donald and almost said, "To support my growing number of dependents." But she didn't. "What do you mean?"

"Why do you want to be a journalist if you have no interest in journalism?" This apparently wasn't the time to admit she'd never been particularly interested in being a journalist. Mostly, she'd been giving thought to what she didn't want to do. "Look," said Mark. "To do this job, you're going to have to read everything, understand? You have to know not just what's going on but what people are *saying* is going on. Two different things. You have to understand the mood of the country—how people are feeling about everything from stay-at-home dads to rendition—so you can bring it to whatever you write. That's the way you connect with viewers and get them interested in the show and, more important, make Bliss and Hap look smart and well-read and funny and interesting and down-to-earth and . . . you get the idea." His phone rang; he glanced at it but didn't pick up.

"Okay," breathed Eve, thinking the writers deserved their capes.

"Look, your take on bouillabaisse was smart. But what you did with soup? You have to be able to do that with overmedicated children, cap and trade, the latest Hollywood 'It Girl'—everything."

"Cap and tray?" .

"Cap and trade. Emissions? Hello?"

No more being ignorant, Eve resolved. She never wanted to see that look on Mark's, or anybody else's, face again. "Right, right. Of course." She'd look up what exchanging hats had to do with pollution at the earliest opportunity.

"Now, to become Queen of the Zeitgeist . . . here." Mark handed Eve a three-page memo on *Smell the Coffee* stationery.

Writers:

In addition to your usual reading (the *Times,* the *News,* the *Washington* and *New York Post*s, *Newsday*), please make an effort to include the following every day, including Sundays:

The Boston Globe
The Miami Herald
The Philadelphia Inquirer
Milwaukee Journal Sentinel
Minneapolis Star Tribune
Chicago Sun-Times
Chicago Tribune
The Plain Dealer
The Dallas Morning News
San Francisco Chronicle
Los Angeles Times

Also, weekly and/or monthly:

Time
Newsweek
Reader's Digest
Vanity Fair
US News and World Report
People
Redbook

Ladies' Home Journal
Woman's Own
Sports Illustrated
GQ
Esquire

(The only title not on the list was *The New Yorker,* which of course was the only one Eve had read.)

In addition, please use Nexis to review daily transcripts from the following:

The Oprah Winfrey Show
Larry King Live
The Tonight Show with Jay Leno
Late Night with David Letterman
Charlie Rose
The Open Mind

Also—please make sure you have read at least seven of the *New York Times* bestsellers and seen five of the top ten box office movies on any given week.

Orla's rather loopy scrawl was at the bottom. Eve got lost in the letters, which morphed from "Orla" to "Or else." But it didn't sound too bad, really. Kind of like being paid to read. The *Daily News* probably couldn't touch Louisa May Alcott, but still. "Okay," she began. "But why are we reading the *Minneapolis Star Tribune*?"

Mark raised an ironic eyebrow. "Because *Smell the Coffee* is not a New York show."

"What do you mean? We're in New York."

"That's only an accident of real estate," said Mark, starting to stack some folders on his desk. "We try not to acknowledge New

York too much because it turns off the viewers. The rest of the country has issues with us. They think we're a bunch of snooty, pseudo-intellectual, nebbishy Woody Allen types. Not that they would use the word 'nebbishy.' "

Eve swiveled in her chair as she considered this. It rang true, unfortunately. Certainly, Ohioans made their fair share of New York jokes.

"Anyway," Mark said. "Can I take it you haven't read the papers the last couple of days?"

"Yes."

Mark sighed and leafed through a stack of tabloids and broadsheets. Each had the same story on its cover, about how police were flummoxed by the Stiletto. Mark directed Eve's attention to a sticky note peeking out from an inside page of the *Daily News*. The headline read, *Morning Show in a Stew Over Bad Fish Dish.*

"They don't know your part in this whole thing, but this reporter might call around, sniffing for the scoop," he said.

"What do I say?"

"Absolutely nothing. You never say anything to the press."

"Never?"

"Never. We have a two-hundred-thousand-dollar-a-year spokeswoman for that."

Eve squinted. Mark had made such a big deal about the cause of journalism. The staff of *Smell the Coffee* was out to uncover stories; it didn't seem fair that they should hamper the efforts of other journalists trying to do the same thing.

"So, okay. Let's get you started," he said. "Now, know this up front. For the near future, you're only going to do non-news segments, all right? Yes, it's the 'fluff'—entertainment, crafts, how-to, maybe some medical stories, but only 'conditions,' not 'diseases'—and you're only going to write for Hap. That's the way it is with new people, so you just sort of have to suck it up. Kevin, the guy who was fired the other day, couldn't seem to grasp that. He was always pressing for hard news and wanting to write for Bliss before he was ready." Mark paused for a moment before continuing. "Bliss is . . . Bliss. It'll be a while before you'll be ready for her. If ever." Eve nodded. The truth was, she was relieved. Why had this Kevin insisted on stepping into the line of fire? She was perfectly happy to duck it.

"Does Bliss do all the hard news stories?" Eve asked.

"No, but most of them. On this show, she wears the pants. And she can spot a flaw in an interview a mile away. That's why people work here for a long time before even trying to write for her. If you've left a stone unturned, or there's a lack of logic in the progression of your questions, she'll alert Giles—that's the executive producer—right on the set during a commercial break. And he'll go straight to Orla Knock, or if she's not here, me. As you can imagine, that's an experience we want to avoid."

Mark launched into more of the basics. Her schedule: in at 3 p.m. for the production meeting, during which that morning's show would be postmortemed and the next day's bookings would be discussed. Then she'd get her assignment, read the research, talk to the guests, and write the intro. The day ended whenever it ended, there was no way of knowing. Segments could fall through, guests often had to be rebooked, news could break—there were any number of reasons why she might have to stay late. It would "probably" never be more than an eleven-hour day, Mark offered cheerfully. Eve felt disappointed; it would be difficult to socialize on this schedule, which entailed working five of every seven nights.

Mark then detailed the heart of the job: the pre-interview. This was the interview, by phone, with the guest booked on the next morning's show. The point of the "pre" was to avoid wasting precious network airtime. Since most segments—even important ones featuring high-ranking public officials—lasted only three or four minutes, they had to be highly choreographed. To this end, the writers spoke to the guests in advance to discover which questions provoked interesting answers and which led down dry holes.

The American public had very little patience, especially in the morning, Mark explained, so the pre-interview was also something of a spy game. The writer was to discern not just the guest's views on the topic at hand, but other things as well: Were they an old hand at live television or a terrified first-timer? Did they talk in paragraphs or were they hopelessly disjointed? Were they accomplished at delivering pithy "sound bites" or did they ramble? The anchors had to know.

"Doesn't sound too hard," Eve said slowly, willing it to be true.

"In theory, it isn't," said Mark. "Of course, since any given segment might have as many as five guests, and since on any given day, you might have two or three segments to write . . ." Eve tried but failed to keep the smile on her face. "Don't freak out," he said. "Today you've only got one segment, one guest. The research is all right here." He handed her a thick folder. "Don't make me regret this, okay?"

In the hallway, Russell and Quirine leaned against the wall, deep in conversation.

"Eve, right?" asked Quirine. Her tone was neither friendly nor unfriendly. Eve nodded. "Much as I hate to be the bearer of bad news, we thought you should know that some people around here might address you as . . ." She dropped her voice. "B.B."

Russell elbowed Quirine in a way that indicated they were good friends. "C'mon now. Don't lay it on the girl so fast."

Quirine shushed him. "I'm just saying. What if she hears it and she doesn't know what they mean? Forewarned is forearmed, no?" Quirine looked up and down the passage, then leaned into Eve and said, "Cybil, one of the PAs, dubbed you the 'Bouillabaisse Bimbo' at the morning meeting. And some of the others are calling you the 'Bouillabaisse Bitch' because of Katrine. I heard that from Tanya."

Before Eve could reply, Russell took off his glasses and rubbed his eyes roughly. "They'll forget it in a day or two, most likely. It's short-attention-span theater around here. And by the way, your intro was quite good. I enjoyed the 'Summer in Marseilles' angle. Very Eric Rohmer."

Quirine smiled archly. "Your screenplay-writing class is making you a one-note."

Just then a woman came around the corner. She seemed to be hiding behind a mass of copper hair and a tangle of folk-art-style accessories.

"Nice of you to join us," said Russell. "Cassandra Martin, this is our new recruit, Eve Weldon. Cassandra covers entertainment."

"Culture," said Cassandra. She offered her hand to Eve but, unlike the others, did not offer even a perfunctory smile. She pushed open the door of her office and disappeared.

"Well, we're off for coffee," said Quirine. Eve would have liked to go with them, but they did not invite her.

Inside her office, she sank down on the chair, placing the folder on the desk. She stared at it, running her palm over the surface. What did it contain? It was like a game of roulette. It could be a scientist booked to talk about some complicated discovery. Or a financial wizard to talk about the recent stock market dive. Given her powers of personal budgeting, that would be a disaster. She crossed her fingers and opened the folder, feeling like she was pulling a trigger. She skimmed the booking sheet: "Metropolitan Museum of Art to host lifetime retrospective of legendary German designer Matthias Klieg." Eve brought a hand to her mouth.

Matthias Klieg was renowned for his architectural clothing that doubled as installation art. For decades, society women had been convincing wealthy husbands to spring for a Klieg original on the assurance that, after wearing it to a certain charity event, it could grace their formal dining room and function as an investment. The Met had gathered dozens of his most famous pieces from living rooms and museums all over the world for an unprecedented display.

Inside the folder, Eve found a series of articles about Klieg and photos of the pieces that would decorate the set. But she hardly glanced at them; she didn't need to. She knew Klieg's career almost by heart, thanks to Penelope, who had worshipped him. Klieg had not only created pieces of radical beauty, he had invented a hybrid medium all his own, which, despite the copycat nature of haute couture, no other house had even attempted to mimic.

Eve had seen a Klieg only once, when she was seven, during the family's trip to France. She and Penelope had spent an afternoon wandering around Paris, a fairy tale of a city. They'd had a picnic by the Seine, captivated by its strange blue-green hue, a color neither could quite remember seeing before. Later, they found the gallery her mother had been looking for. It featured six "dresses," each more audacious and intricate than the last. When the guard wasn't looking, Eve reached out and lightly skimmed "The Ball Gown" with the tip of her finger. It was like touching a bewitched object from a children's story. "The Ball Gown" was Klieg's celebrated, spherical see-through evening dress that, after attending Truman Capote's Black and White Ball on the person of Merle Oberon, had lived its second life as a terrarium in Berlin.

What a job! To think that on her very first day, she was going to talk to Matthias Klieg himself. Then she remembered. Klieg was a notoriously difficult interview. Taciturn and grim, he had long since stopped working and now lived like a recluse. Eve rubbed the spot between her eyebrows, thinking of the freelance writers who would soon finish their stints at CNN and be available again.

· · ·

An hour and a half later, it was time to call the designer at his studio. The phone glared at her like a many-eyed monster, daring her to try. She dialed. A woman answered and put her through.

"*Jah?*"

"Mr. Klieg? Hello, this is Eve Weldon. From *Smell the Coffee?* We're scheduled for a pre-interview? Is now a good time for you, sir?"

"You are an hour late."

Her heart beat fast. "Really?" Eve fumbled with the folder. "I thought I was supposed to call at five-thirty."

"Your booker told me *four-thirty*. Perhaps you cannot tell time?"

Eve flipped through the papers wildly. Was there a note about a change in the time? Had the booker listed on the sheet, someone named Kel Zimmerman, forgotten to tell her? Or, Eve wondered with a sinking heart, had this been some kind of payback for this Katrine person's firing?

"I'm very sorry about the mix-up, sir. I just need a few minutes of your time." This wasn't true but it was the only way she could think to placate him.

"It is impossible. The photographers are here."

"But, but . . ." Eve sputtered, trying to think of something to keep him on the phone. "It's just that I'm curious about 'Peer-Amid,' " she said. "Peer-Amid" was Klieg's landmark piece from 1969, worn by a British countess to President Nixon's inauguration. It was a pyramid-shaped gown (the head of the wearer popping out of its top) of highly burnished gold resin, sprinkled with jeweled hieroglyphics. Since the designer didn't hang up, she continued. "The dress will be on our set tomorrow, as you know, and I've always wondered about your inspiration for it."

Eve had hoped Klieg would pick up the ball and run with it, but he remained silent. She grimaced. What would her father do if this were a deposition? He certainly wouldn't quit. He would apply kind but firm pressure till he got what he wanted, using just the right detail to tease out someone's story. She cleared her throat. "More specifically, my mother used to get British *Vogue* and I read in there once that this dress was based on a pyramid built by Imhotep for King Zoser? But, well, that doesn't seem to be right. Imhotep built pyramids with steps, and yours is smooth-sided. I was thinking yours reminded me more of Cheops's in Giza." She hoped she was remembering correctly her notes from junior year's Art of the Ancient World.

"This is a fair point," he said, his words clipped and precise. "It was Cheops's pyramid I sought to evoke. I wanted the modern woman to know that ancient splendor."

"I see," she said, struggling to take down the last of his response with fingers that had grown clumsy in the weeks since she'd stopped working. "And what about this one with the holes—the one everybody calls 'The Swiss Cheese Dress'?"

"I detest that appellation," he said.

"I understand. Actually, sir—actually, it doesn't look like Swiss cheese to me."

"Well, what then?"

"Maybe I'm making presumptions," said Eve. "But to me it seems like you were thinking of Henry Moore."

"I—well. Yes." There was a note of surprise in his voice. "I met Henry in London. I thought his pieces were so sensual that they would feel divine on the body. So I created this dress. What?" There was some noise on Klieg's end. "Oh for heaven's sake. That's very expensive! Excuse me, Miss Weldon, the photographer from *ArtForum* nearly knocked over a Lalique."

"That's quite all right."

"Out. *Out.*" There was some heated discussion and a sound like a door being closed quite firmly before Klieg spoke to Eve again. "I tell you, most of these philistines don't know me from Max Ernst."

The interview began to flow. Though Klieg remained reserved, he showed flashes of humor and humility. He told her his most "alive" period had been as a young man in Paris in the sixties, when he ran with a diverse crowd of artists, poets, and philosophers, drinking pastis and eating ham sandwiches at the Deux Magots.

"Sounds like a dream life," said Eve.

"It was, eventually. But when I first arrived there, I was, what do you call it? A 'fish out of water.' I did not have many friends and had to work as a dustman before creating my first collection. Things were difficult for a long time before I found my way."

Nearly two hours after they'd begun speaking, Eve came to the end of her questions.

"Goodness," Klieg said. "The booker said we would speak for no more than forty-five minutes."

"I'm sorry."

"It is all right. This was less painful than usual."

"It was an honor for me," said Eve, feeling suddenly compelled to reveal something about herself. "I'm not sure if I'm supposed to tell you this, but you're my first interview. Ever. I'm a fish out of water, too."

"This I would not have guessed," conceded the designer.

After they hung up, Eve rubbed her ear and scrolled through her notes on the computer. Every one of her questions had produced an interesting answer, but she'd have to cull a handful of the best to fit the four minutes allotted. Luckily, her paralegal experience again came in handy. She'd long since mastered the art of boiling down complicated documents and producing pithy summaries. And she was excellent at explaining the ins and outs of difficult cases to laypeople, so much so that her father had put her in charge of the entire firm's client correspondence. In less than an hour, she'd shaped what she hoped was a comprehensive yet streamlined interview.

Then she turned to the intro. How to interest a Phoenix soccer mom in dresses that resembled trapezoids or Calder mobiles? She closed her eyes and took a few deep breaths, trying to clear the decks. She pictured her mind draining like a swimming pool, becoming a clean, light blue space—one of her tricks for dealing with Donald when he got nosy. Dancing into the space came iconic images of Klieg's dresses on Jacqueline Kennedy, Princess Grace, Catherine Deneuve. Maybe that was a way to go, Eve thought. Maybe she should focus on the wearers to spark interest in the clothes. She spent the next hour fashioning and refashioning her copy till she couldn't look at it another second.

She had to wait a good hour before Mark could see her; other writers had finished first. Eve used the time to read the papers and leave a message with Vadis, telling her that she had been hired after all and would do everything she could to make sure Spoilt Picnic would get a spot on the show. Not that she had the slightest idea how to do that.

. . .

Eve swung her crossed leg while Mark read her script, making the odd mark with his red pen as he went. When he was done, he looked up with what seemed like a hint of respect in his deep brown eyes. "Well. The booker said Klieg was a tough interview, but I guess not. This is good. The questions are fantastic. Quite scholarly, for a segment about dresses. Make these few changes and you're all set." He handed back her work.

"Thanks," she said. "So do I get to come back tomorrow?"

"You get to come back tomorrow. And if you do well again, the day after that. But like I said on the phone, you're freelance, which means no benefits, no contract, no nothing. After you've worked a certain number of days, I think it's thirty, you'll be eligible for the Writers Guild, which will give you some protection, but you still always want to be on your toes," he said, leaning forward.

"Got it," said Eve. All she had to do was do what she did today—thirty more times.

"Now get out of here," he said, with a small but genuine smile. She turned to walk out, sensing his eyes on her. It was not a bad feeling.

It was nearly 10 p.m., but Eve felt so energized she walked home. Thirty blocks, in kitten heels.

. . .

The next morning, at exactly two minutes before seven, Eve sat up in bed as if pulled by a string. She padded into the living room and switched on the old black and white she'd found on the curb outside the tenement next door. For all its expense and toughness, New York could be extraordinarily generous. It coughed up regular goodies on stoops and sidewalks, ranging from books to blenders to dining room sets. She'd come across her love seat on Bank Street and a street person had even helped her carry it home. Some items came with droll signs attached. The television bore a Post-it reading, "A good slap turns me on."

She watched the segments executed by the other writers, impressed by the evocative prose of their intros and how much information they worked into the three or four minutes of the interview. She made coffee but couldn't drink it. She drummed her fingers on the bar, then did some stretches and jumping jacks as she waited for 7:48. Finally, the moment arrived. The commercial faded away and Hap McCutcheon appeared.

"Shall we begin 'The Numbered Story'?" boomed Donald, with his impeccable timing.

"Shhhh," said Eve, rotating her shoulders to burn off nervous energy. "My work is about to be televised to the nation."

"What, my dear? Have you—"

"*Shhhhh.*"

(HAP:)
THIS WEEK, THE METROPOLITAN MUSEUM OF ART CELEBRATES ONE OF THE LEGENDS OF THE FASHION INDUSTRY. HIS DRESSES HAVE BEEN WORN BY EVERYONE FROM QUEEN ELIZABETH TO MADONNA. BUT UNLIKE OTHER CREATIONS, THESE GOWNS DON'T RESIDE IN THE CLOSET WHEN THEY'RE NOT BEING WORN.

"You used the phrase 'being worn' twice. Watch that—it's not only repetitive, it's passive voice," said Donald who, annoyingly, was right. Eve hadn't realized he'd be able to hear the TV through her brain.

NO, THESE DRESSES ARE MORE LIKELY TO BE FOUND ON DISPLAY IN THE DRAWING ROOMS OF THE FAMOUS AND THE BOARDROOMS OF FORTUNE 500 COMPANIES. JOINING US NOW, THE MAN WHO HAS SPENT FORTY YEARS CREATING HIGH DRAMA IN THE SPACE WHERE ART AND FASHION MEET—

"Now, that was nice."
"Thank you, Donald."

—LEGENDARY DESIGNER MATTHIAS KLIEG.

The camera pulled back, revealing Klieg. Tall and lithe with solemn gray eyes and gleaming white hair receding from a patrician forehead. He nodded at Hap.

Eve leaned forward and watched as Hap followed her line of questioning precisely. He and Klieg chatted their way through the succession of dresses as if they were old friends. Hap even had Eve convinced he was an authority on Cheops.

"So what did you think?" asked Eve happily when it was over. But Donald was long gone.

. . .

That afternoon Eve decided she could risk the elevator and walk to her office through the gauntlet of *Smell*'s front offices. She noticed or imagined several hard stares as she threaded her way among the cubicles, and her heart started to pound. After the long hike down to writers' row, she saw Mark, Quirine, Cassandra, Steve, and Russell with their heads huddled together. They stopped talking when they saw her.

"Well," said Russell, peering over his glasses at her with new interest. "You certainly know how to make a second impression."

Eve slung her bag off her shoulder. "What's going on?"

Quirine bounced up and down on the balls of her feet. "Go in your office. Now." The others nodded in unison.

Eve pushed open the door. Inside, taking up most of the small room, sat a Matthias Klieg original, threaded onto a slim Lucite pole atop one of the designer's custom platforms.

"Klieg's people sent it over this morning after the interview," said Steve. "I heard it took, like, three guys to get it in and out of the freight elevator."

Eve opened the card taped to the pole, her heart racing.

Dear Miss Eve, .

From one "fish out of water" to another.

I hope you will do me the honor of wearing this to the exhibit's opening gala on Saturday. Please feel free to bring a guest.

Regards,

MK

"It's got to be worth hundreds of thousands," said Russell.

"But, Mark," said Cassandra sharply, "she can't keep it. We're not allowed to accept gifts. Conflict of interest. If she keeps it, we'll have to tell Giles."

What's her problem? wondered Eve. "He just wants me to borrow it," she said. The shimmering teal gown was, in Klieg fashion, a marvel of engineering: Over a silk underdress, a resin shell had been constructed, consisting of a series of waves that surrounded the wearer from the bust down to the knee. The dress sparkled under the fluorescent lights, winking at its drab surroundings. Its surface was awash in seed pearls, crystals, semiprecious stones, and enormous, jewel-encrusted fish.

Quirine approached the dress. "How does he do it?" she asked, peering closely at the place where two waves met. "He's a magician."

Cassandra flounced out of the room. The others, smiling politely, mumbled various things and filed out behind her. Mark stopped in the doorway. He looked at her quizzically. "First the bouillabaisse, now this. Do you always attract so much attention?"

Thinking back over her life before the last few days, Eve almost had to laugh. "Uh, no," she said.

Chapter 6

Eve asked Vadis to be her date at the gala and suddenly it was as if the two failed jobs and anchor vomit had never happened. Eve couldn't contain her elation. She counted the days, then the hours, then the minutes before the party. She was going out on the town in New York.

Because of the elaborate costume, she was allowed to dress in one of the museum's executive offices, and she took special care with her appearance: She put her chin-length hair up with turquoise seahorse pins she'd bought at one of the antiques stores on Bleecker, applied pearly eye shadow that brought out the greenish flecks in her eyes, and swept a deep red lipstick across the pointed pucker of her lips.

"A Klieg's never looked so good," said Vadis as they stood at the entrance to the fete. "Of course, the fact that you're the only one in a Klieg under sixty doesn't hurt." Eve enjoyed the curious looks of fellow party guests. Only five or six other women were wearing Kliegs; the rest were on display around the room, lit from within like multicolored planets, orbited by tuxedos and caviar blini.

Vadis, in a black jersey gown with a plunging neckline, curled her left hand around an imaginary glass and held two fingers of her right straight out as if clutching a cigarette between them, her signal during college that she was ready to party. They made their way over to the bar, accepted two champagne cocktails, and toasted each other amid the churning social whirl.

"*Girl,*" said Vadis, sweeping her eyes over the room, which looked eerily beautiful in low, bluish light, "you've done it."

"Done what?" asked Eve.

"Put us squarely in the position to make shit happen."

"Hmmm?"

"Parties like this . . . we'll meet everyone. I knew I was onto something when I put you up for this job." Vadis took a lusty slurp of her drink.

Eve said nothing. She'd gotten the distinct impression from Mark that being invited to "parties like this" was not just unusual but unheard of. She reached for a shrimp on a passing tray and took a thoughtful bite.

They stood for a few moments, waiting for something to happen. When nothing did, Vadis searched out a promising mark. "Middle-aged ponytail at two o'clock," she said. "*Has* to be in music." She took a couple of strides and struck up a conversation with a self-consciously hip-looking man wearing a gold wristwatch the size of a saucer. A minute or so later, while he removed a business card from his wallet, Vadis turned to Eve with an impish smile and mouthed, *Rolling Stone.*

Eve smiled back, scratching lightly at the stitches on her arm. She looked down at the puffer fish near her waist. A rich orange-brown, its spots appeared traced with diamond dust. Someone jostled her and Eve moved back. The initial interest she'd inspired seemed to have evaporated. She wondered if she should try to enter someone else's conversation, but that didn't look easy. The crowd, mostly older and wearing the safe combination of black and diamonds, was absorbed in itself. Groups of twos and threes gathered, glancing furtively at one another and whis-

pering. Eve heard snippets of conversations: ". . . Went to Field-
ston with my husband and still refused to second his nomination
to the board. . . ." "That acquisition was a *scandal*, an outrage. . . ." She ordered another drink and was just wondering
when Vadis might come back, when a stooped, lanky man with
bifocals and a large Adam's apple appeared next to her.

"Don't tell me," he said, thumping a pencil against the Klieg
catalogue. " 'Deep Blue See'?"

"I'm sorry?"

"What you've got on."

"Oh. Yes," said Eve, uncomfortable under the man's beady
gaze.

"Looks a little big on you. How come you're wearing it?"

"I'm not sure what you mean."

"What I mean is, what's your connection here? Who do you
know?"

Eve wanted to say it was none of his business, but the answer
to his question proved more satisfying. "Well, actually, I know
Mr. Klieg."

"Nice try. Nobody knows him. Now, my friend over there
thinks your father's on the donor committee but I said—"

"Miss Eve," came a voice from her left. Matthias Klieg stepped
between her and the Adam's apple, neatly ending his inquisition.
The designer took her in with raised eyebrows and an abbrevi-
ated bow. "Enchanted."

Eve did a double take. Matthias Klieg, in person! If Penelope
could see her now. Eve straightened her five-foot-three-inch
frame, wanting to show the dress off to its best effect. "Thank
you for inviting me. It was incredibly kind of you."

"It was not my intention to be kind. That dress was to be
worn by Dame Alchist, but she called earlier in the week to say
she was ill, and I hated to display it on a stand. It looks better
when it moves." His eyes moved over the room.

Eve nodded and took a long sip of champagne. She'd so

believed she and Klieg had shared a connection on the phone, a particular intimacy, like strangers who'd been trapped together in an elevator. She tried to think of something to say. "My mother was such a fan of your work." Not very original, but at least it was the truth. Klieg nodded absently, looking bored and, if Eve wasn't mistaken, miserable. "Aren't you enjoying the evening?" she asked. It was a celebration of his life and work, after all. "You look like you'd rather be sweeping the Rue de Montaigne."

This was met by silence. Eve looked away. Then Klieg cleared his throat. "This is not my scene, shall we say," he said, exhaling heavily before swigging what looked like Campari.

"Not as much fun as your Paris days?" Eve ventured.

"Hardly. This is small talk. Small people. Small lives. Nothing irks me more. In Paris, well, forgive my hubris, but I like to think we discussed things that mattered."

"You must have known some interesting people."

"They were the best days of my life." He looked down at the floor. "Inside an old man is always a young man, a young man shaped by his friends. Though now all I have of them are memories."

Eve presumed she was still young herself. But what friends would she have to think so wistfully of when she was sixty-five or whatever Klieg was? She'd called Audrey and Sandy, her friends from the golfing community, a few times since being here, but all they talked about was the new pool by the green and the fact that Ryan seemed mad for Corinne, which they seemed to think would bother her. At this moment they would be at the clubhouse in their Lily Pulitzer dresses, sipping wine spritzers and droning on about whose husband made more money. She'd known them since her father moved the family to Rolling Links after Penelope died. They were nice enough girls, girls she felt comfortable with in the manner of a child who hangs on to a doll she's long since outgrown but whose countenance she couldn't

imagine her bedroom shelf without. But they never asked anything about her or about New York. Recently, she'd given up on
tending their limp friendship from afar. Eve knew she would sur-
vive this shedding of friends, as she was not unaccustomed to
loneliness. But she'd always seen this condition as something to
be withstood for the moment. She'd never thought of it as memories she wasn't storing up for her future.

"Aren't you still in touch with them?" she asked Klieg.

"Not really. A few are dead already. And though we were all
artists, we were a dissimilar group. The sculptors, like Pierre,
used to bicker with the painters. René had a terrible temper
and—"

"Pierre Cavel? René LaForge?"

"Yes. And the musicians butted heads with the actors. Lars
and Ian would debate so loudly that they had no voice left at the
end of the evening."

"Lars Andersen—the Danish experimental pianist? And you
don't mean Ian Bellingham—head of RADA?" Eve couldn't believe the list of names that tripped off Klieg's tongue. Pierre
Cavel, René LaForge, Lars Andersen, Ian Bellingham—they'd
been known as Europe's "Postwar Four." They'd been a symbol
of how Europe's countries could come together after the wreck-
age and form stronger bonds than they'd shared before.

"Yes, they are all quite well known—now. Back then it was a
different story. We faced parents shocked that we'd left home,
disappointed that we hadn't become bankers or doctors. Most of
us were desperate for money, not to mention attention and reassurance. As a result, everyone became determined to establish
the superiority of his own art, even his own art form. We fought
constantly and were thrown out of cafés almost every night."

"But you're smiling."

"I'm thinking of one particular friend. I was quite low in the
pecking order as an aspiring 'dressmaker,' and he took me under
his wing."

"How?"

"He made the others understand that design was not just sewing clothes for life-sized dolls. He explained it to them in an almost academic way—better than I ever could—so they 'got it.' He—helped me." Klieg trailed off here, running his finger around the rim of his glass.

Just then Vadis, looking so pleased with herself she was almost throwing off sparks, sidled up to Eve, taking her by the upper arm. "Can you get away? There's a guy who wants to meet you," she whispered.

Someone wanted to meet her? Lead the way. She turned to go but something in Klieg's posture made her stop. He seemed so alone. "I'm not sure—" she whispered to Vadis.

Vadis cupped Eve's ear. "Look, I don't want you to burn this bridge or anything, but this guy's real cute. And he's a little closer to your age."

Eve glanced at Klieg and tried to read his expression. He was the guest of honor, surely he wanted to mingle? Yet he made no move to circulate. "I'm sorry," she said, "my friend here has asked me to—"

"Please, Miss Eve. I am old but not senile." He turned to go but as his eyes moved over her face he stopped and gazed at her for a long moment, as if seeing her for the first time. Several seconds of this strange suspension went by and then Klieg swallowed as if his throat felt tender. He gave another shallow bow and departed toward a group of cooing, leathery socialites at the bar.

"Okay, try to look cool." Vadis pulled Eve toward the other side of the room. Eve looked over her shoulder toward Klieg but the crowd had swallowed him up. "This guy Alex is connected," assured Vadis. "Rich. And perfect for you. I think he's even got a collar stay on."

It was a slow and awkward walk, what with Eve's resin waves dancing all around her as she moved, but eventually they arrived at their destination.

"This is Zander. A and R for Multiplatinum," Vadis said,

touching the arm of a barrel-chested young man with ruddy cheeks and a goatee, who nodded and held his glass up in greeting. "And this," Vadis continued with emphasis, "is Alex. The next Graydon Carter."

He reached for her hand and brought it to his lips. She noticed how his top lip came to two distinct and perfect points, like twin mountains. Eve tried to adjust her posture into something alluring but her encasement in plastic made it rather difficult. "Alex . . . and Zander?" she asked, finally.

"You picked up on that," said Alex, smiling as he let go of her hand. "Short version: We're both named Alexander. We met in kindergarten. It got confusing when our parents and teachers tried to call one of us, so they decided we should split the name. We did a coin toss when we were seven, with *his* dad officiating, which is why I got boring ole 'Alex.' "

"Would you stop perpetrating this nonsense?" said Zander. "When I introduce myself, people think I'm a magician at children's birthday parties or something."

Alex motioned to Eve's glass. "Looks like you're empty. More champagne?" Eve nodded and Alex sailed off into the crowd. His neatly cut chestnut hair revealed that he was indeed wearing a collar stay.

• • •

Zander and Vadis went off to dance.

"I'd ask you, but I'm not sure if you can rumba in that thing," said Alex.

"Probably not," Eve replied.

"And you're wearing it because . . . ?" he asked.

Eve told the story of the Klieg interview, enjoying holding the stage. Working for her father had rarely occasioned any interesting tales. "The next thing you know, there's this dress in my office and I'm being invited here. And it was my very first interview, too."

"I guess they better watch out who they have you talk to," said Alex. "If you interview Donald Trump, you might get one of those hideous apartment buildings by the West Side Highway. Or the president might give you a state."

"Just as long as I don't have to wear it to a party," said Eve. Alex had a charming laugh. She wondered what he did for a living. At home, one would never ask, relying on back channels for information. New Yorkers, however, seemed quite open about these things.

"And what about you? Vadis said something about Graydon Carter. *Vanity Fair*, right?"

"Yeah. Well, that's probably overstating it a little. Right now, I work for a publishing house. Marketing. But I *am* starting a magazine with some friends."

Eve balanced her champagne flute on the top wave, where it wobbled slightly with her movements. "Really? What kind?"

"Top secret for now. But," he said, winking, "I'll keep you informed if you give me your number."

Vadis and Zander came back from the dance floor, arms looped over each other's necks and laughing. The rest of the evening flew by in a blur of drinking and flirting. Alex, Zander, and Vadis thrust and parried like characters in a thirties movie, though Alex did give Eve a private smile or two and once he traced the outline of a silvery nautilus shell on her dress with his finger while listening to Zander tell a story about valet stroller parking at the Park Slope YMCA. Everyone else laughed, but Eve, hampered by the dress, and not feeling quite up to speed with local mores yet, stood mostly mute. She didn't really mind, though.

Her New York life was starting to happen.

. . .

The next morning, Eve took Highball out for a walk and bought one of everything at the nearest newsstand. She spread the papers out on the living room floor, which was almost completely covered. With discipline she didn't know she had, she read all of the news sections before allowing herself to peruse the arts and gossip pages. And that's when she saw it.

In a column called "On the Town," she spied a series of pictures from the gala. The fourth one down was of her, standing next to Klieg. She had her arms in the air, lengthening her silhouette and showing off the dress to full effect. She didn't remember making such a demonstrative gesture. Eve's eyes dropped to the caption. "Unidentified staffer from *Smell the Coffee* holds attention of evening's honoree." Eve retrieved her scissors from her kitchen jumble drawer, cut the picture out, and stuck it to the refrigerator. She stared at it for several minutes before making coffee.

"Greetings," said Donald, buzzing around her temples. "What about a little dictation? 'The Numbered Story' is ready to pop out of me."

Eve was in a munificent mood. "Let me get some paper." She found the pad and settled down at the bar. "Ready when you are." Her usual reluctance had abated. She would start looking at this as fun, as a unique bond that she and Donald could share. Writer to writer, and all that.

There was a pause, followed by a soft whirring. "One: I came upon a porcelain ladder. Two: It was up to me to scale it. Three: The ladder stands at the corner of Waverly and Waverly. Four: The polished rungs glinted in the sun, daring me to try."

"Um, Donald? You don't need to number the sentences, I can keep track."

"The numbers aren't for you; they're part of the story. Now. Four—"

"Part of the story?" asked Eve, loosening the neck of her favorite of her mother's kimonos, the one with the peacock spreading its feathers across the back. "What do you mean?"

"I told you I wanted to experiment with structure. Continuing on. Five: People went on about their business. Six: They are intimidated by anyone extraordinary."

Who would want to read this? The subject matter was tedious and the numbers were just strange. "Donald, are you sure about this?" Eve asked. "What are these numbers for? I'm not sure they work. They sort of break up the narrative, don't you think?"

"Thank you for that bit of bright and shiny 'Intro to Fiction' analysis. You don't know what you're talking about," he said. "I'm breaking up the 'narrative' in order to call into question the whole *notion* of narrative."

"All right, all right. *Sheesh,*" she said. Then a thought struck. "Before we go on, can I ask you something else?"

"What?"

"Did you know Gregory Corso?"

"Why? You think *he* could have come up with this?"

"Why do you always have to be so competitive about everything? It's just that I walked by a building on Bleecker Street where he used to live. He was about your age. I thought you might have known him, that's all."

"I knew him. I knew all of them."

"And?"

"And what?"

"What did you think of him?" This was like pulling the proverbial teeth.

"Talented, everyone acknowledges that. But troubled. Extremely troubled. Used to pull his pants down in the street as some kind of political statement. You think *I'm* a handful."

"Did you ever share your work with him? Did you ever—?"

"Will you stop hijacking my session with these pointless questions? Can we please get back to my story? Where was I? Eight?"

"Seven." Eve put pen resignedly to paper, wondering why he was so edgy. As he got started again, she also pondered exactly how many blotters of LSD he'd sucked in his day.

"Seven: The higher I got, the smaller they looked. Eight: I pulled myself up, rung after rung, into the clouds. Nine . . ."

. . .

Eve picked up the pace as she neared the corner of Bleecker and MacDougal. According to everything she'd read, she was about to lay eyes on the San Remo, where Penelope had caroused in the sixties, and where Corso and the other founding Beats— Burroughs, Ginsberg, and Kerouac—had held court in the fifties.

Eve had been so busy trying to get a career going that she hadn't had time to track down her mother's haunts the way she'd wanted to. The conversation with Donald had piqued her interest and she was determined to reignite her quest. Plus, today was a beautiful late April day, the kind that heightened the pleasant naughtiness of lingering indoors. There really was nothing to beat a dark bar on a bright afternoon. It was so decadent, so willful. While everyone else jostled hysterically in the parks, *making the most of it,* Eve would spend the next few glorious hours in noir-y dim with sallow strangers. Strangers who might become friends. Because that was the way it happened here. Penelope and Donald both had attested to the effortlessness of connecting with fellow Villagers, who responded warmly to like minds and for whom the next lifelong friendship was but a drink away.

It would all start here, on this corner. Eve tingled as she looked up at the flapping awning. Then her face fell; the San Remo was nowhere to be seen. It had become something called Thai Kitchen. She pressed a curved hand up to the glass to shade her eyes. Dozens of small tables stood lined up on a carpeted floor, each with a tiny bamboo plant in the middle. From the maps spread out on various laps and the cameras slung over shoulders, most of the patrons inside seemed to be tourists.

Luckily, the Gaslight Café, which had showcased Beat poets before becoming a folk club and a haven for a new generation of artists in the sixties, lay just a couple of blocks north on Mac-Dougal. But it too turned out to be a thing of the past, replaced by a chain burrito bar. A man bumped into Eve roughly as she stared in disappointment at the large plastic letters spelling out Taco Bueno.

At least Chumley's remained. Thanks to the Village streets having minds of their own, including some that went north–south until they felt like going east–west, it took some time to find it again, and Eve's feet ached as she sank onto a bar stool. As she rubbed them she realized she was neglecting to affect a welcoming posture, signaling to the assembled that she was open to approach. Somebody might remember her from her first night here, and she wanted to encourage any impulse they might feel to strike up a conversation.

She ordered a sidecar, tossed her hair, and straightened her back. The group on her left was talking about the stock market; the one on the right, the Mets. Neither was her favorite topic, but she did her best to catch the eyes of those on the edges. Their eyes proved uncatchable. She cleared her throat. Nothing. She joined in when the stock marketers laughed loudly, but no one noticed. Finally, she "accidentally" bumped the elbow of the young man next to her.

" 'Scuse me," he said, without even turning to look her way.

Maybe the Village wasn't what it used to be.

. . .

At work, Eve tried to learn the names of her dozens of new co-workers, from Giles Oberoy, the executive producer, to Franka Lemon, the show's line producer, to Jerry Chisolm, the new intern. All in all, the editorial staff—producers, associate producers, bookers, and writers—proved a formidable group. Repartee at meetings sped by so quickly and was so topical it was breathtaking. Perhaps the San Remo spirit lived on, uptown. Eve's colleagues spoke with authority on every subject—and in any language, too. Just the other day an office-wide email had gone out asking if anyone spoke Mandarin; within minutes four people had responded asking which was preferable: Southwestern or Northeastern?

Then came the technical staff, an army of directors, cameramen, tape editors, sound engineers, production assistants, satellite coordinators, and others whose titles she couldn't keep straight.

Eve intended to impress them all, but especially the writers. She knew that privately they questioned her hiring. But if she could earn their respect at work, she thought, the pool of good feeling might spill over into life outside the office. Perhaps, she mused, as she sat squashed between a paint-splattered construction worker and an overperfumed dowager on the subway one day, she had inadvertently stumbled upon a ready-made clique, the kind her mother had run with, the kind Klieg had belonged to in Paris.

The key to all this was pleasing Mark. Much to Eve's relief, Orla Knock did indeed go to L.A. after the management retreat. It was rumored she was in meetings with network brass about something big. Mark continued to coach Eve, often staying late to do so. After the last writer had left for the evening, he would say something like "Want to hang out and go over graphics requests again?" Eve always did. Both because she liked the way he explained things in a commanding yet gentle way and because she was determined to let him know how much she appreciated his faith in her.

And this meant doing every bit of the assigned homework. Eve devoured the morning papers, along with piles of magazines and shelves of books. Periodicals and tomes multiplied around the apartment, taking up every available surface, including much of the floor.

But it wasn't just preparation that was proving to make Eve a good interviewer. She genuinely found other people interesting and enjoyed listening to them. This likely had its roots in the long afternoons during her mother's illness, when they'd talked, really talked, for the first time. The newfound intimacy made Eve feel special and every drop of information she extracted felt like a revelation about life itself.

It was also true that, given the choice, Eve preferred to ask questions rather than answer them. She didn't think of herself as very interesting. Plus, when you revealed yourself, you left yourself open to judgment. If you let someone in, there was always the chance they wouldn't like what they saw.

At first, Donald expressed approval about her new lifestyle; she was expanding her mind. But by week three, he began to carp. *The Dallas Morning News* was all very well, but not if it meant delaying work on "The Numbered Story." Week four brought the complaint that all the new information stored in her memory was leaving him less and less room to deposit his own. This protest was followed by Donald's retaliation: monologues that went on and on just when Eve most needed to concentrate.

Eve suspected that there was something else that upset Donald far more than her new workload. Her other offense, she guessed, was her obsession with two new men. First, Alex. Eve was spending way too much time looking at the phone, willing him to call, frustrated and confused by his silence. Though she couldn't say she was unfamiliar with the inconstant and perplexing ways of young men. Certainly they didn't always do what they said they'd do. But at home, the incestuousness of the golfing community meant it was virtually impossible to hide from those you'd wronged. If a boy who said he'd call didn't (and it was always the boys who called the girls, never the other way around) and you mentioned it to your father, he would no doubt say something pointed to the father of the young man at the next club dinner.

Her other fixation was Hap. These days, when she woke in the morning and when she went to sleep at night, it was Hap McCutcheon she saw: the green eyes fringed with thick lashes, the strong chin with its deep dimple like her father's, and that calm, reassuring voice. Donald accused her of harboring a crush, but that wasn't it. Hap was her job and her job was her crush. It was a real, grown-up, New York job. True to what Mark had said, she was given only Hap segments to write, and usually the

ones in the back half of the show, but she found no humiliation
in it. Hap was not the obtuse ex-jock she had first supposed. As
an interviewer, he was quick and sure, with terrific instincts.
Which one would expect of a major leaguer, according to Steve.

The whole department preferred Hap, if they were honest
about it. They were writers without a byline, invisible to the outside world. They could feed only on the rare praise of the terse
Orla Knock, and on the response of the anchors, who registered
their approval by the extent to which they used the writers' material. Hap made some changes to his intros, but usually it was in
favor of a word that was easier for him to say. And he sometimes
added a question or two of his own to an interview, but only
when it was a story that he personally knew something about.
Each of the writers had gotten numerous "100 percent"s from
Hap—meaning he hadn't changed a word.

Bliss's approach to the writers' work was rather like that of a
lawnmower to grass. Mark, who often took the company line on
things, said Bliss was a perfectionist, plain and simple. Others
insisted she was simply vicious. Either way, Archie, the most
respected and senior member of the department, had scored only
six "100 percent"s from Bliss—six in the eight years he'd been at
the show.

But Eve didn't have time to worry about Bliss. She only had
eyes for Hap, and what he liked from a writer was a preponder-
ance of basic information. So she drafted plain, muscular notes,
beefy with facts. And when there was a particularly difficult concept to convey, Eve found that sports metaphors could be employed to make things clearer, so she'd taken to quizzing Steve
about football, baseball, and basketball on a regular basis.

All the writers, except for Cassandra, took turns helping to
acclimatize her. In this respect Quirine proved the most generous. She summoned Eve into her office one day in May and presented her with a cup of coffee and a cinnamon twist pastry to
celebrate her becoming staff and getting into the Writers Guild.

"You're safe now. You can't be put out into the street because they decide they don't like your hair. You really have to mess up before they can fire you."

"Thanks," said Eve, who was intending to never "mess up" again. They clinked coffee cups and Eve made herself comfortable in Quirine's guest chair, an overstuffed affair in a lovely peach silk that she'd brought in herself to mitigate all "zhat gray." "So finish what you started telling me the other day about Bliss and Hap. Something about lists?"

"This you're going to enjoy," said Quirine, running her hands through her boyishly cut raven hair. "Every month or two, the anchors put out lists for the writers of their likes and dislikes."

"You mean in terms of food? Pets?" asked Eve, which produced in Quirine an explosive snort.

"*Words,*" she said, flinging her hands in the air dramatically. "Let's see, what's an example? Okay, you probably heard that Hap hates puns?"

"Yes."

"Puh-lease," spat someone behind her. It was Cassandra, poking her head in the door. "That's what he says now. A year ago, he loved puns. Hey, I missed the meeting. What story did I get?"

"Celeb roundup with the folks at *People* magazine," said Quirine.

"Well, *that* should keep people in their seats," Cassandra said with a good bit of sarcasm. "Mind if I borrow this?" She picked up a thesaurus from the shelf by the door.

"So why does Hap suddenly hate puns?" asked Eve, enjoying this collegial moment.

"Um, because Bliss put out a list saying she likes them," said Cassandra, as if this should have been perfectly obvious.

Quirine nodded. "As long as they're 'elegant, tasteful, and fresh,' of course." She sighed. "Their lists completely contradict themselves. They're mostly there to one-up each other. Of course, we get caught in the middle, trying to keep them straight."

"And no one in our department has the balls to complain," said Cassandra, turning and leaving.

Eve looked down at her hands, wondering how she'd ever keep up with the lists and everything else. But something else nagged at her, too. "Can I ask you a non-writing question?"

"Of course," said Quirine.

"Am I imagining things or does Cassandra not like me?"

Quirine put her elbows on the desk and cradled her chin in her hands. "She does not like you." Eve's eyes widened. She'd asked the question expecting reassurance, not candor. Quirine laughed. "I'm sorry. I always forget that Americans like some sugar with the medicine. The issue is that Cassandra was mad about Kevin."

"Kevin?"

"The one who was fired the day you came in for your interview."

"They were a couple?"

"He hadn't asked her out yet, but I think she hoped that by seeing him every day, she'd work her magic eventually. Obviously, she never got the chance."

"What does it have to do with me?"

"She thinks if you hadn't come in that day, ready to 'steal' Kevin's job, he'd still be here. And of course they'd be together now, planning a romantic summer vacation."

"Oh." Eve looked down at her lap. Even though Kevin had already been fired before she'd arrived for her interview, she couldn't help feel bad for the doomed couple. "Poor Cassandra. And poor Kevin."

"Don't feel bad for Kevin. He was arrogant and careless."

"How do you mean?"

"Not long before he was let go, he finally got a big news story. And how did he show his appreciation? By including a typo in his script, one that resulted in an on-screen graphic that labeled General Carnegie 'Chairman of the Joint Chiefs of *Stuff*.'"

"Oops."

"Cassandra's affections were misplaced. But aside from that, it didn't help that your Klieg segment resulted in you getting your picture in the paper. Cassandra's incredibly ambitious and, between you and me, the only reason she covers entertainment is because she spent years at casting calls with no takers. What she really wanted was to be an actress."

"I had no idea."

"Of course you didn't. Look, don't take it personally. She gets in these little snits. Probably because she's insecure."

"About what?"

"Well, even though we all have our areas of expertise, it's a point of pride that any of us can jump in and do whatever segment needs doing." Quirine pushed back from her desk and stretched her legs. "Like if Archie is out, in theory, any of us should be able to handle an interview with the vice president. For Bliss. I mean, the next time this country of yours starts a war or something, everyone will have to do hard news, yes? At this point, we've all had to do at least a couple of big stories for her. And she makes changes, but that's just her. Mark and Orla Knock know we're up to the job." Quirine laced her fingers together and stretched her arms overhead. "I'm sorry, what did you ask me?"

"About Cassandra."

"Oh, right. Well, she's the only one who's never been allowed to write for Bliss. Russell overheard Orla tell Mark she wasn't good enough. And she doesn't help herself by being constantly late and hungover at least once a week."

Later that evening, Eve stopped outside Cassandra's closed door. She didn't want to have an enemy. She knocked.

"Come in," said Cassandra. She looked up, her face expressionless. A beat passed, then she picked up the thesaurus and held it out to Eve.

"That's not what I'm here for."

Cassandra put the book down. "Then what can I do for you?"

Eve took a couple of steps into the room. "I just wanted to tell you how much I liked your segment this morning."

Cassandra leaned back. "Really? Why?"

Who reacted to compliments this way? A simple "thank you" was customary. And now Eve was cornered. She didn't even remember which story Cassandra had done. It was probably an actor, promoting a film. But which one? "Your intro. So colorful," she said. Cassandra looked at the ceiling. "The way you wove in the movie clip was perfect, too. . . ." Eve didn't know what else she could say that was vague enough to work. "And I really liked—"

"Please."

"I'm sorry?"

"Be honest," said Cassandra, leaning forward ever so slightly. "You didn't really like my segment, did you?"

"I'm afraid I don't remember it as well as I'd like but—"

"Don't. Don't stoop," said Cassandra. "I'd have more respect for you if you just got on with it and stopped sucking up to everybody all the time."

Eve's face flamed and she withdrew, doing her best to close the door with a click and not a slam.

· · ·

"I thought of you when I saw these," said Mrs. Chin, who worked the Jefferson Market Library's front desk. Eve never forgot her name because she did, in fact, have a soft double chin. But her eyes were kind and her manner most eager, especially for regulars. "They came to us from a deceased local benefactor. Apparently he was quite an avid scholar of life in the mid-century Village. Right up your alley. And I hear there's more where these came from, too. I guess he left quite an estate. But none of these are processed yet, so I can't check them out. You can look at them here, though."

"Thanks," said Eve, lifting several onto the crook of her arm. She took them to her favorite table, in the back by the window. Far from being processed, the books didn't seem to have been cleaned. Eve used her hanky to wipe the fine white dust from the edges of the pages. As she leafed through the tables of contents, she saw that these books were quirkier than what she'd come across before, more color commentary than play-by-play. In moments, she had slipped into the Village of Penelope's time, a kaleidoscope of guitars played on stoops, jazz at coffee bars, and poetry readings given by undiscovered writers at basement cocktail parties. She knew it was a long shot but she still hoped that her mother might be mentioned. Aunt Fern, who had lived in Australia but visited quite often until she died a few years ago, had once said Penelope had possessed real talent as a writer. Over a "girly lunch" at the Vernon Manor Hotel when Eve was twenty, Fern said she wasn't the least surprised that Eve had won the college essay contest; she said Eve was clearly the beneficiary of her mother's gift.

"In fact," she said, her freckled face wide and knowing, "your writing is a lot like hers."

"How so?" asked Eve, putting down her fork.

"Your mother wrote differently than she spoke. With more clarity and confidence. When she lived in New York, she wrote reports on manuscripts for a literary agent, as you know. They pulsed with authority and pizzazz. She always had wonderful suggestions for how to improve books, too; she would have made a wonderful editor, if she'd gotten that far. The agent, unfortunately, was in way over his head and knew it. He never gave Penelope any credit, and often passed off her ideas as his own.

"She wrote other things, too, just for herself. She wouldn't show people, but I used to snoop a bit when I was in the city." She shook her head and tried to look stern. "I don't recommend that behavior, of course. Prying is not right. But with your mother, sometimes it was the only way." Fern opened her pocketbook to fish out a cigarette. "Anyway, eventually I turned up poems, stories, all kinds of things. I take it you never saw any."

"No," said Eve quietly. This was all news to her. She would have given anything—*anything*—to read something her mother had written.

"I suppose she threw them out when she married your father. A lot of women did that back then, put away their fantasies and got on with the business of being a wife. She let most of her friendships from those days slide, too. And I don't think she ever told your father anything about New York. I think he preferred not to know, frankly. And she really did love him, so she tried to forget about it all. I suppose that's a good thing. Awfully hard to have your past competing with your present."

This was the moment that Eve had first wondered: If her mother had loved New York so much, why then had she left?

Eve bent back over the pages, feeling her nose twitch from the dust, on the lookout for any mention of Penelope. Or Donald, of course.

. . .

The very next week, a new Hap list came out, this one expressing an interest in clichés. Or, as he put it, a preference for "tried-and-true expressions to which our audience immediately responds." Eve promptly set about assembling an arsenal of trusty slogans she never used in real life but which now proved highly useful, such as "firestorm of controversy," "a parent's worst nightmare," and the ever popular "unanswered questions." Another device Hap currently enjoyed was alliteration, and thus "triumph and tragedy," "spirit and sacrifice," and "pain and perseverance" became among the most dependable arrows in her quiver.

Each morning, as Eve watched the show with Highball, Hap read these lines with zest. He never betrayed any sign that he'd heard, let alone uttered, the exact same phrases thousands of times before. He gave each his all with a guileless, almost child-like exuberance that Eve found touching. Because of him, people were listening to her. Even if they didn't know it.

Then something even more exciting happened. Mark came into her office with a folder of research and, after they finished talking about her segment, he lingered for a few minutes making small talk, which, for him, was unusual.

Just as Eve was wondering if this was his version of flirting, Mark turned to go. He stepped out into the hall, then he turned back again, slowly. "Have you seen *Transformers: Rise of the Barnyard Animals,* or whatever the heck it's called, yet? I'm way behind on my top ten movies, especially the ones aimed at teenagers."

"I'm behind, too," said Eve, trying to sound casual.

"Maybe we can cross that one off our list in the next couple of weeks?" asked Mark.

Eve nodded.

"Okay, then. See ya, Toulouse." He winked at her and left.

Finally! Eve thought. *He does like me.*

. . .

Late Friday night, she dragged herself up the stairs to her apartment, and down again to take Highball for her nightly constitutional. Poor Highball. She was alone an awful lot these days. Eve tried to give her a longer walk than usual, and was rewarded with another writer's plaque, this one on MacDougal, marking a former home of Louisa May Alcott. When they got home, Eve engaged the dog in a game of fetch and poured herself a bourbon. She was always so revved up after a night at *Smell;* the adrenaline that kicked in from the interviews and writing coursed through her for hours after she left the office. In another life, she would have read herself to sleep, but with all the reading she was doing for work, she simply couldn't face running her eyes over any more words, the spiky letters feeling as if they were practically pricking her eyeballs.

Eve changed into her peignoir and curled up on the settee, just big enough for one person. Everything in her apartment was big enough for just one person, she thought, as she sipped idly and looked out the window at the silhouette of the trees, swaying against the city-lightened sky.

Sometime later, Eve became aware of the phone ringing. This was rare and the noise, just for a moment, confused her. She looked at the clock on the plain wooden mantel and was startled by the time; it was almost 11 a.m. She'd slept the whole night on the couch.

"Hello?"

"Eve?"

"Yes?"

"It's me."

"Dad?"

"My daughter's alive."

"I know, I know," she said, wandering into the kitchen, where she leaned heavily against the small counter. "I'm sorry I haven't called."

It was odd to think she hadn't spoken to him in weeks, considering that before she moved to New York, her father had been practically her entire world. The month she'd graduated from college, his secretary had quit to get married. Eve's two elder brothers were working as junior law associates in Columbus, the younger still in school. Somehow, it had been taken for granted that Eve would help out "old Dad" by answering phones and filing. At his request, she even moved in with him for a couple of years. She hadn't been keen about any of this, but it was difficult to refuse Gin. After Penelope had died, he'd all but closed himself off from the world. He socialized often enough, especially after winning a case or a club tournament, but only in the most superficial ways. Eve doubted he opened up to anyone. She saw it as her duty to keep him company, at least for a while. "A while" had lasted more than a third of her life.

"How are you?" she asked.

"Fine. Out on the green for an early round. Waiting for Smith. He's off settling a squabble between two caddies and left me here to cool my heels." Smith Wainright was one of her father's partners and had lost his own wife six months before Penelope died. Several weeks after Penelope's funeral, he decided he was moving his family to Rolling Links, and Gin had promptly announced he would do the same. In short order, the Weldon family abandoned its three-story Victorian with blue shutters in town for a four-bedroom faux townhouse of a condominium, surrounded by prizewinning thornless roses and overlooking miles of tiny hills dotted with ponds shaped like kidney beans. Eve's new room had come with a bird's-eye view of the sixteenth hole and its men in green pants with little sweaters tied over their shoulders.

"I'm at the eighth hole. Your favorite," Gin continued. "Remember?"

She certainly did. When Eve had been in the sixth grade, her friend Lucy Arbuckle had talked her into "borrowing" a golf cart from an ancient foursome engaged in putting practice. With Lucy behind the wheel, they'd careened around the green at breakneck speed till one side of the cart ran over the edge of a sand trap, momentarily tilting the entire cart at a forty-five-degree angle and throwing Eve overboard. She'd landed very hard on her palm and sprained her wrist. A small crowd gathered and began to shout. She was still in shock when her father arrived, plunked himself down in the sand in his new pants, and cradled her in his arms as if she were a newborn. He'd actually shaken off his usual haze and remained focused, all the way to the infirmary where she was iced and bandaged. He even fed her soup that night rather than make her eat with her left hand.

"Of course I remember," said Eve, padding back out to the living room with a hot cup of tea and sitting on the deep windowsill. And then in a small voice, "I didn't think you did."

There was a short silence on the other end. "So you're still in the Big Apple. That . . . place."

"Yes, I am."

"Vadis taking good care of you?"

"She sure is."

"Because you can come back, anytime you want."

"I can?"

"Of course. I've found some help. She's good, but she's no you."

"Thanks."

There was a little cough. "I was thinking maybe I didn't tell you often enough how much I appreciated your work. And if that's why you left, well . . . perhaps I could do better on that score."

"That's nice of you to say." Eve ruminated on the fact that she'd never heard from Alex, and on Donald's incessant needling. Compared to them, her father proved to be surprisingly sensitive.

They chatted a bit about her brothers and Gin seemed impressed that Eve could now talk with some authority about both sports and politics, things he enjoyed that she'd never known much about.

". . . Well, we'll see if you're right about the Yankees' front office. I'm still skeptical," he said.

"You bet."

They were silent for a moment and Eve sensed Gin was struggling with what to say. "Still not sure about you—*there*," he said, finally. "I just can't see you as a New Yorker, honey. I know your mother enjoyed it, but to me it's a strange place. Cold."

"It does seem that way sometimes. But I think things could change," she said, thinking of how Mark had finally asked her out.

After they hung up, Eve went back into the kitchen to dump out her now-cold tea and make a fresh pot. As she poured milk into the bottom of the cup, she considered what exactly made someone a New Yorker anyway. A certain salary? A particular address? A table full of friends, perhaps. Or maybe it was being able to order a complicated sandwich at warp speed and having your money ready for the deli man so you didn't cause those behind you to wait one millisecond longer than absolutely necessary. That was probably the most likely.

．．．

"What a jerk."

"Who?"

"That father of yours," said Donald. "Trying to quash your life's journey to make his own more comfortable. Trying to lure you from your destiny so that you can serve his interests."

"That's not fair," she said. "He misses me and wants me home. What's wrong with that?"

"Nothing, if it were true. But you and I both know the moment he got you back he'd try to bribe you into being a lawyer again. He wants cheap help."

"Which is exactly what you want. Me, as your unpaid servant."

"It is absurd to compare filing for your father to the chance to apprentice with a revolutionary artist. In fact—"

The front door slammed satisfyingly behind her. Too late, she realized she was in the hallway without her shoes. She sank down on the top step of the landing, ready to wait it out until Donald disappeared. As she sat there, examining the chipped polish on her toes, she found herself thinking about her dad. Maybe he just wanted "cheap help" or maybe he really missed her. Either way, it was nice to know she had options.

Chapter 7

Matthias Klieg's atelier took up the bottom floor of his home, a baroque townhouse on the Upper East Side. Eve stood in the foyer, craning her neck. Since the gala some weeks ago, she and Klieg's people had been trying to work out a time when they could pick up the underdress she'd worn with "Deep Blue See." Finally she'd offered to deliver it herself.

Klieg's chief of staff, Maxine, a tall, stately woman in a pencil skirt and flats, smiled as she accepted the box. She put it on a small table and considered Eve. "Mr. Klieg is at work in the studio. Would you like to say hello?"

Eve was surprised. Hadn't Klieg famously stopped designing years ago? She followed Maxine into a spacious, neutral-hued room. Antique chairs and settees sat in small clusters, a chandelier hung on a velvet rope, and floor-to-ceiling windows let in sparkling shafts of light. Eve perched on a tufted ottoman and accepted a cup of mint tea offered by a valet.

Klieg strolled around a platform, chin in hand, considering a model draped in champagne organza with a bored expression on her face. So far, it didn't look like much. Two assistants kept several paces behind Klieg, trying to anticipate his needs for pins and sticky tape. This process continued for some seven or eight minutes before the designer spoke.

"At the shoulder or the hip?" he asked, stopping to hold a rosette up to the dress.

No one answered.

"Miss Eve. Shoulder or hip?"

Eve clattered the cup back in its saucer. "I'm sure I have no idea."

"Yes, you do. Any girl who can pair an Yves Saint Laurent shift with, what is that, a Ben Reig bolero, can't be completely hopeless." He did not look at her as he said this.

Eve approached the platform. She tried to read Klieg's expression to determine which option he preferred, but his face betrayed nothing. She took the rosette he held out and stood on tiptoe to hold it against the model's shoulder. Then she brought it down to the hip. She went back and forth several times, suppressing a smile when she caught Klieg turning his head this way and that, following her movements. He looked comically earnest.

"Here's the thing," she began. "If the dress were only for this model, I'd put it at the hip, because she's so slender. For another woman, the shoulder might be better, because it could balance a delicate jaw. On another woman, the waist might be best."

Klieg nodded. They stood silently, staring at the nascent creation.

"Forgive me if this is an obtuse suggestion, but could the rosette be detachable? Perhaps each woman could decide for herself how to wear it," said Eve.

"Interactive fashion?" Klieg raised one white eyebrow.

"I think any woman would feel honored to have a hand in something you created."

"Hmm." Klieg walked around the model twice more, seeming to disappear into a private world. In the end, he said he would take the rosette idea under advisement. As the model stepped off the platform and headed behind a screen to change, he approached Eve slowly, squinting at her with the same pained, quizzical expression as he had at the gala, just before they'd parted company. "Thank you for your assistance, Miss Eve." He shook her hand.

Eve knew the encounter was already far more than she had a right to, but she couldn't bring herself to leave. "Thank you, Mr. Klieg. This was a remarkable experience." She turned and walked slowly toward the foyer, trying to squeeze every ounce out of the moment.

Maxine poked her head in and said something to Klieg. She was either irritated or German was always spoken with a slight hiss. The designer grunted and they seemed to bicker briefly. Eve reached the threshold.

"Miss Eve?" said Klieg at last. "I'm afraid I forget my manners. You've come all this way to return my garment. May I offer you lunch on the patio?"

· · ·

They sat at a small wrought-iron table on wide paving stones overlooking a tiny English garden. It was pleasantly cool compared to the streets on this unexpectedly warm day. The cook, Marie, brought out omelets *aux fines herbes,* a baguette, and a chilled Riesling. Eve accepted a piece of bread and spread it with beautiful, pale butter.

Klieg said nothing, but after a few sips of wine, Eve thought she might risk a question she hoped wouldn't sound impertinent. "Why did you stop designing the installation dresses? Not that what you're doing now isn't beautiful. I just wondered, why the change?"

Klieg put down his glass. "I had an epiphany."

"About what?"

"First you have to tell me something."

"All right."

"And you must be honest."

"Of course." Eve put down her fork and looked at him.

"How did you find wearing 'Deep Blue See'?"

"I loved it." Klieg said nothing but continued eating his omelet. Eve tried to dial up the enthusiasm. "It was incredible. Every eye was on me. I felt like a princess." Klieg put down his own fork and cocked his head. She had the unnerving feeling that he was looking into a secret room inside of her that she'd never told anyone about. "Well," she said finally. "I—I guess I wasn't all that comfortable?" She coughed. "Physically." Small bonfires erupted on her cheeks.

"Ah."

"You're not surprised."

"Not at all. In fact, this is the answer to your question."

"I don't understand."

"When I designed those pieces, I was thinking of myself. My art, the statement I wanted to make. Getting the world to notice me. I did not care anything for the woman who'd have to wear them. How she'd hold a drink, flirt with a man. Or visit the loo, if you don't mind me bringing up something so vulgar over lunch."

Eve smiled. "And then?"

"In my latter career, I designed for the woman: what would make her look good. Feel good."

"It sounds like you regret your early work."

"Heavens, no." He sat back and looked at the square of sky above the patio. "How can I explain? I had to do that work. It was in me and it had to come out. It was, if I may say, a significant contribution to the art form, and my early pieces advanced the notion of what wearable design could be. But they were of a particular moment in my life. They could only have been done by a young man."

"What do you mean?"

"As we age—and you can't know this yet. But as we age, we start to care about too many things." He took a sip of wine. "It all seems so precious. Every little thing. That tiny purple flower there, bending over the brick. You see it? Or the way the sun makes your hair look wet." Reflexively, Eve put a hand to her head. "Everything we see feels so significant, yet so fragile," Klieg continued. "We become acutely aware of everything we have lost, and our longing for it only increases over time. When we care so much *about* so much, passion is diluted. I could never focus the way I did when I was young and free. I could be bold then because I had more . . . room. You see?"

"I think so." Eve glimpsed Maxine watching them from the kitchen window. When their eyes met, Maxine looked away.

"It is part of development," said Klieg. "That feeling of being immortal, it lets you take the chances you will no longer take when you have a husband and children and a legacy. So my advice to you, Miss Eve, is this: Be bold while you are young."

Klieg asked her about *Smell the Coffee* and whom else she'd interviewed. As with Alex, the topic brought the storyteller out in Eve. The more she worked, the more entertaining stories she had, especially about celebrities. She didn't get to talk to big stars; usually it was just "movie of the week" folk, but even they constituted a minor brush with notoriety. The famous behaved differently in phone interviews; they were far more relaxed than on television. There was a "just between us" feel that arose from the meeting of two disembodied voices, and Eve had used that to lure some interesting tidbits from her subjects. She told Klieg about an up-and-coming actor she'd interviewed who had met his wife on a movie set. Unfortunately, she was engaged to the director and the entire shoot had taken on a cloak-and-dagger feel as the two actors tried to steal time together without the director knowing. By the end of the story, Klieg had stopped eating and was actually leaning forward in his chair.

"Fascinating," he said. "Though they sound like a very ill-bred pair, making a mockery of the woman's fiancé. Discretion used to be customary in such matters."

"Were you ever married?" asked Eve, wondering idly if he might be gay but also picturing him with any of the dozens of beauties he'd dressed in his time.

Klieg leaned back again, folded his napkin, and placed it on the table. "Yes." A cloud passed over their little patch of sky and threw the patio into momentary dimness. Klieg looked at his watch. "Do you mind? I have some calls to make." He scraped his chair back with a bit more force than necessary. They stood and faced each other and Maxine hurried out with a furrowed brow.

Lunch was over.

. . .

"How about we get back to 'The Numbered Story'?" asked Eve. "I have to go out in a while, but I have time before I need to leave."

Donald didn't have to be asked twice. "Capital idea. We've got to finish this one quickly, in fact, because I have another I want to start before I forget it. It's very hard to keep track of things in the state I'm in. Now, what number had we gotten to?"

"Let's see. Twenty-six," Eve replied, flipping through the pages of their legal pad. " 'A school of fish swam by and offered encouragement.' " Eve knew better than to ask why there were fish in the sky.

"Ah, yes." Donald sighed approvingly. "Here we go. Twenty-seven: Scumbag. Twenty-eight: Asshole. Twenty-nine: Mother-fucker."

Eve put down her pen. *Ugh.* She knew enough not to complain about the blue language, but there was so much else wrong. "Sorry, but are you sure this approach is a good one?" she asked. "I mean, a numbered story about a man climbing a ladder to nowhere on Waverly Place? Look, I have a suggestion. We start the story earlier, get to know this poor fellow, understand him. . . ."

"I'm afraid," said Donald in his most exaggeratedly patient tone, "that this is just a *tiny* bit over your head. You may think you're a writer now with your big television job but that carries no water with me. And you're certainly no editor. No one edits me, ever. Now—back to it. Thirty . . ."

Eve sighed. "All right, all right. May I just ask, how many sentences are there?"

"I would think you could figure that out for yourself. One hundred. Now, *thirty* . . ."

. . .

In mid-July, the mercury skyrocketed to 93 degrees, where it sat for a week like a stubborn child. Manhattan lay prostrate under a white sky, and almost everyone dissolved into a listlessness that bordered on catatonia.

Eve, used to the summer breezes that moved across the open spaces of the Midwest, felt as though she were pushing her way through the days, the tall buildings holding the humidity close. Yet she had to take the dog out, and when she did, she would often come across a new plaque. Today it had been Frank O'Hara and, even more exciting, Allen Ginsberg himself over in the East Village.

When she came home, she asked Donald what he remembered about each. It turned out that O'Hara, who was not just a poet but a museum curator and champion of everyone from de Kooning to Pollock, had died even before Donald, the result of a car accident. In fact, Donald said O'Hara's early death had triggered his first thoughts about mortality.

"Little did I know how soon my own bend in the road would come . . ." he said, his voice growing more and more distant before fading out completely.

. . .

The hot weather had an unfortunate effect on work, too. Consumed by the heat that had invaded the entire East Coast, *Smell* featured endless segments on air-conditioner maintenance and quirky cooling techniques.

There was only one bright spot on the horizon.

"A drink with your boss? You must be joking," huffed Donald.

"Mark's not really my boss. The boss is still in L.A. Mark's just filling in," Eve said, clearing the mail that had accumulated from the bar and setting down her pad for another stab at "The Numbered Story." The truth was, she was excited. There had always been a hint of something between her and Mark; she'd just felt it. Mark had been vague when he'd suggested they see a movie, and she wondered if he was ever going to propose something concrete. Then, finally, yesterday he'd suggested a drink tonight. Of course, Alex had never called, so this was her chance to finally go out on a real New York date. Plus, Mark really was handsome, albeit in a way that it took a while to notice. And he was nice. Extremely nice.

"Nice. *Nice,*" Donald spat the word in her inner ear. "What's happened to sexual politics since I left? Women never used that word to describe the male power structure in my day. The thought of socializing with—let alone flirting with, *sleeping* with—the oligarch was verboten. What we knew is that—"

"Let's get on with dictation," said Eve, cutting him off. "We wouldn't want my wayward love life to deprive the world of your brilliance."

Donald grumbled, letting her know he was onto her, but picked up the thread of his profanity-laden tale. After the sixth vulgarity in as many sentences, Eve had to say something.

"You're absolutely sure about this approach?" she asked, rubbing the back of her neck. "You might want to consider that times have changed. I mean, writers in your day, all you had to do was use the f-word and the, uh, the c-word to cause a stir. Now it takes a little more than that."

Silence. Eve felt slightly guilty. She hadn't meant to sound so critical. Donald's writing had some potential, she thought. If only as an early example of a new kind of fiction that had revolutionized an art form. And if he worked on it now, and accepted a suggestion or two, he might even generate something satisfying in its own right. Maybe.

"Do you mean 'fuck'? And 'cunt'?" he hissed.

"Stop it."

"God, you're such a prude," said Donald. "*You can take the girl out of the Midwest* . . . All the mooning you do over Mark, and that Alex person. You think being such a priss is going to get you a boyfriend?"

Eve put the pen down on the paper. Having a man in her life, if and when it happened, she realized, was going to be yet another thing made more complicated by Donald.

    . . .

That evening, Eve was the last to finish her segments, and by the time she and Mark left the office it was close to one-thirty in the morning. They set off through the hushed streets, the new moon hanging like a glowing eyelash in the sky. Eve took a deep breath of night air and noticed that the streetlights were kinder to Mark than the office fluorescents. They softened the worry lines on his forehead and the shadows beneath his eyes.

As they approached the bar, Eve wondered what the moment would be like when the conversation turned from professional to personal. They worked so closely yet knew so little about one another. She was just pondering why this was when they pushed through the doors and she saw them: Russell, Quirine, Steve, and Cassandra, all piled into a booth together.

"Hey, everyone." Mark said, squeezing in on the side next to Quirine and Cassandra, while Eve stood awkwardly. She tried to perch on the three available inches of bench not used by Russell and Steve but had to brace herself with her left leg. Her foot slipped on a puddle of spilled beer.

"Whoa, careful now." Mark hopped up and dragged a chair over from another table. "That's better," he said, settling her in it.

"Thanks," she said, wondering whether he would have done the same for Quirine. She certainly hoped he wouldn't for Cassandra.

"Next round's on me. We're celebrating," Mark said, waving over the waitress.

"What can I get you?" she asked, giving her nose ring an unappetizing twist. Everyone gave their orders, finding they had to repeat and clarify them, frustrated by this obstacle to hearing the news. Eve was intensely curious; Mark hadn't even hinted he had anything to announce on the way over, let alone that it was something important enough to warrant summoning the whole department.

"Celebrating what?" asked Russell, as soon as the waitress departed.

"You may have been wondering why Orla Knock has been gone for so long. Turns out she's been promoted to Vice President of Entertainment Programming," Mark said, looking around the table. "She'll be staying in L.A." A beat of silence was followed by an ebullient eruption.

"Yes! Whoops," said Steve, slamming his pint of ale on the table and wiping a few errant drops off Eve's sleeve. "That witch was always out to get me."

"Me, too," said Cassandra bitterly, hooded eyes flashing. "Always complaining about the angle of my interviews. Always telling me to focus more on industry news instead of advice for young actors—"

Russell shook his head, cutting off his colleagues' grievances. "Uh-uh," he said, pushing his glasses firmly onto his nose with his forefinger. "I know you think that but she wasn't out to get anybody. She was distrustful of *everybody,* which, let's face it, is true of a lot of women in management. And understandably so," he hastened to add when Quirine gave him a look. "Personally, I think that's why she's been sent out west. She'd bumped heads with everyone in New York."

A flood of relief swept over Eve. She'd been carrying a pit in her stomach ever since she'd started at *Smell,* waiting for the day Orla came back.

"But wait," said Cassandra. "Why would she want to do entertainment? She's a news person." Everyone exchanged questioning looks.

"Yes, but she gave that interview to some online place last year where she said her real dream was to do arts programming. Remember?" said Quirine.

Russell smothered a laugh. "Last season, the network ran a sitcom on Friday nights about a family of crickets—played by people. So if she thinks she's going to be doing *Masterpiece Theatre* out there in L.A., she's on drugs."

"Who cares?" cut in Steve. "What I want to know is, what does this mean for us? Mark?"

The waitress reappeared. She placed the glasses on the table in the wrong order and then rearranged them, still incorrectly, in a manner that was less than apologetic. Finally, she toddled off and everyone's attention refocused on Mark.

"Okay. If you think I'm the new managing editor . . ." he began, his face betraying nothing. "You're right. Giles mentioned it might happen last week, and confirmed it yesterday."

There was a burst of applause and a clinking of glasses. Quirine, elegant as always in a generous cowl-neck that showed off her delicate clavicle, gave Mark a quick kiss on the cheek. "That's great. You deserve it," she murmured, patting his hand. If Quirine hadn't mentioned her boyfriend Victor a number of times, Eve might have wondered if she too had feelings for Mark.

"So maybe this is it? A reordering of the cosmos? Maybe we'll finally graduate from our status as the bastard children of network news?" asked Steve.

"'Bastard children of network news'—now, *that's* a shopworn cliché," chastised Cassandra, who was immediately interrupted by Russell's "Hello? Ree-dun-dant."

"What—what do you mean?" asked Eve, wanting very much to join in. "I know the writers get blamed when a segment goes poorly, but 'bastard children'? Are things really that bad?"

"Let me clue you in to something," began Steve. "We, the writers, are the dirty little secret of television news. No one," he held his forefinger up to his mouth and blew a loud *shhhh*, "is to know we exist."

"Why not?" asked Eve.

"Because," said Quirine, "the great illusion is that these anchors—who, by the way, are called 'presenters' in Europe, where they don't believe in this kind of pretense—aren't reading to the viewers, but speaking. We are never supposed to lift the curtain and show how much behind-the-scenes help they have." Quirine continued, looking at Eve, "It's probably what you assumed before you got here, no? That they just spoke their own thoughts?"

Eve nodded.

"Don't be embarrassed. It's what they want you to think," said Quirine. "And it's silly. There's no way anyone could anchor a show like ours—with twelve segments a day and who knows how many guests—without someone else doing the writing and interviewing. There aren't enough hours in the day."

"Want to know how far they'll go to preserve the impression that anchors are solo acts?" asked Russell. "Let me tell you about when we took the show on the road for May sweeps two years ago. We were at Euro Disney—I know, I know. It was hideous, just hideous," he said as Quirine and Cassandra made gagging noises. "And we were told to fan out across the place and interview employees for tips on how to enjoy the park."

"I got a tip from this really cute cub from Le Jamboree des Country Bears," said Steve. "She told me that if you see two lines for a ride, always take the one on the left. Most people gravitate to the one on the right, like driving on the road, so the one on the left moves faster."

"So that night," said Cassandra, downing a slug of merlot, "we get together in Russell's hotel room and make a list of everything we'd learned to put into the show."

"Right," said Russell, "and I wrote something like 'Our writers have scoured the park for tips you can use to have a great time. And here are the top ten.' "

"Innocuous, no?" chimed in Quirine, putting down her gimlet. "But the next morning, when Giles saw the script, guess what happened?"

"What?" breathed Eve.

"He changed the word 'writers' to . . . 'staffers.' "

"No." But Eve suddenly remembered the caption under her picture with Klieg in the paper. She'd been called "an unidentified *Smell the Coffee* staffer."

"Yes," came the unanimous reply.

"They never mention writers on the air. Ever. They'll give a nod to the producers, bookers, and production assistants," said Steve. "They'll mention the director and even the prop guys. But never us."

Eve had been disappointed to see the gang when she first walked in, but now she was glad they were here. She was learning a lot. And since the Village was turning out to be a dry hole when it came to meeting people, this band of writers might yet be her best chance at a social circle.

"And what about the production meetings?" she asked.

"What do you mean?" asked Mark.

"Giles consistently compliments every other department except ours. Now, why is that? The writers aren't exactly a secret to the staff of the show."

"No, but we do have the temerity to be in a union," said Russell. "We make more than the bookers and a lot of the producers. Plus we don't constantly put in 'face time' with Giles the way the other departments do. We get on with our—not inconsiderable—work."

Quesadillas arrived, but they sat, congealing. The writers seemed hungrier to get things out than take them in. They were sorry for themselves, true. But they were also prickly, dramatic characters worthy of *The Happy Island,* Eve decided. She felt a sudden surge of affection for them.

"Hey, you guys, c'mon. I told you not to bombard Eve with all this stuff, remember? You'll scare her," said Mark, who had been quiet for the last few minutes. Eve was thrilled that he'd actually been concerned about keeping her.

Cassandra rolled her eyes again. "Please. You think we should all be grateful just to have jobs. Admit it."

"Yeah, well, he does have a point," said Russell. "In theory, this is one of the greatest jobs ever. Steve—you got to talk to DiMaggio, for God's sake. And Cassandra, you interviewed Paul Newman before he died."

"And, at the risk of giving you swelled heads: You're all extremely talented," said Mark. "Each of you could be at *The New York Times* or *Newsweek* or even writing novels. But you're not. You're at *Smell the Coffee.* There has to be a reason." The others grunted into their drinks. "Okay, what about this?" he continued. "You can't open a paper today without reading about the latest round of news layoffs. If we hadn't snuck Eve in while Orla was away, we'd probably have lost another position in this department and we'd each be writing *four* segments a night." This sobered the table, and the writers bowed their heads in tacit agreement.

"But that doesn't mean this job doesn't suck sometimes. Mark, you can't deny it. Tell Eve what's going to happen if she ever starts writing for Bliss," pushed Cassandra. Mark shook his head. "Fine, *I* will," she said. "When you start writing for Bliss, and be glad you're not near ready to yet. But if you ever are, get ready for major pain. No matter how talented you are—"

"And you are, Eve," interrupted Russell. "Still green, but you've gotten some interesting shit out of some pretty boring people. Personally, I think it's because you're the last earnest girl left in New York."

A chorus of "Mmm-hmm"s went up, which Cassandra quashed with an *"Anyway."* "No matter how talented you are, this woman will treat your work like a pile on the sidewalk to be stepped over. Even when you give her what she wants, it's not what she wants." Eve thought this had to be bluster, since Cassandra wasn't yet allowed to write for Bliss. But the others nodded with heavy heads.

"She doesn't want what she wants?" asked Eve. "What does that mean?"

Quirine elaborated. "It means you rack your brains to come up with an intro that is perfectly suited to her. Something even her husband would swear she'd written. You're feeling good. And the next morning, you watch as she fixes those big blue eyes on the camera. She pauses dramatically and says . . . something totally different."

"It's as if she punishes you if you out-Bliss Bliss," Steve said, nodding.

"You should confront her. Tell her to knock it off," said Cassandra to Mark, sounding a little slurry.

"Yeah, thanks for that," he said, not even looking at her.

"I'm serious. You're the boss now. Tell her we want some fucking respect."

The writers exchanged looks. Eve wondered why they couldn't just enjoy the fact that for the most part, Hap appreciated their work. But perhaps that was a writer's nature, to focus on the bad review.

"So, given the circumstances, what is it you want?" Eve's voice sounded hoarse and she coughed. "I mean *we*. What do we want?" she asked the table at large.

Quirine swirled her glass. "This is a question." There followed an uncomfortable silence.

Finally, Russell spoke up. "I guess what we want is what

everybody wants. Some kind of . . . credit. Acknowledgment. I know they're never gonna say, 'Hey, by the way, folks at home, we've got a team of great writers here who help make our anchors look like rock stars.' But could Bliss go through just one segment—anybody's—the way it was written more than once a century? Could Giles throw us a bone at a production meeting? Or when they're thanking the whole staff at the end of the Christmas Day show, could they say the word 'writers'?"

Everyone nodded into their drinks.

Eve thought for a moment. "It seems to me," she began. The others, lost in private meditations on their unjust treatment, didn't look up. "It seems to me . . . ironic."

"What?" asked Russell.

"It's ironic," she said, feeling very wise and very drunk. "That we—writers, of all people—should be without a voice."

The group gazed at her as though she were the Oracle at Delphi. Either that or they were just very drunk, too.

. . .

The others melted away into the night, citing exhaustion, waiting boyfriends, or suspicious girlfriends, leaving Eve alone with Mark as she nursed her last drink.

"Mind if we get out of here?" he asked. Eve nodded, pushing the glass away, still half full. It sounded like he wanted the second half of their evening to begin.

"You seemed a little out of sorts tonight, given that it was a celebration," she offered as he helped her on with her sweater. His hand brushed her neck lightly and sparks flew down her spine. How long had it been since she'd been touched? Months.

"I guess it was because it suddenly hit me: I'm gonna be you guys' *boss*," he said as they headed out the double doors to the empty street.

"And you're not sure what you should and shouldn't say anymore," she said.

"Exactly. I mean, I'm aware of the downsides of this gig as much as anyone. Hey—taxi!" But the cab turned in the other direction, its red taillights disappearing down the street. "But I know what it's like to lose a job. And that was worse. Much worse than a job that's occasionally superficial and thankless."

Eve couldn't imagine Mark being fired. "Really? What—?"

"Damn. Do you think we should walk over to Third? This is ridiculous."

He was certainly eager. She wondered if he was going to ask her to go over to his place. She certainly hoped so, since hers was out of the question.

They got to Third Avenue and found a taxi waiting at the light. "Well, good night," said Mark, opening the door for her. "Thanks for coming out."

Eve hoped her face didn't betray her disappointment. "You don't want to maybe . . . hang out? A little while longer?"

"I don't think that's a good idea."

"Why not?"

"Like you said, I'm your boss now."

"Does it really matter?"

He sighed, seeming to acknowledge that this discussion had been coming. "Look, I really like you, I do. I think you know that. You're beautiful, and incredibly sweet. Smarter than most people at the show." He paused for a moment, seeming to consider something. "You want to know something?"

"What?"

"That day when Orla Knock came in? Asking me about the two other writers we had on file? And I told her they were doing vacation relief at CNN?"

"Yes."

Mark flicked his eyes down the street, then brought them back to her face. "I lied. I didn't even call them."

"Really?" The thought thrilled her more than anything he'd ever said or any look he'd ever given her.

"Yes, really. But I don't want to mess this job up, or complicate it more than it already is. Orla was never anyone's friend. But I *am* you guys' friend, so I just want to avoid any possible weirdness, okay? For everyone's sake." He gave her a winsome little smile and guided her into the taxi. "Okay, Toulouse?"

Eve nearly teared up at the use of his pet name for her. She nodded and waved halfheartedly as the door slammed shut. As the taxi cruised downtown, for once Eve didn't see the mythical city around her. All she saw were the smudges on the window.

Chapter 8

Something was wrong when the highlight of one's weekend involved walking the dog and looking for plaques on old buildings. Yet even as Eve lamented how things had ended before they began with Mark, she couldn't help but be a little moved to discover Pound and Millay, who had also lived alongside one another on her mother's shelves. She felt energized by them and decided to try for something harder: to track down some lesser-known writers, especially among the Beat generation. Eve took to carrying a small pad of paper to scribble down the addresses of the homes she found and had filled three pages so far.

On Saturday afternoon, she and Highball found themselves on a previously unvisited block of Jane Street, in front of a consignment store called Full Circle. It lured her with a Peggy Hunt lace cocktail dress in the window. They entered and Eve ran her fingers over the sheer black netting that overlaid the champagne taffeta bodice.

"I don't know about that for you."

Eve turned around. A young woman behind the counter was addressing a lumpy customer who'd just stepped out of a dressing room wearing what looked like a hand-painted Mexican blouse and skirt, probably from the forties.

"Excuse me?" said the customer.

"The print on the skirt makes you look wider. And the wooden buttons add bulk at your bust. It's not flattering." The content was harsh, no doubt, but the young woman's delivery was so sincere that it almost muted the hurtfulness of her message. "Try the bias-cut yellow sundress over there instead." The customer frowned at her reflection and stomped back into the changing room.

Eve approached the counter, which displayed an array of rhinestones, pearls, and cameos, set against slabs of black velvet. She picked up a carved green Bakelite cocktail ring and tried it on.

"Now, that's something," said the proprietress. Like Eve, she was spare of build, although she possessed a coltish, animated quality that made her presence seem quite vivid. She pushed back a curtain of blond hair, somewhat stiff with dye, to reveal large brown eyes, rimmed in black kohl like Cleopatra's.

"It certainly is unusual," said Eve. She slid the ring off and put it back.

"I mean your cardigan." She gestured at Eve's cashmere sweater, with its appliquéd pieces of antique Asian textiles. "I can't remember the name, but that's the one where the label is sewed into the waist instead of the collar, right?" Eve shrugged out of it and handed it over. "Carruthers. I knew it. Can't imagine what you paid for it."

"It was my mother's."

The girl gave a low whistle. "She has great taste."

"Had, actually."

"Oh. I'm so sorry." She sounded like she really *was* sorry.

"Thanks," said Eve. She admired some brooches for a minute or two. "May I ask you something?"

"Sure."

"Why did you warn that woman away from that outfit?" Eve whispered the question because the woman was still in the store, prowling somewhere in the back and making disgruntled noises.

"It wasn't right on her."

"It wasn't *that* bad."

"But it wasn't absolutely right. And that wouldn't be fair to her. Or the dress."

"Not fair to the dress?"

"That dress deserves the right person. She's beautiful, but delicate. I worry about her. She's not exactly a kid anymore and the next person who takes her home could be the last partner she'll ever have. I want her to be with the right one at the . . . end." She pressed a button that popped open the cash register, and began making stacks of bills. Looking down, she said, "I anthropomorphize clothes. I realize this is not normal, but there it is."

Eve stuck out her hand. "Eve Weldon."

"Gwendolyn Montgomery." They shook but before either could say anything further, the dressing room door burst open and out came the customer, this time in a sky blue polyester pantsuit, circa 1975.

"Now, that," said Gwendolyn under her breath, "is a match made in heaven."

• • •

The answering machine light was blinking when she got home. Eve pressed the button, kicked off her shoes, and headed into the kitchen.

"Eve. Is this you?" She stopped in her tracks. "Not sure if I dialed right. Anyway, Alex here. From the Met gala thingy. I know it was months ago but it's been a crazy summer. Wondering if you want to hang tonight. Call me."

Eve looked at the machine, overcome with excitement. *Finally.* Of course, it happened just when she'd stopped thinking about him, but that was life for you. She lifted Highball's front paws and began to dance around the apartment. Then something occurred to her. Asking her out at the last minute, after all these weeks, was not a good sign. At the very least, he assumed she didn't have plans. And of course, she didn't. Vadis was still on

the road. Quirine had once said they should take in a movie together but hadn't mentioned it since. And Mark? Well.

Eve definitely wanted to go out. But if she accepted Alex's invitation, it would be tantamount to admitting her status as social
pariah. She sat at the bar, frowning in thought.

Donald appeared with a slight pulsing next to her left ear. She
knew what he was going to say: She should stay home and help
him tackle his next story.

"As it happens," he huffed, "that's not it at all."

"It isn't?"

"No."

"What were you going to say, then?"

"I think you should go."

"Go where?"

"On this date."

"You do?"

"This generation," he groaned. "Such ceremony! One of the
young women who lived here before you, she actually bought a
book on how to trap a man. She had to say no to every boy three
times before accepting an invitation, wouldn't spend the night
for three months, and all kinds of other nonsense. All part of
some scheme to lasso a husband. Pathetic. In my day, things were
much more free. Girls said what they meant and did what they
wanted. They walked home in their Saturday night clothes on
Sunday morning and didn't care who saw them. Take my advice
and loosen up. If you like this young man, accept his offer and
try to have some fun for a change."

Eve was touched. Donald had often been kind, but rarely had
he given any real thought to her happiness, and certainly not at
the expense of his own. Heart beating fast, she picked up the
phone and dialed Alex before either she or Donald could change
their minds. He answered on the third ring and didn't sound in
the least bit surprised to find her on the line.

. . .

He buzzed at five after eight.

"Be right down," she said, preempting any suggestion he might have about coming up. She looked in the mirror once more, taking in the shirred red cocktail dress and royal blue bouclé jacket.

"I'm sure you look very lovely," said Donald.

"Thank you."

"I wonder . . ."

"Yes?"

"Could you perhaps tell me what you look like?"

Eve pressed her lips together. What everyone always remarked on first was her slight build, ebony hair, and pale skin. Like any girl, often she felt quite pretty, but sometimes plain. Her father said she was the most beautiful girl in the world. Of course, most dads thought that of their daughters. But then again, Alex had picked her out of everyone—actresses and models included—at the Met gala.

"How do you imagine me?" she asked.

"Ah. Well, you're a Midwest girl. So I picture you as corn-fed. Long blond hair, strong shoulders, large hands. Sturdy. I like to think of you that way. Am I close?"

"On the nose," said Eve, smiling to herself. She couldn't blame him. She herself had often imagined Donald as something of a Beat caricature: clad in a black turtleneck, slapping a pair of bongo drums.

"Well then. Have a good time." Donald's tone was upbeat yet wistful, like a father trying to affect bravery while sending his daughter off on her first date.

"I will."

"But remember one thing."

"Yes?"

"Actually two things."

"Okay."

"Everyone will disappoint you. And in the end, we're all alone."

Typical.

She kissed Highball on the forehead, turned out the light, and left.

. . .

Alex stood on the sidewalk, gazing down the block toward the sunset over the Hudson River, which was just visible at the end of the street, and now shimmered a smoky, soft purple. She cleared her throat and he turned.

"Ah," he said, as if reregistering what she looked like, and not without pleasure. "The belle of the ball." She gripped the rickety iron railing and made her way down the stoop. Standing on the bottom step, she was exactly his height. He kissed her on each cheek. "Ready?" Eve nodded and Alex led her to a waiting taxi. As they pulled away from the curb, Alex lowered his window and Eve did the same. The evening moved in, warm and close. Couples held hands, store windows twinkled, and high above them, plastic bags rattled in the trees like maracas.

"I'm sorry I didn't call sooner," he said. "Been dealing with magazine stuff, up against the clock. I really did want to see you before this."

"That's all right," said Eve, glad he'd mentioned it and sorry for all the times she'd cursed him. She liked his linen sports jacket and two-tone shoes. It wasn't a vintage look, but there was something retro about it. Something imaginative.

"That's where I lived as a kid," Alex said, pointing at a Federal-style townhouse. "My parents were kind of boho and didn't want to live on the Upper East Side like all their friends. If owning an entire townhouse on West Ninth Street can be considered boho." A couple more blocks went by, one with a deli on the corner. "That's where Zander and I used to steal gum when we were in junior high . . . and there," he said, pointing at Washington Square Park, "is where I broke my arm when I was sixteen. Skateboarding."

"I broke up a dogfight there. Got a scar from the stitches to prove it," said Eve, holding out her arm.

"You're tougher than you look," said Alex, running his index finger along the slightly raised skin.

They passed 38 Washington Square South. "That's where Eugene O'Neill lived," said Eve. "And he also lived down there, at 133 MacDougal."

"How do you know that? Or I mean—why?"

"I walk my dog a lot."

"Huh?"

"I walk past all those plaques on old buildings that tell you about the famous people who've lived there."

"What plaques?"

"The reddish oval ones. Usually near the front door somewhere. You're a lifelong New Yorker and you never noticed?"

"Guess not." Alex scanned the buildings outside looking for one but they were all offices and NYU dorms.

The car moved through the traffic on Delancey and Eve became aware that they were approaching the on-ramp of a bridge.

"Where are we going?" she asked.

"Brooklyn. Buddy of mine's just opened up a place near me and I said I'd support him. Sound okay?"

"Of course. Wait—you say the place is near you?"

"Yeah, near my apartment."

"You live in Brooklyn and you came all the way over to get me?"

"Of course," said Alex, patting her hand.

As they reached the middle of the East River, Eve peered out the back window and the bridge behind them looked strangely narrow, like pulled taffy. Moments later, they were deposited in a maze of wide, buzzing streets, which coursed with fewer taxis but more trucks, more pizza places but fewer manicurists. If Manhattan was a slender, delicate girl, Brooklyn came off like her burly, ever-so-slightly coarse older brother.

They pulled up in front of a plain, two-story brick building that might have once been an office or a school. Its front door was padlocked and two of the windows were boarded up. Alex knocked on one of the windows with two sharp raps. Then he led Eve down the steps and around the side to a big metal door. He knocked six times. A slip of paper slid out the crack beneath the door. Alex opened it and grinned. Eve read it over his shoulder.

Which high school team's banner hangs over the men's room door at The Yachtsman?

He wrote *Choate,* and slid the paper back under the door, which, after one or two beats, opened. They found themselves in a pitch-black hallway on what felt like smooth wood floors.

"Hey," said a voice in the dark.

"Who's that, Ted?"

"Yeah. Just head toward the music, man. They're all down there."

Alex led Eve by the hand toward the sound of twenties jazz. After about fifteen seconds, a door opened and they stumbled into a small but beautifully appointed room dominated by a long bar of dark wood. Small tables were scattered around, each surrounded by four striped, silk-upholstered club chairs. About two dozen young men in khakis and girls in pencil skirts and cardigans looked up, a few breaking into smiles at the sight of Alex. He pulled Eve lightly through the crowd, shaking hands and kissing cheeks, introducing her to nearly everyone with some detail of their shared past. It seemed they were all either classmates, campmates, clubmates, or colleagues at some time or another. But Alex appeared to occupy a special place among the group; the others eagerly confirmed his observations and laughed at even the smallest of his jokes. A couple of girls looked at him with umbrage and several others brushed their eyes over Eve with naked curiosity.

They sat down at a free table and were immediately swarmed

by a pair of ruddy young men whom Alex introduced as Paul and David and a round, playful girl named Barbara who went by Bix. "We haven't seen you in *forever,*" they mock-whined at Alex.

A burly carrottop in black slacks, a white shirt, and a long white apron appeared with teacups on a silver tray.

"Speakeasy theme," he said. "Like it?"

"It's terrific, Tom," said Alex, holding his cup high in a toast.

Eve sniffed her own cup and detected scotch, a young one, but nice. She felt like she'd stepped into a time machine. "Wonderful," she said. "I can just imagine Fitzgerald in that corner over there, writing *Flappers and Philosophers.*"

"If it's good for business, I'm all for it," said Tom absently, wandering off into the din.

"Tom was at Trinity with us but I don't think literature was his strong suit," said Alex, and the other three laughed.

Paul pulled out a cigarette. "I think the ponies were his strong suit. Remember how much money he lost sophomore year?" Everyone laughed again and Eve did, too, even though she hadn't been there. It felt good to join in.

"What do you do?" Bix asked her.

"Eve works at *Smell the Coffee,*" said Alex, and the others looked at her with interest.

"What's Bliss Jones like?" asked David.

The inevitable question. "What can I say? She's a legend," replied Eve. This was what she'd heard Mark say to Steve's aunt when she visited, and somehow she felt it unseemly to criticize a member of the *Smell* family to relative strangers.

"No dirt?" asked Paul.

"Maybe when I get to know you better. Either that or after a few drinks," replied Eve, and Paul jokingly signaled for another round.

"Hey, maybe you should have your launch party here," said David to Alex.

"If we ever launch," said Alex.

"Now will you tell me what kind of magazine it is? I've been curious since the gala," said Eve.

Bix, who was balancing on the armrest of Eve's chair, chimed in. "Yeah, c'mon. Enough already. No one's gonna swipe the idea from you."

Alex smiled and shook his head. "Okay, okay, you win. I'm sick of being pestered. But only because Eve is so pretty and charming." He winked at her. "Here's the concept: *The New Yorker*—for kids." He sat back, folding his arms across his chest.

"Go on," said Paul.

"Short stories by great young writers and adults who write well about kids. In-depth articles on the Tao of Saturday morning cartoons and the fairness of curfews. Stuff like that." Alex leaned forward and began playing with a coaster as he explained more of his ideas. "We're calling it *Our Turn*."

Eve had no idea if it would work, but she was pretty sure from all the periodicals she read these days that there was nothing like it out there. "Where'd you get this idea?" she asked.

"A couple of years ago I read this article about how, in previous generations, kids couldn't wait to grow up; they wanted to be like adults. But now parents want to be like kids. They dress like teenagers and act like them, too. It's getting ridiculous. So I thought it might be cool to get back to the way things used to be, when aspiring to be an adult was a *good* thing. Plus there've been a couple of literary magazines that have started up in Brooklyn. No one thought they had a chance, but they seem to be doing okay."

Whatever Eve had expected, it wasn't this rather sober, sophisticated idea. "How far along are you?" she asked.

"We're cramming to get the layout done so we can get it off to the printers and get it on stands next month. September's big in the mag world. I've got six guys on computers in my apartment as we speak. The art alone is a nightmare. I'm the brains—and most of the cash—but they're doing the heavy lifting."

"How much money you got sunk into this?" asked Paul.

"Too much," said Alex.

"What happens if it doesn't work? I mean, what's the failure rate for magazines?"

"We'll be fine." Alex smiled as he said this, but there was metal in his voice. Eve wondered if he had a bit of a temper. Not that it was necessarily a bad thing. In New York, it was probably essential, if only to make it clear you were no pushover.

David chimed in, "It's gonna be great."

"I think it's fantastic," said Bix.

Tom brought more scotch and there was a toast along with congratulatory noises. "To Alex," they all said. A few moments later, Paul, David, and Bix waved at some friends who'd just come in and excused themselves.

"I'm impressed," said Eve quietly.

"Thanks," said Alex. He ran a fingertip over a daisy on his cup. "I'm just so *ready*."

"For what?"

"To get out. Do my own thing. Stand on my own two feet. You just get to a point, you know?"

"Yes, I do," said Eve.

Past midnight, they arrived at her building. The overhead light above Eve's front door was out again, and the whites of Alex's eyes, so close to hers, glowed like moon rocks. Eve faced him and he pressed her against the door. He put his hand gently on the side of her neck, his fingers reaching up into the roots of her hair. "Did I ever tell you about the first time I saw you?" he whispered.

Eve's knees went buckly. "No."

"It was the moment you walked into the room in that dress. This tiny girl, like a doll in a plastic case."

Eve closed her eyes and breathed in through her mouth.

"And I was thinking . . ." he said, his lips hovering near her left ear.

"Yes?"

"I was thinking that we talked a lot that night."

"We did."

"So it was kind of like a first date."

"Mmmm."

"Which would make this our second."

"Mmmm."

"So what do you think?" he asked, running his thumb around the edge of her lower lip. Before she could speak, he lifted her chin and gave her a soft, melony kiss. Fireworks exploded behind her eyelids. She hadn't been kissed like this in a long time, maybe ever. For a fleeting moment, she thought about saying yes. Donald was the one who suggested she go on this date; maybe he'd keep quiet.

"I'm sorry," said Eve, leaning away and trying to catch her breath. "It's just . . . my bathroom. It flooded last night. The rugs are still sopping."

"I don't mind wet feet." He kissed the corner of her mouth. "Unless the problem is that you have *cold* feet?"

"No, really. It's not that. It's awful up there. You just don't know how awful." She bit her lower lip.

"That's okay, doll." Alex kissed her forehead. "I don't mind a little anticipation. Next time, then?"

"Next time," she breathed. "For sure."

When she opened her eyes, he was gone.

Chapter 9

Eve stepped out of the bath, toweled off, and donned a kimono. "Okay," she said, putting a fresh yellow pad on her lap for a new story. She needed distraction to keep from waiting for the phone to ring. Donald said there was no way Alex would call the day after their date, and Eve had to admit he was probably right.

Of course, Donald might have said anything to get on with his work. He assured her that his next tale would be a towering achievement, unlike any of his previous work. Eve only hoped it turned out better than "The Numbered Story." (After eighty-eight sentences, man finally reaches top of ladder, discovers a leopard cub with no claws that turns into a beautiful princess whom he steeps in hot water, making a tea that he gives away free to beggars. So much for Donald's feminist diatribes.) She pulled herself into a cross-legged position on her bed and patted the spot next to her. Highball jumped up and curled herself into a little ball. "Hit it."

The whirring began. " 'Rock, Paper, Scissors: A Love Story That Does Not End Well.' "

"Nice title."

"Thank you. It all begins with Paper. Paper, that which holds all the ideas in the world. Paper, so precious, so slender and—don't put any commas in this—so vulnerable. Paper . . ."

For heaven's sake—Eve stopped her thought before it could be detected. "Great. Continue," she said instead. On went the description of "Paper" for several more cryptic minutes.

"Ah! But it is not a Paper Paradise. For Scissors comes on the scene. Scissors, young, fresh from the smoke-spouting factory, the natural enemy of Paper, cuts a swath across the land. Scissors so sharp so sparkling so lethal. They will meet at a dinner party."

A hundred thoughts fought to express themselves in Eve's head. About how obscure this was, yet again, and how fruitless. But she wouldn't let them cross her consciousness; she wouldn't let Donald know because he'd hit the roof, which would only delay finishing the work. She bit her tongue and did nothing but take down his words for the next few minutes. Her hand began to ache.

"Soon too soon the moment comes. Paper and Scissors meet. Everyone in the room wonders what will happen."

"Donald, do you mind if we—"

She felt what she could only describe as a light slap on her temple. Donald swept on for several minutes, building up steam as he went. "The others stare with wide eyes, spoiling for a fight. Will it come before the salad course? Before the fish?"

"Donald—I need a break." The story's aggressive lack of emotional underpinning and self-conscious cleverness were too much. Maybe humor would help. "Salad, fish. You're making me hungry."

"What?" he asked, missing the joke.

Loath as she was to open her favorite can of literary worms again, maybe she could save them both hours of time. "Your approach is . . . I don't know how to put it without hurting your feelings." She looked for just the right word. "Kind of unsatisfying."

"I'm afraid this is over your head, little one. This technique is a continuation of the ideas, the themes, of my greatest work. There will be eager hands, and eager minds, waiting for it."

Eve groaned. "I don't think so. It might not be good enough." Highball snorted in her sleep and rolled over.

"Oh, yes, Miss *Smell the Coffee*. By all means, do tell me about *great writing*."

Eve was surprised at how defensive she felt about her job. "Maybe what I write isn't high art or anything, but we do some pretty important stories. It's a national conversation, and in a splintered country, there aren't many of those. Plus, unlike in your day, people wake up today and aren't absolutely, positively sure the world is still there. Understand? We let them know that it is. We get people's day started with good information and a little fun. And at least I know whom I'm writing for."

"The mother of four in Sheboygan? Please."

"What's wrong with the mother of four in Sheboygan?"

"If she's so great, why did you move to New York?"

Eve was hurt that he would bring up something so personal during a spat. "You *know* why."

Donald seemed to realize his error. "Penelope," he said softly. Eve pulled a large down pillow onto her lap and hugged it. "You feel like she's still here, don't you?"

"Kind of."

"You still long for her. All these years later."

"It just seemed like she always had a better place to be, inside her mind somewhere. A place we could never go. Then, when she got sick, everything changed. For once, she let me in." Eve felt the blood begin to pulse in her face. "And that's why it's so unfair. Just as I was getting to know her, she left. And I was all alone." Eve rocked back and forth, a couple of hot tears melting into the pillow. "My father never talked about her. Neither did my brothers. *Ever*."

Highball woke, snuffled for a few minutes around her ear, and then attempted to lick the part of Eve's cheek that was visible. Eve trembled. Where had all this emotion come from? She sounded angry. And she was not an angry person.

"Hah," said Donald.

"Hah what?"

"*Hah*. You have plenty of anger. By the way, you're not the only one to lose a mother, you know. It's nothing to take personally."

Nothing to take personally? Of course it was personal.

"Young lady, you need to get over this victim mentality. It's poison and it will infect your whole life."

"I'm no psychiatrist," said Eve, wiping a hand across her eyes. "But I would say that sounds like projection."

"Hmph."

"Hmph."

Several moments went by during which neither spoke.

"I am sorry, my dear," said Donald. "I did not mean to upset you. Try to relax."

"It's okay. I'm okay." Eve pulled the pillowcase from the pillow, used it to dry her face, and then dropped it into the hamper. She took some deep breaths and went to brew some tea.

"No one knows better than I that you are a lost lamb beleaguered by emotional trip wires that it behooves us both for me to skirt," Donald continued soothingly. But this condescension just upset Eve all over again.

"I'm not a lost lamb, for heaven's sake. Look, forget what I said, I came here for the same reason as everyone else—including *you*, my friend. I came here to make it. To do something interesting with my life."

"Much as I hate to rub you the wrong way again, your job is not interesting."

"Yes, it is." It was. Wasn't it?

Smell the Coffee was encumbered, as was most of television, by its consumer-driven ethos. It was exactly the opposite of the

Beats, who'd so fiercely rebelled against the mindlessness of consumer culture. It was easy for "news you can use" to look shoddy, craven, by comparison. Yet while the world had certainly benefited from the prying open of assumptions the Beats achieved, they weren't perfect, either. For one thing, where were the women? Where were the plaques for Joan Vollmer Burroughs, or Joan Haverty Kerouac or Carolyn Robinson Cassady? Or Elise Cowen or Hettie Jones?

Eve had read that someone had asked Gregory Corso why there weren't more women acknowledged as Beat architects. He'd replied that there had been plenty of girls around, but only men were allowed to be rebels. Girls who tried to be were "locked up" by their families. The Beat men didn't exactly care, though; they seemed to have eyes only for each other.

Whereas *Smell the Coffee* had more women on staff than men. Both Bliss Jones and Orla Knock were formidable. Orla was gone, true, but from what everyone said, she was raising hell out in L.A. *Smell the Coffee* also had flexible, child-care-friendly hours. And most stories were female-driven, because household budgets were determined by women. Women earned money now and so had consumer clout, which was *something*, at least. And they weren't locked up for speaking their minds.

Now, if somehow the rebellious impulse of the Beats and the power of women could ever come together, wouldn't that be something? Eve would like to work on that show.

"At least they pay me enough to live in the Village," she said. "How many writing jobs do that?" The kettle screamed. "When was the last time you had a writer in here anyway? The eighties?"

"I don't remember," said Donald. "And are you sure they pay you enough to live here? Haven't you been worried lately?"

This was true, unfortunately. The salary had seemed more than adequate when she'd started. But that was before Eve had understood exactly how long her hours would be. And before she'd had to hire Denise, a dreadlocked local dog walker, to take

Highball out several times a week because she was gone so much. Denise charged extra for keeping Highball at her apartment all day, but Eve couldn't chance the girl coming into her place to pick the dog up.

Then there was the bombshell from De Fief. Though Eve's apartment was expensive by Ohio standards, it was a bargain for the Village. The gang at *Smell* had whistled when she told them her rent; it was well below market rate. But the other day, a letter had arrived from De Fief informing Eve that as of January the rent would jump a stunning eighteen percent because a recent check of the records revealed that it hadn't been raised to the maximum amount under the law on the leases of the previous six tenants. They'd come and gone so quickly (no surprise there) that the paperwork simply hadn't kept pace.

"And then there's the fact that they don't treat you with any respect," said Donald, firmly onto something now. "'The Right Makeup for Your Astrological Sign'? 'Is Your Carpet Killing Your Toddler?' All they give you is crap. When will you get a real story?"

This stung even more. When she'd first started at *Smell*, Eve had told Mark she'd be happy with any segment, and she was. She'd been so grateful to have the job at all. Now she was beginning to feel itchy. She wanted to graduate from being tolerated to being respected, sought after. And being respected at *Smell* meant one thing: writing hard news and writing it for Bliss Jones. But every time she brought it up, Mark put her off. "Everything's covered today, thanks," he'd say, and hand her another research folder on "Crafts to Do with Your Pets."

"Don't you think you've earned the right to do some real news?" asked Donald. Eve didn't respond. "Are you or are you not ready to write for this Bliss Jones character? She's not God on the mountain, after all."

"No, *you're* God on the mountain," said Eve.

"What?"

"Nothing. I'm ready to write for her. But it takes a long time before you're allowed to even try. I was told that at the beginning. It's the way it is." Even as she said this, she wondered if Archie or even Quirine had had to wait this long. "I just have to keep doing a good job. They'll notice."

"Your doormat tendencies are exhausting. I realize as a child it was difficult to get your mother's attention. But you can't let the resulting neediness define your life. Certainly not in New York. You can't get by being 'the good little girl' in this town. You must demand what you want. In my day, the women . . ."

Eve suddenly remembered there were some blouses waiting for her at the dry cleaner. She found the ticket, threw on some clothes, and headed out the door, Donald still nattering on.

• • •

A few days later, unable to keep from staring at the phone, Eve took Highball out for an extra walk. She took long strides, energized by a general sense of righteous indignation, mostly about men. Donald was irritating. Mark was patronizing. And then there was Alex. They'd had a good time, so why hadn't he called yet? Was he *that* put off that she didn't let him come upstairs? Did he think her hopelessly old-fashioned?

After she'd circled past James Baldwin's and Edmund Wilson's houses twice, Eve made her way over to Full Circle. She needed the company of women. Gwendolyn saw her through the window and waved her in.

"This is so strange," she said, leaning over the counter. "I was thinking about you just this morning. We got in some new stuff I think you might like. Haven't had time to unpack it yet. You got a minute?"

"I have lots of minutes."

They spent the rest of the afternoon trying on the choicest pieces whenever there were no customers. After closing time, Gwendolyn lowered the shades and made some tea while Eve described her magical date with Alex. "I'm pretty sure he's going to call, but it's awful waiting."

"Why don't you just call him?" asked Gwendolyn.

"I couldn't possibly."

"Why not?"

Eve stirred some honey into her tea as she pondered this. She'd learned how to send back a weak scotch and soda to the bartender, even at the Plaza. She'd learned how to get the best of anyone who tried to poach her taxi. She'd learned how to talk on the phone with all kinds of people. Maybe she *would* call Alex.

. . .

When she arrived home, she found an envelope made of thick, luxurious paper with her name on it on the small table in the vestibule. There was no stamp; it seemed to have been delivered by messenger. She opened it quickly.

Dear Miss Eventual,
I fear I ended our lunch some weeks ago rather rudely. May I
make up for it by asking you to join me at Lincoln Center for La
Bohème a week from Friday?
MK

The surprise was enough to make her plop down on the stairs and reread the note three times, hand on cheek.

. . .

Mark assigned her a cooking segment, her first since the bouillabaisse.

"I think someone's ready for panini!" he trilled, handing her the folder with the recipes and the dossier of the chef who would be demonstrating them. He seemed to think this was a sign of well-deserved esteem. "I told you you'd work your way back to covering food. Good job."

This was patently ridiculous. Eve had done well on the writing of the bouillabaisse segment; her only problem had been with the cooking. The show had long since hired a new food producer, so she wouldn't be expected to actually grill the panini. She gave Mark a look that evidently he chose not to see.

"Feel free to have fun with this one," he said, picking up the phone to make a call.

"What about new trends at Montessori schools?" Eve asked.

Mark checked a phone number and began dialing. "Quirine's got that."

"I know, but she's also got two other stories. Let me take one of hers. How about the latest on cap and trade?" She knew all about it now.

"No, really, she's fine. Just do the panini." His tone said, "On your way now." Eve turned to leave, shaking her head. What was the problem? She was better than panini; she knew she was. Yet after several months of good work, her status in the department remained stuck at the bottom.

Along with Cassandra.

. . .

Klieg's box offered a perfect view of the stage and the glittering audience below.

"This is spectacular," said Eve, gazing at the enormous modernist snowflake chandeliers overhead. She'd chosen a deep purple Claire McCardell dress with a fitted bodice and a tulle ballerina skirt for the evening and fantasized that she'd detected a nod of approval when she and Klieg had met in the lobby, though in fact his greeting was terse.

He surreptitiously opened a bottle of champagne with practiced ease if little enthusiasm and handed Eve a glass. He drank without toasting.

"Thank you so much for inviting me tonight," said Eve.

"It was Maxine's idea," he said, setting the bottle down and pulling out his libretto. Just then, the box's door opened. In stepped a young man with conservatively cut dark blond hair. He looked at Eve for a moment, then he and Klieg spoke several sentences to each other in rapid German. After a slightly unpleasant pause, he sat on the chair behind Eve.

Klieg focused once again on his libretto. "This is Günter. My nephew."

"Pleased to meet you," said Eve, turning around in her seat. Günter inclined his head slightly but said nothing.

"Günter is a veterinarian," said Klieg. "In America to work at Plum Island for the year. Helping to understand foreign animal diseases. He is supposed to be some kind of expert. My brother insists he spend time in the city with me to absorb some culture. I'm not sure he can be converted to opera in his mid-thirties, but I said I would try."

Eve turned to Günter again, tilting her head to try to look into his downcast eyes. "Do you speak English?"

Günter nodded.

"He speaks it very well but thinks it's not good enough," said Klieg. "He is a perfectionist." Klieg did not make this sound like a compliment.

Eve gave up and opened her own program. She thought of Alex. She hadn't had to call him, after all. He'd called the previous week to apologize, saying he'd been spending every night working. They'd since gone out twice more, late, after she got off from work. Alex had taken her to late night jazz at the Blue Note and a midnight poetry reading in the East Village. His kisses had made her swoon but both nights he'd gone back to Brooklyn to work on the magazine, which was a couple of weeks away from going to press.

She wished she were at the opera with Alex. This private little nook was just the place for a stolen kiss in the dark. At least they were going out again in a few days. Dinner with Bix and Paul, then a birthday party for some friend of theirs and then . . . ? Back to his place, she hoped. Denise had agreed to take Highball for the night. It would be forty dollars well spent.

Klieg remained buried in his libretto. There were a good ten minutes to go before curtain-up, and Eve couldn't bear to spend the entire time mute. And why should they? They'd gotten along well enough the two times they'd met. Though for some reason, Klieg seemed to find it slightly painful to be near her. Probably after so many years as a recluse, it was difficult to be around new people.

She decided to take matters into her own hands. "I interviewed a young actress last week," Eve began. Klieg nodded but kept reading. "Not a particularly talented one. She told me she's about to launch a clothing line. She seemed to think it quite easy to reinvent herself as a designer."

Klieg didn't take his eyes off his program. "Such ventures constitute an affront. The added insult is that she will likely do very well, at least at first. Until distributors realize she's not talented at this, either." Finally he looked at her. "The traditional way is to fail first and then work one's way up. It was good enough for me."

"Did you ever fail? Really?"

"My first collection very nearly ended my career."

"No."

"Yes."

"When was this?"

"In the early sixties."

"Well—what happened?" Eve felt frustrated at having to pull every morsel out of him.

Finally, Klieg closed his libretto. "I had taken every centime of my money from street sweeping and fixing shoes and even selling my blood, and poured it into one show, at a local park. It contained my first experiments with spheres and other shapes. There was a clumsy but promising trapezoid, I remember. The collection had to do well and bring in at least a few orders, or I would have to go back home to Germany. I cannot tell you how much this idea pained me. The word of mouth before the show was favorable and I believed I had a very good chance of success." Klieg shifted in his chair, facing her slightly more directly.

Eve put her glass down and leaned in.

"The big day came. A handful of critics, mostly there to catch a glimpse of my rather notorious friends, took the front row. I sent my garments down the runway. There were gasps from the audience; this I expected. It was something new and they would rely on the critics to decide what they felt. But the critics just sat with crossed arms and blank faces. Then they went home and wrote the worst reviews you can imagine: They called my work silly. Childish. Not scandalous, which would have been all right. People will buy clothes that shock. But when you are dubbed ridiculous, this is almost impossible to recover from." Klieg took a sip of champagne and coughed as if some had gone down the wrong pipe.

"How awful. What did you do?"

"I turned to my friends, of course. Only they did not provide as much comfort as I had hoped. Perhaps they thought failure was contagious. The only one who stood by me was Donald. He spent a week sleeping on my floor, lent me money, and did his best to cheer me up. In the end, though, I had to return to Germany. I had to earn some real money, so with my 'tail between my legs,' as they say, I went to work for my father. Delivering heating oil."

Eve was so wrapped up in the story that she'd almost missed it: Donald. *Donald?* It must be a coincidence. There were thousands and thousands of Donalds in the world. But she had to ask.

"Mr. Klieg—" Just then the lights dimmed, the orchestra began its overture, and the curtain lifted, revealing the Parisian garret of Marcello and Rodolfo. The players took the stage but Eve barely saw them. In her mind, she ran a quick calculation: In the early sixties, Donald would have been in his early thirties. He'd mentioned once in passing that he'd spent time in Europe. Had it been Paris?

An hour later, when the lights finally came back on, Günter excused himself to the bathroom. Klieg launched into a critique of the costumes, but Eve stopped him with a hand on his arm.

"I'm sorry, I'm just curious. What you said earlier . . ." she began.

Klieg's expression indicated he'd noted the urgency she'd tried to conceal in her voice. "Yes?"

"You said you had a friend who helped you in your hour of need. Was it the same friend you mentioned at the gala?"

"I am not sure. . . ."

"The one who explained to Pierre Cavel and René LaForge and the others about what it meant to be a designer? Who helped them appreciate your work?"

"Oh . . . yes."

"You said his name was Donald."

"Yes."

"Donald what?"

"Donald Béliveau." Eve's shoulders sank, but Klieg went on, seemingly caught up in memories. "He was the only American in our group. Full of lingering postwar bravado that only the Americans had. Hubris, really."

Eve reached into her bag for her compact. "He was what, a painter? Sculptor?"

"Heavens, no. Donald had no visual sense. He couldn't even pick out a necktie."

"What, then?"

"He was a writer."

"What kind?" she asked, dabbing her nose lightly.

"*Experimental,* he insisted on calling it. His work was a mass of symbols and deconstructions. Nursery rhymes for the insane." The hairs stood up on the back of Eve's neck and she put the compact down. "A nightmare for the reader," Klieg continued.

"What happened to him?" asked Eve.

The lights dimmed and Günter slipped back into the box.

"I think the opera's about to begin again," said Klieg.

But Eve couldn't help herself. "*Please.*" She could feel Günter glaring at her from behind. She had no idea what his problem was, and right now, she didn't care.

Klieg furrowed his brow. "My goodness, why is this so interesting? I can't think of another young person who's ever asked so many questions about things that happened before her time." He picked up his glass and put it down again without drinking. "Well, if you must know, it was not a happy story. He died suddenly. Here in New York." He sighed. "I was still living in Paris at the time."

"Mr. Klieg?" Eve couldn't keep her hunch to herself a moment longer. "Are you sure you're not talking about Donald Bellows?"

Klieg's eyes widened. "Why—yes, actually. I always forget that he'd used a different surname in Paris. Americans were still hailed as heroes on the Continent back then, and most of them couldn't resist taking advantage of this. Not Donald. He enjoyed doing things the hard way, didn't want any special favors. So he took a French name and, since he spoke beautiful French, often got away with it. Only his intimates knew his real identity. But . . ." He blinked now in astonishment. "How could you know? I didn't think anyone as young as you would have heard of Donald."

Eve, trying to keep her voice even, explained about living in Donald's apartment, making it sound as though the landlord had told her. "So I've become interested in him."

"I suppose I can understand that," Klieg said. "But what exactly do you find intriguing?"

"I guess it's just that it feels so intimate, to live where someone else once did. I stare up at the same bedroom ceiling he did and hang my clothes where he hung his. I feel"—she shrugged—"connected to him."

"I see." For the first time Klieg held her gaze. "I admire your sensitivity, I must say. Perhaps this is why you are such a good interviewer." He smiled, just a little.

Eve was bursting with questions. She remembered how Donald disappeared during Klieg's segment on *Smell the Coffee*. Had he been pulled away by the forces he couldn't control or had he departed on purpose? And if so, why? Was there bad blood between them? She was just deciding what to ask next when the second act began. The orchestra played a lilting melody and the performers took their places. The story of Paris's young artists, passionate and poor, jealous and heroic, powerless in the face of fate, unfolded in a swirl of music, color, and light. Eve glanced at Klieg. His eyes were glossy. She felt a wave of compassion come over her and it was all she could do to stop herself from putting her arms around his neck right there in their box, high up in the dark.

. . .

Late in the evening, the end finally came, and with it, Mimi's death. The audience rose for three standing ovations before shuffling out. Even Günter seemed moved, either that or he had something in his eye. He and his uncle spoke in German and then he turned to go. As an afterthought, he offered his hand to Eve. She expected it to be limp in keeping with his mood, but his grasp was strong and warm.

"A pleasure," he said, but did not wait for her to reply before going.

Klieg remained in his seat. Eve found a tissue in her bag and handed it to him.

"Thank you," he said. "I don't know what's wrong with me. I think all this time in America has robbed me of my stoicism. My brother in Cologne would be horrified."

"I think the opera got to everyone," Eve offered, seeing a woman down below put her head on her husband's shoulder and weep openly.

"I've seen *La Bohème* many times. But tonight, your questions, they made me think of my own time in Paris, my own friends."

"How did you and Donald meet, if I may ask?" Eve asked quietly, after he seemed to collect himself.

They'd first laid eyes on one another at a dinner party in the Sixth Arrondissement in '61. "I was just twenty-one. Everyone had brought elaborate flower arrangements or chocolate. I had made the faux pas of bringing wine, which you never do at a French dinner party. It didn't help that it was a cheap bottle, all I could afford. But Donald walked in, and with great ceremony set a silver bowl on the table. We looked inside and found not food, but tiny pieces of paper, each with a different word on it. He called it a 'word salad.'" Eve smiled. That was *so* Donald. "He served each guest with great fanfare and there was general delight. Except for our hostess, I'm afraid. She was at a loss for what wine to serve with it."

This image of Donald was charming, so different than his often surly pose now. Eve poured the last of the champagne for them.

"What did you think of his work?"

"He certainly tried very hard."

"But did you think he had talent?"

Klieg twisted his glass, watching the golden liquid swirl in the bottom. "I'm afraid not."

This was the answer Eve had been expecting, even hoping for. It confirmed she had a right to be impatient with Donald, to be frustrated by his demands that she help with his work. And yet, she felt pained by the revelation, too. Donald had died too young; apparently without even having a legacy worth preserving.

"I take it you weren't a fan of his 'deconstructed style'?" she asked.

"No."

"Too clever, too self-conscious?"

"Among other things."

"Why do you think he didn't put any emotion into his work?" Eve pressed, unable to help herself. "Isn't that strange for an artist? I mean, look at your designs. Especially the early ones. They overflowed with exuberance and humor and optimism."

Klieg folded his libretto in half and pushed it into the pocket of his jacket, which hung on a wall hook overhead. He stood.

Eve, puzzled, stood too. "I mean, isn't art supposed to move us as well as challenge us?" she asked. "I get the idea he had no emotions at all. Like he was just some kind of word machine without a heart."

Klieg took a step toward the door, and when he spoke, he did not look at her. "You probably should not offer opinions on that which you do not fully understand," he said softly.

. . .

As soon as Eve got home, she took Highball and headed out in the direction of the river. She didn't want to risk thinking about Klieg in Donald's presence. Instinct told her to keep this development to herself, at least for now. For one thing, it was delicious to finally have a secret, to know something about Donald that he didn't know she knew. It was still rare for her to come across anything even tangentially about him in any library books. Spending time with somebody who'd known Donald well could provide a wealth of information. But this would make Donald feel vulnerable, which would doubtless make him even more fractious than usual. And there were endless ways he could retaliate if he felt his power slipping.

It was early September now and the ginkgo leaves, shaped like little geisha fans, began to scatter themselves on the sidewalk. The air smelled earthen and damp, like the inside of a cave. She enjoyed these late-night ambles through the quiet streets. Without the traffic and tourists, this was when the Village felt most timeless.

The evening with Klieg, like their lunch in the spring, had ended strangely. But despite this, it represented something of a breakthrough. It was the first time she'd been with Klieg and not felt awed. Even though several people in the audience had spotted him and nudged one another, she had all but forgotten she was sitting next to someone famous.

The truth was, Klieg was a mortal, and a thorny one at that. There was something disquieting about the way he spoke of the past. Unlike those of Eve's grandfather, who used to spout happy tales of his barefoot boyhood like a geyser, Klieg's accounts were halting and seemed to carry hidden, anguished layers of meaning. Yet it appeared that on some level he yearned to talk about the old days. It was as if he hadn't spoken of them for so long, he had become afraid of losing them completely.

Eve wanted to hear more, more about Klieg and definitely more about Donald. And somehow she knew she would. Their relationship had changed tonight. She knew, even as Klieg had guided her down the stairs a little too quickly, that they would see one another again.

Back home, Eve was feeling expansive; she wanted to take a little dictation in this mood. Donald might have no real talent, no great legacy to defend, but was that the only criteria to consider? What about desire? Drive? Dedication? She pulled out the pad and a pen and settled into bed.

"Donald?" she called softly. "Donald?" But he did not answer.

. . .

The next morning, it dawned on her how astonished, how proud, Penelope would have been to know that her daughter had just spent the evening on the town in New York with none other than Matthias Klieg.

Eve padded to the closet and pulled down the family album she kept on a high shelf. She sat cross-legged on the bed in her pale blue Chinese print pajamas and flipped through the heavy black pages, looking at the pictures affixed with little white corner-shaped stickers. There were many of her brothers, each with their father's square jaw and chin dimple, and a family portrait taken at the Vernon Manor on her parents' fifteenth anniversary, when Eve was seven. There were also a dozen or so pictures of her mother: with Gin and his partners and their wives at various benefits, a half-smile as she looked just over the camera lens; on a hammock in the backyard, reading a book and wearing capris with apple red polish on her toes; at the beach in California under an enormous umbrella, the children in the foreground, building sandcastles in the sun. She was still so fresh-looking then; no one would have guessed that in just a couple of months, she would get desperately sick.

It started with weakness on one side of Penelope's body. Her jet black hair took on an ashy cast, and in a matter of days, her luminous skin grew thin and veins sprouted across the backs of her hands. There was vomiting and double vision and loss of memory. She begged off from hosting parties for Gin's partners and their wives, and her hothouse flowers began to droop. Soon after, her bed had been relocated to the den so she wouldn't have to negotiate the stairs, and she lay on it, breathing shallowly, drinking water from a glass on her bedside table through an extra-long straw. A brain tumor, they said. There would be surgery, but first, medication to control the swelling. The doctors gave her special pills to take at specific intervals, without which it was said she would lapse into unconsciousness and soon after, well, they didn't tell little girls things like that.

Gin's pain took the form of distraction. He was unable to focus on cases, and his partners insisted he cut back his hours at the office. But aside from providing the pills like clockwork, he proved mostly useless. Words failed him, so instead he brought his wife tray after tray of objects, usually things she had no use for. There were beautiful plates of fruit she could not eat and stacks of books she hadn't the strength to pick up. In desperation, he brought in jewelry from her box to wear and souvenirs from their trips abroad to hold in her slight, shaky hands. Not knowing how to talk to his children about what was happening, he encouraged them to spend as much time "in the fresh air" as possible, and the boys, who were on numerous teams, complied with resignation if not with enthusiasm.

But not Eve. Instead of heading to the library, where she usually listened to the "story lady," she came home every day, right after school, taking up a post next to Penelope's bed. At first, they spoke of everyday things. Her fingers worrying the top of the sheet, her mother would ask about how the new gardener was faring with the dahlias or whether her father had remembered PTA night at the boys' school.

One cool day, Eve reached for a hot water bottle next to the bed and knocked over one of the books that Gin had left in a stack on the floor. It was by someone named Dawn Powell and it was old and frayed but she liked the title, *The Happy Island*, which sounded like a place you'd want to go. She also liked the cover, a cabaret singer and piano player surrounded by patrons swilling drinks at checkered tables.

The dust jacket called the book's characters "schemers and dreamers on crossed paths, embroiled in a series of dramas, double-crossings, and hullabaloos that would make the towns of Sodom and Gomorrah seem like mere suburbs of li'l old New York." Eve laughed at the word "hullabaloo" and Penelope smiled. "Dawn Powell was from Ohio, just like us," she said.

Eve opened the book and began to read aloud, enjoying wrapping her tongue around names like *Van Deusen* and *Dol Lloyd*, and places like *Hamburger Mary's* and *The Studio Club*. The book read like a fairy tale, though a strange and brittle one. The characters were clever and arch but vulnerable because of their secrets. One of them, a nightclub singer named Prudence Bly, had left Silver City, Ohio—it seemed everyone was from Ohio—and all it represented, for New York. Eve loved the way her transformation was described: "Overnight she erased Silver City and overnight invented a new personality into which she stepped and, like her grandmother, kept this dress on day and night."

"Before you were born, *I* was a New Yorker," Penelope said, closing her eyes, her lashes fanning over the tiny strawberry-shaped birthmark under her left lower lid. "Did you know that, honey?"

Eve did know. Based on what she'd gathered from after-dinner-coffee conversations among the grown-ups, her mother—Penelope Easton, as she was known back then—had had something of a colorful past "back East" before being claimed by her father, who'd made "an honest woman out of her." Which was odd, because Eve had never heard even one story about her mother lying.

"What was it like there?"

Penelope opened her eyes to the ceiling, a canvas for a mental picture she seemed to paint. "I don't think I can tell you, at least not in a way that would make any sense. New York is different for everyone. You need to see it for yourself."

Eve kept reading, all afternoon and into the evening, when Gin brought in a deck of cards and shooed her out. But the next day she started again, and a few days after that, they finished the book and she picked up another. Over the weeks, Eve worked her way through the Powell collection, but with each volume, progress became slower because so many passages touched off recollections. In contrast to her short-term memory, Penelope's long-term recall seemed to catch fire. In hoarse whispers, she mused about the charmers and the strivers, the rascals and criminals she had known, the kind of people "you find only in the Big Apple."

Penelope's tone grew wistful as she spoke of a young man named Mack. "Now, you can't say anything to your father about this. But I did love someone else once. He was a writer and the leader of our gang. Talented, gregarious, audacious. The women were mad about him, but for some reason he only had eyes for me." Penelope waxed on for several minutes about romantic strolls through the Village with Mack in the mid-sixties, perusing sidewalk art displays, listening to the folksingers around the fountain in Washington Square Park, and wandering the Italian section with its old men gossiping on the bocce courts and kids playing stickball. "Mack couldn't walk past a game without waving for the broom handle," she said, marveling at the memory. "He'd whack the ball and that thing would sail onto a roof two blocks away,"

"What happened to him?" asked Eve.

Penelope pressed her lips together and blinked hard one or

two times. "I came back here for the wedding of an old friend. I was one of her bridesmaids and your dad was one of the groomsmen. He pulled out my chair, took me on drives through the countryside and out to the Amish markets." A bird flew out of a tree in the garden and Penelope turned her head toward the window. "I went back to New York, but not long after, a day came when I just knew it was time to come back home."

"Because you'd fallen in love with Daddy?"

"Sure, sweetheart."

Eve was happy to hear it. "And Mack?"

"We went our separate ways."

"You told him you loved Daddy better?"

"I wrote him a note. It was easier." Penelope closed her eyes and sighed.

"Is easier better?" asked Eve. But her mother was asleep.

Several weeks later, as Eve read aloud from *Turn, Magic Wheel*, Penelope began to perspire and her eyelids to flutter. In a whisper, she told Eve to get her father. Soon the room was full of men and equipment. Eve held her mother's hand as she was wheeled through the living room. She had to stand aside when they got to the front door, and just before her mother slipped through, she gestured toward the book, still clutched in Eve's hands. "You finish. You finish for both of us," she said.

In the days and weeks that followed, Eve made her way through the shelves, reading the rest of her mother's books, almost all, she would later realize, by New York writers. She read in her playhouse at the bottom of the garden or tucked up in her small room at the top of the stairs. She read while the funeral arrangements were made, while the lawyers and their wives milled around casseroles in the formal dining room, and while the corn rose in the fields and everyone else moved on.

Now Eve closed the album and placed it carefully on the floor beside the bed. She lay back and blinked up at the ceiling, head aswirl with pasts—hers, Klieg's, and Donald's.

Chapter 10

They ate at a minimalist Japanese place on the East Side, Bix and Eve sitting across a booth from Paul and Alex. It was a relief to be out with people her own age, people very much in the here and now. Much of the chatter broke down along gender lines but Bix proved to be a delightful companion. She wrote grant proposals for a nonprofit that distributed the hand-me-downs of wealthy New York children to the disadvantaged. She laughed easily and listened well.

"Alex really likes you, you know," she said as they washed their hands in the ladies' room.

"How do you know?" asked Eve.

"He's handsome, thoughtful, passionate. Let's just say girls come pretty easily to him. He's got a different one every couple of weeks, without making much of an effort. And we, and by that I mean his college friends, *never* get to meet them. Yet he's brought you to us twice. So yeah, I'd say he thinks you're pretty special."

After dinner, Eve had hoped they would go to one of the historic bars that she hadn't yet seen, like Pete's Tavern or the Algonquin. But everyone else wanted to go straight to the party, which turned out to be in a basement apartment in the Village.

Alex kissed her in the coat closet. "I missed you this week," he said, and led her to the kitchen counter that served as the bar, where he mixed her a Manhattan. When the hosts dimmed the lights to show an arty video of the birthday boy, Alex nudged a friend off the couch so Eve could have a seat. The party was moving into high gear at 1 a.m. when he took her aside. "Want to get out of here?" he asked.

Out on the sidewalk, the fresh air was invigorating. They walked, holding hands. No taxis were in sight, but Eve thought they'd find one on Seventh Avenue for the trip over to Brooklyn.

"Hey, look. We're in front of your building," said Alex.

"So we are," said Eve as she continued to walk. Alex stopped her. "Can I come up?" he asked.

"I don't think that's such a good idea."

"C'mon."

"Sorry."

"I'm not, like, expecting anything, if that's what you're worried about. We can snuggle up and watch a movie. Order in. Play cards. Whatever you want."

"That sounds fantastic. Let's do it at your place."

"Don't you have to walk your dog?"

Eve blushed. "Actually, she's with a friend for the night."

He smiled. "Oh, she is, is she? Well, more room for the two of us." He nuzzled her ear.

"The thing is," Eve said, resting her head on his shoulder, "I'd love to see your apartment." She couldn't make it any clearer.

"The guys will be there all night. A half-dozen stinky, cranky computer geeks. We go to press next week. After that, you can come over for a whole weekend if you want."

"My place just isn't good for company," Eve offered, trying to sound both apologetic and firm.

Alex thrust his fists into the pockets of his wool jacket and gave her a look of utter confusion. "Most girls, like, *love* cuddling up for a movie."

"Another time, really," she said.

He stood firm, squinting at her. "You know what?" he said. "I have to go to the bathroom."

"There's a coffeehouse down the street. Right on the corner."

"You're not gonna let me use your place?"

"No, I'm sorry."

"What are you, one of those 'Rules Girls'? Not willing to spend a night together until there's a ring on your finger? I thought that was long over but I've somehow dated three of them in the last two years. They just string you along, head games all the way."

"That's not it. Believe me."

"Then you're *afraid* to let me up."

"What?"

"The Midwest girl is afraid I'm some kind of New York psycho? Afraid I might hurt you?"

"Obviously not," said Eve, thinking this was getting ridiculous. "I'm more than happy to go to your place. Remember?"

"That's pretty convenient, since you knew we couldn't go there until the magazine was done."

"Alex, for heaven's sake. I'm crazy about you. I want to be with you. But we just can't go up to my apartment."

"Oh my God." His eyes opened wide.

"What?"

"I get it."

"Get what?"

"You've got another guy up there."

"No, I don't."

"A boyfriend? Oh, no wait: a husband."

"*No.*"

"The last two times we went out, you insisted on seeing yourself home. Why didn't I put it together? It's so obvious to me now. You're cheating on some poor slob with me. Or vice versa. Maybe *I'm* the poor slob. Christ." He kicked the stoop, seeming stunned, like he'd never even conceived of this kind of affront happening to him before.

"Where is this coming from?" asked Eve. The sudden bile in his tone had taken her by surprise. She'd guessed he had a temper, but he was starting to sound unhinged. "Are things not going well with the magazine?"

Alex's face was blotchy. "Fuck you."

The words hit Eve like a slap and she flinched. She was stunned at this side of him, one she never would have suspected was there. "What's wrong with you?"

"Nothing's wrong with *me*."

Eve swallowed and tried to regain her composure. "Let's go somewhere and talk about it."

"I'm done with the talking."

"Well, then I don't know what to tell you."

"You know, I could call up ten girls right now and go to their place."

Eve looked at him evenly for several seconds. "Then why don't you do that?" she asked, then stalked up the steps to the front door and went in without looking back.

. . .

Eve couldn't help but fume. How could she have misjudged Alex so badly? How could he have misunderstood her so completely? Only after they were apart for a few days did she admit to the absurd fantasies she'd concocted around him. The two of them celebrating Christmas together, New Year's Eve in Times Square. Even going to work for him at his magazine, penning clever, esoteric "writery" stuff. Becoming a fabulous New York couple.

It was odd. She hadn't spared a second thought for Ryan after leaving Ohio, had only answered his letters with the odd postcard, but Alex had gotten under her skin. Or, if not actually Alex, the notion of Alex certainly had. And it wasn't just him; it was his circle of friends. Eve sincerely liked Bix and would have enjoyed seeing her again, with or without Alex. But she didn't even know Bix's last name, let alone her phone number.

Donald was sympathetic at first but by day four, when Eve, in a fit of pique, actually pulled down a suitcase from the top shelf of the closet, he lost his patience.

"Collect yourself! You're not going home over this nonsense. Look, he was just a boy. All right? Not your personal key to the city. You have to stop expecting so much of people. Alex wasn't worthy, can't you see that? And neither is Mark, I hope you've realized. Or this patsy Hap McCutcheon. And certainly not Vadis. God help this city if she's what passes for a 'real New Yorker' these days. They're just people, wandering around and bumping into the furniture like everybody else."

Eve was only half listening. The unzipped suitcase lay on the bed. She picked out a couple of stray buttons in the corner and bounced them in her palm.

"At your age you shouldn't be looking for attachments anyway. You should be enjoying the clichés of your relative youth: playing the field, sowing your wild oats, spreading your wings. . . ."

But this kind of talk just depressed Eve. She closed the suitcase, stoop-shouldered, too tired to even maintain her annoyance. She hated everyone, everything.

The evening was unexpectedly warm for fall, and she peeled off her cardigan as she toddled into the living room. The window was open a few inches, allowing in barbecue smells and party sounds from the other end of the courtyard.

"Donald?" she said, taking a seat at the bar.

"Yes?"

"Where do you go?"

"What do you mean?"

"Where do you go when you're not here? When you're not with me. Do you have . . . friends?" He said nothing. "Hello?"

"I cannot say."

"Don't be coy about this, please. I've had a bad couple of days. Throw me a bone."

"I didn't say I *would* not tell you. I said I cannot."

"But I mean, are there others there, wherever it is? Other writers maybe? Like John Clellon Holmes? I saw his plaque the other day. Or what about Lucien Carr? He died within the last couple of years."

"Good God, child, *no*. And if I did, I might run screaming. Lucien *killed* a man, you know. In Riverside Park. Kerouac helped him dispose of the knife. Jack went to jail and his father wouldn't post bail. So this gal Edie Parker's father said *he'd* post it if Jack married his daughter. They were married in the clink! Annulled months later. Utter hooligans."

Eve thought they sounded rather exciting. She'd like to see Mark wave a knife at Giles. "Tell me more."

After repeated coaxing, Donald relayed a story about a long, strange night with Kerouac and the rest. It had started with a card game during which the stakes kept escalating. When most everyone was out of money, someone dug up some antique swords and the dares became physical. Drunken thrusting and parrying ensued, concurrent with boisterous arguing about how important fear was for good writing.

"And who got nicked in the arm?" he asked. "*I* did. And all I did was come in with the scotch and sandwiches."

Without realizing it, Donald had just admitted to being, well, the person sent out for scotch and sandwiches. It explained a lot and made Eve wish she could give him a hug.

"Ginsberg called the Beats 'the Libertine Circle.' That's *one* way to put it," he said when he was done.

Eve found that, without thinking, she'd been taking down the stories as Donald related them. She scanned them and an idea dawned on her.

Would he do it?

Or was he too jealous of those better known?

"Did you just wonder if I was jealous? Heavens, no. They were wildly talented, yes. But so was I, obviously. I *am* jealous of the time they had. That's what I wish for."

"You didn't get enough," agreed Eve. "It's not fair." But privately she thought, and always had, that there was something else that made him sad. Pain that was rooted in his life, not his death. "So you don't see anybody else, wherever it is you go?"

"No."

"What *is* it like, then?"

"It's not like anything; I don't 'go' anywhere. I don't understand it and usually have no control over it. This existence is as much of a mystery to me as the last."

Eve wandered back into the bedroom and lay down. She had never been particularly religious, save for those bedtime prayers as a child, but she had always imagined that *some* secrets were revealed in the hereafter. Highball jumped up beside her, laying her chin on Eve's stomach.

"Isn't there some kind of . . . I don't know. Explanation?"

"Hah! My dear, anyone who thinks we get all the answers in the afterlife is in for a rude awakening."

Eve turned out the light and closed her eyes even though it was early. She wanted to ask more questions but already felt herself slipping toward sleep.

"Take it from me, little one," said Donald, just before she dropped off. "Don't put off anything, banking on eternal peace in the great beyond. You focus on the present."

. . .

"I'm just making tea. Take a load off," said Gwendolyn. She pulled her embroidered pale yellow shawl with its foot-long fringe around her as she disappeared into the alcove.

Eve hopped up onto one of the tall stools behind the counter and dropped her bag on the floor.

"What's new in here?" she asked, looking around the store. It was an exuberant space and a bit of a funhouse, with platforms creating various levels, hidden crannies stuffed with memorabilia, and scarves draped out of baskets hanging from the ceiling. The temperature had finally dropped, and the old radiators were reluctantly stirring, going back and forth from ice cold to hissing with heat.

"That red silk with the notched bodice, I just got in." Gwendolyn gestured toward a mannequin in the corner as she handed Eve a mug. "Victoria Royal, from Hong Kong. The stories she could tell. And we got a few accessories the other day, too. An old lady on Morton Street died and her niece brought a bunch of her stuff in. But a lot of it is fur and that can be tricky. I'm not sure I can sell a mink choker."

"So why did you take it?"

"I can't help myself. I try to be more judicious, but I can't stand turning anybody away. Telling them their things aren't good enough is like telling them *they're* not good enough, and that's above my pay grade."

Eve had begun to pop into Full Circle around midmorning every week or two before heading up to work. She and Gwendolyn would unpack whatever had come in and chat about books and boys. Eve was still upset over Alex and was wondering why a bona fide New York boyfriend was so hard to come by. Gwendolyn had suffered two hideous breakups in the last year and was avoiding men altogether.

"I've been thinking about this since the last time we talked," said Gwendolyn, using her label gun to stab price tags onto purses. "And maybe it's because it's been a while since I've been in a, quote-unquote, successful relationship, but I don't see why you'd bother with an Alex anyway when you have a Matthias Klieg in your life. Sophisticated, soulful, wealthy beyond belief. If he can get it up at all, I'd say you were in business."

"Gwen! Please," coughed Eve, feeling the hot tea, all orange and clove, rise into her nasal passages. "I could never think of him that way. It's completely wrong. Sacrilegious."

"Okay, okay," Gwendolyn said with an impish grin.

"Honestly." Eve dabbed at her mouth with a napkin. "As if I'd take relationship advice from you anyway, with that track record of yours."

"Hey. Give me a break. I'm an only child. I have an excuse for being clueless about men. But you'd think someone who grew up with two brothers would understand them a little better."

"Three."

"Even more so."

"Maybe I would if they ever included me," said Eve. "But they never did. I wish I'd been an only child. I'd have traded lives with you in a second." She walked over to the red dress for a closer inspection.

"Are you nuts?" Gwendolyn put down the label gun. "I was so lonely."

"So was I."

"Because your brothers didn't talk to you."

"Right."

"So what happened when you talked to them?"

"What do you mean?"

"I mean when you knocked on the door and barged into their room. Did they just sit there, stone-faced, and make no response?"

"I was not exactly a barger."

Gwendolyn sighed and rotated her shoulders back. "Look, I don't know you that well, but it sounds like that's at least as much your fault as your brothers', isn't it? Not everything happens to you. One does make choices, you know. I mean, older siblings ignore younger ones; it's what they do. And it's the job of the younger ones to refuse to be ignored."

"This hem has come undone, right here," said Eve, fingering the back of the red dress.

"Hey. Did you hear what I just said?" asked Gwendolyn.

"Yes." She'd heard.

Gwendolyn sighed and opened a drawer under the counter that held dozens of needles and hundreds of spools of thread.

"You get uncomfortable whenever the focus is on you. Do you realize that?" She picked out a ripe red and threaded the needle as she joined Eve at the mannequin.

"I can do that," said Eve, taking the needle.

"You can?"

"I have to touch up my mom's stuff all the time. And I used to sew buttons on my dad's shirts and mend his sweaters. I kind of like it, actually." Eve bent to the task, making swift, even little loops. In two minutes, the dress was good as new. She bit off the thread with her teeth in a practiced motion.

"You're good." Gwendolyn bumped her hip against Eve's.

"Thanks," said Eve. She bumped back.

"I'm sorry for shooting my mouth off. I forget not everyone can take it."

Eve wound the dangling thread around the spool and handed it over. "I can take it," she said.

. . .

On Saturday, Eve called Gin, and when he answered it was clear he was happy to hear from her. Eve made a big pile of her shoes in the living room and, while they spoke, gave them their weekly polish from a set of pots and brushes she kept in a sturdy wooden box. Soon they were chatting in easy, relaxed fashion about her brothers, the new exhibit at the Cleveland Museum of Art, and, amazingly, a little about Penelope.

Eve brought the subject up, rather tentatively, sticking to simple remembrances of her mother's sometimes eccentric behavior. Gin chimed in with the story about the time Penelope heard gunfire in the kitchen. She had run to the neighbors and used their phone to summon the police, who arrived to find six exploded eggs she'd been hard-boiling. She'd forgotten about them while outside on the lawn building a Victorian-style birdhouse from a kit she'd ordered from England. One of the officers, laughing, stayed to help her affix the roof.

"Boiling eggs. She did *try* to be a wife," Gin said with a chuckle.

"She did."

Eve wouldn't say six hundred and fifty miles had made them closer, exactly, but perhaps less far apart.

. . .

Eve was usually the first to arrive at work, except for Mark, but today not even Mark was there yet. She flicked on the light in her office and found a memo on her desk. It was titled "New guest vetting procedures." She could guess what this was about. For weeks there had been rumors that the network brass was unhappy with some of the show's less-than-attractive interview subjects. And a week ago, according to one of the associate producers, several viewers had actually called to complain about a female guest in a camisole out of which peeked a sprinkling of black underarm hair, insisting the sight made eating breakfast impossible. Eve scanned the missive with mounting irritation.

Writers:

As of today, bookers will step up efforts to identify potentially "distracting" guests who may interfere with the unfettered flow of information to our audience. This will include searching newspapers, periodicals, and the Internet for visual representation of potential interviews.

Where pictures are unavailable, writers will now make their own efforts to determine what impression a guest will potentially make. This may occur through polite questioning or a request for a faxed photo to determine whether he/she exhibits the following:

Weight issues. *Those with a BMI of 26 or over (eyeball it), no longer acceptable (unless segment deals with obesity and guest is serving as an example and has signed a release).*

Facial hair. *Well-trimmed mustache or beard
acceptable; goatees, sideburns, or nose hair—alert
Franka Lemon.*
Eyewear. *If guest wears glasses, please check that they
are nonreflective. Make him/her aware that contacts
are preferred, blue or green highly desirable.*
Visible piercings and tattoos. *Out of the question,
unless for recording artist in* Billboard Top 10.
Accent. *British, highly acceptable, esp. London &
Sussex; other Northern European, use your judgment;
pronounced Southern European, Caribbean, or
Asian—alert Franka.*

Giles

Eve sighed and stuck the memo to her corkboard along with
the dozens of others. Then she realized the light on her phone
was blinking. She entered her voicemail password thinking it
might be Vadis, who was due back from the tour any day.

"Eve, it's Mark. Small crisis here." He was speaking quickly.
"My mom's in the hospital. Seems to be some kind of heart
thing. It looks like she's going to be fine but my dad's away on
business and I want to wait with her until he gets here. I've left
the assignments on my desk—wouldn't you know there's major
breaking news today—and I need you to get the list and tell
everyone what they're doing today, okay? Archie will be in later
to edit. I'll call you to check in. Thanks so much."

Saying a silent prayer for Mark's mother, Eve went into his office. The list, which he'd printed out and left on his keyboard, was
entirely predictable. Archie was doing the latest on the Middle
East peace negotiations and a toy recall for Bliss. Russell was to
interview the author of *A Psychoanalytical Approach to Quan-
tum Physics*. It had taken him two weeks to get through the book
and the interview with the author promised to take up most of
the afternoon. On Quirine's plate: a consortium of heirloom veg-

etable growers about to march on Washington to save small
farms for Bliss and the annual *Forbes* list of "America's Most
Powerful CEOs Forty and Under" for Hap. Steve had a segment
about a football player who'd been killed in a home invasion for
Hap and the latest sports steroid scandal for Bliss. Eve was to
tackle the best pillows for your hair type and then interview the
cast of the new sci-fi movie *Starship Kibbutz,* both for Hap. The
tape of the movie, or "screener," was next to the assignment list
on Mark's desk.

Just as Eve realized that Cassandra had no assignment, she
spied a handwritten scrawl at the bottom of the page.

> Cassandra—Stiletto latest, incl. police chief & criminal psy-
> chologist (Bliss)

Eve stared at the paper. Obviously, this was the "breaking
news" Mark had been referring to. The Stiletto, in heels and, this
time, a mini skirt, had struck again, overnight in the East Village.
So much for *Smell* never acknowledging New York. It seemed
half the stories were related to the city in some way.

The Stiletto had now attacked seven times, each assault more
violent than the last. The first couple of times, he'd only bran-
dished his knife. Then, back in April, he'd slashed his fourth victim on the arm (which Bliss was reporting when she was cut
down by Eve's rancid bouillabaisse). Over the summer, he'd
slashed two women in the torso, and last night, he'd pierced his
victim's neck. She was alive, thankfully. Nevertheless, it was the
story of the day. And Cassandra was going to do it. For Bliss.

Eve opened the folder of Stiletto research. Inside were Nexis
printouts of recent articles on similar crime waves and dossiers
on NYPD Chief Sebastian Pell and Columbia Presbyterian criminal psychologist Dr. Shin Tang. Pell was to give the details of the
latest attack, while Tang was booked for the bulk of the segment,
to try to shed light on what kind of person the Stiletto might be.

Stuck to Tang's bio was a Post-it, on which a booker had written: *No prior TV appearances, no pic avail.*

Eve closed the folder and ran her palm over it. She wanted this segment. She deserved it. On the other side of the closed office door, she could hear the writers arriving. They made their way down the hall, chatting about what they'd done with their mornings and about the day ahead. Any minute now they'd poke their heads in, looking for Mark and their assignments. She strained to hear if Cassandra was among them, but it appeared she was running late. Again.

Eve would give her ten minutes.

. . .

Archie raised an eyebrow. "You're doing the Stiletto? Well, good for you."

"Thanks."

"Let me know if you need any help."

"I will. But the first pre is in five minutes, so I guess I better get to it."

Her heart beating fast, Eve headed back to her office and plunked down at her desk. She kicked off her pumps, which had begun to pinch, and unbuttoned her tweed peplum jacket. What she was doing wasn't technically ethical. But this was her chance to finally show Mark—and everyone else—what she could do. If she executed this segment well, Mark would have to admit she was ready for hard news and ready for Bliss, and everything would change. He might, though he was the boss, even allow his old feelings for her to stir.

Anyway, she'd asked him for months for a real story. This was apparently the only way to get one.

Plus, Donald said she had to stop being a doormat and demand what she wanted. If he were here right now, he'd no doubt applaud her. Gwendolyn would, too. The thought gave her the final push she needed.

She skimmed the Stiletto articles as quickly as she could and dialed the police chief. The phone was answered by a deputy, who informed her that Chief Pell was on the line with another morning show and two camera crews were waiting outside his office to tape interviews.

"I'll hold," she said through gritted teeth.

Seventeen minutes later, Pell finally picked up. He sounded harried and annoyed and Eve's usual powers to charm a guest out of extra information fizzled. The chief stuck to a clear script, answering each of her questions in a brisk, rote monotone that told her he'd just given the exact same information to ABC, NBC, and CBS. He cut their talk short when the *New York Times* reporter showed up.

Cassandra came in, eyes bloodshot and carrying the world's largest Coke, which she sucked at greedily, not unlike someone who was dehydrated after a night of drinking. "Archie says you're handing out the assignments today. I've had a shitty morning. What am I doing?"

Eve held out the *Starship Kibbutz* screener, which Cassandra grabbed before weaving off down the hall.

Any guilt Eve might have felt over what she was doing evaporated. Cassandra clearly wouldn't appreciate the honor of doing a big segment for Bliss. She looked like she was going to spend half the evening in the ladies' room, head hovering over the toilet.

Eve turned her attention to the next order of business: the stack of scripts and transcripts of Bliss Jones's most recent segments. Eve had ordered them from research, planning to compare the transcripts of what Bliss said on the air with the writers' segments as they'd been written. She was going to crack the case and figure out just what Bliss Jones wanted.

Twenty minutes later, Eve's brain felt like a packed bleacher at a football game. She had a mental picture of Donald's and Hap's rear ends grumpily scooting over to make room for Bliss's. She felt as though her skull would burst, but it was worth it; she thought she'd figured out something important. In nearly every segment, Bliss pushed beyond whatever the writer had done. She'd rework the intro so that it promised more—often too much—and during the interview, she'd press past the writers' suggested questions into new territory. Sometimes it was fascinating territory, other times boring. Often it was neutral. So why did she do it? Maybe she couldn't stand to feel like a "throat," as anchors were sometimes called derogatorily. Maybe she just wanted to beat the other morning shows. Either way, one thing seemed clear: Bliss didn't just want to report news; she wanted to *make* news.

But what if Eve herself could push the story into new territory? What if she could come up with questions that were better and smarter than they could possibly have on any of the other shows? What if she could unearth something from the guest that would actually make news? She wasn't contemplating getting anywhere near a "100 percent." But if she could do a decent job of this, Mark would have to put her into the Bliss rotation. She'd have proven herself.

Was that a good enough reason to do what she was doing? She paced the room. The walls pressed in. She shook her head and rotated her shoulders. Now was not the time for doubts. She sat down and dialed criminal profiler Dr. Shin Tang.

He picked up on the first ring and they exchanged the usual pleasantries. Dr. Tang spoke with a slight accent, but Eve decided it was nothing that required the attention of Franka Lemon. She mentally crossed her fingers and embarked on her first question.

"I know you've been keeping up with the Stiletto case and analyzing the victims' accounts for clues. What theories have you come up with about what kind of person the Stiletto might be?"

Dr. Tang began to explain the Stiletto's probable profile. He seemed to ponder each sentence before he spoke it. Eve encouraged him, nodding to herself as she took it all down. Gently, she probed his reasoning, testing his various theories, all the while feeling more and more certain he knew what he was talking about.

Forty minutes into their talk, the doctor trailed off from an answer about the increasing violence of the attacks. "It almost makes me wonder . . ."

"Yes?" Eve asked.

He paused. "No, I'm sorry. That is all, Miss Weldon. You have the information."

"It sounds like you wanted to say something else."

"Uh . . . no. It wasn't anything."

"Look, Dr. Tang," she began gently. "I understand if there's something you're not sure you should say. Why not tell me about it? Maybe together we can figure out whether it belongs in the segment. There won't be any pressure from me if you're not comfortable."

There was a long silence. "Well, Miss Weldon, and only because you are less abrasive than most of the newspeople I've encountered in the last few weeks, I suppose it couldn't hurt for you and me to deliberate together what should be discussed on the air," he said finally. "I was going to offer some advice to women who find themselves confronted by the Stiletto."

Eve straightened in her chair. "Yes?"

"I'm afraid I still hesitate. The police dislike this kind of thing, you see. I was quoted once in a newspaper giving certain suggestions, and I got a very nasty call from the commissioner's office. The police almost never advise victims to defend themselves, and, statistically speaking, they are probably right. If one does fight back, it can infuriate the attacker and he may become more violent."

"Statistically speaking? But you think this case may be different, am I right?" pressed Eve. "Then get it off your chest and let's talk about it."

The doctor sighed deeply. For a moment, her heart beating fast, Eve thought she'd pushed too hard. But then he continued.

"Well, for what it's worth, here's what I have come to believe. Now, it's just a theory, you understand, but I think it's sound. . . ."

Eve's fingers flew across the keyboard as she took it all down. When she was done, she took a deep breath.

"Sir, I think this is vital information. Important for our audience to hear. May I put this in the interview? May Bliss Jones ask you about this tomorrow?"

It took him a long time to answer. "You really believe it could help somebody?"

"Yes. I really do."

"All right, then."

After they hung up, Eve scrolled through her notes, knee bouncing with excitement. Now this, the other shows wouldn't have. This was information that could help the women of New York. This was going to impress Bliss Jones.

Chapter 11

I think what everyone wants to know is, why would a mugger wear *high heels*?"

Eve stood wrapped in her kimono, frowning at the television. It was 7:06, and Bliss had just begun the interview with Chief Pell. She had changed sixteen words of Eve's intro, but things could have been worse.

"Well, that's the question that's perplexed us for months. We've never seen anything like it, Bliss. But now—*now*—I'm hoping we've cracked the case," said Chief Pell with a tight smile.

Bliss, looking sensational in a cherry red blazer and lip gloss, leaned in close to her quarry, her trademark move when combined with a delicate frown and the rhythmic tapping of pen on armrest. She was watching the police chief with focused intensity. He gazed back, seemingly transfixed.

"Well, let's hear it." Bliss's voice was as crisp as the bacon frying across the country at this hour. "You think you've solved the mystery? It sure has taken a while."

Sheesh. More aggressively worded than what Eve had as her first suggested question, but still, so far, Bliss was sticking to the script. How could she not, though, really? The question was obvious.

"Well, yes," began Pell. "It has taken us longer than we would have liked. But we've been at it twenty-four hours a day because we're dedicated to protecting the citizens of New York City and we believe—"

"Yes, yes. As a citizen of New York City, I thank you," Bliss said dryly. "Now tell us—what's with the high heels? Even when he's *not* wearing women's clothing, he's got the heels on. It makes no sense. They don't exactly make for a speedy getaway."

For heaven's sake, why was she being so testy? Eve always felt uncomfortable when Bliss went into Jack Russell terrier mode. She seemed to revel in prodding interview subjects like the embers of a sputtering fire, until she had extracted from them every last spark of information, or, if circumstances demanded, humiliation.

The police chief shuffled in his seat. "We think the high heels are his disguise."

Bliss leaned in, her visage reflected in the police chief's badge. "What do you mean? That no one will recognize an armed felon if he's wearing pumps?"

"No, Bliss. The shoes are not his visual disguise, they're his audio disguise."

"His audio disguise?" Bliss asked, betraying no hint that she'd read all of Pell's answers earlier in Eve's briefing note; that she and the chief were, in a sense, two actors performing a play. "What do you mean?"

"Well," began Pell, warming to the subject, "this is what I mean. What does a mugger—or any street criminal—depend on? The element of surprise. He needs to sneak up on his victim. This attacker has found a clever, and utterly unique, way of doing this."

"Go on."

"Well, Bliss, I'm sure you're an alert, 'big city' woman." Bliss narrowed her eyes at him, signaling displeasure at being patronized. "When you're walking down the street at night and you hear footsteps coming up behind you, what do you do?"

"I look over my shoulder to see who it is."

"Of course you do. Now imagine you're walking down the same street at night but the footsteps you hear behind you are the click-click of high heels. What do you do?"

"Well," began Bliss, acerbically acquiescent in her role, "I would assume there was a woman behind me. And as women don't tend to be muggers or rapists, I most likely would not turn around."

"Exactly," replied the chief. "And that's what he's counting on. He comes up behind a woman wearing these heels, lulling her into a false sense of security, and then sticks a knife in her back and demands money. It's diabolical."

"Well," said Bliss sardonically, "it's certainly something we haven't seen before. And your theory would appear to hold some water. Now, sir, stay with us for a moment while we turn to our other guest, criminal psychiatrist Dr. Shin Tang of Columbia Presbyterian Hospital."

The camera panned over to Dr. Tang, in the armchair next to Chief Pell. He was much as Eve had pictured him from his voice on the phone: sixtyish with a thick mop of shiny black hair parted deeply on the side . . . and a mole the size of a small pancake next to his left nostril. *Damn.*

"All right, Dr. Tang, you heard what Chief Pell has told us about the Stiletto's methods. Any theories on how he came up with the idea of wearing high heels? It's not exactly a typical MO."

Again Bliss's tone was more aggressive than desirable, but this time there could be dire consequences. Eve had spent a good part of the briefing note explaining that Dr. Tang needed careful handling. He was nervous not only because it was his first TV interview, but because the commissioner, whom he'd once angered, would be sitting right next to him. Bliss, Eve had made clear, should tread lightly. Eve fretted; would the lucid, nuanced answers Tang had given her during the pre-interview quiver and disintegrate under the hot lights and confrontational style of Bliss Jones? It had happened before, as all the writers could attest.

"Well, Ms. Jones, we do have one interesting supposition about that. Very often, we find, clever ideas come about by accident. So we believe the attacker might have been wearing high heels for some unrelated reason, perhaps with a full complement of women's clothing, as he sometimes does now. In any case, we think that perhaps while doing so, he walked up behind a woman on the street, noted that she didn't turn around, and realized he could use this information for nefarious purposes."

Bliss's brow was so tightly knit, Eve almost expected a pair of mittens to pop out of it at any moment. "And why would this person be wearing women's clothing to begin with? And why only sometimes? Are you saying we're looking at a part-time drag queen doubling as a violent felon?"

Eve bit her bottom lip. She hadn't put the "drag queen" bit in; it sounded like a slur.

Dr. Tang also looked uncomfortable. "Well, I—I don't want to say for sure; but it is possible that this man is experimenting with women's clothing as some kind of coping mechanism for a psychological issue. The shoes are different. They are a constant, which would indicate that they are most likely a strategic choice. Whereas the clothing, which comes and goes, might be explained by a half-dozen scenarios."

"Like what?"

What was the point of this antagonism? And going down this unproductive path? Dr. Tang was now shrinking back in his seat and beginning to sweat.

"We're—we're just trying to consider all the possibilities."

Eve's heart sank. Tang was obviously feeling so besieged now that when asked about his big theory, he might well balk. She prayed he wouldn't. He had to realize how important this information could be for the city's women. As he told Eve, he had a daughter walking these streets. Bliss opened her mouth and Eve held herself still. If Tang delivered here, *Smell the Coffee* would make news.

During their pre-interview, Dr. Tang had proposed a fascinating hypothesis: If the mugger had spent significant time as a cross-dresser, whatever the reason, he might have adopted some feminine personality characteristics. Scientists had seen this before. For instance, he might have developed an aversion to physical violence. The doctor guessed, and he insisted it was only a guess, that the attacker was relying on the element of surprise and his knife to overwhelm his victims, and might find going *mano a mano* abhorrent. Which meant, the doctor speculated, that a woman who fought back might stand a reasonable chance of overcoming him. In any case, Tang had told her, no woman who found herself a victim should ever let the man take her to a secondary location. That was inevitably where rape or bloodshed occurred. She must stand up to him or get away from him, if only for that reason.

Eve rewrapped the kimono around her, waiting for Bliss to ask the question: *Doctor, I understand you have a theory about how victims might defend themselves? We're aware the police are concerned about this kind of speculation, but we think our viewers will want to hear all the information before making up their minds and we ask Chief Pell to indulge us here.*

Bliss leaned forward as if anticipating a choice morsel. She paused dramatically and pressed her lips together.

"Very interesting, Dr. Tang. Thank you." Bliss leaned back abruptly. Why was she wrapping up? There must be at least two minutes before commercial. "Now," she began again, pulling out some papers from underneath her script, "Chief Pell, back to you for a moment. If you don't mind, I want to revisit the issue we were discussing when you were here a couple of months ago. We were talking about the scandal at the Department of Corrections, about the officers who themselves turned out to have criminal records, and allegations of money laundering within prison walls. You never quite answered my question. . . ."

"*Goddamn it.*" Eve turned the set off with such ferocity that the knob came away in her hand.

. . .

That subterranean snake, otherwise known as the subway, slithered unaccountably slowly that day, and Eve arrived late for work, barely making it in time for the production meeting. She snuck in at the back of the room. Giles was detailing an upcoming November sweeps trip, spotlighting the best Christmas shopping from coast to coast. Immediately a general mumble began, as everyone speculated on whether they'd be on the trip, which cities had the best stores, and which hotels in those cities had the best room service.

Suddenly, everyone stopped talking. Bliss Jones had entered the room through the far door behind Giles. He turned, startled. "Well, *hello,*" he said, standing. "Bliss. How nice. Welcome." Giles dispensed these words like hopeful little pellets as he made his way toward the anchor and then stopped abruptly when her expression said he'd come close enough. It was disheartening to see the executive producer behaving like a beaten dog but not altogether surprising. Just last week, Russell had explained the somewhat twisted relationship between top managers and top talent at the network. He said that although the executive producer was "the boss," the one who called the shots on programming, who interfaced with the network brass and handled the budget, a star anchor (if the ratings were good) actually possessed more clout. It was the anchor the public knew, the anchor who was the face of the show, the anchor with the glamour quotient and the astronomical paycheck. If the anchor and executive producer both went to the network president with a dispute, it was almost guaranteed the president would side with the "talent."

"Hi, troops." Bliss nodded to the room.

"Can we get you something?" Giles asked. "A water maybe? We're just talking about the sweeps shopping trip and I think you'll be pleased—"

"I'm not here about sweeps," replied Bliss.

Eve tried to take in what was happening but found herself starstruck. Bliss Jones was in the room! And she looked exactly the way she did on television! There were no marks or shadows on her skin, which glowed with health and vigor. The hair was teased enough to appear lustrous but not hard, and the purply-blue eyes sparkled like amethysts thanks to perfectly blended cinnamon eye shadow and expertly drawn brown liner. They did not move from Giles's face. "I need to ask you about what happened this morning."

There was a mass intake of breath.

"I'm sorry?" Giles appeared to have only barely recovered from the initial shock of Bliss's appearance and now struggled with this new blow.

"The Stiletto segment," Bliss returned.

"I'm not sure I know what you mean."

"It was unacceptable."

Eve felt the blood come to a halt in her veins.

"Shall we take this in my office?" Giles asked.

"I don't have time. I'm on my way out. But before I go, I need to know how a brand-new writer came to handle the lead story."

"We don't have any brand-new writers."

"Well, I certainly don't recognize this name." She looked at a sheet of paper in her hand. "It's right here on the briefing note. Eve Weldon. Who is that?"

"She's right over there," Cassandra piped up prettily, pointing in Eve's direction.

Every head in the room swiveled in neat formation.

"Right. I'm Eve Weldon," said Eve in a voice that sounded as if it were coming from very far away. She forced herself to meet Bliss's gaze. The anchor gave her a once-over that felt like a punch in the stomach. Then she turned back to Giles.

"This is not someone who has ever written for me before, yet suddenly she is handling the top story, one that includes violent crime, an untested guest, and Chief Pell, who is one of the world's most evasive and self-aggrandizing public officials. This alone is of great concern to me."

Eve looked back at the ground, focusing on a tiny patch of beige carpet, trying to count the fibers in it.

"And then, making it far worse, is the fact that the interview, as prepared, was disastrous, bordering on dangerous."

What? Archie himself had told her she'd done an excellent job. That's why she'd been confident Mark wouldn't be angry with her if he found out what she'd done. She glanced around looking for Archie in hopes of finding some support, but he wasn't there. Mark himself was looking at her with mounting alarm.

"Dangerous?" said Giles.

"Yes. I won't go into it here, but the line of questioning proposed was downright irresponsible and could have gotten the network in serious trouble."

"Bliss, I'm sure—"

But Bliss looked down at her watch and cut him off with a slicing gesture of her hand. "I really do have to run. I just want to make sure nothing like this happens again." She turned to the room with a wry smile. "Bye, gang." And she was gone.

There was an excruciating pause during which Giles took a long swig from his water bottle. "Where were we?" he asked. The meeting hobbled along but Eve couldn't follow a thing that was said.

As they filed out, Giles turned to Mark. "In my office," he said, and Mark shot Eve a look of utter blackness.

. . .

Quirine and Russell slid behind Eve into her office and shut the door.

Eve tried to think up something to say, but before she could, Quirine pulled Eve into a hug. Not a stiff, acquaintance hug, but a deep, body-to-body embrace. The gesture brought tears to Eve's eyes.

Russell cleared his throat. "That was frickin' ridiculous. I've never seen anything like it. What got into that woman?" Eve closed her eyes tight. Russell put a hand on her back. "Can I just ask, what exactly—"

"Shhh." Quirine cut him off. "She can tell us later. Right now, let's just give her some peace before she deals with Mark."

"No, it's okay," said Eve, pulling away. She told them what she'd done.

Russell let out a low whistle. "Wowsa."

Quirine pushed a lock of Eve's hair behind her ear. "I think that's a first around here. Much as Cassandra deserved to have her segment taken away, I don't think anyone else in the department would have dared do what you did."

Great, thought Eve.

Just then, the phone rang. It was Mark.

. . .

Eve sat down without looking at him. He was silent for several moments. Then, quite suddenly, he leaned forward, his face red. "Do you have any idea what you've done? I don't know what's worse. That you broke the chain of command. That you violated my trust. That the writers were already in the doghouse and you've managed to put us in the basement of the doghouse. Or the fact that you turned in a segment that was slipshod. Maybe even irresponsible."

Now this last accusation was completely unfair. She wanted to ask Mark if he'd even read the segment, or talked to Archie about it. But this was not the time to defend herself.

"You realize you deserve to be fired, right?"

Eve nodded, miserable.

"And I would fire you, but to make the 'cause' argument with the union, I'd have to explain what you did yesterday, switching the assignments. Which would only make me look like an idiot in my new job and make the department look even worse. Right now they just think I took a chance on you and 'neglected' to explain about you to Bliss, the way Orla Knock used to do with her new writers." Eve shifted her weight back and forth. Mark looked up at the ceiling. "God, when I think of you here, sitting at my desk, tampering with my list. It makes me sick."

Eve felt sick, too. She saw it from his side and was horrified. All the arguments she might have made about how Cassandra had been late again, about how Eve herself was ready for a big story and ready to write for Bliss and how unfair it was that he never gave her anything serious to do, just felt empty and hollow. Why, oh why, had she done it?

"I'm sorry," she whispered.

He acted as though he hadn't heard her. "So I'm not firing you. But you might as well look for another job. You're not going anywhere here. And don't even think about asking for a reference."

Eve nodded. She pushed herself up from her chair and backed out of the door.

. . .

They went to the same bar as the night Mark announced his promotion. This wasn't a night for wine; they ordered straight scotch and sat at a small table in the back, Eve between Quirine and Russell. Nervous energy coursed through her and she chewed, hamster-like, on the end of a tiny red straw.

"So, back to your question," said Russell, after the waitress had left. "Yes, I think Mark will be as good as his word. I think you're going to have a rough time of it; he's not going to be very pleasant."

"I for one think he's so angry because he feels guilty," said Quirine.

Eve looked at her. "What do you mean?"

"Oh, on some level he understands what you did. He knows he kept you waiting for a lot longer than was probably fair. Maybe he was afraid to give you a big story because Cassandra has more seniority and he didn't want an earful from her if you leapfrogged over her. She can be quite combative, you know."

"It's depressing," said Russell. "I mean, I think Mark is a

great guy and I know he means well, but he's terrified of conflict. And I don't think that bodes well for the department. He went from zero to company man in sixty seconds."

"He's definitely afraid to make waves," said Quirine. "I heard he lost his temper once when he was at the *Daily News*. Screamed at his boss in the newsroom. I think it was during his divorce, which was apparently highly acrimonious. Anyway, he wound up being fired. I guess the lesson he took from that was to keep quiet and keep management happy."

The three sat a few moments in silence. *Divorce?* Eve really hadn't known the first thing about Mark, she realized.

"Anyway," said Russell. "I'll keep an eye out for jobs for you, Eve. I've got friends at the other networks, though I think things are pretty tight right now."

"Yes, I am afraid this is bad timing," said Quirine, putting her hand on Eve's forearm. "Didn't CBS just announce layoffs?"

. . .

Eve woke Saturday morning overwhelmed by homesickness. She lay on the bed, blinking at the window, the expanse of brick on the other side of the courtyard, and the sliver of sky visible above it. What she would give to see the endless green hills of Rolling Links. To show up for work at her father's office, where she was treated with the respect accorded the boss's daughter. Or to go out with a nice, undemanding young man, someone she could invite in at the end of a date.

The sharpest pang she felt was, as ever, Penelope's absence. All of this would be so much easier if she could talk to her mother about it. Giving in to the misery swirling through her, Eve wondered for the millionth time why her mother had had to die. She rolled over, shut her eyes, and drifted off into memory.

The bedroom was dim, save for a small circle of light from the lamp on the night table. They'd fallen asleep together, a book open between them. Eve opened her eyes and looked at Penelope, serene in slumber. But something was wrong. Her mother's breathing was labored and a fine sheen had broken out on her skin.

"Mom? Mom?" Eve reached out and shook Penelope's shoulder. Penelope did not stir. Eve looked at the clock. It was nearly 6 p.m.; her mother was supposed to take a pill at 4:45. She grabbed for the bottle but it was empty.

She leapt off the bed. "Daddy?" she called as she ran through the house. Then she remembered: Gin had rushed off to the office for an emergency meeting about a case. Her brothers weren't home, either. Eve, pulse racing, forced herself to concentrate. She found another bottle of pills in the medicine cabinet of the guest powder room. Each tablet had to be broken in half and dissolved in water. She tried to snap a pill in two with her fingers, but she only wound up crushing it into soft flakes. The same thing happened with a second pill.

She took a deep breath and headed into the kitchen, where she found a paring knife and used it to slice a pill right down the middle. She put half of it into a tall glass and filled it with water, stirring hard with a milkshake spoon until it became microscopic fragments swirling evenly in the liquid.

Eve carried the glass down the hall using both hands and placed it on the night table. She shook her mother for all she was worth, then pried her mouth open and poured the water in slowly. At first, Penelope coughed it right out again, soaking her nightgown. But after a few moments, she began to drink slowly, then deeply.

When the glass was empty, she clutched it to her chest, fell back against the pillows, and looked at her daughter. "God, honey, are you all right?"

Eve realized she was crying. "Yes. Are *you*?"

"Yes, yes. I'm all right." She looked as though she'd been away, somewhere mystifying, and was surprised to find herself home again. "Where's your father?"

"At the office."

"Your brothers?"

"I don't know."

"You did this all by yourself? The pill—everything?"

"Yes," said Eve, taking the glass back and putting it on the table.

Penelope cupped Eve's chin tenderly in her hand and regarded her daughter, her very irises seeming to widen. She held Eve's gaze and did not let go, even when they heard the front door open and Gin come running down the hall.

Eve pulled herself back to the present. She dabbed at her eyes with a tissue and headed into the living room, where she looked at the map of the Village she had tacked up over the fireplace. Some time ago, she'd starting pushing a tiny red pin into the map, to mark the location of each of the writers' plaques she'd found. Now she was looking at a constellation of the authors who'd kept Penelope company for so much of her life.

Eve hugged herself, running her eyes along the streets she and her mother had both called home, so many decades apart.

. . .

The coffeehouse was packed and it was hard to hold the empty chair across from her. Vadis, finally back from her extended tour with Spoilt Picnic, was twenty minutes late, and Eve ordered a second café au lait and drummed her nails on the table as she skimmed the want ads. Nothing in television at all, unless you were something called a "satellite truck operator."

"Sorry," said Vadis, leaning down for an air kiss. She seemed in very good spirits. Her ebony hair was longer and she wore a concert T-shirt under her trench coat. "I've just had so much shit to do after being away. I've only got about forty-five minutes. Got to go to the post office and yell at whoever forgot to restart delivering my mail. I've been back four days and haven't gotten a thing."

"Well, you look great," said Eve, realizing she'd missed Vadis. There was something infectious about her energy and determination.

"You, on the other hand, have looked better." She waved at a waiter, signaling she'd have what Eve was having. "Everything okay?"

"Fine, fine," Eve replied, trying her best to sound breezy. She couldn't bear just yet to tell Vadis that her little charity project had turned out to be a bust. "So tell me about the tour."

Apparently, Spoilt Picnic had played to packed venues, albeit small ones, all over. The tour had extended beyond its original Northeast scope and had hit the mid-Atlantic states and some of the South. They'd garnered some decent reviews and Vadis had enjoyed the nonmusical gifts of the lead guitarist ever since Baltimore.

"Jeremy is amazing. And he actually does better press interviews than Geoff, who's the lead singer. So I thought when they're on *Smell the Coffee,* maybe Bliss could interview both Jeremy and Geoff before they launch into their big hit. I'd like to get them on right before the CD comes out next month. What do you think?"

Eve didn't know which was worse: that it seemed the main reason Vadis had made time for her was because she wanted something or the fact that Eve couldn't provide it. "Sounds great," she said. "Except for one thing."

"What?"

"Orla Knock doesn't work at *Smell the Coffee* anymore." Eve took a long time detailing Orla's move into the entertainment division in L.A., hoping Vadis might forget what they were talking about.

"Wow. I have to call her. Sounds like another great contact," said Vadis, dabbing the corners of her mouth with her napkin. "But anyway. You can still do it, right?"

"Do what?"

"Talk to whoever books music for the show. I've got some

great video of the guys in concert that I shot. You can give it to them."

Eve took another sip of coffee. "I don't think I'm the best person to ask anyone for anything right now."

"What do you mean?" asked Vadis.

Eve told Vadis about her misadventures in television. She thought she saw a glimmer of admiration in her friend's eyes when she explained about taking the Stiletto segment away from Cassandra, but then she came to the part about how Mark had told her to find another job.

"I'm really sorry that I can't help you," said Eve. "Please believe me that I wish I could, but I'm persona non grata around there." All Vadis had spoken about in the last few months was Spoilt Picnic; she'd been counting on getting them on TV. She had no other clients. This had to be a bad blow.

"Yeah, all right," said Vadis. "Just so long as you're not expecting me to help *you.*"

"Huh?"

"I have the feeling you're working up to asking me to help you find the new job that Mark's advised you to get."

"Absolutely not!" said Eve. This was actually the truth. Eve realized, with some surprise, that she had not been expecting Vadis to help her again. She'd been here months without her; she wasn't suddenly going to fall back into dependency. Whatever she was going to do, she was going to do it on her own.

Vadis looked at her watch. "I really do have to go."

"Coffee's on me," said Eve.

"Thanks," said Vadis. "Look, sorry I was such a bitch just now. I'm just really tired after all that traveling. And I'm sorry about your job. We'll think of something, okay?"

Eve nodded as Vadis stood and turned to leave. Eve caught her arm. "I'll make up for this," she said. "I promise. One of these days, I'll be the one helping you."

. . .

It was Sunday afternoon and Eve sat on the floor, listening to the rain and flipping through the many sections of the paper. She'd read all the news, and was now perusing the gallery listings in the arts pages. When she'd first arrived in New York, she'd gone quite often, hoping they would provide an opening to meet the locals in a way that bars had not, but the cliques that gathered there turned out to be as hermetically sealed as those at Chumley's and the Cedar Tavern. The art, though, riveted and energized her in a way she hadn't experienced since senior year of college when she'd immersed herself in her thesis, "Collectivism After Modernism: The Art of Social Imagination After 1945."

She wondered if there was something good in Chelsea. Maybe she could call Gwendolyn and they could go together. She needed to get out of the house. There were plenty of offerings; a mixed-media installation looked good, and so did a group show of new artists. Then Eve saw a name she recognized.

René LaForge retrospective: rare collection of the late postmodernist sculptor. October 1–16.

Today was the sixteenth.

Eve said Donald's name, but he seemed to be on hiatus, as he had been for the last few days. She reached for the phone and dialed.

"Hello?"

"Matthias Klieg, please."

"Who is calling?" Eve gave her name. "Ah, Miss Weldon. This is Maxine. What can I do for you?" Eve explained about the LaForge show. "I am sure Mr. Klieg would be interested. He has a lunch that should be over in about two hours. Shall I have him meet you at the gallery?"

Eve wondered if anyone held that much sway over Klieg. "Are you sure he'll want to come?"

"I believe so. He has been meaning to call you, I think,

but . . ." It seemed Maxine thought better of whatever she was going to say. "Anyway, it is good that you have called."

· · ·

The wind and rain had increased through the afternoon and the gallery was nearly empty. Eve and Klieg strolled around the large white space.

"I remember this one," said Klieg, pointing at an intricate copper piece. Three layers of lacy trees and tiny deer extended from a wire attached to the wall. "Rene was inspired by the Bois de Boulogne."

"Is there any of his early work here?" asked Eve, looking around. "Everything looks so assured, so precise."

"Ah," said Klieg, continuing to walk again. "Unlike most of us, René had no awkward phase. His first pieces are hardly distinguishable from his last."

Eve hesitated to bring up a delicate topic, but she wanted to go back to things they'd discussed at the opera. "So he never had a bad review?"

"You mean like I did?" Klieg looked sideways at her.

"Like you did."

"No, I'm afraid he could not quite understand what that was like."

"What was it like?"

Klieg's eyes widened and he tilted back on his heels for a moment. "Well. I bore the scars for quite some time. I felt I couldn't trust my own judgment. And that is one of the worst feelings one can experience."

"Boy, are you right," mumbled Eve, taking in an abstract piece that looked like a ball of yarn or maybe the universe. They strolled separately for a few minutes before Eve worked her way back over to Klieg. "You told me you had to return to Germany to earn money for a new collection," she said. "That must have been difficult."

"Yes. Going home so soon after striking out on one's own is

no picnic, as you say here. But it was not as terrible as it might have been," said Klieg, pondering a steel orb with pinpricks all over it. "Louisa came with me."

"Louisa?"

"She was a cashier at the Deux Magots. Graceful as a ballerina and so kind to us starving artists. I can't tell you how much charcuterie and cheese she took from the kitchen for us, smuggled in napkins and stuffed into our satchels."

"This is when you were hanging around with René, Lars Andersen, and the others?"

"Yes."

"And . . . Donald."

Klieg leaned in close to admire the soldering on a complicated piece of blocks and pulleys but said nothing. Maybe he hadn't heard her.

Eve tried again. "How close were the two of you?"

Klieg looked at the ceiling. "He was quite, how shall I put it, ornery? He made a dramatic point of disparaging the everyday: the search for an affordable garret, the bills, the boring part-time jobs all artists must suffer. He would never let us wallow in those things; he insisted we talk about only the extraordinary."

"I guess that's what he was attempting to do in his work?"

"I suppose, in his maladroit way, yes."

"But why did everything have to be so opaque? I don't want to upset you," said Eve, remembering the way their opera evening ended. "But I can't help but wonder. Why didn't he write from the heart more, reveal something of himself the way the great artists do?"

"He did, in his early work."

"He did?"

"Yes."

"What happened?"

Klieg was silent for a few moments before he spoke. "He changed gears."

"Why? When?"

"It must have been about 1964 or so. He decided that words were inadequate to convey emotion." When Eve looked perplexed, he continued. "This is typical of a young artist—to throw out everything because he's discovered a new, more fruitful path." Klieg stepped back from the sculpture and took in the whole.

What had happened to Donald in 1964? Eve wanted to ask, but feared Klieg would shut down again. She opted for safer ground. "Tell me more about you and Louisa."

"We married. When I could afford to, I moved us back to Paris. And eventually, we came here."

"Why?" asked Eve.

"Louisa wanted to. She found being back in Paris . . . difficult. And of course, there is a certain kind of person who just won't be happy unless she lives in New York at least once in her life."

"Yes." Eve smiled.

"I suppose I was like that as well. It was irresistible to see if I could 'make it' here. I did find success, of course, and worked a great deal. That was part of it. And we did so enjoy ourselves. The opera became a habit of ours. It was her seat you took some weeks ago, our season tickets. We took walks in Central Park, ate dinner at Café Carlyle every Sunday, went for drives in the Hudson Valley. We kept up most of our routines until just before she died. . . ."

Eve's ears pricked up when he said "Café Carlyle." But before she could ask him about it or the million other questions that sprang to mind, Klieg surprised her by resting a hand lightly on her shoulder.

"Many in the press have asked me about my personal life, but I have always declined to talk about it. I don't know why, but you . . ." Eve nodded. She had heard this many times from her interview subjects. "Maxine worries about me, thinking I am too closed off. She was most pleased about your invitation today."

"I'm glad you were able to come," said Eve.

"Shall we have a drink?" he asked. "Someplace nearby, perhaps."

They collected their coats and umbrellas. Before they headed out into the storm, Klieg looked at the rain pelting the windows and the trees turned inside out by the wind. "Let me tell you, Miss Eve, the past is a guest who visits whenever he pleases. For a long time, I managed to keep the door locked. But no more, it seems."

. . .

Eve awoke to find the apartment stone cold. It felt like the heat was on the fritz. She decided to try the fireplace, though Mrs. Swan had once told her that most of them didn't work. This had disappointed Eve, who'd cultivated a romantic image of herself tucked up in her Village apartment on a winter's night, fire blazing, shadows swaying on the wall.

Amazingly, the deli carried logs—these institutions had turned out to be marvelous places—and Eve loaded them along with balls of newspaper onto the grate and lit a match. The orange flame crisped the paper and set its teeth into the wood. A moment later, enormous clouds of black smoke came billowing into the room.

"Oh my God!" Coughing, her throat burning, Eve picked up Highball, shoved her into the hall, and slammed the door. Then she opened every window and ran to the kitchen, where she grabbed her biggest pot from the shelf over the stove. She began to fill it with water. "Come on, come on," she urged the lazy spigot.

"What's the hassle, baby?" asked Donald, appearing for the first time in days.

"The fireplace. It's"—she broke off, throwing some water into her mouth—"not working. I've got to call 911—"

"Now, now. Hold on. When did you light it?"

"I don't know. About three minutes ago?" She broke out into another coughing fit.

"Give it a couple more. It's cranky. It needs to burn off the gunk inside the chimney, then it works just fine."

Eve, nearly gagging, ventured back into the living room. Another puff of smoke burst from the fireplace and then, suddenly, the blackness began to abate. She used pillows to shoo the remaining smoke out the windows, and the room slowly began to clear. When the air was breathable again, she let in the confused Highball, who sniffed the air warily.

"You were right," said Eve, holding her hands up to the dancing fire. "It's okay now."

"That brings back such memories. This funny little apartment with all its idiosyncrasies. How I miss it. Does the closet in the hallway still smell like teriyaki?"

"Yes," said Eve, laughing.

After she changed, she made herself some tea and found their current yellow pad. "As a thank-you, how about we get back to 'Rock, Paper, Scissors'?"

"It's gratifying to see you so eager," Donald said as Eve sat down on her bed. "But I worry you're not in the right frame of mind. After all the unpleasantness at work, are you sure you wouldn't rather just relax?"

"You're sweet," she said. "But I could use the diversion."

"Ah. Well then, onward. But if you'll permit me to say just one thing about it. I want you to know I support what you did."

"Lighting the fire?"

"No. At work. Taking the big story for yourself."

Eve had almost forgotten she'd been thinking of Donald when she did it. Even now, his support still gave her a small measure of comfort. "Thanks."

"My generation had a rather different relationship to the Establishment than yours, you know. We saw how the individual could be crushed by the machine. In my circle, we did not hesitate to resort to drastic measures when the situation called for it. We felt our power and we used it."

"Writers really mattered back then, didn't they?"

"They were covered in the papers like Hollywood stars."

"It seems like they weren't afraid of anything." Eve thought of the beaten-down *Smell the Coffee* writers.

"Probably because we had real community back then. Manhattan was smaller. So was the Village. We stuck together, took care of each other. And restaurants and bars took care of us, too. They gave us food and drink when we were hard up. They took pride in having a stake in the career of up-and-coming young talent."

"Nobody remembers those times anymore," said Eve, thinking of the plaques. Every time she'd mentioned them to someone, they'd shrugged. Alex had never noticed them. Nor had Vadis. Or even the *Smell* writers. "It's fifty years ago now. Soon it'll be lost for good. Unless . . ."

"Yes?"

Now was the time. She hadn't planned for it, but there might never be another moment that would feel this natural. She cleared her throat and employed the lightest possible tone. "Have you ever thought about writing a memoir?"

"No."

"Why not?"

"I'm an artist. My fiction is my statement."

"Well, plenty of artists have written memoirs. And think about it, you've lived such an interesting life. Everyone you knew in New York. Plus Paris! Your days with Lars and René and—"

"How do you know about *them*?"

"The library," she lied, hoping to steamroller right over this revelation to prevent him from questioning this further. "You could tell stories about all of it. The Beats. The Postwar Four. How the movements were related. Funny anecdotes about everyone."

"I don't—"

"And how about this? We put your stories in the *body* of the memoir. You discuss your artistic process and then illustrate the fruits of it, all in one book. Let the reader go behind the scenes with the artist."

"Listen here—"

"This could be a whole new way to go, something more for the times as they are now. You've been gone a long time; things have changed. Drop the veil. Let the reader in."

There was a pause. Eve rubbed the sides of her upper arms. She rarely gave directives, rarely spoke in such short, punchy sentences. It felt good.

"I'm not interested in a memoir. I want to continue with my stories. Now, will you or will you not help me?"

Highball, who'd been watching her intently from the foot of the bed, high-stepped her way over the gathered ridges of the coverlet. She yawned, stretched, and sat, her pointed snout an inch from Eve's own nose. The dog's breath was warm against her cheek, her wagging tail like a feather duster, tickling the sides of her thighs.

"Of course I'll help you." Eve sighed, trying to take his decision with good grace, already planning to bring the subject up again soon. She picked up her pen and they returned to the story, at the key moment when Paper and Scissors finally meet.

"Everyone is waiting for the fight, for the collision," began Donald. "Paper and Scissors size each other up and . . . smile broadly. They get along like a house on fire. The dinner guests are disappointed; there is nothing to see! Paper recognizes in Scissors a kindred soul, a metaphysical twin. By all rights they should be mortal enemies and this is what makes it even more delicious."

This story seemed to come closer to saying something than the previous ones, as though the metaphors might actually be about something real, but it still didn't make much sense. "I realize Paper and Scissors are supposed to represent something," she said when Donald paused for a moment. "But can we make it clearer what that is? I think that would help."

"How many times have I told you? I am not here to spoon-feed the reader. If he can't keep up, that's his tough luck." He continued with his dictation.

Eve shook her head but took down his words, just as she had so many times before. This time, though, she felt something stirring within her. She'd always been curious about whether his work was worth publishing, but she hadn't cared on an emotional level. Now she began to, just a little. Not so much that his stories would be published, but that *he* would be. Which made it all the more frustrating that the work was so, well, bad.

Chapter 12

November arrived and the chill sank its claws into the city. The sky hung low like a sheet of iron, and the last of the colored leaves that had carpeted the streets suffered the indignity of being swept into large garbage bags that now lined the sidewalks like shiny black fists. Eve bought a pretty winter coat, at Full Circle of course, a high-collared bouclé affair with jeweled buttons.

As she paid for the coat, Gwendolyn invited her over for dinner the following Saturday night. She lived at the corner of Christopher and Greenwich in a rent-controlled apartment she'd inherited from her grandmother. It was on the ninth floor, with a beautiful view of the Jefferson Market Library and, beyond, the Empire State Building. Unlike Eve's radiators, Gwendolyn's hissed their productivity loudly, and her windows were thrown open wide like arms around the city. Eve leaned out and breathed in the crisp air, before tucking into a deep bowl of pasta and a hearty Shiraz. They spent the evening playing go fish, and afterward, Eve quizzed Gwendolyn for an entrepreneurship exam at the New School.

Gwendolyn was planning to buy Full Circle and was single-minded in pursuing her goal. Gwendolyn, Alex, Vadis: It struck Eve that young New Yorkers were far more intent on going it alone than Ohioans. Would she ever want to do the same? She wouldn't even know how to begin.

. . .

At the library, Mrs. Chin informed Eve that more boxes had come in from the collector.

"I know I promised you these a while ago," she said, reaching for the books, which she'd put aside under the counter. "But there's a backlog of material, and with the latest round of budget cuts, we've fewer people handling processing. I hope you'll forgive me."

"That's okay," said Eve. "Thanks for flagging them for me." She carried the stack over to her usual table. The third book she flipped through, *Village Artists and Their Associations, 1940–1970*, sparked an idea. Maybe there was a way to *back* Donald into a memoir without him realizing what she was doing. Maybe she could read up on his contemporaries and ask him about them quite innocently, drawing him out in casual fashion.

The book proved extraordinarily helpful for tracing connections. For instance, she quickly determined that Donald was in something called the Free Voices Brigade, along with William Burroughs and someone named Simon Thuen, who was also in the Unchained Essayists of Eighth Street. And Simon was part of the Village Scribes along with Gregory Corso and someone named Floyd Sommers, whose style was described as "freemodern." This sounded promising and Eve wrote it down in her notebook. By the end of the afternoon, she had seven pages of names and affiliations.

At home that night, she took up her place at the bar and called out for Donald.

"You rang?" he said. His flash of humor indicated a good mood.

"I've been reading about my mother's times at the library, as you know," said Eve. "And I was wondering if I could toss out some names I found in a book today to see if any ring a bell. Just for fun."

Donald grunted a tacit assent. The first ten or so names she mentioned produced either no memory at all or spirited denunciations that were capped by such proclamations as "fink," "horse's ass," or the dreaded "sellout."

"What about Mike McGuire?" asked Eve. "He was in, let's see, Unchained Essayists and his name also pops up in several articles about minor Beats. Seems he was sort of the tail end."

"McGuire . . . yes," said Donald.

"What do you remember about him?" asked Eve.

"Poet. A bit younger than I, ten years or so, not the kind of person I would ordinarily notice. But he stood out. He rode just up to the line of brashness. He spoke a lot but also listened well. He possessed boundless energy, too, as if extra blood were pumping through his veins."

"What else?" Eve flipped the page and kept scribbling.

"I used to see him at El Faro and places like that. Have you been there? I hope it still exists. Marvelously cracked, very bohemian. Anyway, he always had a pencil behind his ear and a handkerchief in his breast pocket. He had a job writing advertising copy, took a lot of ribbing for it from the counterculture set. He also gambled a bit on the ponies. When he was flush, he'd buy the whole room a round. He was quite the glad-hander but he carried poems in his pocket and the only time he grew shy was when he tried to show them to me."

"Why did he want to show them to you?"

"They were—only vaguely, mind you—an homage to my style."

"Were they any good?"

There was a beat of silence. "He struggled a bit in terms of adapting my ideas to his own voice, which is what every writer must do, this dance between influence and the essential self. But I suppose I must admit there was . . . potential there. And I remember something else."

"Yes?"

"After a reading I gave on Bedford Street, the hostess took me aside and told me that before I'd arrived, McGuire had addressed the room. He urged those gathered to not only read my stories but to try my theories on for size in their own work. He said something to the effect that for him, nothing had been as freeing as my particular restrictions."

"He really admired you."

"Kind, very kind, he was. I wish now I'd paid a bit more attention to him. I was so busy trying to curry favor with those older and more successful than I that I forgot to complete the circle, to support those coming up behind."

Eve sat up straighter on the bar stool. "I'd love to talk to him. I wonder where he is now."

"I'm not sure. He left town, as I remember, went traveling probably, as most of us did at one point or another. But perhaps he returned."

. . .

The next week at work, Eve kept her head low and said little. Whenever she had a moment, she worked on her résumé, but the rest of the time, her stories ranged from "Perfume for Your Daughter's Dolls" to "Eating for Seven: Snacks for Moms Expecting Sextuplets" to "Fourteen Kinds of Thanksgiving Relishes." She did not get to go on the sweeps shopping trip to Chicago with Quirine and Cassandra. And editing sessions with Mark became a daily misery; he was immune to her talent and to any small joke she might offer.

Still, every once in a while she felt compelled to try to improve the atmosphere between them.

"Hey, did you see?" she said, leaning against the doorway of his office. "They finally moved Orla Knock's stuff out. After all this time. I guess you'll be getting her office, right?" The wall-to-wall windows would be a vast improvement over Mark's airless box.

"No," said Mark, turning his attention to a stack of folders. "They've got some marketing guy they're giving it to."

"What? Marketing's not editorial. That office is the managing editor's office and you're the managing editor."

"I know that, Eve." Mark said, starting to tap away at his keyboard. "Apparently, they're reorganizing the floor."

Eve shook her head. This seemed like yet another slap in the face to the department. She wanted Mark to march into Giles Oberoy's office and demand the office for himself. But after the embarrassment she'd caused the department, he probably didn't think he could demand anything.

"Mark, I—" she began.

"Kind of busy here," he said.

. . .

Quirine and Russell were being extra nice. Quirine invited her to a play and they had dinner afterward. She made for lively company. She could tell you the best places to go camping in Vietnam as well as a foolproof way to get an annoying song out of your head. And Eve was further surprised when Russell and his wife, Susan, invited her over for dinner at their place on the Upper West Side. Susan, at about thirty, was ten or so years younger than Russell but had a focused air that made her seem if anything more mature. She was a pixielike redhead who worked for a cookbook publisher, and she treated them to a delicious tilapia in banana leaves that she was testing for a new volume. Quirine came too, bringing Victor, a graduate student of historical preservation at Pratt. He was olive-skinned with a halo of corkscrew curls and an easy manner, and when Eve insisted on washing the dishes, he took up a post next to her to dry them, turning the whole thing into a friendly competition to see who was faster. It ended with the two of them engaged in some playful splashing, and though a few soapy droplets splattered Eve's Ossie Clark dress, she didn't mind a bit.

Socially, things finally seemed to be picking up. She even had a date.

Oliver was a musician who played guitar for several bands whenever one of their own members was sick or out of town. He'd been sitting two bar stools over at the Chelsea Corner, where Eve and Klieg had gone for a drink after the LaForge show. When Klieg had excused himself to the restroom, Oliver had leaned across to her.

"Isn't he a little old for you?"

"He's my *friend*," said Eve, irritated.

The young man was handsome, with hair the color of wheat, like many of the boys back home. There were so few blond men in New York; he made for a nice change, if nothing else.

"I was just kidding." He grabbed at the bowl of popcorn between them. "Seen any good art today?" he asked, nodding at the sheaf of gallery leaflets she'd put on the bar. They chatted about a space they'd both liked and a particular piece there, an impressionistic nude of a water nymph. It was two-for-one happy hour, and he bought Eve another drink. "Cheers," he said as the bartender put their glasses down. They toasted. Just before Klieg returned, Oliver asked for her number.

It took more than three weeks for him to call, but Eve was prepared for the angst this time and found it easier to bear. She kept her voice casual as they spoke on the phone, a subtle wink that *Yes, yes, we both know this is how the game is played.*

He suggested they go out the following Tuesday night. She'd earned a personal day by now and took pleasure in informing Mark that she was taking it.

Highball took up a post just outside the closet and nodded or shook her head at various outfits Eve tried on. In the end, they chose a deep rose wool shift from the sixties and paired it with drop pearl earrings and a black satin clutch. Eve knew better than to expect Oliver to be some kind of knight in shining armor, but an evening of pleasant conversation, an evening spent doing what the young and eligible were supposed to do in New York, was more than enough.

Donald groused. "What about 'Rock, Paper, Scissors'? We're at a critical point in the story. Do you not see that, unlike your quasi-romantic escapades, my work has lasting meaning . . . ?"

Donald was frustratingly inconsistent. One minute he was eager for her to "sow her wild oats," the next he was irked because she had a date. She assuaged him with a barrage of soothing words until he left, which took far longer than it should have. She was so nervous about being late for Oliver that she dropped her keys twice as she attempted to lock the door.

She arrived at the appointed corner and, confused, checked the address to make sure she was in the right place. Pushing through the glass door, she found herself inside a giant box of an Italian restaurant, a chain establishment, with a salad bar occupying a large central area. Aside from several families with small children dotted around the cavernous room, it was mostly empty.

"Hey, you made it," Oliver said, rising from a small bench next to a sign saying *Hostess Station* and kissing her on the cheek. He wore jeans and a T-shirt advertising some band called Freak Show, and high-top sneakers. Perhaps he noted some surprise in her expression because he hastily explained, "I know it's not romantic, but there's a method to my madness. You'll see."

"Ah," said Eve.

The hostess, in a green uniform, matching visor, and black sneakers, approached. "Table for two?"

"Actually, two tables for one," said Oliver. When the hostess looked confused, he reached for his wallet, pulled out two orange slips of paper, and handed them over.

"Uh-*huh*," she said, handing them back. "This way." She grabbed two poster-sized menus and led them across the room.

Oliver whispered to Eve as they walked, "Each coupon is good for a dinner entrée on separate visits on Tuesday nights. I figure if we're at separate tables, we're technically on separate 'visits.' Starving artists have to be on their toes in this town. Score, huh?"

They spent the next hour and a half at adjacent tables, eating bland manicotti with watery sauce and talking sideways at each other. Between multiple visits to the salad bar, where he seemed interested in nothing but bacon and croutons, Oliver waxed on about a guitar he wanted to buy and how tough the competition was for studio work. He was wildly self-absorbed and failed to ask her even one question about herself. By the end, Eve's stomach was complaining bitterly and her neck was in spasm.

Oliver suggested dessert but Eve had had enough. She stood and fished some money out of her wallet. When he asked what she was doing, she explained that she had an impatient short-story-dictating ghost waiting at home and really had to go.

. . .

The following week, Eve suffered through a particularly grueling night at work, her eyes nearly crossed from exhaustion. Every segment she worked on was rebooked after she'd written it, forcing her to start all over again. At eleven-thirty, just as she was gathering up her things, news broke of an avalanche in Colorado, from which six skiers had miraculously escaped. *Damn, damn, damn.* Now she'd have to wait till the bookers tracked down the survivors at the hospital. An hour later, when Sharon, the booker, finally gave her the information on the four survivors willing to talk, Eve placed four calls. Four times she asked, "What did you think when you heard the ski patrol's voice coming through the snow and you knew you were going to be saved?" And four times she'd heard, recorded, and put into a briefing note, "Uh, um, you know, it was, like, you know, awesome."

It was after one-thirty by the time she dragged herself up the stairs, dreading having to go right back out again for Highball's nightly walk. She braced herself for the usual bombardment of paws about her thighs and cracked open the door. A finger of light shot across the room, fanning out as she kicked the door open, but no dog appeared. Her eyes darted around the living room. "Highball?" Eve's coat and bag slid down her arms and onto the floor with a plunk. The dog was never *not* by the door to greet her. Eve padded around, looking behind the bar and in the narrow space between the small fridge and the kitchen wall. Heart pounding, she ran into the bedroom, checking the closet and under the bed. "Highball?" No dog. Eve headed toward the bathroom but found her footsteps slowing. She had the feeling there was something terribly wrong. "You here?" she whispered as she pushed the door open and flicked on the light.

There, holding herself eerily still in the corner by the claw-foot tub, sat Highball. She was staring straight ahead with glassy, unseeing eyes. Eve felt an icicle plunge into her stomach. She crouched beside the dog, but Highball didn't so much as glance at her. As Eve reached out to touch her fur, the dog shook her head violently, her ears flapping like birds' wings.

Eve pulled back, startled. "Highball! What is it?" The dog brought her back leg forward and directed it into her ear and began to dig frantically. Eve prayed it wasn't an ear infection, not at this time of night. She pulled Highball's leg away and lifted up the shaggy ear to look inside. No sign of any irritation. But Highball began to dig again and to whimper piteously. Eve grabbed her face and looked into the deep chocolate eyes. What she saw was pure fear.

"What's wrong?" cried Eve. Her skin was crawling, her forehead sweating.

And then she knew.

"Donald!" she shouted. "Get out—get out of there now!" No response. She held Highball's face, searching her eyes again frantically, wondering if she could actually see Donald, knowing she wouldn't. He wasn't possessing the dog, just as he never possessed her. He was simply poking around in the corners, like a homeless man in a garbage can. But it was enough to petrify Highball. "I mean it! *You. Leave. Her. Right. Now!*" Eve was shrieking in a voice she didn't recognize. Thank goodness Mrs. Swan was still out of town or Eve would have woken the old woman up. The black and white tiles of the bathroom began to swim. Eve steadied herself by gripping the edge of the tub. "Out!"

Everything went still. She felt a familiar channel open, signaling Donald's arrival. But something was different. Suddenly, she was aware of a hundred smells: the saltiness of a speck of dried olive stuck to the side of the tub from a bath-time martini, the metallic scent of aspirin in the medicine cabinet, even the bitter damp of the morning's coffee grounds still in the machine in the kitchen. *Heavens,* she thought. *Is he bringing Highball with him?*

Then suddenly, with a firm click, Donald was in and the smells disappeared. Eve looked into Highball's eyes again and saw that the terror had been replaced by mild confusion. Eve collapsed against the wall, breathing hard, crushing the dog to her chest.

"Don't be so dramatic," said Donald, tickling her cerebellum. "The four-legged one is fine. Believe me, there's very little in there to disturb. I must say the trip over knocked the wind out of me, though. Never tried anything like that before."

"How dare you do that to her? What the hell were you thinking?" Eve demanded hoarsely, covering Highball's ears.

"I simply had to stretch my legs," Donald replied, with defensive nonchalance. "You're never around when I need you and I was bored to tears. We were supposed to continue working, remember? You've been putting me off for days and—"

"Don't! Don't say another word," hissed Eve, setting Highball down and marching into the living room. She grabbed the leash. "If you weren't already dead, I'd—I'd—" She stepped into the hallway with the dog and slammed the door behind them.

. . .

She was still breathing hard as she hustled Highball onto the street. Her heart pounded with outrage so hard it sent vibrations out to her extremities, through her skin, and into the air. The brownstones' wrought-iron gates, the spiky shadows they threw onto the ground, the awning of the bakery on the corner— everything seemed to be humming, as if she were walking through a Van Gogh. Highball still looked anxious and walked tentatively, as though across a bed of nails.

In the kind of stupor that follows trauma, they made their way westward through the cold, still night. The moon hovered, its outline smeared across a sullen sky. The last few maidenhair leaves dusted the ground while the first Christmas wreaths adorned townhouse doors, as if fall and winter were clasping hands for a brief moment before fall let go and winter went on alone.

They turned onto Bethune. Eve's head was throbbing, her mind flitting like a bird from branch to branch. Donald had shocked her with his indifference to Highball.

They marched on. When she looked down at her watch, she was stunned to see that twenty minutes had passed. Goose bumps invaded her flesh; in all the commotion she'd forgotten to put her coat back on. And she had no idea where they were now. Little West Twelfth? Gansevoort? Everything looked different, dream-like. Remnants of chimney smoke from the evening's fires per-fumed the air like incense, and the trees stretched across to each other, creating a vaulted ceiling over the street like an al fresco cathedral.

Eve realized another sound had joined the click of her boots and the faint scratching of Highball's nails on the sidewalk. The noise made its way in from the edges. Where was it coming from? Somewhere back and to the left, around the corner. She recognized the hollow clipping echoing up from the ground: a horse. A police horse, out on patrol.

The sound transported her. A horse on cobblestones: It was a sound you'd have heard on these streets two hundred years ago.

A lonely prance through empty streets, a fugue in the night. Eve let her mind wander with her feet, imagining she was on her way home from dinner at the home of, say, Willa Cather. Perhaps Robert Frost had entertained them with a poem—

Her trance was interrupted by Highball's abrupt yank toward the curb. She pulled more forcefully than usual, and the leash, which was wrapped tightly around Eve's hand, cut sharply into the soft place between her thumb and index finger. The dog crouched, arranged and rearranged her back feet to get them into proper position. While Eve would never relish this part of their relationship, she dreaded it far less than she once had. The key was not to think about what you were doing: Simply grab and go. Eve was just congratulating herself on this bit of vulgar wisdom when she glanced down. Highball's run-in with Donald must have triggered some kind of shock to her system; the pile that was forming was three times its usual size. Eve reached for the sandwich bags she kept in a pocket attached to the leash and waited for it to end. At last, Highball shook her hindquarters daintily, and Eve bent over and began her work, though the Baggie seemed hardly capable of meeting the challenge.

The clip-clopping was almost upon them. But it sounded odd, as if the horse was laboring, or teetering on the edge of something. Suddenly, Highball gave a sharp yelp and tugged hard on the leash, almost pulling Eve over. The moon flickered and the shadows of the privet branches shot out like streamers. Eve turned, but there was no horse. Only a very tall man. A very tall man in high-heeled shoes.

"Your money." Eve had to tilt her head back to take him in. His skin was pale, his hair spiky black. He was wearing leggings with a baggy sequined sweater under a wool peacoat. She stared at him, mute. "Look, are you retarded? Give me your money and do it fucking now." He pushed up his sleeves, revealing a mean set of tracks going up his left arm and jagged scars across his wrist.

Eve willed herself to follow what was happening but it was

impossible. She was face-to-face with the Stiletto, a moment of crossed paths worthy of Dawn Powell. Eve wished she could see Chief Pell's face at this moment. Not to mention Bliss's.

In a movement, he crossed to her, spun her around, and put the knife to her back. She felt its tip press through her blouse, grazing her flesh. His sour breath wound its way up her nostrils and deep inside her brain.

"Stop fucking around." He jerked her arm sharply upward, sending ripples of pain out from the socket. She felt like a roast squab, his for the pulling.

"I don't have any money," said Eve, craning her neck. Wasn't anyone hearing this? "I'm—I'm just walking my dog and—" Highball. She was in danger, too. Eve dropped the leash and nudged the dog with her foot. *Run, girl, run.*

But Highball stood her ground and began to bark. The Stiletto kicked her hard. Highball yelped and then whimpered softly.

"That dog makes another sound and I'll kill it." He was sounding unhinged now, reckless. Like he didn't know where this was going. "And as for you. No money, what good are you?" With a jolt, Eve felt the knife press into the flesh just to the right of her upper spine. Her skin gave momentary resistance before allowing itself to be pierced—just slightly, she thought. She cried out, but he slapped a hand over her mouth. It smelled of sweat and Chanel No. 5. Her eyes closed. Pain radiated out from the knife wound like the scorching rays of the sun. She tried to wriggle out of his grasp, but he was far too strong. This was it, she realized. It was all over. She threw her head back and looked up through the tree branches to the stars. Her knees gave way and she felt herself slipping into darkness.

Suddenly, the hand on her chin wasn't his, but Penelope's. They were on her bed, facing one another, the glass of water between them.

"You did this all by yourself? The pill—everything?" Penelope had asked.

"Yes," Eve had said.

Penelope's expression was pure wonder and tenderness. "There's the girl," she'd said softly. "There's the girl."

Eve's eyes flew open.

Here's the girl.

She pulled free, barely noticing the knife's twist on its way out. Then she stepped back and launched herself straight into the Stiletto's solar plexus.

"What the fu—" He was on the ground, writhing beneath her. She reached for his neck and as she deflected his kicks and jabs she noticed that he, like dear Dr. Tang, had a mole on his face. A big, brown mole. It seemed to be growing and stretching, now covering all of one cheek. His neck twisted wildly, his body bucking like a rodeo horse. She almost went flying, but the more he struggled, the stronger she became.

He struck out and she felt her jaw explode, refueling her anger. Eve gripped his neck, pressing her thumbs deep into his Adam's apple. He coughed and began to throw up. Tears mixed in with the vomit. "Stop . . . *stuughugh*," he said. He thrashed a moment longer, then seized up, looking directly at her. They locked eyes in a moment of spine-tingling, intimate madness.

Then, suddenly, he seemed to deflate like a punctured balloon and lay spent beneath her, his surrender hitting her like a double shot of whiskey. The world went swirly and she closed her eyes tight.

A shriek intruded. A black and white car came barreling around the corner and slammed to a stop in front of them.

"Freeze," said a voice inside. A squat, olive-skinned police officer pushed open the driver's-side door and leapt out. "Off her. Now," she ordered, as her partner jumped out the other door. He was tall and angular. For some reason, he was aiming a gun at Eve's head.

"You heard the officer," he said. "Get up and back away with your hands in the air. Slowly. Four steps. Let's go."

Eve stood up on legs that felt like rivers and stumbled backwards. Her fingertips brushed the heavens and her breath came
quick and shallow. From somewhere behind her, she became
aware of yowling.

"That your dog?" asked the woman officer. Eve nodded.
"Shut it up." Eve came down beside Highball. She checked the
dog's rib cage, which seemed all right if tender, and whispered
soothing nonsense in her ear, while the male officer strode over
to the heap on the sidewalk.

"Uh, hello? Miss? You all right? Jesus, what's that smell?" he
asked, leaning over. Then he looked a little closer. "Oh my God,"
he said, taking a step backward. "Oh my God. Oh my God!"

• • •

Itching from the dressing the paramedics had applied to her
wound, Eve sat in the back seat of the police car with Highball,
whose chin lay on her lap. The emergency crew had been kind
and attentive, even trying to wipe her sweating face. But Eve had
waved them away; she couldn't bear to be touched. The police
insisted on taking her to the station as quickly as possible, so
the paramedics gave her some aspirin and made the officers promise to bring her to the ER as soon as they were done with her.

Eve gazed out the open window, grateful for the air. They
coasted along blocks she knew so well—there was Mark Twain's
home and Hart Crane's—and yet everything looked different.
Colors burned softer yet brighter. Traffic lights winked at the in-
tersections. The corner playground rose up like a castle.

Gradually, snatches of the car's conversation began to pene-
trate her swarming mind. "—did it. Nabbed the goddamn
Stiletto—" "—in Crowley's patrol car right *now*—" "—cannot
believe it—" "—my collar—" "—excuse me, *my* collar—" "—
our collar—" "—reporters—" "—call my wife—"

They pulled up outside a low gray building bearing a large in-
signia on West Tenth Street: the Sixth Precinct. Eve could see the

Stiletto out on the sidewalk, being hustled inside. He was bent in half, dragging his feet, which were encased in some kind of paper booties, while an officer held his black pumps aloft in a Ziploc bag and waved them at the throng waiting by the entrance. "Check it out, the Stiletto's stilettos!" Flashbulbs and questions erupted: "How—?" "Where—?" "They're holding the presses for this—" "When—?" "Who—?"

"Talk to *her*," the officer said, pointing at Eve's car. "But first she's ours."

The woman officer, Fernandez, got out of the car. She strode around the back and opened Eve's door. "Miss," she said, suddenly formal. "This way, please."

Eve placed Highball gingerly on the sidewalk and took a deep breath. She swung her legs out of the car and felt an explosion of flashbulbs cover her with warm pops. Shading her eyes against the brightness, she placed one foot on the sidewalk, then the other. More pops came, showering her face and shoulders. She stood. Sound was drained from the world; the only noise was the liquid thumping of shutters clicking, bulbs bursting, and her own heart beating. *Flash.* Highball blinked. Eve strode toward the door, turning her head from side to side, her eyes rolling over the sea of eager faces. *Flash. Flash.* An earnest-looking young man tried to take her picture, but was pushed out of the way by those taller and stronger. Eve stopped in front of his lens. She turned and waited until he'd righted himself. She winked.

Finally, she arrived at the precinct door. As she crossed the threshold, several officers surged around her. Some smiled, others dipped their chins in respect. A few looked at her with what seemed like concern. Eve's temples pounded and her skin burned. She clenched and unclenched the muscles in her jaw.

"Give us some room, guys." Fernandez grabbed Eve's elbow. "I'll be the one taking you to meet the captain. Can I get you something to drink?"

Eve realized she was exceedingly thirsty. "Yes, please."

"Anything. Anything you want," said Fernandez.

"Just water," said Eve.

"No problem. I'll get you a bottle as soon as you're settled. Now, ah . . . before we go into the captain's office, you want to freshen up? It might be a good idea. . . ." Fernandez trailed off. "I'll hold the dog for you. You can use the officers' bathroom. It's right here."

Eve nodded and pushed open the thick metal door. When she reached the sinks, she gazed into the mirror. There was a large purple bruise along her jawline. But there was something else, something strange. Brown lines across her cheekbones. Stripes of . . . what? She dabbed her pinkie in the stuff. No. *It couldn't be.*

Eve spun the "H" tap as far as it would go; the water was ice cold. As it warmed, she wiped her face with paper towels, feeling the adrenaline still rocketing through her. She stared like a stranger into her own eyes. Her hair was wild as a lion's mane, but her clothes were pristine, as if just off the hanger.

She rinsed her face and hands, giddiness bubbling up from within. She giggled. Laughed like a crazy person. The sound slammed into the tiles and bounced back, filling the space, rattling her eardrums.

She came back out, collected Highball, and turned to Fernandez.

"Let's go," she said.

Chapter 13

Eve peered into the blackness, aware of heavy breathing in her ear. Her heart racing, her breath coming fast, she flailed in a panic only to connect with Highball, passed out on the pillow next to her. The dog yelped and Eve reached out to embrace her hastily.

"Sorry, girl, sorry," she said, exhaling sharply. She was in her bedroom; everything was fine. She'd had a dream. A really strange one.

She took in the glowing dial on the nightstand: 7:06. She'd overslept. In the more than seven months she'd worked at *Smell,* her internal alarm had never failed to wake her at 6:58. Other writers slept in and taped the show, but not Eve. Now she might miss the avalanche survivors. She threw her legs over the side of the bed, but as soon as she stood, she fell back on the mattress, feeling as if her legs had lost the ability to support her. She pushed herself up again and lurched out to the living room. She turned on the TV at 7:08. She had missed the news headlines but was in time to catch Tex Franklin finishing up the weather report. A cold, bright day, highs in the mid-forties . . .

Eve put some coffee on and refilled Highball's water bowl,

almost falling over as she leaned over to put it down. The wooziness wouldn't quit. At 7:09, Hap read her intro to the avalanche story. When the survivors appeared via satellite, there were only three instead of four. Either one of them had suffered a case of stage fright or there was a technical problem, Eve guessed. Unfortunately, the script included questions for four survivors, and Hap, seemingly off his game, proved incapable of matching up the appropriate question to the correct guest. Eve kicked the floor when he asked the one with the broken leg about his bruised ribs; she cursed when he joked with the single one about whether his wife would ever let him ski again. When it was over, she poured some coffee and considered the damage. The segment wasn't a complete disaster but, to be safe, she'd take the stairs.

Eve thought of going back to sleep as she usually did, but felt so achy she decided on a hot shower first. In the bathroom, she punched on the shower radio, poised as ever for breaking news, which would mean having to get to work informed and, worse, early. Traffic report. She turned on the hot water and waited for it to warm. Déjà vu stole round her along with the steam. She stepped into the tub, and put her head under the pounding stream. She leaned out to lather her hair. Weather. She rinsed off. Now sports. She combed through an extra-big dollop of conditioner. More sports. She rinsed again, stepped out of the tub, and reached for a towel. Still more sports. She leaned over and draped the towel over her wet head, giving it a vigorous rub, momentarily drowning out all sound save the roar in her ears. And then she pulled the towel off.

"—Updating our top story. Police say the man who has been stalking New York City for the last nine months—the knife-wielding mugger known as the Stiletto—has been caught. Caught in Greenwich Village just a few hours ago by a young woman who, from all reports, is barely half his size. How did this dainty vigilante manage to overpower such a dangerous criminal? In a word, 'dog poop.' Mike George is standing by now on the block of the Village where it all happened. Mike?"

Eve sank down on the edge of the tub, the cold porcelain pressing into her shower-hot skin. Like a drunken episode re-called mid-hangover, it all rushed back with alarming hazy-clarity, including how one of the ER doctors had given her a bottle of sleeping pills. Of which she had taken how many exactly?

Still listening to the radio, she began to dry her back when she felt the towel catch on something. She reached back to touch it and found gauze, which must have been taped over the stitches. Eve headed back into the living room.

"—stunning news this morning," Bliss Jones was saying. "As you heard in the news block, one of New York City's most bizarre criminals, the Stiletto, has been apprehended. And, what is so gratifying to us here is that he was nabbed by one of our own. Yes, the heroine is a valued staffer here at *Smell the Coffee*. Her name is Eventual Weldon"—here they put Eve's corporate ID photo on the screen, the pixels so enlarged that she looked as though she'd been rendered by Lichtenstein—"and we want to let you know that we'll have an *exclusive* interview with her to-morrow morning. You won't hear her story anywhere but here. So! Stay tuned for that. Now, coming up in our next hour, we turn our attention to airfares. . . ."

Eve steadied herself against the bar. She wrapped the towel around her more tightly and glanced at the answering machine. She'd turned off the ringer before falling into bed as she always did, and now—*twenty-three messages.*

5:32 a.m. "Hi, this is Kathleen Swanson from Channel 11. I'm looking for Eve Weldon. We'd like to talk to you about your part in the capture of the Stiletto. Please call."

This was followed by messages from four or five other local news stations.

5:49 a.m. "Hello, Ms. Weldon. This is Jill Mimeux from the City section of the *Times*. I apologize for calling so early, but we'd like to get in a feature on you for this Sunday. Please call at your earliest convenience."

5:52 a.m. "Hey, it's Mary." It was Mary Lauder, a booker at

Smell the Coffee. "How are you? Call the office ASAP. You're leading the show tomorrow."

Just as the last of the messages finished playing, the phone rang again, sounding a bit tuckered out. She let the machine pick up.

"I cannot believe this." It was Vadis. "We need to talk, pronto. . . ." Eve picked up.

After promising Vadis exclusive duties as her publicist or spokesperson or whatever—the opportunity to help her friend had come far sooner than she ever could have guessed—Eve noticed Highball standing by the door, whining urgently. She threw on a rush outfit: a camisole and some silk lounge pants, her wool kimono and her favorite Turkish slippers with the upturned toes. As she closed the apartment door behind them, she heard the phone ring again.

They made their way down the dim stairs, through the front hall, past the mailboxes. Eve turned the knob of the heavy oak front door and pulled. In fell an enormous bald man with three cameras around his neck. He had evidently been sitting with his back against the door, and now landed with a thud at her feet, which sent Highball into a frenzy of barking. Immediately, voices pierced the morning. "There she is!"

A dozen reporters and photographers, who'd been camped out on the sidewalk and the adjacent stoops, darted through the blue light, snapping pictures and yelling, "Eve! Over here!" *Snap, snap.* It felt strange to be greeted by perfect strangers as though they knew the name of her favorite childhood doll. "What's it like to be a hero?" "What gave you the idea to use dog shit as a weapon?" "What would you like to say to the Stiletto this morning?"

She picked up Highball and pushed her way down the steps till she reached the sidewalk. Plumes of steam pumped out of the reporters' mouths as they shouted more questions and the photographers asked her to turn this way and that. Eve lowered Highball to the ground, where she promptly peed on a man's shoe.

"Seen the early editions yet?" A tall woman with wild red hair and large, black-rimmed glasses waved the morning papers at Eve.

The New York Times: Mugging Victim Said to Capture "Stiletto"

The *Daily News:* Sassy Village Gal to Stiletto: "Poo on You!"

The *Gotham Gazette:* Stiletto's Spree's "Crappy" Ending [and, in smaller letters] Arresting Citizen: Who Is Eve Weldon?

"Hey, Fred. Snap her looking at herself on the covers," called out a reporter in an enormous down parka to his young photographer.

Each paper had the same picture splashed across the front: Eve, in three-quarter profile, winking at the camera over the brown stripes on her cheeks. She pulled her eyes away from the image and found herself looking at the young man who'd shot it. He gazed at her with round green eyes.

"Seth Finkelstein from Overnight Newsservice." He extended a hand. "I just want to thank you for last night. Everybody picked up my picture. That's never happened to me before."

She smiled at him but another man demanded her attention. "Ms. Weldon. Please, over here." He pulled a pen out of the breast pocket of his trench coat. "Cliff Landy, *Daily News.* So far, we've only heard from the police. Everybody wants to hear from you. Would you take us through the events of last night, starting from the moment you first laid eyes on the Stiletto?"

She opened her mouth, then stopped short. Bliss's voice echoed from within: "We'll have an *exclusive* interview with Eve Weldon. You won't hear her story anywhere else but here." And it hit her: In a stunning turn of events, *Smell the Coffee* now needed her more than she needed it. She was the big story. This was going to fix everything!

Eve cleared her throat and addressed the crowd. "I'm sorry,

everyone, but I'm afraid I'm unable to do any press at the moment."

. . .

She spent the day lying in bed, trying to go light on the painkillers. She called her father but there was no answer and she didn't want to say what she had to say on an answering machine.

Just as she hung up, the phone rang. It was Gwendolyn, screaming so loud Eve had to hold the phone away from her ear.

"Are you all right?!"

"I'm fine."

"The dog?"

"Also fine. We're fine, fine. Just tired."

"I can't believe this. I picked up the paper on the way to the store and there you are on the cover. It's amazing! What are the odds? You take that Stiletto segment for yourself and then a few weeks later, boom, you're face-to-face with the real thing. Did you tell him that? Oh, what am I saying? Of course you didn't. I'm sorry I'm talking so much but I'm just blown away!"

Of all the reactions Eve had encountered, this was by far the most genuine. And the sweetest. "It's okay. In fact, it's great. You're making me laugh. And thanks to the painkillers, laughter doesn't hurt."

"What can I do? Bring you food? A heating pad? I can close the store for an hour and come by."

"Honestly, there's nothing. I'm going to order in and take a nap. And then this afternoon I have to do a pre-interview for the show tomorrow."

It took a good ten minutes to make Gwendolyn stand down, although she did send flowers, which arrived at the same time as Eve's wonton soup, saving her a trip downstairs.

. . .

"How does it feel to be on the other end of one of these things?" Quirine asked.

"Surreal," said Eve, stretching out on the bed. "I can't quite believe I'm doing this."

Quirine asked her to describe everything that happened the previous night, starting with the moment she first realized she was face-to-face with the Stiletto. Eve offered a few recollections, not wanting to bore Quirine or make too much of herself. Quirine listened, waited a beat, and then prompted, "And?" Not rudely, but quietly insistent. Eve supplied more details, fleshing out the tale till it came closer to her actual experience. Each facet of the story followed suit; if Eve omitted—or even skimmed over—anything important or interesting, Quirine would say simply, "And?" Eve surmised that this was Quirine's interview technique, and it was a good one. You couldn't help but want to fill up the silence that hung in the air after each gentle "And?"

They spoke for nearly two hours. At the end, Quirine said there was someone who wanted to talk to her and that she'd transfer the call.

"Eve?" It was Mark.

"Oh—hello."

"I, ah. I just want to say how glad I am that you're all right. I can't even imagine what you've been through. We're all really proud of you." He seemed to grasp for words. "Whatever's passed between us, I want you to know that."

Eve felt tears coming. "Thank you, Mark."

"I'll be at the studio in the morning. I don't want you to be alone out there." He coughed. "If that's okay."

"It's very much okay."

. . .

As instructed, at 6 a.m. on the dot, Eve arrived at the studio and went straight to hair and makeup, where Parminder Singh slathered her face with base the consistency of cement.

"Jeez, honey, that guy really decked you," she said as she tapped extra concealer on the bruise along her jaw.

"Do I look awful?" asked Eve.

"Actually, it looks kind of cute. You're just a little swollen. We can contour it with powder," Parminder said, sorting through various pots of color.

Lark Carmichael popped her head in. "Well, well, we meet again." She patted Eve on the shoulder as she gazed at her in the mirror.

"Lark, hi," said Eve, relieved to see a familiar face. So far, there'd been no sign of Mark.

"So you're the lady of the hour, huh?"

"I guess."

"Just want to tell you, I know we haven't seen each other since the day of your tryout, but I've always felt bad about not being able to warn you about the bad fish that day," said Lark, twisting her long cornrows absently. "But I had that cold—remember? I couldn't smell a thing. If they'd refused to hire you over it, I would have felt terrible."

"That's sweet of you, but it was my own fault. Anyway, they hired me and . . ."

"The rest is history," finished Lark, picking up an enormous powder brush and running it across the back of her hand. "So, Parminder, did you tell Eve what Giles wanted you to do with the makeup?"

"No, I didn't," said Parminder tersely, sweeping deep gray shadow into the creases of Eve's lids. "It's beneath mentioning."

"What? What are you talking about?" asked Eve, turning to look at Lark.

"Hold still," said Parminder.

"Giles wanted her to paint brown stripes across your cheekbones—you know, like in the newspaper."

"You're not going to, are you?" asked Eve, pulling away from the brush. Parminder grabbed Eve's chin and pulled her back into position.

"Don't worry. She's not," replied Lark. "I told Giles we

couldn't light you right if you were half my color and half your color. Total lie, but he bought it."

"Whew."

"But between you and me, he's really keyed up," continued Lark, checking her teeth in the mirror. "Been talking about nothing but you. So, if I were you, I would give a great interview this morning. Should be no problem, right? You've written enough of 'em."

. . .

To Eve's surprise, the famous "green room," where guests waited before heading to the set, wasn't green at all, but soft mauve. Several low upholstered chairs sat in a semicircle facing a big-screen monitor on the far wall. A small conference table held a beautiful spread: dainty croissants, strawberry butter, imported jams, fruit salad, and mini Danish of every variety. She couldn't imagine eating, but some cold water sounded good. Eve picked up an enormous pitcher. Her hand shook as she tipped it over a glass and a good slosh of the water spilled, soaking an entire platter of tiny turnovers. One of which had a hand on it. A hand belonging to Bliss Jones.

"Oh my God. I'm so sorry," said Eve, looking up.

Bliss looked down at her, her radiant beauty even more startling close up. Eve saw herself, pulled and distorted, in the glossy irises. She held out a napkin.

Bliss held her gaze steadily for a moment and raised one perfect eyebrow. Then she popped a green grape into her mouth, turned on her heel, and left.

. . .

How could she ever have thought the studio was chilly? The last time she'd been here, it had seemed as dark and cold as the far reaches of the solar system. Now, in the studio's "library" setting, the bright lights made her feel like she was sitting directly on the sun. Tiny beads of sweat broke out on her upper lip. Eve craned her neck around the astronaut-like robotic camera to her left. She could see Bliss on the couch some thirty feet away, tossing to Tex Franklin.

"After the weather, what America has been waiting for: my exclusive interview with the young woman who caught the Stiletto, our own Eve Weldon. You won't want to miss this."

A movement caught Eve's eye: Mark appeared next to one of the cameras. He waved and mouthed, *Sorry I'm late.* She waved back, relieved. He gave her a thumbs-up sign.

As soon as the stage manager gave the all clear, Bliss was off the couch like a hare, clicking her way across the shiny black linoleum. She sat down across from Eve, nodded briskly at no one in particular, and began looking through Quirine's script. Bliss's personal makeup artist appeared to touch up the anchor's face. Bliss's expression didn't budge as she was prodded, painted, and dabbed. Eve thought of show dogs staring resolutely at some fixed point on the horizon while handlers cleaned inside their ears and under their tails. Bliss ran a red pen through the pages of questions, scribbling notes in the margin.

The stage manager, wiry and sporting assertive sideburns, lifted his chin at Eve and pulled off his headset. "Hey there," he whispered, shaking her hand. "I'm Sam. You okay?"

Eve liked his smile. "Sure." Truth was, she was starting to feel sick. She tried to pretend that there were only she, Bliss, and Sam in the world. That there weren't millions of people watching.

"Knock 'em dead," said Sam before shouting to the room at large, "Okay, people. Places! Weather cut-in is over in five. Four, Three, Two . . ." On "One," he pointed silently to Bliss. Eve saw the intro pop up in the TelePrompTer.

(BLISS:)
THANKS, TEX.
WE ARE PRIVILEGED TO HAVE AN

EXTRAORDINARY STAFF HERE AT
SMELL THE COFFEE . . . FROM OUR
PRODUCTION ASSISTANTS TO OUR
BOOKERS TO OUR EXECUTIVE
PRODUCER, IT'S AN INCREDIBLE
GROUP.
WE NEVER DREAMED, THOUGH,
THAT WE'D HAVE A BONA FIDE
HEROINE WITHIN OUR RANKS.
BUT, AS MANY OF YOU HAVE
HEARD, ONE OF OUR STAFFERS,
EVENTUAL WELDON, IS
RESPONSIBLE FOR PUTTING AN
END TO ONE OF THE MOST
PERPLEXING CRIME SPREES IN
NEW YORK IN RECENT MEMORY. IN
THE WEE HOURS OF YESTERDAY
MORNING, SHE SINGLE-HANDEDLY
APPREHENDED THE MUGGER
KNOWN AS THE STILETTO. AND
SHE WAS ARMED WITH ONLY
SPUNK AND, SHALL WE SAY,
IMAGINATION. EVENTUAL WELDON
JOINS US NOW.

Very nice, thought Eve. *Thanks, Quirine!*

Bliss turned her laser-bright eyes on Eve along with a smile that almost made her swoon. "How wonderful to have you here this morning. Of course, we work together every day, but it's truly marvelous to see you under these circumstances."

"Um—thank you, Bliss," Eve replied, trying to keep from betraying her utter surprise at these words, considering they'd crossed paths exactly twice, both times unpleasant.

"Now—set the scene for us." Bliss leaned forward into Eve's

airspace, cocking her head almost coquettishly. "You were walking your dog, I understand, at about two o'clock yesterday morning, when you heard footsteps coming up behind you. What happened next?"

Eve cleared her throat quietly. She knew what was expected of her and she was determined to provide it. "Well, Bliss, I turned around and I couldn't believe what I was seeing. . . ." Eve launched into the interview she always hoped her guests would give, answering each question fully, passionately, but stopping in time to let Bliss direct the conversation. Bliss took Eve through the moment when she realized she was face-to-face with the Stiletto, how it felt to have the knife in her back, the fury she'd felt when Highball was kicked, and the surge of strength that allowed her to topple her attacker.

"This man was practically twice your size. How did you manage it?" asked Bliss, giving the impression she found Eve more fascinating than any other person in the history of the world.

"I think I simply surprised him," Eve replied. "He was holding me at knifepoint; he assumed I was powerless. So when I turned on him suddenly with my dog's business in a bag, well . . . I think it was the last thing he was expecting." She very much wanted to say more, to explain what she'd learned from Dr. Tang, but to do that would mean making Bliss look bad. And she wasn't going to do that. This morning was all about job security.

Bliss smiled for a fraction of a second, almost like a muscle contraction. She regarded Eve carefully. It was the look Bliss gave before going off script.

"Eve, I wonder if I could ask you to do something?"

"Of course."

"I'd like you to stand up"—*Stand up?*—"and demonstrate for us exactly how you got the Stiletto on his back. It just seems so incredible."

Eve, startled, remained mute for a moment. Asking a guest to do something physical, something that hadn't even been discussed in the pre-interview? This was unheard of. Sam's eyes were wide. The robotic cameras pulled back, giving her space.

"All right," she managed. She rose to her feet and smoothed her dress. She looked around the room. "Well, let's see. He was behind me and I sort of . . ." How was she going to do this? Then she spied the "library's" coat stand, a few feet behind her chair. She walked over and stood with her back to it. She took a deep breath, turned abruptly, threw it to the ground, and straddled it, narrating as she went. The cameras spun wildly, trying to keep up.

At first she felt foolish, but a gust of exhilaration carried her through. When she was done, she pulled herself up off the ground with as much composure as she could muster and returned to her seat. She felt like she'd passed some kind of test. She knew her segment had been given a healthy seven minutes, and now that Bliss's little deviation was over, she planned to enjoy every one she had left. She was especially excited about setting her story in a larger context to help other crime victims— something Quirine had suggested during their pre-interview.

It was an idea Bliss, a longtime advocate for victims' groups, would love, and she was leading Eve right there. They finished the part about the police hailing her as a hero, which provided a perfect segue to the larger issue of victims performing as a vital function of law enforcement.

But then Bliss shuffled the rest of Quirine's questions beneath a sheaf of scrawled notes.

"A remarkable story, Eve, truly. Now, shifting gears a little. We have some examples here of how the press has covered your bravery. Let's show them to everyone at home."

Eve glimpsed on the floor monitor what the audience was seeing: the photo of her winking in war paint, and more pictures taken outside her apartment, in which she was wearing her kimono and slippers. There was even a shot of her—looking captivated and incredulous—seeing herself on the front page for the first time.

"It seems to me you're quite enjoying this moment in the sun," said Bliss. "And who could blame you? So I thought we could talk for a moment about the strange—and limited—nature of sudden celebrity. Your thoughts?"

Eve stared at her and Bliss stared back. Dead air hung heavy between them.

"Let me put it a different way," Bliss began, her voice lilting but insistent. "I wonder if you could talk a bit about the temptation to prolong this moment in the limelight. You know, from your perspective as a behind-the-scenes *staffer*."

Eve didn't like Bliss's condescending tone. She glanced at Mark, who seemed to be chewing the inside of his cheek. She remembered Steve that night at the bar: *They never mention writers on the air. Ever.*

"You there?" asked Bliss.

Eve felt herself flush as she remembered the look Bliss had given her at the production meeting when she barged in to complain about the Dr. Tang interview. The one that felt like a punch to the gut.

"Actually," said Eve, her voice low, "I'm a writer."

"I'm sorry?"

Mark shook his head wildly. Eve cleared her throat and averted her eyes from him. "I'm a writer here at *Smell the Coffee*. Not a 'staffer.' A writer."

"I'm not sure what you're getting at," replied Bliss, whose arteries seemed to be hardening before the world's eyes.

"Well." Eve sat up straight. "I'd just like to set the record straight. I'm a writer here, one of seven. And what we do—as you know, Bliss—is write everything that you and Hap say." A red glow spread over Bliss's face like a rash, and Sam took a step backwards as if he'd been pushed. "We write the introductions to the segments, we interview the guests the day before you do, and then we write up questions for you to ask. I don't think people at home know that."

Eve pulled a piece of folded paper out of her breast pocket. She kept waiting for Bliss to interrupt her, but she didn't. "There's Mark and Archie and Cassandra and Steve and Russell and Quirine. Quirine is the one who wrote this segment," continued Eve. "She did a terrific job and I actually have her questions right here. I think she's hit on some very interesting points that we should talk about with the—" Eve glanced at her watch. "Minute we have left."

Bliss remained frozen. Eve could hear Giles pushing his way into the studio, and striding across it muttering as loudly as he dared to without the floor microphones picking it up. Mark shook his head violently and made slicing motions across his throat.

"So let's see here. Quirine came up with a great question . . . what was it?" Eve unfolded the piece of paper, noticing out of the corner of her eye that Giles had arrived and was waving urgently at his star anchor. "Ah, here it is. Number seven: 'What is the message of your story? What would you like others to take from it?' Now, I think that's a great question. And here's what I would say: Seize opportunity. I didn't have size on my side the other night, or strength. But I had the element of surprise and I used it." She suddenly thought of Donald dropping dead on a beautiful afternoon, a life, and career, cut short. "A lot of times, we don't have any choice about things, but when we do have a choice, we shouldn't be afraid . . ." Here she remembered Klieg's little speech over lunch on the patio. "To be bold, I guess."

Bliss seemed to have died with her eyes open. Giles was bouncing on the balls of his feet. Sam rotated his index finger rapidly, indicating they had to wind things up.

"Oh," said Eve. "I see we're out of time. Well . . . I guess— I guess I'd like to thank myself for being here," she finished brightly.

Eve looked at Mark, expecting him to be apoplectic. Sure enough, his hands were thrust into the hair at his temples, which was sticking straight out. But she thought she saw something else in his eyes. Along with horror and disbelief, it looked like amazement. And maybe, if she wasn't imagining things, even a touch of admiration.

Sam pressed his right headphone into his ear, listening to the control room. Then he gave a thumbs-up. "Okay, and . . . we're out," he said, exhaling loudly.

Eve blinked once or twice and gazed around. It appeared the studio universe had just suffered something akin to the Big Bang.

Chapter 14

Claire, Giles's beaky assistant, gripped Eve's elbow like a vise and hustled her out the giant doors used for moving large props in and out of the studio and onto the sidewalk. Claire flagged a cab and did not let go of Eve until she was safely inside.

"Don't set foot in the building until you receive a call from us." She closed the door and banged on the hood of the car.

When the cab pulled up in front of her building, Eve saw Vadis gesturing animatedly to a small gaggle of reporters and handing out business cards with the speed of an Atlantic City blackjack dealer. Everyone turned when they saw Eve get out of the car.

"There she is!"

"What happened after they cut to commercial?"

"What do you have to say to Bliss Jones? What do you have to say to the Stiletto?"

Eve pulled Vadis aside as best she could. "What are you doing here?"

"Are you kidding? I saw the show and came right over. Let's get the hell upstairs so we can talk."

"No," said Eve. "Let's get out of here. To a coffee shop or something." She grabbed Vadis's arm and pulled.

"What?" Vadis yanked her arm away. "And have these guys follow us? No way." She turned her palms upwards. "Let's. Go. Up. Stairs."

"We . . . can't," replied Eve, starting to feel dizzy. She needed a drink, badly. How could it be only 7:55 a.m.?

"Why on earth not?" Vadis asked, over the reporters' din.

"It's Highball. She's injured from the attack and—and needs to rest."

"Oh, for God's sake." But Vadis's tone had softened and Eve knew she wouldn't have to embroider further on her excuse. "All right, let's go."

. . .

They wound up at a diner over by the West Side Highway, at a table in the back in case any reporters had managed to follow them.

"I can't get over it," said Vadis, slathering grape jelly on some rye toast. "You, this little mouse, and—and then *this*." She chewed a bite thoughtfully. "The thing is, we have to act fast."

Eve pulled at a corn muffin, which was dry and crumbled all over the plate. Her thoughts felt similarly fragmented. She couldn't believe what had happened in the last thirty hours. No, not what had happened. What she'd done.

"Hello?" Vadis was waving at her from across the table.

"I'm sorry, what did you say?"

"I said we have to get on the ball."

"What do you mean?" Eve pushed her plate away.

"A moment like this only comes along once. We have to make the most of it."

"A moment like what? When you kiss your whole career goodbye?"

"Are you kidding? This is going to *make* your career."

"Huh?"

"You're the name on everyone's lips. People want to see more of you. We can parlay this."

"How?"

"You've just become a symbol. For everyone who's had enough. You've shown people that they don't have to take it!" As she said this, Vadis lifted her arms overhead in a kind of Olympic flourish.

"Don't have to take what?"

"Any of it!" said Vadis. "It's like that movie *Network*, except with a cute girl instead of some old man."

Eve felt completely lost.

"Oh, baby," continued Vadis, her internal wheels spinning fast now. "I see specials. Magazines, a book, even. We're going to create the Eventual Weldon brand. We start with some well-placed interviews. Not with those small-timers back there, but with people who can help us and who let us set the parameters."

"I don't know if I can do any interviews," said Eve, putting down the coffee she'd just started to lift to her lips. "At *Smell the Coffee,* we're not allowed to talk to the media. If I even still have a job there, which I seriously doubt—"

"Honey, forget *Smell the Coffee.* By the time I'm done with you, someone will be offering you your own show."

"What?"

"We're going to take your little heroine act to the moon. The problem is, this city has a short memory. Next week some cop will save a bank full of people from armed robbers and you'll be history. So we need to get cracking." She dumped four packets of sugar into the fresh cup the waitress had poured and turned her attention to her exploding datebook. "I'm thinking Janet at the *Times,* Frank at *Newsweek,* maybe I can even get Karen at *Vanity Fair.* . . ."

. . .

When she got home, several reporters remained on her stoop. They leapt into action, brandishing pens and microphones, but Eve only shook her head at them and went inside. She pulled herself up the stairs by the railing and stumbled in the door feeling like she was a hundred years old. The bed swallowed her whole and within minutes she fell fast asleep, coat and shoes still on.

Sometime later, she didn't know when, she stirred.

"There's the girl," came a whisper in her ear.

"Donald . . ." she mumbled.

"Shhh. Back to sleep," he said softly, and soon she was dreaming again.

She came to for real hours later, sweltering in her coat. She rolled out of it and kicked off her shoes. In the bathroom she threw cold water on her face.

"Better?" he asked.

"Mmmmm. I don't know. It's been a—I don't think I can even explain it."

"No need to. I've seen it all. In your dreams. You were so god-damned brave. I'm in awe, little one. And so relieved that you're all right. If anything happened to you, I don't know what I . . ."

"Thank you, Donald."

"And the attack, why, it was like something out of one of my stories. Your weapon, a prime metaphor for the scatological nature of society today . . ."

"I . . . guess." Eve was relieved that amid all the insanity, Donald was behaving as one would expect, which was to inflate his own importance.

"And then—the interview," said Donald.

"Um-hmm."

"It's like you have taken to heart everything I've been trying to teach through my work."

"It is?"

"Yes, standing up to that vile news harpy, right there in the temple of her mediocrity. You are a champion. A firebrand." He sounded like Vadis. "And the fact that I have inspired you in this way is so gratifying. . . ."

Eve wandered into the living room and collapsed on the love seat. "Is this your way of saying you want to do some dictation?"

"In your present state? Of course not." There was a pause.

"Of course, if you'd like to get your mind off all this hullabaloo, I'd be more than happy to oblige you."

"Why not?" sighed Eve, rolling her shoulders back. She could use a break from fretting about everything that had happened and the fear of what was to come. She found their current pad—the last of twelve in the packet—underneath the seat cushion and scanned the last few paragraphs of "Rock, Paper, Scissors." The story had been creeping up on Eve, growing more and more interesting despite its stubborn opacity.

"Where were we?" Donald asked.

"Let's see." Eve located the last few lines of the story. " 'Paper and Scissors live in harmony. It is a relationship that confounds the critics but thrills the gods.' "

"Ah, yes. Here we go: Their closeness is not romantic but it is nevertheless a love affair. The skies of Paris smile down on the pair, the trees along the Champs-Élysées wave at them. The monuments all stand at attention when they pass by and at night the lights twinkle their names in Morse code."

"Hang on." Eve took a sip of her drink. ". . . Morse code. Okay."

"One night they leave a restaurant very late, so late it is early, and take one of their walking trips by the river. There is a hush in the air. The streets are empty and the city feels ancient, sacred. The skies go from black to silver and the stars begin to fade. The river stirs as if waking up and sends waves crashing to shore. They see something in the water, glinting in the new dawn. An island? But there has never been one there before. Paper and Scissors look at one another and decide it is worth the risk. They jump in.

"The current is strangely colored, a dark blue-green shot through with black, like rare sapphirine, which some say lies beneath the streets here. It has ideas of its own about whether it will be crossed. The water buffets and rolls them, almost pulling them under. They are half dead before they make it to the middle. But there, before them, shiny and trembling, lies a tiny island.

"Rock.

"They pull themselves up and collapse on her, exhausted by their swim. They rest in tiny hollows on her surface; her dimples cradle them tenderly. Beneath their weary bodies, they feel her breathe, deep and steady.

" 'Will you join us?' they ask her, each speaking before realizing the other has also opened his mouth.

" 'Yes! I cannot hang on here much longer. Please take me with you!' she cries over the roar of the current. Paper and Scissors lower themselves into the water and are nearly sucked away. Their strength is spent from the trip over. Rock reaches out to them and the three clasp hands. The current tries to force their hands apart, to cull the herd. But they hold firm. Together, they possess just enough might to make it across. Slowly, laboriously, their little circle moves through the waves until it reaches the shore.

"When at last they stagger out of the water, they find they are tinted with its odd hue. It clings to their hair, their limbs, their eyes; they know in an instant that it will mark them forever.

"The journey has left them famished. Paper and Scissors are poor and can only afford to make a picnic, but it transforms before their eyes. Cold sausages become pâté, and water, wine. Passersby gasp, but not at the enchantment of the food. *Isn't Paper supposed to wrap Rock?* they wonder. *Isn't Rock supposed to smash Scissors? But look at them, they don't even try. They are an affront.*

"The three ignore the stares. They have been through hell and high water and have their own idea of destiny. They run through the streets, laughing."

Donald's transmission had a dreamy quality to it and Eve became positive that it was no mere construction. There was something here, an emotional resonance that "The Numbered Story" and the other works hadn't had. But what was it?

"Suddenly, the wind picks up, and around them, the trees begin to laugh. They shake merrily, letting go the blossoms in their hair and turning the sidewalk into a flower girl's trail. The sky overhead is licked by pink and orange flames. Sound drains. Colors deepen. A bird cries and flies out of a tree. It is as if the world mirrors their happiness: Nature herself celebrates the improbability and purity of their friendship." He paused. "They form a nation of three, a country at peace."

Eve rubbed her hands together to relieve a cramp and waited, mesmerized, for him to continue. After several moments of silence, she said his name, but he did not respond. Whether he'd been pulled away by the forces he did not understand, or the subject matter had simply overwhelmed him, she didn't know.

. . .

She looked at the phone for quite a while before dialing.

"Hi, Dad."

"This is a nice surprise."

"You didn't watch my show yesterday by any chance, did you?"

"Sweetie, I'm sorry. I just got back from a four-day retreat with the partners. No TV, no computers. We even had to turn our cellphones off. Did I miss a big story you did?"

"You could say that." Eve told him everything, trying to get it out quickly, to skip over the worst moments and emphasize her rapid recovery. "My stitches will come out in a few days and everything and—"

"Stitches. My God. *Stitches.*" There was a long pause. "Why don't you come home and we'll have Dr. Olsen take a look at them?"

"I'm fine, really."

"He's very good, you know. He took care of you when you hurt your wrist, remember?"

Why was her father so focused on the stitches, the least interesting part of her tale? Perhaps he found the rest of it inconceivable.

"The doctors here are pretty good, Dad."

"I thought you'd *want* to come home at a time like this."

"Oh." Eve stood up and started to pace. "To be honest, I never even thought of it."

"Ouch, kid."

"I'm sorry." Why had she said that?

"No, no. You have every right." He sighed and there was a long pause. "I guess I've never really been there for you, not the way a dad should be. After your mother . . . I suppose I dropped the ball."

Eve couldn't believe what she was hearing. "You did the best you could. I know that."

"If you came home, I could do better."

Eve sat on the floor and tucked her knees under her chin. "That's so nice to hear. It really is. But I don't want to leave New York," she said, pulling Highball in close.

"Your mother told me that once. Eventually, I changed her mind." He paused. "Get it, *eventually*?" he asked.

"I get it."

"Though maybe it wasn't me who convinced her."

"What do you mean?"

"When we first met, she was here for a friend's wedding, staying with her parents for a few days. She spent the whole time itching to get back to the Big Apple. Suddenly, a few months later, she calls me and says she's coming back. And this time she's going to stay. That's when we started seeing each other. We were so happy. Though sometimes I caught her crying when she thought she was alone. But my friends said all girls do that, and what did I know? When you kids were born, she'd come alive for a while, but it never lasted. You were too young to notice, of course. How far away she was."

Eve wondered how he could possibly think that she hadn't noticed, but realized it was probably less painful for him to believe than the truth, so she said nothing.

"And there were certain things that would just set her off. You'd step on a trip wire, without even knowing it, and she'd clam up. Go hide in her room. Weird things. A song playing on the radio. A poem in *The New Yorker*. The Vietnam War once, for heaven's sake. There didn't seem to be any rhyme or reason to what would upset her." He sighed again, a long exhale that seemed to let all the air out of his body. "Anyway, I got the feeling it all had something to do with New York. I offered to take her there once, for our anniversary, and she said, 'God, no.' Something must have happened, but she never wanted to talk about it. Not that I was one for asking about things."

He sounded miserable. Eve didn't know what was more surprising: her father's insights or his candor.

"Oh, Dad."

"Anyway. I won't push. If you want to live in that treacherous town, you stay there. But please be more careful. No more walks late at night. And remember, there's always a place for you here. And a job."

"Thank you."

"You're really all right?"

"Yes."

"I guess I'll go on the computer and read all about it." He paused again. "Think about coming for Christmas. Okay? I miss you, sweetheart."

"I miss you, too," said Eve.

. . .

It was nearly six o'clock and she was starving. The fridge held little more than a yogurt and some almonds, of which she grabbed a handful. She collapsed on the love seat and turned on the TV.

CHANNEL 2:

GOOD EVENING.

WE BEGIN TONIGHT WITH NEW

DETAILS ABOUT THE END OF THE
STILETTO'S REIGN . . . AND A LOOK
AT THE YOUNG WOMAN
RESPONSIBLE.
A WOMAN WHO TOOK TO THE
AIRWAVES THIS MORNING . . . AND
MADE WAVES.

CHANNEL 4:
—WE BEGIN TONIGHT WITH A
CITY FULL OF RELIEVED WOMEN.
WOMEN GRATEFUL TO ONE OF
THEIR OWN FOR PUTTING AN END
TO THE STILETTO'S CRIME SPREE.

CHANNEL 7:
—BEGIN TONIGHT WITH THE
YOUNG WOMAN WHO FOILED THE
STILETTO LAST NIGHT, AND HER
RATHER LIVELY TV DEBUT THIS
MORNING.

Before she was able to take it all in, the phone rang. She let the machine pick up. "Are you watching TV?" It was Mark's voice.

She dashed for the phone. "Uh . . . which channel?"

"Any channel. It started with the noon broadcasts, then the five's, now the six's."

"I'm watching," she said. It was so thoughtful of him to think of her when she felt so alone, so isolated.

He breathed slowly and loudly, in and out. "Were you put on earth just to screw up my life?"

"What?"

"Do you have any idea what happened today after you detonated your little bomb in the studio? As soon as the show was over, I was dragged into Giles's office and ordered to explain."

"Explain what?"

"Explain why you did what you did. They thought it was my idea."

"Oh God, Mark. No," said Eve, looking at the TV, which now showed tape of her straddling the coat rack. She cringed and turned it off.

"And then all the other writers were called in—individually—in an effort to detect some sort of *plot*." Eve was suddenly aware of traffic behind Mark's voice.

"Mark, where are you?"

"On my cell outside. I can't risk talking to you from the office." Everything suddenly felt cloak-and-dagger, as if they were two characters in a Le Carré novel. "Can I ask you something?" Mark's tone turned bitter. "Why the hell didn't you think about the writers when you went off on Bliss like that?"

"The writers are exactly who I *was* thinking about," replied Eve hotly. Didn't he know that? A man she'd harbored a crush on for more than half a year should know that. "Look," said Eve. "I'll call Giles and tell him you had nothing to do with it. And I'll call the writers to apolo—"

"No—don't. Do not call anybody. And I've told all of the writers not to contact you. That could ruin everything. You wait till you hear from me."

"Am I . . ." She almost couldn't bring herself to say it. "Going to be fired?"

"I don't know. If they were going to fire you, I think they would have done it already. Something weird is going on. There were a bunch of executives running in and out of meetings today. I heard the PR department sent out for pizza and they're still huddled upstairs. Just lay low and try not to attract any more attention. And I'm sure this goes without saying, but absolutely no press. Okay?"

"Of course." She coiled herself into the fetal position on the settee and closed her eyes, listening to static on the line for several moments after he hung up.

. . .

Around nine o'clock, the phone rang right next to her ear, startling her awake. She'd been dreaming about the Stiletto and her heart was pounding.

"Hello?" The voice on the other end was so muffled she could hardly understand. "What?"

"We're in my office," said Quirine in a low voice. "We're not supposed to call you. But we had to."

"No matter what happens," said Russell, "you did a great thing today. And whatever Mark says, we know why you did it."

"Steve's father even called, and they haven't spoken in years," said Quirine. "He was so moved by hearing his son mentioned on the show."

Eve began to feel better. They spoke for a few more minutes and then Russell said he heard Mark in the hall and that they better hang up.

"Thanks for calling," said Eve, suddenly missing them both intensely. "You don't know how much I appreciate it."

Highball whined and paced the room, signaling she needed a walk. Downstairs, another cream envelope rested on the vestibule table.

Dear Miss Eve,

I have read about your adventures with keen interest and am relieved that you are safe.

Would you and your brave canine companion be well enough to come to dinner Friday evening?

Until then, count me "another grateful New Yorker."

MK

Eve tucked the note into the inside pocket of her coat and went into the crisp night, once again brushing past the reporters gathered on the sidewalk.

. . .

Mercifully, Gwendolyn didn't ask to come over. Instead, she invited Eve for lunch at her place. Gwendolyn met her at the door, took her coat, and offered her at least five different things to drink as well as a feast of takeout that spanned the nationalities from Greek to Chinese to Indian.

"I didn't know what you'd be in the mood for, but whatever we don't eat you can take home. In case you don't feel like cooking for a while."

"Thanks," said Eve, helping herself to stuffed grape leaves and samosas and realizing she was starving. "I want some of everything."

Gwendolyn wanted to hear the Stiletto story in its entirety, and for the first time, Eve came close to explaining it exactly as she had experienced it, including the tangle of thoughts and memories that had confounded and incited her.

When she was done, Gwendolyn put a hand on hers. "Did you ever think . . ."

"What?"

"How proud your mother would be of you?"

Eve put her glass of wine down and turned to her friend. "That," she said quietly, "is possibly the loveliest thought, ever."

. . .

Highball did not like water. She scraped against the edge of the tub, eyes wide with panic, trying to claw her way out. On previous attempts to bathe the dog, this was the point at which Eve had conceded defeat. But not today. They were going to an early dinner at Klieg's and everyone had to look her best.

Klieg's driver, André, greeted Eve at her front door with an umbrella to protect her from the snow that fell slowly and heavily through the darkening afternoon. He opened the car door for them and Highball hopped inside as if she'd been doing it all her life. When they arrived at the townhouse, Marie ushered them in. "Mr. Klieg is on the telephone and asks that you and your companion wait upstairs in the drawing room. It's at the top of the stairs, all the way to the left."

They climbed the steps up to the residence. Eve couldn't resist poking her head in several rooms, including a library. In contrast to the grand, airy first floor, this room felt like a cozy wooden co-coon. Diamond-patterned windows of deep purple and green glass filtered the light from the streetlamps to a soft glow. Books lined the walls from floor to ceiling and two large leather arm-chairs took up the center of the space. One chair was perfectly smooth; the other, which Klieg evidently favored, was marked by a soft depression in the center. A stack of books towered on a table next to it. Eve touched her index finger to the spines, find-ing biographies of artists and emperors, and a picture book of the jewelry of sixteenth-century India.

Eve sank down onto the chair and ran her hands along the armrests. From this vantage point, she spied a deep shelf in the far corner that held dozens of framed photographs. She walked over and studied them. There were shots of Klieg at various times in his life, receiving awards or bowing with models at the end of a show. There were pictures of what looked like Klieg's family back in Germany at weddings and Christmases. And there were several shots of Klieg with a pale sylph of a woman with short, dark hair, cut like Audrey Hepburn's in *Roman Holiday*. Eve stared hard at her for several moments.

She scanned the other pictures for more shots of the woman. There was one photo so far back she couldn't properly see it. She reached in and carefully brought it out without knocking over any of the others. It was a black-and-white of Klieg and the girl in front of the café Deux Magots, which was hung with bunting. The girl wore a simple but elegant geometric print dress with a sweet-heart neckline and full skirt. Around them stood several other young men, most with slightly longer hair than Klieg's. Some in ties, others in turtlenecks. Most with cigarettes. She heard a noise.

Klieg, in slacks and a sweater, strode into the room and Eve turned to face him. They'd always shaken hands when they met but this time he gripped her lightly by the shoulders and leaned down for a dry kiss on each cheek. "Here she is, the heroine."

Eve blushed slightly. "I hope you don't mind I came in here. It's just such a wonderful room."

"Not at all. Now tell me, your stitches. Do they give you much pain?"

"I barely feel them."

"And this is your crime-fighting partner, I presume?" Klieg said, looking at the dog.

"Yes." Eve instructed Highball to sit and was relieved when, with great earnestness, she managed it on the first try.

"*Liebe,*" said Klieg, patting the dog lightly on the head. "So much valor in such a small package."

"She's a fighter, all right," said Eve.

"Ready to eat?" Klieg asked. "I've had Marie lay a table in front of the fire."

"Yes, but first, could you tell me about some of these pictures?" Eve held up the photograph she'd been staring at. "This woman in the middle, she's in so many of them. . . ."

"Ah. Yes." He paused and cleared his throat. "This is Louisa. On Bastille Day." He smiled sadly, then blinked once or twice and said, "There is something about you that reminds me so much of her."

"I suppose we do look alike."

"Yes, but it's something else. A spirit, perhaps. There is an expression you wear when you are listening intently, and this especially makes me think of her." Eve felt a tingle as if a feather had passed across her neck. They stood side by side, looking at the photograph. In the quiet of the library, Eve could hear Klieg's soft, regular breathing. "The first time you and I met, at the gala, it took my breath away. It almost hurt."

Eve remembered his confused, haunted expression. "Why didn't you ever tell me?"

"I do not know. Perhaps I did not want you to think I was expressing untoward interest in a lady as young as yourself."

"Hmm." Eve found this rather sweet. She wondered how long he'd been alone. "When did she die?"

"It was 1987. She was just forty-five."

Eve noticed there were no children among the photographs. "Did you two ever have kids?"

"No," said Klieg. "We wanted to but could not."

"I'm sorry." The naked pain in his tone made Eve want to change the subject. "I was wondering," she said a few moments later, "if Donald might be in here somewhere?"

Klieg tapped his finger on the young man to Louisa's left. Eve leaned in, and felt goose bumps rise on her flesh.

He looked right into the camera with dark, shrewd eyes under a gray beret and over a long, delicate pipe. His face was thin yet not feminine and a short, well-trimmed beard distinguished him from the clean-shaven crowd. But Eve went back to his eyes. They didn't twinkle or beckon but pierced like the eyes of a man who'd taken one step back from the human condition and saw it more clearly than everyone else. Or at least thought he did.

"Incredible," she said, under her breath. Klieg went on to point out the others: René LaForge, Lars Andersen, Ian Bellingham. All destined for fame, for world-class success. All except Donald, who didn't possess the talent.

Klieg held his hand out for the picture and cleared his throat. "I don't want to be rude but we really should go in."

The table boasted a small crown of lamb, roasted potatoes, salad, and three place settings.

"Let's eat while it's hot," said Klieg. He did the honors, carving the lamb beautifully and even placing one pink chop on a small china plate on the floor for Highball. The dog picked it up delicately and trotted off behind a curtain, presumably in case her impromptu benefactor changed his mind.

Eve accepted a plate full of food, just her third home-cooked meal in New York. "I don't know where to start," she said, and stabbed a potato with a fork. The crisp skin gave way to a soft, flaky interior.

"Marie is wonderful at this traditional European cooking. Almost as good as Louisa was."

Eve touched her napkin to the side of her mouth. "What else did Louisa enjoy?"

"She did wonderful embroidery. She trained birds. And when she was young, she wrote poetry."

"I wish I could have met her," said Eve. Klieg nodded and took a sip of wine. Eve thought about the picture. "So she and Donald knew each other, too."

"Yes."

"Were they friends?"

Klieg split open a roll and began to butter it. "Not particularly. They liked each other well enough, but . . ." Eve wanted more details but just then the far door opened. "At last," said Klieg, looking relieved and irritated at once when Günter walked in.

"Hello, Uncle," he said. Then he glanced at Eve. "And hello to you as well." The way he omitted her name made Eve wonder if he even remembered it.

Klieg filled Günter's plate and the young man began to eat in focused silence. He cut his meat into piece after piece of the same size. He chewed each the exact same number of times, and followed up with precisely one piece of potato and one sip of red wine. He kept his elbows at his sides and dabbed at his mouth regularly with his napkin. Except for his concerted lack of sociability, Eve thought, he was the model dinner companion.

Klieg spoke up again. "Günter, for heaven's sake, you remember Eve. What's more, she is in all the newspapers. Did you not read the articles I left out for you?"

Günter only nodded. His lack of interest wasn't exactly surprising. Eve had harbored a hope that her celebrity might arouse the interest of the opposite sex, but Donald had quashed this by offering that, sadly, most men liked heroes well enough but they didn't necessarily want to date one. Perhaps it was just as well. After Alex and the depressing evening with Oliver, Eve thought she would just as happily shelve the whole idea of a boyfriend for the time being.

"Gunter, here is another interesting fact about our new friend. She is a *ghostwriter.*"

Eve almost choked on her wine. Her mind reeled as she tapped her napkin to her chin. Had he found out about Donald and their stories? How could he know such a thing? Then she realized that her imagination had gone haywire; Klieg was simply using the word incorrectly.

"Actually," she said, "a ghostwriter is someone who writes a book that is credited to another person. What I write is television news scripts that other people read."

"Perhaps you would explain to my nephew what that involves exactly," said Klieg. "He asked me before you arrived but I found I could not enlighten him."

Günter made a face that indicated he certainly had not asked this question but wasn't going to make a scene. Eve described a typical day at *Smell the Coffee,* from research to interviewing to preparing intros, wondering if she'd ever have another one of those days again. She kept it brief for Günter's sake and was rewarded with another one of his glorious nods.

"And you?" Eve asked. "How is your lab work going?"

"As well as can be expected," said Günter.

They ate in silence for a few moments, Klieg clearly growing embarrassed. "Günter is here to contribute to an important new group, but he is reluctant to embrace the opportunity and become part of the team. Do they do things differently than his colleagues at home?" Klieg shrugged his shoulders. "Perhaps. But is this not the point of coming?"

"I told you I prefer not to discuss it, Uncle."

"He is finding it difficult to make friends over here," said Klieg to Eve, ignoring his nephew's directive. "And it is strange to me because his sensitivity to animals is unparalleled. Even as a boy, rabbits and field mice would follow him in the meadow behind his father's house." The way Klieg talked about his nephew right in front of him was embarrassing, but Eve couldn't bring herself to shush him in his own home. In any case, the designer swept on. "And the meadow is where he usually was. I used to try to interest him in my world, thinking one day he might take over my business. He is far and away the brightest of all his cousins. But every time I showed him how to sketch or drape, he grew so restless I would have to send him outside to burn off some energy. He would rather climb a tree or run up a hill than hang a bolt of beautiful fabric on a mannequin."

Eve had to smile at his incomprehension, as if most boys would choose silk over sports. "Not everyone's cut out to do what you do," she said. She meant only to get Klieg off his nephew's back but too late she realized that to Günter she might well sound obsequious. She looked at him but it seemed as though he wasn't paying the least bit of attention.

"True," said Klieg. "But each generation hopes that, if necessary, the next will finish its story. Now that I don't work, Günter could have kept the business going, for both of us."

"Weren't you working that day in your atelier?"

"That was simply dabbling, to keep my muscles loose and my mind sharp. To ward off the Alzheimer's. My company . . . well, that's all but dead."

Eve put down her fork and took a sip of wine. She wanted to follow up on what Klieg had said a moment before. "Doesn't each generation finish its own story?" she asked.

"Well." He looked thoughtful. "Sometimes the dreams of our youth—dreams of good work and self-discovery—are interrupted. These dreams are among the most powerful motivators in life. They are the things that keep us going when the real world crashes in, and because of this, they become, what's the word? Indelible?" Eve nodded and he continued. "If they are thwarted, a part of us spends the rest of our lives trying to get back on that first course. To recapture the hope that tantalized us when we were most impressionable. If we fail to do so, it can cause great anguish." He coughed and took a sip of water. "And so we hope that those who come after us may set things right, pick up where we left off. To continue our story and complete our destiny."

"Interrupted how?" asked Eve.

"By making mistakes. By losing faith. Being untrue to ourselves. Any number of things—"

Suddenly, one of the curtains moved and Günter jumped, almost spilling his wine. Eve giggled and tried to turn it into a cough when he looked at her sharply. It was only Highball, done with her bone and on patrol for another handout.

"*Ein Hund,*" said Günter. Highball made a beeline for this new target. Günter pushed his chair away from the table and gave her a tender caress under the chin. "*Guter Hund.*" He lowered himself onto the floor, where he sat, cross-legged, and hand-fed her every remaining piece of meat off his plate while the dog gazed at him adoringly.

Klieg gave Eve a look that said, "It is an endless mystery that we are related" and "Thank you for providing this distraction," all at once. She smiled and gladly accepted seconds.

. . .

Over the next few days, Eve lay low. Fear of unemployment sapped her energy. She stayed home, drapes drawn, curled up on the bed with Highball. She also reread a good bit of Dawn Powell, though her worries kept pulling her mind off the words.

She hoped someone from *Smell the Coffee* would call, but the phone remained stubbornly silent. Just what was going on?

. . .

The buzzer rang. Finally, the tamales she'd ordered for lunch.

"Be right down," said Eve into the intercom.

"Let me in," said Vadis.

"What are you doing here?"

"I'll tell you when I'm up there."

"I'll come down."

"No! We need to talk in private."

"Hang on." Eve pulled on her coat and boots.

"That's the famous Vadis?" asked Donald.

"Yes."

"Why not invite her up?"

Eve, who had just been picking up her purse, stopped mid-motion. "Yeah, right."

"My dear, you underestimate me."

She put the purse down. "You'd be good?"

"I won't say a word."

"No matter what she says?"

"No matter what she says."

"Well . . ." Eve really didn't feel like going out. She looked around at the apartment. It wasn't spotless but it was definitely suitable for company.

"Unless she tries to bully you, that is. I can't have my girl treated with disrespect—"

Eve picked up her purse and left.

• • •

"What are you doing down here? Let's go upstairs." Vadis practically tried to barge past her.

"I wish you'd called," said Eve, blocking her path. "It's really not a good time."

"Yeah, well, stuff is happening and we have decisions to make. So I don't care if your place is a mess or your pipes sprang a leak or whatever. Let's go."

"I could really use a drink," said Eve. "How about the White Horse? Nobody'll be there now."

"What the fuck is it?" asked Vadis, looking at her with utter bewilderment. "You're hiding an escaped felon up there? Or, I know—you've got a sweatshop in your living room. Dozens of little immigrant kids, making all your cute little clothes. What the hell is going on?"

"Please. Let's go." Eve made her way down the stoop to the sidewalk. Vadis didn't move. They looked at each other for a long moment. Finally, Vadis huffed in exasperation and stalked down the stairs.

The middle room at the White Horse was empty and they took the table under the painting of Dylan Thomas. Eve ordered a hamburger and, with a pang of guilt, realized the tamale man was going to find no one home.

"I've got some exciting stuff to tell you about," said Vadis.

"Ah," said Eve, reaching for her bourbon and hot water.

"I couldn't get the big books like *Vanity Fair* or *Newsweek*, because they're waiting to see where this goes. But I did get *New York* and *Time Out*."

"Uh-huh," said Eve.

"And that's not even the best part. I think we might be able to get you on *Dateline*. Not by yourself, but as part of a story they're doing on citizens who fight crime." Eve took a deep sip of her drink. "Well?" prodded Vadis. "Great, right?"

"Great," agreed Eve. "You're a terrific publicist."

"Why do I get the feeling there's a 'but' coming?"

"I can't do any interviews right now."

"Right now is all there is."

"I can't believe it's that dire."

"Look, it's been five days since anyone's seen your face. That's a good thing; you've piqued their curiosity. The papers have kept you on their covers, scrounging around to create stories with no new information. That's fine, but pretty soon they'll need something fresh. Meanwhile, the magazines go to press soon, and if you don't hit it, a whole cycle goes by and then, bam. Everyone's forgotten about you. So it's now or never."

Eve put her elbows on the table and rubbed her temples. She

couldn't believe she was going to have to say what she was going to have to say.

"I really appreciate everything you've done, but I can't do it."

"Why not?" said Vadis, leaning back abruptly and crossing her arms over her chest.

"I'm trying to keep my job. If I blab to the press, I'll be fired for sure."

"Don't you think you'll be fired anyway?"

"I don't know. Maybe. But it doesn't matter. I gave my word to Mark that I'd keep quiet."

"Why? What does he care?"

"The whole department got into trouble because of me. Anything I do could just make things worse."

"You've got to be kidding. Who cares about them? You've got to start thinking about yourself. Trust me, Mark does not have your best interests at heart. He just wants to make his own life easier."

Vadis had a point. At this juncture, as painful as it was to admit, it was safe to say that Mark did not care about her. He was angry; he didn't trust her; he'd already told her to find another job.

Vadis, detecting Eve's weakening, pounced. "How do you think this town works, anyway? You think anyone here actually cares about anyone else? No one has time. When you're sprinting for the gold, you don't stop to give CPR to the runner who's having a coronary. I thought you'd figured that out by now. Let Mark eat your dust."

Eve shook her head. "I can't break my promise. If I do, I might get the writers in even more trouble and I couldn't live with that."

"What about your promise to me?"

"What?"

" 'One day I'll be the one helping you,' you intoned so righteously."

"Oh," said Eve, not quite meeting her friend's eye. "I know. I know what I said. But please don't ask this."

"In no small part because of you, I never got Picnic on *Smell*.

They're still struggling to break out. If you do what I tell you now, we could both make some serious money. Don't you owe me at least that? After I got you out from under Daddy's thumb? Got you a job?"

The thought of "serious money" gave Eve momentary pause. "Everything you say is true," she said finally. "But I just can't."

"Yeah, right," said Vadis. "Whatever. Forget my advice. Looks like you already *are* thinking about yourself." Vadis stood, threw her coat over her arm, and left.

. . .

Eve roused herself three times a day for dog walks and sustenance. When she ventured onto the sidewalk, she wore a hat pulled low to keep away the cold and prevent her from being recognized, though passersby often stared and several asked for her autograph. There were usually a couple of reporters outside, too. Eve had to admire their persistence if nothing else.

Two days later, she came home from buying logs to a message from Mark.

"Giles wants to see you. Tomorrow, two o'clock. And don't ask me what he's going to say. I have no clue."

. . .

The fire stairs were grungier than ever and seemed to have multiplied; Eve found herself panting well before she got to *Smell the Coffee*'s floor. By the time she arrived, though, she'd almost convinced herself things were going to be all right. She thought of all the free publicity *Smell* had received in the last few days, not to mention the fact that the city was minus one violent criminal. Didn't all that count for something? Wouldn't she have to be considered an asset to the show?

As she threaded her way through the rows of cubicles, she caught sight of Quirine and Russell going into the tape room, but they didn't see her. Several colleagues stared at her with open curiosity. Others refused to meet her eye, though two production assistants gave her small smiles.

Eve stopped at Claire's desk. She expected to be kept waiting a few minutes and planned to use the time to do some deep breathing.

"Go right in," said Claire, barely looking up.

Giles's office was twice the size of the one that had belonged to Orla Knock. It was lined with banks of television sets tuned to what appeared to be every channel in the world, even foreign ones. Giles sat looking at some papers at the far end behind a gleaming Lucite desk and under a shelf of Emmy awards that gazed down upon them like an assembly of tiny tribal elders. Eve put her hand on the back of the chair that faced the desk.

"No need to sit," said Giles, without looking up. "For legal reasons, we have to meet face-to-face for me to fire you."

"I'm fired?" she said, looking at the thinning hair, gray mixed with a few diehard strands of blond, atop his head.

"Of course you're fired. What did you think?"

"I thought, well, I mean—"

"I am going to do you a favor, though."

"Yes?"

"I'm going to save you some time. Don't bother with the other morning shows, don't bother with the other networks, and don't bother with any of the local stations, either. Nobody's hiring you. Got it?"

Eve nodded.

"When you leave, you'll see Malcolm outside," Giles continued, finally deigning to look at her. Malcolm was the security guard posted to their floor. "He'll escort you to your office, where you'll collect your things. You will not touch your computer or phone. When you're done, he'll take you downstairs and onto the sidewalk. And you will surrender your ID."

Eve stood for a moment, letting her mind become a clean, blue space and hoping to come up with the perfect parting line.

Nothing came. She tried seeing the child inside of Giles. No dice. Donald had been totally wrong about that one. Giles returned to his paperwork and she walked out. Malcolm, holding a large cardboard box, tilted his head at her.

"Tough day, huh?"

She nodded up at him and began the long trudge to her office.

Inside, she retrieved the pictures of her parents and Highball that she'd kept on her desk. From her drawers, she took the paper, pens, and stapler she had bought with her own money, since the network did not provide them. Except for a black cardigan hanging on the back of her door, there really wasn't much else. Her belongings barely filled a quarter of the box. Malcolm, ever gallant, took it from her and they headed back to the main offices.

On the way out, she passed Mark's door. She paused and he looked up at her for a moment. Then he went back to work.

. . .

The elevator doors opened and Eve walked into the lobby with Malcolm behind her. As she headed toward the revolving door, she caught sight of Cassandra coming out of the kiosk with a newspaper and a pack of cigarettes. Eve picked up the pace.

"Hey," Cassandra called out. "Wait."

Eve stopped but didn't turn. Cassandra walked around her until they were facing one another.

"I'll be outside," Malcolm said, and shuffled off.

"What?" asked Eve, bracing herself.

Cassandra swayed slightly, putting her weight on one foot and then the other. "I heard they fired you. I just wanted to say goodbye."

"Okay."

Cassandra lightly tapped the rolled-up paper against her thigh. She waited until a couple of men in suits walked by before continuing. "So I got a call from Page Six today. They wanted a quote about you and Bliss Jones."

Eve narrowed her eyes. "You didn't give them one."

"Actually, I did." Cassandra looked this way and that. "I told them Bliss had it coming and that any other writer would have, and should have, done what you did."

"You did?"

Cassandra nodded.

"Won't Mark be furious?"

"Fuck him."

"You're not serious."

"Look, it's no secret you and I aren't best friends. But you at least have balls. Which is more than I can say for him." She pushed a lock of copper hair out of her eyes. "And anyway, they'll never know. I spoke anonymously," said Cassandra. "As a *Smell the Coffee* 'staffer.' " She delivered a wicked smile so disarming that Eve smiled back.

"Well," Eve said. "Good luck."

Cassandra's expression became sober once again. "Yeah. You, too."

. . .

Out on the sidewalk, Malcolm handed Eve her box and took her ID. With a pink face, he gave her an embarrassed pat on the shoulder and retreated inside.

She looked around at the crowds zooming by, the men with their briefcases and camel-hair coats, the women in their sleek blowouts and high-heeled boots, and she remembered how daunting she'd once found them, the big-striding New Yorkers of Midtown. Now she could keep up with them easily. The problem was, she had nowhere to go.

Chapter 15

For a brief moment after the Stiletto, Eve had felt she owned Manhattan. Maybe everyone who came here thought that at some point. But in truth, it was impossible. The most you could rule was your own roost. And sometimes not even that, as she was now reminded.

Donald began to push on her the names of literary agents and editors to contact about his work. Dutifully, she consulted the phone book and made some calls, but unfortunately, they all turned out to be dead.

She also left a message with Vadis to tell her she'd been fired, and to explore what media options might still be available.

Vadis never called back.

. . .

She was grateful, as ever, for Gwendolyn and her easy friendship. Eve and Highball dropped by Full Circle on a regular basis and Highball soon showed real talent as a store dog. Customers often brought in their own dogs and Highball entertained them so well that shoppers stayed longer than they'd planned—and bought more.

"I still can't believe it. That they fired you," said Gwendolyn for the third time that week. They were sitting at the counter reading the paper and eating croissants. "I mean, I can, but it sucks. It makes them look small. Frankly, you were so good in your interview, I think they should have found a way to use you on air. Like as a justice correspondent, or whatever."

"Well, the justice correspondent at the network is an actual lawyer. And has covered Washington for decades, so . . ."

"Well, okay, maybe not that. But something. You really were good."

"Thanks. But do you mind if we stop talking about it?"

"No problem. You're right. We've talked this subject to death."

"How's class?"

Gwendolyn dipped her paper toward the trash and swept some flaky crumbs from it. "Finals are coming up. Brutal. I'm not near ready and don't have enough time to study. Usually I can hit the books while I'm here, but with the holidays, it's going to be too busy for that."

"Let me help," said Eve.

"Help how?"

"I can be here. Help customers while you study. I probably couldn't do much with the books, but I could ring people up, sew buttons, run errands, whatever you need. I don't have a job, re-member?"

"You'd do that for me?"

"Of course."

"I'll pay you, of course. I can carve something out of my check."

"I wouldn't dream of it," said Eve, without thinking. "This is just a friend helping out a friend." Gwendolyn jumped off her stool and stood before her, her large brown eyes full of relief. Eve stepped off her own stool and the two embraced. It felt good to help someone else. Over Gwendolyn's shoulder, Eve caught sight of herself in the full-length mirror on the opposite wall. Given everything that had happened, she looked unaccountably happy.

. . .

These days Eve slept in, no longer automatically jumping out of bed at 6:58 with her heart pounding. But she still bought all the papers and paged through them carefully first thing in the morning before heading over to Full Circle. Knowing what was going on in the world was top-grade social lubricant in New York, where one of the most terrifying things that could happen socially was to have a reference about a *Times* op-ed piece go sailing right over your head.

She read both the national and international coverage first, but it was the media pages that she perused with special attention, wondering if she'd see something about Giles being demoted or Bliss suffering some kind of mental breakdown. But today it was another familiar name that caught her attention.

NET EXEC "KNOCKED" FOR A LOOP

The buzz out west is that Orla Knock, Vice President of Entertainment at America's third-placed network, is about to be shown the door. The official reason: Ratings that tanked this season and a roster of mid-season replacements that appears hopeless. But savvy industry watchers know most of those shows were greenlighted well before Knock's arrival in L.A. The unofficial reason, according to a source: Knock does not get along with her superiors, particularly the male ones, who have evidently decided that a hefty payout is worth every penny if they can rid themselves of this famously exhausting firebrand.

Eve exhaled. Orla Knock fired, too. Who was safe? Perhaps only the Marks of the world.

. . .

December stormed in and with it, the wearisome five-minute routine of putting on a hat and scarf, waterproof boots and mittens. Most of which proved fruitless. The rain came in sideways under her umbrella and the wind laughed in her sleeves. It wasn't as cold as the Midwest, but the dampness coming off the river made it feel worse, somehow.

De Fief's letter came as quickly and sharply as a guillotine. Eve read it in the vestibule so as not to alert Donald. Her rent would increase 18 percent beginning in January, and an inability to produce the new amount would immediately be met with eviction proceedings. Eve leaned against the wall. She'd managed to save some money the past few months, but hadn't been very diligent about it. And her efforts to line up a new job were going nowhere. Hoping Giles's threat had been just that, she'd sent résumés to the other networks and the local stations and had followed up with phone calls, but had received not so much as a flicker of interest.

. . .

Donald had stayed away for several days. Now, at last, he was back, sounding cheerless, almost defeated. His brave front, which usually manifested itself as a staccato rhythm, had quieted to something softer, almost a kneading. Or was it pleading? But presently, she felt him do his best to shake it off and return to normal. A week later, he declared he was ready to work again.

Eve felt around under the settee for the pad. "We left off with Rock, Paper, and Scissors running through the streets," she said, turning the pages. "Let's see. 'The sky overhead is licked by pink and orange flames. It is as if the world mirrors their happiness: Nature herself celebrates the unlikelihood and purity of their friendship. Sound drains. Colors deepen. A bird cries and flies out of a tree.' "

Eve held her pen tightly.

"Destiny does not like being flouted and will track down those who ignore her," Donald growled, and Eve recoiled slightly, rubbing her ear. "One evening, after a literary salon, they say their good-nights. Paper goes to embrace Rock and finds he is compelled to wrap her after all. It is his right; it is their fate to come together this way, after all. He will wrap her and in the morning they will find Scissors and tell him that they are now a two within the three. But as Paper stretches to take Rock in, she vanishes. It is as if she has disintegrated in his arms.

"Paper searches the city, high and low. Every café, every club, every garret of a friend. He is worried now. She is not teasing; she is not being coy. She is gone. At last he goes to the home of Scissors, to recruit his help in the hunt. It will mean confessing what he tried to do, but he is willing to take this chance." The words, which had been coming fast, suddenly slowed and grew halting. "All this time, he has flouted destiny. Now destiny repays the favor."

Eve took down the last of his words and, her heart racing, asked, "Why? What?"

"Quiet," said Donald, sounding labored.

Eve gave him a few moments to compose himself. Softly, she said, "Please don't get angry with me, but what is this about?"

"Not this again."

"Please tell me, what is this story about? It's different from the others. You'll give me that, won't you? Is it about your childhood? Are these characters your family?"

"Stop."

"Why won't you tell me anything about yourself?" she asked quietly.

"Do not interrogate me. If you are tired, we can postpone the dictation. But no more questions."

"Have you given any more thought to doing the memoir? Honestly, it would be so interesting."

"We don't have time for a memoir. Now that you've begun the search for an agent, we must move swiftly. As soon as the literary world becomes aware that unpublished works of mine exist, they will want to see them as soon as possible. And we must be ready with the complete collection. All the stories work together and must flow in the proper order. There are probably letters in the mail to us right now."

Eve brought a knuckle between her teeth. The agent search. She'd told Donald that she'd compiled a list of agents who handled experimental fiction and who were actually alive. She'd promised to send out query letters as soon as she had time to draft them, but had completely forgotten. She tried to stifle this thought before he could detect it, but—

"*What?*" he asked. "You haven't even begun to look?"

"I'm sorry."

"You've been lying to me."

"No, I haven't. It just slipped my mind. Believe it or not, you are not the center of my universe. I've had a rough few weeks."

"You've been playing me for a fool." Donald's pulse through her mind burned like a tiny electric snake.

"Don't be so dramatic."

"You've let me down in the worst possible way! You have all the power here; I cannot go into the world and verify what you tell me. I am completely dependent on you and you betrayed me."

"I have the power? *I?* You must be joking. You completely control my life." How could he not see he was the cause of her isolation? He was the looming scandal, the ex-con in the family, the bones in the backyard. Vadis and Mrs. Swan both had good reason to think she was nuts because of him. And if she could have invited Alex up, they might be together to this day. Eve stood and began to pace around the room in a tight circle, the only kind this claustrophobic apartment would allow. "Why do I put up with this? Why? So you can finish this useless work that no one wants."

"You little horror! Can you not see that these stories are the inheritors of the great ideas and themes of my most important work? It may be too much for your ordinary little brain, and only I know how truly ordinary it is, but—"

"You're fooling yourself!" Eve felt her stream of words slice through Donald's, stopping them cold. "You might once have been ahead of your time. You might have pushed boundaries and 'remade the short story' if you'd lived. Maybe. But from what I hear, you were never really talented. Your friends were, but not you!"

"From what you hear? What have you heard, you insolent—"

"And even if you did have a modicum of talent, you'd have to come up with a whole new approach to get published now. You can't hide behind these stupid metaphors anymore. Others have trodden this path since you died. You're going to have to produce something different to get anybody's attention now. Something real."

"Real? What the hell do you mean by that?"

"You really want to know? Your work is soulless. There's no emotion, no guts, no you. There are pretty words but it's cold; it's boring. And self-indulgent. You refuse to put anything of yourself out there. To be vulnerable. To be true. You may have something to say but you never say it!"

There was a terrible hush, which became more and more ominous as Eve contemplated the various ways Donald might respond. He'd triggered more than a few headaches, even when he was in a good mood, but when angry he might—

"I refuse to be true? *I?*" he boomed, a crack of thunder across her cerebellum. Eve had to steady herself on the doorframe of the kitchen.

"Yes," she whispered against the headache that threatened to break her mind in half.

"What about you? I've never met anyone so inauthentic. Such

a needy little people-pleaser. You spend years slaving for a father who doesn't respect you, get a job writing things for other people to say, which they ignore. Understandably, too. You moon for weeks over insipid, spineless boys. You fret because that carnivore Vadis is annoyed at you. And you let everyone else—Mark, Giles, even De Fief—walk all over you."

"What are you talking about? I captured the Stiletto! And then went on national TV and stood up for my colleagues and myself. I spoke up—and paid the price."

"Only because you're such a nervous Nellie! So concerned about what other people will think. After you were fired, you should have gone to the tabloids. You should have screamed bloody murder about what they did to you! But you didn't do any of that. And why? Because you're weak. Just like that poor mother of yours."

"Don't you *dare* talk about my mother!" Eve was free-falling into the blackness of anger. "And may I remind you that this nervous Nellie is the only prayer you have of your work ever being published? So how's this for bloody murder?" She took a breath. "I'm moving out."

Eve fetched her suitcase from the closet and threw it open on the bed. "To think I've been worrying about how to scrape together the rent for this place so I could stay with you." She began stuffing clothes and dog toys into the case. The toys were grimy and belonged nowhere near her silks and wools, but she didn't care. Highball wove around the floor in little figure eights, whimpering. "To think of all the times you kept me from doing work or getting sleep. To think of all the friends I haven't been able to have over because of you. Not to mention the dates. How many people think I'm just plain weird because of you!" She threw in some books and her toothbrush. "You're the strange one, you know. There's something wrong with you. Something happened, I don't know what. But I bet it was in 1964." At this she felt something like a little whip of surprise inside her left temple. She pressed it hard, trying to make the pain go away. "I'm right, aren't I? And whatever it was ruined you as an artist. And as a man."

Eve put Highball's food in a shopping bag and grabbed her coat.

"It's time for me to live my own life—finally. To do what I want to do. To find an apartment that feels like a home, where I don't have to tiptoe around some bully. I'll be okay, you know. I have all the time in the world! But you—"

She found she couldn't finish the sentence. She stood in the doorway with Highball, breathing hard, waiting for Donald to respond. She took in the apartment: the crown moldings, the tall, narrow windows, the black lacquer bar with its bottle of Kentucky Pride bourbon on top. The room seemed to shimmer in the fading light. She trembled, her eyes watering.

Why wasn't he saying anything? Didn't he realize this was it?

Oh, hell, she thought. She stepped into the hall and slammed the door.

Chapter 16

Eve used the pay phone at the laundromat to avoid the cold. She wanted to call Gwendolyn, but she'd gone upstate to spend Christmas with her parents and Eve didn't have the number. She fumbled with shaking hands for the address book in her purse and flicked through the sparsely filled-in pages.

"Hello?"

"Vadis, great, you're there."

"Who is this?"

"It's Eve." Vadis didn't hang up, which was encouraging. "I know we're not on the best of terms, but I was wondering if I could ask you a favor," said Eve. Silence. "I've had a problem in my apartment. The wiring blew and there's no light. Or—heat." More silence. "Could I possibly stay with you for a day or two? Just till I figure out something else."

There was no sound for several moments save for the whirring of the dryers all around her.

"Gee, I'd love to help you out but I've got a problem in *my* apartment."

"What's wrong?" asked Eve.

"They're fumigating. Yeah. And sanding the floors. And caulking the tile in the bathroom." There was a pause. "Sorry."

Someone came into the laundromat, and a shock of cold air hit Eve full in the face. She pulled her coat around her and looked down at Highball, who was licking something on her boot. So it had come to this. What had she been thinking? Donald was right: Everyone will disappoint you. And in the end, we're all alone.

Eve pressed the phone very close to her mouth. "You know something?" she said. "When I got here, I was so lonely. I envied you so much: You could talk to anybody, you knew everybody. But you know what I think now? I think *you're* the lonely one. You just don't know it yet." She hung up and rooted in her coin purse for another quarter.

. . .

Quirine lived in a tenement building on the Lower East Side. A narrow staircase led past landings with cracked, frosted-glass windows and metal doors painted green. Her apartment, on the third floor, was small but charming. There was no central lighting in any of the rooms, but floor lamps dotted the corners, throwing discs of light upon the sponged ruby-colored walls.

Victor had moved in, making things a bit tight, but Quirine said since she would soon be taking Victor to Paris to meet her family for the holidays, Eve could have the place to herself for a couple of weeks.

Waking up on the couch the first morning, she sighed and stretched. The house was quiet; Quirine and Victor were out Christmas shopping. Eve thought contentedly of her night's sleep. It had been deep and full, with no one peeking at her dreams. The kind of sleep possible only in a place without ghosts.

She tensed, reflexively bracing for retaliation. But none came. Her head remained tranquil and completely her own, like her childhood playhouse at the back of the garden. She exhaled with relief, threw on her kimono, and looked around for Highball, who was sprawled contentedly across an orange cashmere pillow on the living room floor.

She found a note on the coffee table, next to the morning papers. "*Coffee in kitchen. —Q.*" Eve smiled. A roommate who could write for herself—a definite improvement. A roommate who made the coffee—absolute decadence.

Eve poured herself a mug and settled on the couch with the papers, flipping straight to the job and apartment listings. She ran her finger down the pages, but the paucity of work in which she could make use of her interview and writing skills was shocking. The only thing more upsetting was the price of apartments. She should have known this, of course; New Yorkers talked about it all the time. It was just that, until you needed one, you didn't really pay attention. Finally she gave up and turned to the news pages.

A *Daily News* headline on page 3 leapt out at her immediately: EXCLUSIVE: STILETTO'S SHARP PAIN. Eve put down the coffee. She hadn't thought much about the Stiletto since their fateful encounter. Somehow the drama of what had happened with Bliss and her subsequent firing had drowned out everything else. Now her breath came fast, bringing back all the fear and fury of the attack. She scanned the piece, her eyes moving so quickly they tripped over the words.

It turns out walking around in high heels wasn't the first time the Stiletto (aka Matt Buntwiffel, 32) experienced pain. In a jailhouse meeting with his lawyer and criminal psychologist Dr. Shin Tang of Columbia Presbyterian, a law enforcement source tells the *News,* Buntwiffel disclosed a life of torment. The child of parents who drank heavily, his only source of love was his twin sister, Mary. . . .

. When they were six, the two were play wrestling in a tree house at their home in Columbia County, New York, when Mary plunged to the ground, fatally breaking her neck. Matt was blamed by his grieving parents and began to blame himself . . . gradually slid into a life of drugs . . . their expense pushed him to steal.

Cut to the night Buntwiffel wore heels for the first time (ex-

perts say he may have been trying to "replace" Mary by sometimes wearing her clothing and shoes) . . . and walked up behind a woman on Grand Street who didn't turn around . . .
giving him an idea for raising money to feed his drug habit . . .
claims his attacks were "harrowing" and that the guilt is unbearable . . . now on suicide watch . . .

Eve inhaled sharply. Highball stirred, left her pillow and nuzzled Eve's knee. Eve had never thought of the Stiletto having a
real name before, let alone a childhood. But of course, everyone
had one.

Even Donald, probably.

                    . . .

In the late afternoon of Christmas Eve, she ventured out for
something to eat. On the sidewalk, parents carried presents and
bottles of wine to family gatherings, young children skipping several yards in front. Laughter and music and cooking smells filled
the streets. Eve ducked into the gourmet market, where she ordered a single serving of turkey, sweet potatoes, and green beans.
The total came to more than fifteen dollars and she winced.

She trudged back to the apartment, body clenched against the
gathering storm. Her hat blew off her head and danced away but
she couldn't summon the energy to chase it.

Back at Quirine's, she stood at the counter, making unappetizing track marks through the potatoes with her fork, and
thought for the thousandth time of Gin, the simplicity of home,
and her easy job.

"Merry Christmas, Dad," she said when he picked up the
phone.

"It's my girl," said Gin. "Wish you were here today."

"I know. Me, too," said Eve. It was the truth. She had very
much wanted to go home. But after De Fief's letter, she needed to
save every dollar. And she was too proud to ask her father to pay
for the plane tickets, even though he'd have agreed without ques-

tion. She was too old for such a thing, surely. So she'd told him she had plans. "What are you doing today?"

"Leaving to pick up Jennifer in about an hour." Jennifer was Gin's girlfriend. She was a divorcée, and a realtor. It had taken him years after Penelope's death to begin dating, and even then he'd only attempted it sporadically, always keeping the women at arm's length. But over the last few months, he seemed to be growing close to Jennifer, and Eve wondered if this might be because he no longer had his daughter to lean on. "We're going over to Bryce's. His new sweetie is supposed to be some cook."

"That sounds really nice."

"And you?"

"Going to be with my friends. All my friends," said Eve.

"Well, look at you. That's terrific. And maybe at Easter we'll see you back here?"

"Definitely," she said. "If not sooner."

She went back to her meal, lost in thought about what Klieg had said about interrupted narratives. Penelope's story line, the one about the young girl finding herself in New York City, had been cut short, and she'd sunken into a state of distraction and melancholy that lasted until she died. Would Penelope be glad Eve was here, trying to carry on her New York story? Why had she abandoned her own in the first place? Eve wasn't any closer to the answer than when she'd arrived, and could only speculate that it was something truly awful. Like being fired and lonely and exhausted.

She looked out the window at the couple fixing dinner across the airshaft and wondered whether Donald was as forlorn as she was. Of course, he had no idea it was Christmas. Dates, holidays, rituals—all irrelevant to him now. He was probably, as he'd once explained to her, in the limbo-like state that he was powerless to comprehend or control.

Much like she was.

Well, she wasn't completely powerless, she thought, putting down her fork. She put the plastic cover back on the turkey, slid it into the fridge, and picked up the phone.

. . .

In the doorway, Klieg put his warm, smooth palms on Eve's cold
cheeks and pressed, smiling down at her. "What bad luck," he
said, referring to her story that she'd had to call off her dinner
party because her pipes had frozen. He stepped aside so she
could enter. "But as it happens, this works out very well."

Eve let Highball off her leash. "It's no trouble that we're here?"

"Far from it. Günter was supposed to go to Germany to be
with his parents, but his flight was canceled due to the weather."
He gestured at the snow blowing sideways outside, before closing the door.

"Weren't you going as well?" asked Eve, shrugging out of her
wrap.

"No. My brother, Henrik, and I are not on the best of terms."
It was clear he didn't want to discuss it. "So it is just Günter and
me this evening, and frankly, we could use the buffer."

Eve had stopped on the way to buy Klieg a present, a new edi-
tion of Dawn Powell's *The Happy Island*. "It's one of my favorites. I hope you'll like it," she said, handing it to him.

"It goes on the top of my stack," said Klieg, and led the way
up to the drawing room, where the Christmas tree rose high into
the air and glittered with white lights and tasteful silver drops.
He poured champagne and after they toasted he smiled wanly
at her.

Just then Günter entered. He'd shaved off the tips of his rather
long sideburns since Eve had last seen him, and there was a tiny
patch of very white skin just in front of each ear. As Eve reached
out to shake his hand, she inadvertently swayed forward on her
toes. "Excuse me," she said, trying not to look foolish as she
used his chest to brace herself.

"Hello," he said, tightening his mouth slightly in what might
have been a smile or a grimace. He dropped his hand to his
blazer pocket, pulled out a rubber ball shaped like a Christmas

ornament, and looked questioningly at Eve. When she nodded, he threw it for Highball, who skidded after it, up and down the highly glossed wood floor. They made small talk for a few minutes and watched the dog, Eve trying to assess relations between Klieg and his nephew. There seemed to be some kind of holiday cease-fire but still little warmth.

Marie served dinner in the formal dining room, which looked enchanting, with tapered candles at least two feet high running down the center of the table and the wainscoting draped with evergreen garlands. A roast goose held center stage on the sideboard along with a suckling pig. These were surrounded by silver bowls of jellies, white sausages, macaroni salads, and wire baskets of bread called Christstollen.

Klieg took a seat at the head of the table, Eve and Günter on either side. Klieg bowed his head and delivered a short prayer in German, and Eve was touched by the earnestness of his tone and the humility of his posture. She wondered what he prayed for.

Klieg poured them all big glasses of wine so dark it looked almost black. "How should we translate *Dickbauch*?" he asked his nephew.

"Fat stomach," said Günter. Eve looked quizzically back and forth between them and Günter continued. "It is what the superstitious aspire to on the holiday. Tradition states that those who do not eat well on Christmas Eve will be haunted by demons during the night. Hence, enough food for an army, even for just three," he said, cutting through a crispy piece of goose. "Of course, some suffer demons either way," he said, under his breath.

Klieg did not seem to have heard the last part. In fact he appeared cheered by his nephew's relatively lengthy speech. "Ah, yes," he said, wiping his mouth. "We have many traditions and fables surrounding this day. Legend has it that in Germany on Christmas Eve the rivers turn to wine, the animals speak, mountains split open to reveal precious gems, and church bells can be heard ringing from the bottom of the sea."

Eve smiled, thinking it sounded as magical as New York had appeared to her when she'd first arrived. And sometimes, despite everything, enchantment still revealed itself slyly through cracks in the everyday.

Klieg took a sip of water and continued, "Unfortunately, only the pure of heart can see these magical happenings."

Günter nodded silently, just once, then occupied himself with his usual exercise in textbook dining while feeding Highball none too surreptitiously under the table.

Since she took a sip of wine at every awkward silence, by the end of dinner Eve was quite drunk. But afterward, when Klieg urged her, she accepted a glass of brandy by the fire in the drawing room. Highball curled up by the large window, the coolest spot in the room, and Klieg went to the antique gramophone and put on what sounded like German folk music. He swayed to the lilting accordion melody. "Remember this dance, Günter?" he asked, his eyes twinkling slightly as he looked at his nephew in the flickering light. "You were quite good at it as a child."

"Only because Louisa was such a good teacher."

"How did Louisa come to be an expert at German folk dance?" asked Eve.

"It was the enthusiasm of the émigré, I suppose," said Klieg. "We did not live in Germany very long but while we were there she was determined to become part of things. The dancing she kept up long after we left."

Günter got up to poke the fire.

"While you are up, why not show Eve how it's done?" said Klieg.

Eve wanted to crawl under one of the damask pillows on the Regency sofa. Günter might be behaving civilly but this was no reason to push it. Indeed, he said nothing, just busied himself scraping ash with a small, flat shovel.

"Günter. *Es ist Weihnachten,*" prodded Klieg.

"Yes, Uncle." Günter straightened and came toward Eve. "It

will be my pleasure." He offered his hand and led her to the open area just in front of the hearth, where he faced her. *"Frölicher Kreis,"* he said.

"I'm sorry?" Eve couldn't say she'd ever been a fan of the German language; its rasp seemed almost deliberately unpleasant. But there was something provocative about Günter's particular elocution. Some months ago, when talking about an ex-boyfriend, Gwendolyn had used the term "sexy ugly," and Eve thought this was as good a way as any to describe the sound of Günter speaking his native tongue.

"It means 'the Happy Circle.' It is supposed to be a dance for eight." He held up his palms to face her and nodded for her to do the same. He took a step backward and she did, too, so their arms were fully extended. Then, waiting for the beat, they stepped in, and out again. In, then out again. Suddenly, he came around the side, put a stiff arm around her waist, and began to promenade her quickly in a small circle.

Eve looked over her shoulder at Klieg as they moved past him. He smiled, but at something, or someone, far beyond them.

After a few moments, Günter's posture relaxed slightly. Eve leaned in. "Why are you so difficult with your uncle?" she whispered under the music.

"You do not know what you are talking about," he replied.

"He's an old man. Can't you be a bit kinder to him?"

"It is he who is unkind to me."

"I can't believe that. I mean, I know he can be moody, but he means well."

"He only brings himself to be pleasant when you are around."

"What do you mean?" she asked as they faced one another again with their palms touching.

"He mopes all day. When he does talk, it is to complain. Except, every once in a while, he waxes poetic. About you," said Günter, as they stepped in and out again. "As if you are the child he never had or something." Eve looked at Klieg, who was nodding to the music, but Günter wasn't done. "I used to be special to him. I was the only child of the next generation, which is why he wanted to groom me for his business. But even though I wouldn't pin his dresses for him, he adored me. Spoiled me terribly."

"So what happened?"

"When Louisa died, he sank into a bad humor. This was to be expected, of course. But it never ended. Even I, who always brought a smile to his face, could do nothing to cheer him. I tried so often to please him, but it was impossible."

"That must have been difficult."

"And now. I accepted this post in New York to be near him. It is not easy for me at the lab, but I stay with it because all I want is to have back what we once had, the closeness. Our whole family feels it is now or never, that if the rift continues much longer, we will lose him forever. So I keep trying. But it seems there is only one person who can make him smile, and it is not me."

"I'm sorry." Eve realized for the first time that it was pain, far more than anger, that animated Günter.

"What is the connection between you?" asked Günter. "You have an uncanny similarity to my aunt; even I have noticed this. At first I thought that was it. But when I see you together, it seems there is something else."

"I don't really know," said Eve.

Suddenly, he whirled around and placed his hand on her shoulder and put hers on his own. They clasped hands underneath and went round and round. "Perhaps you hope he will fall in love with you? Perhaps you think you will get his money?"

Eve dropped her arms and stepped back, looking at him with utter incredulity.

"I'm sorry," Günter said. "That was rude. I forget myself. Please." He held out his hand. She took it reluctantly, thinking he really did look repentant and not wanting Klieg to know anything was wrong.

"I think he likes me because I let him tell his stories," she said as they picked up the steps again. "People need to do that, you know."

"Does he have stories to tell?"

"Yes."

"About what?"

"Why don't you ask him and see for yourself?"

"I have tried. Uncle doesn't make it easy. Half the time, he seems lost, in another place. Like right now," he said, nodding toward Klieg, whose eyes were closed. "Sometimes I don't even think he sees me."

Eve thought of herself as a child, playing on the floor of her mother's room, facing Penelope's back. "I'm sure that hurts," she said. She recognized by the music that it was time to go back to the promenade, and she turned, putting her hand against the small of her back for him to grasp.

"What about you?" Günter asked as they walked the circle.

"What do you mean?"

"Something is wrong, is it not?" Without his help, the fire sputtered and the room had grown dim.

"What makes you say that?" she asked, stumbling slightly.

"You seem different tonight. I noticed during dinner. Though you did your best to appear your usual charming self, I have a feeling something is not right."

Eve's cheeks grew hot and she looked over her shoulder at Klieg. His eyes were closed and his chin rested against his chest. It was easy enough to explain her melancholy if she chose to; she'd been fired from her job, after all. But that wasn't it. "You really want to know?" she asked, and Günter nodded. Eve stopped walking and faced him, aware of the wine coursing through her and glad that in the undulating darkness she couldn't see his eyes. Out of nowhere, she was overwhelmed with emotion and pressed her palms into her eyes.

"Someone has broken your heart?" guessed Günter, with surprising gentleness. She shook her head vigorously. Günter remained silent, gazing at her. Eve felt a hot tear slide down her cheek. "A boyfriend?"

"No, God no. Of course not." What an idea. "I mean, not really."

"But a great love, nonetheless."

Eve shrugged her shoulders helplessly. Günter nodded and the song ended. The needle on the record made a scratching sound.

• • •

Eve lay under a blanket on a divan in the library, dark save for the glow of a second, smaller Christmas tree. The twinkling lights threw giant shadows of needles across the walls and ceiling, making the room feel like a glade in a forest.

Before Klieg had gone up to bed, he'd suggested she spend the night, since it was so late. None of the guest rooms were made up and he'd offered her his own, but Eve said she'd be quite happy in the library. She lay for several minutes, looking up at the ceiling. Unable to sleep, she threw off the covers and made her way to the shelf with the photographs, the sea of tiny faces staring back from across the decades. She flicked on a reading light. From somewhere outside, carolers made their way through the night. "*Silent night, holy night . . .*"

She found the picture she was looking for and searched Donald's face. She pressed his image lightly with her fingernail and the photo bounced back, as if something thick had been shoved in behind it. She turned it over, and slid the back of the frame out from the sides. Out slipped another picture, folded in half.

It was Klieg and Donald, Louisa between them. It looked like it was taken the same day as the other one; everyone was in the same clothes, though Donald's pipe was missing. The three smiled, pressing in close to fit inside the frame. They looked young and jaunty, all bold fronts and endless possibilities. Looking into Donald's eyes gave Eve a chill, the intimacy of it almost too much to bear. She dropped her gaze to the bottom of the pic-

ture and noticed something: Donald and Louisa were holding
hands. Klieg and Louisa were not.

A throat cleared.

"I was on my way to get some hot water and honey. . . ."
Klieg appeared in the doorway. "I saw the light."

The carolers began a new song.

"*It came upon the midnight clear*
That glorious song of old . . ."

He saw immediately what she had in her hand.

"You said Donald and Louisa weren't friends."

Klieg gazed at her for several long moments. Then he walked
toward her and sat on one of the leather chairs. Eve took the
other. They faced each other for several moments.

"I do not think I can talk about this." He sighed and folded
his hands. He sat silent for several long moments. "But I suppose
I can try. What's the difference anymore?" He dipped his head.
"Our group in Paris consisted of painters, sculptors, actors. Big
talents, big egos. As a relative youngster, and a designer, not to
mention a German, I was the outsider. I was not disliked, but I
was thought of as, at best, a mascot. Yet Donald took a liking
to me. We shared an architectural approach to our work. The
others shook their heads, they did not understand our relationship. The writer and the dressmaker."

Eve knew all this but Klieg seemed to be in a trance.

"I think it was because we had more than a philosophy in
common. We'd grown up in similar families. We'd come to feel
we were alone in the world at a young age and recognized this in
each other. If this doesn't sound too strange, it was a little like a
love affair."

Eve nodded.

"We did everything together, walked every inch of the city and
talked all night over bottles of wine at Montmartre. Paris was for

us what New York is for so many: that hypnotic place that binds those who cherish it in the same way. We could not get enough of it or each other. A few days apart felt like years." He rubbed his eyes. "And then one day a new cashier started at the Deux Magots."

"Louisa."

"Immediately we sensed that she was a once-in-a-lifetime woman, the kind who could change a man's destiny. Parisian girls could be a proud, haughty bunch, especially with foreigners, but Louisa was not. She came from a small village north of Toulouse and it was as if she was the only earnest girl left. She took a real interest in those around her and showed true kindness when anyone was in need. And that spelled danger. But we ignored this, of course." He paused, remembering. "We spent every afternoon at the Deux Magots. Donald would look at the poems she was trying to write—I'm not sure how much talent she had, but she was so, so hopeful about it. And I would sketch dresses for her. After she got off work, we'd fly around the city from bar to café, salon to party, laughing and debating. We'd come home at dawn, staggering up to Louisa's flat for 'café pour trois.' Black coffee in tiny cups and whatever Louisa had stolen from the restaurant would be our breakfast. We were so young, so ridiculously young. We thought we could go on like this forever."

"But you couldn't," said Eve.

"I became aware that I had done what was verboten: I had fallen in love with Louisa. I agonized. What should I do? How could I hurt Donald? How could I jeopardize the friendship that existed between the three of us? Then my collection failed, as I told you, and something inside me broke. I decided if nothing else, I must at least have this woman. So one evening, I went to her flat to surprise her. I brought flowers, gladiolas. She wasn't home but I knew where she kept her extra key and let myself in. Only to put the flowers in water, I told myself. I looked down and realized that I'd stepped on something. An envelope, slipped under the door." His voice had grown hoarse.

"Go on," said Eve, handing him her glass of water.

Klieg took a drink. "I opened it. I had no right to but I did. I read the letter inside. And I knew that if Louisa read it, I would lose her."

"Why? What did it say?"

"It was from Donald. He too was in love with her."

"But how did you know Louisa would pick Donald over you?" Eve asked, bringing her knees up under her chin.

"Because he had said all the right things. That he was ready to use words as a bridge instead of a wall, to say what he felt. He had written a new collection of stories, stories from the heart, not just the mind. He said it was she, Louisa, who had inspired him to reveal himself this way, and he included one of the stories with his letter. He implored her to meet him that very night, so he could declare himself in person. He promised that if she didn't come, he would never bother her again. He said he would never ask anything of her and he would never speak of it to anyone. He said that the three of us would go on as we had always been, *les Trois Mousquetaires.*"

"Do you really think she would have gone to meet him?"

"Oh yes. Because while Louisa loved us both, it was Donald she was *in* love with. I knew; I could see that, despite our pledge, the two of them belonged together. But there was a problem. She was often frustrated by his inability to communicate, yet she was not the type to make demands. If she'd been bolder, she would have told him that he was the one she wanted. And she might have shown her poems to an editor and . . . who knows?

"In any case, with his letter, Donald made it clear that for her, he had changed his disposition. I doubt he ever used the word 'love' before or after. If he'd lived long enough to become famous, that letter would have become quite valuable. If I had not torn it to pieces, that is." Klieg allowed himself a mirthless laugh.

Eve couldn't believe what she was hearing. "What happened next?" she asked, hardly able to breathe.

"Louisa came home and we ate dinner together on her little

terrace overlooking the courtyard. I knew I had to act fast and I did. I asked her to marry me."

From outside, the carolers' voices drifted up:

"And man, at war with man, hears not
The tidings which they bring
O hush the noise, ye men of strife . . ."

"That whole evening, I felt sick. As the hours ticked by, I kept thinking of Donald, somewhere out there in the dark, waiting for her. At the end of the night, Louisa agreed to be my wife. I should have rejoiced but I felt only torment. And this became a harbinger for our marriage. As wonderful as she was, and as well as we were suited, our time together was shadowed by my guilt. A piece of her always seemed to be somewhere else, with her real love." Klieg brought his elbows to his knees and placed his face in his hands.

"Did Donald find out about you two?"

"Yes. Some days later he dragged himself away from his self-imposed isolation and came to the café. He saw us embracing by the espresso machine."

"What did he do?"

Klieg shook his head. "Nothing. He kissed us each on the cheek and demanded the biggest *pain au chocolat* in the case, got himself a newspaper, and took a seat at his favorite table. Never once did he mention the letter or his feelings. He even helped Louisa and me pack for Germany." Klieg's shoulders sagged and he sat back, spent. "I have often wondered if I would have been so selfless if the situation had been reversed. But if Donald had taken Louisa from me, I do not know what I would have done." Again, the low, bitter laugh. "I might have tried to kill him with my scissors."

Eve brought a hand to her mouth.

Donald . . . the writer . . . *Paper.*

Klieg . . . the designer . . . *Scissors.*

Eve looked at the creased picture in her hand: Louisa, with her dimples . . . *Rock?*

Eve reached out, putting a hand on Klieg's knee. "You told me at the gallery that day that something happened to Donald in 1964. Something that led him to distrust words, to decide that they couldn't communicate feelings. And that after that he never again attempted to express emotion in his stories. You said you didn't know what had happened. But it was you taking the letter, wasn't it? That's what happened in 1964. Donald believed she'd read his words and that they hadn't moved her. Maybe that they even caused her to reject him."

"Yes." Klieg's face crumpled now. "In one night I destroyed everything. I cast three lives off course. Louisa died with a broken heart because she missed Donald. Donald died without Louisa and without achieving the dreams he had of becoming famous. Everyone lost because of what I did, and perhaps the world lost, too. Lost a great artist."

A beat passed and then Eve was brought up short by this last claim. "What do you mean, lost a great artist? You said Donald didn't have talent."

"Of course he had talent! He possessed one of the most original minds of his generation," said Klieg, his face ashen.

"Then why did you lie?" asked Eve, blinking fast, bringing a hand to her forehead.

"Because I couldn't face what I did. It was easier to believe Donald was average, that I had silenced only a mediocre voice." He swallowed. His eyes, when he finally looked at her, were like glass. "That is why I stopped working years ago. Why should I have this enormous success when he did not? The shame caught up with me. Because I had Louisa, I was happy and able to create. Because he lost her, he became for all intents and purposes a failure. Both of us bitter and, in our hearts, lonely," he whispered.

Eve looked at Klieg for a long moment, flooded with a mix of emotions. She was stunned, and incensed on Donald's behalf. Yet Klieg looked so utterly defeated, she couldn't help but feel sorry for him. They sat for several minutes in silence, listening to the carolers' voices growing faint as they moved off down the street.

Finally, Eve stood. "I'm sorry," she said, wiping her face. "I can never thank you enough for your honesty, but now I have to go." She put on her shoes and lay a hand on his shoulder. "Everything's going to be all right, though. It really is," she said, though she was not at all sure that it would be.

As she ran lightly down the stairs with Highball at her heels, she could just make out the end of the song.

> "O ye, beneath life's crushing load
> Whose forms are bending low
> Who toil along the climbing way
> With painful steps and slow
> Look now! For glad and golden hours
> Come swiftly on the wing
> O rest beside the weary road
> And hear the angels sing!"

. . .

It wasn't easy in the predawn hours of a stormy Christmas Day to get a taxi to take her and Highball all the way down to the Lower East Side, wait while she packed up her bags, and then drive them all the way back up to the Village. It was after 3 a.m. when she stopped on the last stair, dipped her chin to her chest, and closed her eyes. Highball looked up at her and whined softly. Eve swallowed, rotated her shoulders a few times, and fumbled through her keys. The door opened with a sigh of protest. A quick entry was definitely best, Eve thought, like jumping off the high dive before you had a chance to think about it. She strode with purpose down the hall and into the bedroom, where she dropped her luggage.

Seeing her rooms again was like walking into a museum dedicated to "The Previous Life of Eve Weldon": the pieces, a catalogue of her recent past, perfectly preserved. All that was missing were little bronze plaques: "Bed slept in by Eve Weldon, always, unfortunately, quite alone." "Vanity mirror gazed into by Eve

Weldon. Known to look fondly upon thirties hats." She came back down the little hall and her eyes swept over the living room: "Art deco bar, drunk at rather too frequently by Eve Weldon. Also served as desk for dictation of—"

Her heart stopped. The bottle of bourbon that had been standing on the bar when she left two weeks ago now lay on its side, its contents spilled. Eve turned the bottle upright with a shaky hand. "Donald?" she whispered. No answer. She leaned over and saw an inky bourbon stain on the floor with a thin film of dust over it. *"Donald?"* Still nothing.

Eve's mind raced. She sat at the bar, afraid that her extended absence had killed him, or whatever the equivalent would be. If it had, she'd never forgive herself. She bounced her knee and counted the minutes. After nearly half an hour with each of her senses turned up a notch, she thought she felt a tentative creeping in her head. It moved forward, then back, then forward again. A moment later she heard a muted static, like the first time Donald had made contact.

"EEEE-wshhhhhh. EEEE-wshhhhhh—effort to—*wshhhh-hhh*—promise—*wshhhhhhh*—pour—*wshhhhhhh* " The voice was so faint she thought she was dreaming it. Had her absence weakened Donald this much?

Promise . . . pour. What was he saying? Of course. The day she had saved Highball at the dog run and got that cut on her arm, Donald had pledged that one day he'd pour her a drink.

"Someday, I will surprise you," he'd said then.

"But I—*wshhhhhhh*—bit of trouble," he gurgled now.

"Donald? Can you hear me?" murmured Eve.

"Yeeeee . . ." His voice was faint but clearer.

"Were you trying to pour me a drink?"

"Yes."

"Did you know I was coming home?"

"No."

Eve perched on a bar stool. The moment felt crucial yet fragile. If it were a reunion with a long-lost love, this would be the time to look into each other's eyes and read what was there, for better or worse. But she couldn't do that with Donald. She closed her eyes and let her mind become the empty blue space. When she sensed thoughts intruding, she pushed them out. She held the space empty for as long as she could, then felt a trickle of feeling snake through. Regret, maybe. Whether it was hers or Donald's, she couldn't tell. Soon it ran into a rivulet of something else, something that felt like hope. The two streams swirled slowly around each other, finally giving up their separateness.

Eve had no idea how long she sat there, but as church bells struck the half hour, words found their place again. "Well," she whispered finally. "It's the best drink I never drank."

Donald's small chuckle sent a tingle through her head.

"The perfect Christmas present," she said.

"Is it Christmas?"

"Yes."

"Merry Christmas."

Eve stood up and began to light some candles. She didn't feel like turning on the lights.

"I have another present for you," said Donald. "With you gone, I've had a lot of time to think. To face facts."

"Meaning?"

"Meaning I've gotten it through my thick head that I've departed your world. My existence is different; my tasks must change. I've got to do what ghosts"—he'd never used this word about himself before—"do. Open doors. Make floorboards groan. Warble 'boo' or some such."

This last part nearly made Eve laugh out loud. "You can't be serious. Why would you want to do those things?"

"You won't always be here, that much is clear. So I must get over silly notions about my stories and move on."

"Stop. And listen," she continued, walking toward the bathroom. "I'm going to take a bath and make a pot of tea. And then—'Rock, Paper, Scissors.'"

"What?"

"We're going to finish your story," she said as she turned on the hot water full blast. The steam rose, warming her skin and bending her hair.

"That's all over now. I can't make this work. As you've been trying to tell me, once it was fresh, but now it's nothing special."

"Stop. Right now. You possessed the most original mind of your generation. You didn't get enough time to perfect your craft like your Paris friends did. But we can work on that. And we can help readers understand it in context, how you came up with that style and what it was like to write that way before anybody else did . . . if we do the memoir."

"But a memoir would take months, a year. It would be a mammoth job. Why would you want to do that?"

"Because I think you have a story we can sell. And even if it never sells, I want to hear it. For myself," she said. "So, are we in agreement?"

"I suppose we are."

After a long soak, Eve donned a silk chemise and brewed some oolong. As it steeped, she took a rag and cleaned the bourbon from the bar and floor. Then something occurred to her, something she couldn't believe she hadn't thought of before.

"When we're done with this work, where am I going to say I found it? And how are we going to convince them it's yours when you've been gone for so long?"

"Ah. Not a problem," said Donald. "You can use my Royal Mercury. My typewriter. It's behind a cupboard in the bedroom."

"You hid your typewriter? Why?"

"It was my most precious possession, and with all the impoverished would-be writers in the building, I was worried it would be stolen. As a matter of fact, it was, once or twice. My neighbors said they'd just 'borrowed' it but that was but a euphemism." Eve walked into the bedroom. "If you type the new material on my old machine, it will match my previous work," he said. "You can claim you found it hidden under a floorboard or something. No one will be surprised to hear that. Writers always squirrel away their work, usually because they can't stand to look at it anymore but can't bear to throw it out. We used to tell each other about our hiding places, but only other writers, not spouses or friends. They would never understand. e. e. cummings used to put his unfinished work in the dumbwaiter. Djuna Barnes, under the floorboards of, of course, her boudoir." He mumbled something about T. S. Eliot. "And that's just Patchin Place! Half the buildings in the Village are home to one minor masterpiece or another. Or at least some worthy experiments. The stories I could tell you."

"Donald, the *typewriter*."

"All right, all right." He guided her to the back wall of the low cupboard she used for hatpins and lace collars. As he'd promised, if the wall was pounded on the right side, the left side popped out and the whole thing came loose. Behind it, the Royal Mercury reposed like Sleeping Beauty, resting not on a pillow but on two large shoeboxes and reams of loose paper, some of which was blank and some of which appeared to contain stories.

"What's in these boxes?" Eve asked, blowing the dust off everything and carrying it to the bed.

"Nothing interesting. Ignore them," Donald replied as she took the top off one of them.

Inside were dozens of letters, press clippings, and small leather notebooks. His journals, she thought. The other box contained hundreds of pictures, bundled together in bunches with thick red rubber bands. Eve slipped the band off the first bundle, all black-and-whites. The top picture was of a towheaded boy in a suburban backyard. He looked about three. He was wearing a tiny straw cowboy hat and a red bandanna around his neck. His brow was furrowed as he tried to thread a toy gun into a leather holster. Next to him stood a sturdy woman, staring off into the distance with a grim look on her face. On the back Eve read, *Donnie and Mommy on D's birthday at Maple Drive House, 1936.*

"Donnie?"

"Don't," he groaned.

Next came a second-grade class picture: sixteen or so children smiling broadly, with Donald, his hair slightly darker now, in the back row. Other snapshots showed Donald putting a model schooner together with a pair of tweezers and playing the piano. Then came one from what looked like a junior high play, Donald playing the Stage Manager in *Our Town*. At the end of the bundle, Eve found a picture of a group of teenaged boys and men dressed in fishing gear. A banner hung overhead, reading *Oakfield's Father & Son Tackle Day, 1947*. Each father held the top of a fishing rod, his son grasping it underneath. Eve ran her eyes over the faces, looking for Donald. There he was, on the right-hand side. He was holding his rod all alone.

Eve felt her breath catch in her throat. She ran her finger along the curve of Donald's chin, moved by the stoicism of his expression. She wanted to crush this boy to her chest, bake him a five-layer cake, wade into the river with him and pull out fish with her bare hands.

She pressed a tissue into the corner of her eye and pulled the band off another bundle. There was a picture of Donald behind a desk at what looked like a college newspaper, frowning at a layout, a pencil behind his ear. After it, dozens of pictures taken in Paris, like those belonging to Klieg: groups of young people around tables, men in fedoras and women in cropped jackets with funnel necks. In one picture, a perfectly pressed Klieg toasted Donald with a cloudy glass of pastis.

"Here's a picture of you and . . . Mr. Klieg." She tried to sound surprised.

"Ah yes," said Donald. "Matthias." Donald spoke the name with such melancholy Eve caught her breath. "He was a little younger than the rest of us. He wanted to make clothes, and was laughed at by some of the more insecure members of our crowd. But he began to trail me, like a puppy. He would show me his work. We'd get a table away from the others and he would open his portfolio. I saw brilliance there. Rough, to be sure, but brilliance. A rare intellect. And an old soul.

"His parents traveled a lot when he and his brother were young, and he cared for his brother Henrik like a father. He would do the same for anyone who needed it. Even cats! The dreadful strays he picked up. He bought them cream, not milk, even when he was broke."

Eve smiled at this. She found a picture of Louisa standing beside Donald, who was seated at a café table. Donald was gazing up at her and smiling.

"Donald, who's the woman with the short hair? She's lovely," said Eve innocently.

Donald seemed to weigh his response. "That would be Louisa," he said finally. "A cashier at Les Deux Magots."

"And . . . ?"

"And a friend. Also a writer. She wrote poems. Hundreds of them. She kept them in a trunk under her bed."

"Did she ever publish them?"

"Not that I know of. She was afraid to let anyone but me see her work. I tried to encourage her but I was not successful."

Eve gazed at a picture of Louisa and Donald on a boat. Louisa wore a blue and burgundy floral dress—a YSL, by the looks of it. Her head lay on Donald's shoulder and she grinned like a child. "Did you love her?"

"I would have died for her."

Eve let this sink in for a moment. "May I ask what happened?"

"Nothing."

"Please. *Please* tell me."

"She, Matthias, and I became inseparable. Matthias and I would spend all day at the café, then drive with her all night to the beach, where we'd wade into the waves and drink champagne while we watched the sunrise. We called ourselves the Three Musketeers, *les Trois Mousquetaires*. Whenever we met, we'd salute one another and proclaim 'All for one and one for all.'"

"Then what?"

"I made a fatal mistake: I fell in love with her."

"Did you tell her?"

"Not for a long time. I knew that Matthias had fallen for her as well, and I couldn't bear to hurt him. I hoped she would see my feelings in the stories I showed her, but she never did. Because of course they were rather incomprehensible. Nevertheless, I believed that she felt something for me. She used to darn my shirts and once she embroidered a little heart inside the collar that only I could see. And then there was the way she touched my arm when I was helping her with her poems. Now I look back on it and think it was just simpatico between writers, but then I was so sure . . ."

Eve got back up onto the bed, putting her teacup on the nightstand.

"And then I did the stupidest thing I could have done. I wrote her a letter, stating my feelings. It was a simple little thing; a child could have written it. I included a new kind of short story as well, a very honest, inelegant little thing. In the letter, I said if she felt anything for me, she should meet me that night, and that if she did not come, I would never mention it again. Can you imagine such a thing? But it was only worth risking our troika if she was as in love with me as I with her."

Eve drained the last of her tea and put her head on her pillow.

"You can guess where this is going. Louisa did not come and a few days later I found out why. She had agreed to marry Matthias."

"And you kept your promise and never mentioned it."

"Yes, I kept that promise. I should have fought for her; I see that now."

"But you wanted to honor your word. And be a good friend to Mr. Klieg."

"Ah, but you see, I was not a good friend. Matthias's first collection had been a failure and now I was glad. Yes! I was glad that he received not one order and had to go back to Germany for three years to work for his father. I could have offered to let them stay with me. But I couldn't face sharing Paris, let alone a room, with the two of them. Louisa went with him, of course. We kept in touch for a while but I couldn't stand the stab of my guilt that I hadn't done more for him. Finally I stopped writing back."

Eve hugged her pillow. "Did you ever see each other again?"

"Yes. Once. In the late sixties or early seventies. I had returned to New York by then, trying to start again, to climb the ladder of success into the clouds so I could forget everything else. But I went back to Paris for a symposium. Matthias and Louisa, with money and a new collection, were also back and we ran into each other at a café in the Fifth Arrondissement. The magic between the three of us had evaporated, of course. We held ourselves stiffly and our jokes fell flat. I think we were all relieved when it was over."

"Oh, Donald."

"So now, little one, you know the truth. If you've ever wondered what kind of man I was, what kind of life I lived that made me the kind of spirit I am . . . now you know. I tried to woo a woman who found me unlovable, which I was. I went behind my best friend's back to do so and let him down when he needed me most. You once said something was wrong with me, and you were right. When I had the luck of being alive, I wasted it being wretched."

Eve lay flat on her back, staring up at the ceiling. "You're too hard on yourself," she said.

"My only consolation is that Louisa chose Matthias. If she'd picked me, she would have become a widow far too early. . . ."

Before Eve could reply, she felt Donald's pulse grow weaker and weaker until finally he disappeared.

Outside, the dawn broke. The first rays of sun peeked in and she rose to close the drapes. Then she fell back into bed, pulling up the covers and curling herself around Highball, who licked away her tears with a tongue soft as an angel's wing.

Chapter 17

Eve received a call from the DA's office advising her that a plea deal had been reached in the Matt Buntwiffel case and that there would be no trial. He would be going to a psychiatric hospital in the new year, and all that would be required of Eve was signing some kind of document that she'd been notified of this fact. The man on the phone seemed to assume she'd be furious, but she could not bring herself to be.

"Thank you," she said before hanging up. She imagined Matt finally getting to unburden himself to someone about his childhood. Maybe he'd come to understand it, even free himself from it. What more could anybody ask for? Eve hung up and rubbed her arms with vigor to soothe the goose bumps that had suddenly risen.

. . .

She wrote her first increased rent check, for January, and to her horror found her bank account half depleted. Reality set in, a clammy feeling along her neck and shoulders. If she didn't find a source of regular income fast, she was going to have to leave the apartment. She shrugged on her coat and went down to the stoop to think.

She couldn't ask her father for money, couldn't ask him to finance her life in New York when what he wanted was to have her back home. Plus, even asking would be a giant step backwards. And Klieg? She wasn't sure yet what to do about him. She felt great sympathy for him yet what he'd done to Donald made her boil every time she thought about it, which she made sure never to do in Donald's presence. He was far too fragile now for anything like that, and she needed him to be strong for the memoir.

Good manners had dictated she send Klieg a thank-you note for Christmas. At the end she'd written, *What about this as a New Year's resolution: telling Günter everything?* Klieg hadn't replied. She wondered if she'd been too presumptuous. He might actually be annoyed with her now. Anyway, even if she could bring herself to ask Klieg for money—which would only prove to Günter that he'd been correct in his hideous assumption—and even if Klieg said yes, what could she ask for? A month's rent? Two? It was hardly a real solution.

That night, she went out for drinks with Quirine and Victor, just back from Paris. They told funny stories of Victor's American-style faux pas with Quirine's parents and Eve wished she could offer some charming anecdotes of her own, but she could only try halfheartedly to put a comical spin on her money troubles. Victor said he thought there might be a secretarial position opening up at Pratt in a few weeks and he'd see what he could find out.

The next day, Eve began pounding the pavement, hitting the bakery, the dry cleaner, and even a couple of law offices. Working in a law office again would be, in her mind, a horrible regression, yet if she got an offer, she would take it.

But no one was hiring.

．　．　．

New Year's passed quietly. Eve slipped into her mother's Malcolm Starr cocktail dress with its white silk bodice covered in jet beads over a full black tulle skirt and played fetch with Highball and twenty questions with Donald. In the process, she polished off an entire bottle of champagne, which knocked her out by eleven-thirty.

On January 2, she went back to job hunting, and it was as she ran a pen down the listings in the *Times* that she was struck with a thought that stopped her dead. The memoir. How much time did she have to get it done? At the rate she was going, she'd probably be able to make the February rent, but March looked sketchy. And if she was even a day late, De Fief would surely start proceedings to have her evicted. And that was if he did things the nice way. If not, she could find herself out on the streets within a matter of minutes, like the hockey boys who'd departed suddenly last April, leaving Highball behind.

The realization lit a fire under Eve. First, she informed Donald they'd be on a rigorous interview and dictation schedule. Then she bought a new set of pads and wrote down every anecdote Klieg had ever mentioned that involved Donald. She also visited the library almost every night, redoubling her efforts to learn about Donald's times and his contemporaries, both the famous and the forgotten, to understand where he fit in among them and within his era in general. When she finished all the books, she looked up newspaper articles on microfilm. You never knew where you'd find something important.

. . .

Eve arrived at Full Circle. "Hello?" she called out as she closed the door against the bitter wind outside.

"Hey!" Like a jack-in-the-box, Gwendolyn popped out of the alcove, her blond hair now topped by inch-long dark roots.

Eve clapped, overjoyed. "I'm so glad you're back!" She ran over to Gwendolyn and threw her arms around her and the two rocked back and forth for a moment, saying nothing.

When they parted, Gwendolyn ran the back of her fingers

briefly down Eve's cheek. "I've been feeling really bad. I wanted to invite you to come up to spend Christmas with us. I called a few times and your number just rang and rang. You weren't alone for the holiday, were you?"

"Actually, Mr. Klieg invited me over for Christmas dinner," said Eve. "It was an incredible evening."

They had fun pulling out red dresses and sweaters for a pre–Valentine's Day display and catching up with one another. Eve told Gwendolyn more about Christmas at Klieg's but not the revelations about Donald. Though she'd confided more than she ever thought she would about her family and her childhood and the feelings she harbored about both, there were some things that simply had to remain private. While Gwendolyn possessed an open heart and generous spirit, Donald presented a bridge even she would be unlikely to cross. And though Eve reasoned that she could probably invite Gwendolyn over and trust Donald not to reveal himself, she couldn't bear to make him keep quiet. After everything he'd been through, she wasn't about to make him feel like a pariah in his own home.

. . .

The bakery called her back offering a part-time counter and delivery position. It meant a lot of time out in the elements and didn't pay very well, but what choice did she have? She'd have to keep plugging and hope that something else came along. She told herself to be grateful that at long last, she finally had something.

. . .

It had been a long afternoon on her feet delivering cupcakes and turnovers, and Eve sank gratefully into a chair at the coffeehouse when her shift was over. She wrapped her hands around the steaming mug of tea and made her way through the papers that hung on wooden poles along the wall.

A *Post* headline trumpeted a name she recognized.

"BLISSFUL" JONES: MORNING ANCHOR SNAGS
RECORD-BREAKING CONTRACT

Good luck keeping up with the Bliss Joneses. The morning star has just signed a four-year, $60 million deal. Industry watchers had been wondering what, if any, fallout there would be from Jones's brief but oft-replayed embarrassment last fall, when she seemed to fall into a catatonic state while being skewered by Eve Weldon, a *Smell the Coffee* staffer who had just apprehended the knife-wielding mugger known as the Stiletto. (See latest on Buntwiffel, page 11.)

Now we know. Insiders say ratings for *STC* actually saw an uptick after the imbroglio, and the brass have evidently decided to reward Jones, who was reportedly threatening to bolt to NBC or CBS.

On an unrelated note, or so a spokeswoman assures us (wink, wink), the network has also announced job cuts to the morning show. Among those to be slashed: production assistants, graphic artists, secretaries, and writers.

How do you like that? Eve thought. *The writers finally got a mention.*

As soon as she got home, she left messages for Quirine and Russell, letting them know she hoped they were spared.

. . .

Eve set a demanding goal of ten pages a day; if they could do that every day till the end of February, when she might have to leave the apartment, she'd have a manuscript that she could take to an agent. Donald remained reluctant to share his more intimate secrets, but Eve finally hit on the idea of using her *Smell* interview methods to extract what she needed. She wrote down all her questions before their sessions and circled him back whenever necessary to make sure he answered each one.

This approach produced a couple of grumbles, but slowly, Donald ventured into the personal. He talked about his childhood in southern Illinois, the parents who fought and the father who left, the discovery of writing in high school thanks to an encouraging teacher, life typing up army reports during the Korean War, the guilt he felt at creating military propaganda, his disappointment when so many of the Beat writers he'd known abandoned New York for San Francisco, and his subsequent decision to move to Europe.

He shared his impressions of the twenty-one-year-old Klieg, who was a tormented soul when he arrived in the City of Light. His father had decided his son's interest in fashion meant he was gay, which had made him abusive. Klieg came to Paris to escape, and his deliverance into a circle of fellow artists constituted his salvation. Donald, a bit older, had been in Paris for a few years. He was just beginning to tire of it when he met Klieg at a dinner party, and he delighted in reexperiencing the city through the fledgling designer's wide eyes.

As for Louisa, she'd arrived in town with nothing but a suitcase and a few francs. A cousin got her the café job, but she had never dealt with customers before and suffered a couple of difficult months at the hands of the world's most discriminating diners. Donald and Klieg took the delicate-featured beauty on as their project, helping her make change when the café was busy and both learning something about humility in the process. Louisa returned the favor by giving Donald surprisingly sophisticated feedback on his stories and serving as Klieg's first fit model.

"How quickly did you sense that she would present a problem for you both?" asked Eve.

"It took some time," admitted Donald. "I actually believed, when it came to friendship, that three was a more solid number than two. Like three legs of a stool, we seemed more sturdy, more stable, as a trio. Each time two of us disagreed, we had a built-in mediator. One of the three of us always had money, or wine, or a better idea. Good moods became infectious; bad ones easily put down. If not for the jealousy of a heart in love, I would have been happy to go on that way forever."

Over the next few days, Donald spoke thoughtfully of Lars, René, and the others. How they'd escaped their own dreary towns to create a family of the like-minded in Paris at the dawn of a new era. The way he described his friends reminded Eve of how Dawn Powell portrayed her characters: He was witty, unsentimental, and though he often skewered them, it was obvious he loved them.

Donald widened his scope: Over the course of several sessions, he presented a detailed analysis of how the euphoria of victory that buoyed postwar Paris gave way to the acknowledgment of the genocide that had occurred on its doorstep. This, he said, had prompted the artistic community to seek new tools in order to express this incomprehensible reality. For Donald, it led to the development of his unique deconstructed style, a metaphor for how the old rules—for writing, for the world—had been rendered utterly moot, right under everyone's noses.

Eve's pulse began to hum within her. The combination of Donald's intimate stories of writers and artists he had known, plus this macro view of postwar culture, was unique. Add to that his own work, which was becoming deeper—and more honest— by the day. His dictation was colorful and concise, but now he welcomed her contributions as an editor and she was able to enrich and shape his work. This, she thought, hand racing across the page, was starting to feel like a real book.

· · ·

In the second week of February, Eve arrived home to a postcard from Klieg, postmarked Capri. It showed two empty beach chairs on a stretch of powder white sand in front of a glinting blue ocean.

Took your advice. Told Günter all. World did not end. Now we attempt old-fashioned family vacation but we are burned from the sun. We fly to Germany tomorrow, eager for clouds.

I hope you are well and that despite everything I may still count you as a friend.

—MK

Eve sat down on the stairs and fanned herself with the postcard, considering the question. It didn't take very long. The fact that she was so relieved to hear from him told her what she needed to know. They were still friends, she decided. Of course they were.

Klieg's infractions were long ago, and at some point, well, enough was enough.

. . .

Eve was enjoying her fifteen-minute break, sitting on a sack of flour in the back of the bakery, talking to the bakers and inhaling the scent of butter and cinnamon. As she finished her coffee, she flipped to the TV page of the *Daily News* and found the latest dispatch from her previous life.

OPPORTUNITY KNOCKS ANEW

We were the first to tell you how former network VP Orla Knock was forced out from her entertainment position in L.A. The good news: Her payout was apparently hefty enough to finance a new venture. Knock has announced the opening of OK Productions, based in Chelsea, which has just inked a deal to produce arts-related documentaries for PBS. Now's your chance to learn the secret history of zydeco music and go inside the Royal Danish Ballet. Must be nice to not have to work for "the man" anymore. Welcome back, Orla!

Arts programming, thought Eve. *Just like she wanted.* It was nice to know that being fired by the network didn't necessarily have to be the end of the world.

. . .

"Another two boxes came in," said Mrs. Chin. "Getting down to the dregs now, though. Mostly mimeographed literary neighborhood quarterlies." She handed Eve a pile of leaflets. "I'm not even sure if we'll shelve these, we might just store them. But you might as well have a look. And I'm told there's one last box coming. Should be here next week."

"Thank you," said Eve, pulling the stack across the counter toward her. "Do you happen to know the name of the collector?" Maybe he'd been someone Donald had known.

Mrs. Chin shook her head. "I don't. But I can certainly ask."

The literary quarterlies hardly qualified as "dregs"; in fact, they were charming. Though uneven, vulgar at times, they pulsated with the energy of the Village of the fifties and sixties. Some contained socialist rants, others racy limericks or cartoons. Many presented first-person accounts of dramatic encounters between writers at local watering holes: fistfights over women, births of minor political parties, authors getting into verbal duels of stunning technical virtuosity in front of agog onlookers.

An hour or so into her work, she came across Mike McGuire again. His name appeared in *The Free Voices Brigade, 3rd Quarter, 1965.* His name, and more than a dash of Donald's style. It was a series of spare, oblique poems about longing. She skimmed them before taking the leaflets to the copy machine, armed with a fistful of quarters.

She fed them in, one by one, and a realization took hold: Donald had possessed a genuine disciple. And if there was one, perhaps there were more. The fact that he might have had influence after all, despite what she'd read in that book so many months ago, could prove helpful in selling his memoir. Not to mention that Donald was someone who could tell you behind which bathroom tiles Chandler Brossard hid the only novel that was a worthy follow-up to *Who Walk in Darkness,* and who could also explain, from the inside, the machinations of how the Beat movement fed into the sixties counterculture in a two-continent, postwar movement that had taken the world by storm.

It was ten days until March 1, when the next rent check was due.

As the machine clicked and hummed, an idea formed in the air around her. A plan that could save them both.

Chapter 18

The cake was gorgeous. Inside, yellow sponge had been layered with fresh strawberries and real whipped cream. Outside, a perfect coating of white fondant, and red letters with flecks of sparkle in them, spelling out *Congratulations!* Even with her employee discount, it cost Eve twenty-two dollars. She hoped it would be worth it.

She exited the elevator on the eighth floor and followed the signs for OK Productions. Glass doors fronted the suite. Inside, there was the sound of hammers banging against walls and the smell of fresh paint. No one was at the reception desk, so Eve filed past it and down a wide hallway. At the end, she found the office she was looking for. She stood outside for a moment and took a deep breath before tapping the door with her knuckle.

"Yes?" came a familiar voice from inside.

"Delivery for Orla Knock," said Eve.

"Come in."

Eve stepped in, the enormous pink box shaking slightly in her hands. They locked eyes and Eve wondered if Orla would remember her. The question was answered immediately.

"You," said Orla.

"Yes."

"Eve . . . something, wasn't it?"

"Weldon. Yes."

There was a pause while this sank in. "You're delivering cakes now." Orla said this as though reading the absolutely fitting last line of a novel.

"Yes," said Eve, trying to affect more dignity than she felt. "But it's only temporary."

"Until when?"

Eve searched for some spin that would mitigate her embarrassment. "Until I don't have to anymore," she said at last.

Orla looked tanner for her time in Los Angeles and now sported an armful of silver bangles and large ropes of turquoise beads. But the West didn't seem to have dampened her essential New Yorkiness: Her persona still appeared to be clad head to toe in black.

Eve handed her a slip to sign for the cake. Orla scribbled her familiar signature and handed it back. "Who's this from? I don't see a card."

"It's from me," said Eve. She put the box on the corner of the desk as Orla looked at her quizzically.

"May I sit down for a moment?" asked Eve.

"Why?"

"I have something I'd like to discuss with you."

"I suppose. But I'm doing a conference call in about three minutes."

Eve took a seat. She gazed briefly around the bright corner office with its large windows on two sides and the many pictures resting along the walls, waiting to be hung. Boxes were stacked in the corners and an enormous corkboard burst with rows of Post-its and memos.

"I'll be brief, then," said Eve. "I've been reading about your new venture. And I have a proposal for you."

"You don't say," said Orla, betraying neither interest nor disinterest.

"I noticed that while your series has the visual arts covered, everything from commercial posters to architecture—and music, too—you're not doing anything on literature."

"Literature is inherently less interesting on television."

"Maybe. But the writers themselves are just as interesting—if not more—than any of the fine artists. For one thing, they're more articulate." Orla shifted in her chair but said nothing. Eve cleared her throat. "Anyway. I've come into possession of a rather important unpublished manuscript. By a writer present at one of the most significant cultural moments in modern memory, both in the United States and Europe." Eve summed up Donald's life and named some of the famous artists he'd known. She even explained about the connection between Klieg and Donald and that Klieg would most likely provide one heck of an interview about his old friend.

"The manuscript's got all kinds of illuminating, never-before-heard stories about lots of famous people. And it details hiding places of work that his New York writer friends weren't ready to show anyone. Under floorboards, behind mantelpieces, false bookshelves. So much, just waiting to be discovered. I've included a full list of what's likely out there."

"But how could one possibly verify something like th—"

"I've already made contact with the tenants over on East Seventh Street and Avenue D, and 14 St. Luke's Place, which were home to Herbert Huncke and Marianne Moore, respectively. The manuscript was absolutely right." Eve opened her shoulder bag and pulled out a folder containing copies of what she'd found. She handed them over to Orla. "It's a virtual treasure map."

There was a noncommittal silence as Orla leafed through the pages—notebook writings by Huncke, which described how he'd come up with the term "Beat generation," and a poem by Moore. "And just who did you say is the author of this astonishing manuscript?" Orla put down the papers.

"His name is Donald Bellows. Here's a short version of his

bio." Eve handed Orla a Xerox of his entry from the Village writers book. "This says his symbol-based approach was only a germ, but there's a good deal of undiscovered writing included in the memoir and I can assure you it went far beyond a germ. And he was the first to do it. Here are some samples, if you want to know what I'm talking about. And here's the work of one of his acolytes, a young man who sought to build on his ideas and encouraged others to do so as well." Eve handed over copies of everything, along with a complete proposal of what the documentary could cover.

Orla used the pages to fan her face. "And how did you come to possess this manuscript?"

"I found it in my apartment, which is where Mr. Bellows used to live. It was behind a panel in a cabinet. He died without family and with no estate. I've checked with a lawyer. I'm the rightful owner of this material."

Orla skimmed "Rock, Paper, Scissors."

"I think to be complete, your series, which I believe is called *Unknown Treasures,* should have something literary, which I realize is well-trodden territory," said Eve. Orla put the pages down on the desk with what looked like a bored expression. "But this would be something new, something the world has literally never seen before."

"And why do you care? What would you get out of this?"

"I want to work on it. I want to work for you."

"You worked for me once. Things didn't go so well."

This was the blow she'd been anticipating, and she was prepared. "Look, I made a mistake about the fish my first day, I admit. I was intimidated by everything at *Smell the Coffee.* I was new in town, in over my head, and afraid to say something in case I was wrong and looked stupid. But I earned my way into that department. You can ask anyone, even Mark. I'm a good writer, a quick study, and I work hard." She paused, looking down at the cake. "Even at this. You can call my manager at the bakery. The number's on the box."

Orla squinted at her.

"I've taken up enough of your time for today," said Eve, standing. She thought it best if she was the one to end this meeting. "But I'll be honest about something. I can't work for anyone else in television. Giles Oberoy has made sure no one will hire me. That's why I'm delivering cakes. He fired me for not kowtowing to Bliss Jones during our interview. It wasn't fair," Eve said, running her palms down the front of her thighs. She paused a moment. "Just like maybe them firing you wasn't fair."

She backed out and shut the door quietly behind her.

• • •

Nearly a week had gone by since their meeting and Orla hadn't called. Eve wanted to kick herself. Why had she been so stupid as to leave all that material behind? Even if Orla decided she liked the idea, she could just keep everything and do it herself. She had only pieces of the manuscript, but she had enough to work something out if she really wanted to.

In any case, Orla probably wasn't interested at all. That's what it usually meant when you didn't hear from people.

Eve drafted a new list of literary agents, but none was interested in seeing anything short of a full manuscript. And she and Donald weren't anywhere near done.

"Donald?" Silence greeted Eve as she entered her apartment. She trudged to her room, crawled onto the bed, and sandwiched her head between two pillows. She felt Highball jump lightly onto the mattress and lie down, pressing her warm, soft bulk into Eve's ribs.

So this was what the end looked like. It had been there all along really, just waiting for her to see it. This past year had been a masquerade, one long session of dress-up. But now it was time to take off the drapey dress, kick off the sloshy shoes, and admit it was over. Strangely, she thought as she moved the top pillow for some air, the moment didn't feel as bad as she'd thought it would. She might even call it a relief. It was clear now: Her time away from home had served the purpose it was meant to. To shake her out of her zombie-like malaise.

And home wasn't so bad! Those wide-open spaces. Family she had come to appreciate. It wasn't like she'd be going back with her tail between her legs. She wouldn't live in Rolling Links, for one thing. She'd move into the city. Gin would be so happy to have her back, he might even pay for grad school instead of law school. That way she could study writing. Working on the book, she'd been bitten by the bug. She wouldn't mind becoming an editor, either. Or she could get another job in television; after all, she hadn't been blackballed in the Midwest.

The next few days would be a time of goodbyes. Or would they? Undoubtedly easiest for everyone would be for her to simply slink out of town. It would be impossible to say goodbye to Gwendolyn face-to-face anyway. She'd never had a friend like her. For a moment, Eve contemplated moving to Queens or some other borough. At least they'd be only a subway ride from one another. But the thought made her shudder. The whole point had been to live in the Village.

Besides Gwendolyn, who'd really miss her? Klieg was all right now. He and Günter were still in Germany, spending time as a family with Klieg's brother, Henrik—they'd made up—and his wife, Claudia. They were having *eine wunderbare Zeit*, according to Klieg's latest postcard.

Quirine? She would be a little sad, but she and Victor were in major cocooning mode. Likewise Russell and Susan. Couples were different.

As for Vadis, the one who started it all, the one who talked Eve into believing she could make it here like the "thousands of others doing it every day"? Eve tried to wonder what Vadis was doing these days but couldn't bring herself to care.

And Donald. She literally could not imagine life without him. But he'd be fine without her, eventually. He acted as though he was excited at the thought of having his memoir published, but he was probably just going along because she was enjoying it so. If she left, he'd soon have a new tenant to harass. And now that he'd honed his physical skills, his fun would increase exponentially.

These things that she told herself swirled through her mind and acted on her like a sleeping pill, gently sucking away her instinct to struggle against fate.

. . .

She felt silly even sitting at the library. There was no way she could finish the stupid book. Even if she managed to complete it once she got back to Ohio, and even if she managed to find a publisher, she'd have no way of ever telling Donald.

"Did you ever get that last box?" she asked when she reached the front of the line at the desk.

"Been saving it for you," said Mrs. Chin. "Here." The box was smaller than the others, perhaps a foot square, but it had the same cavelike smell.

"Thank you," said Eve, picking it up. She turned to go, then remembered her question. "Did you ever find out who the benefactor was?"

"His name's on just about everything inside that box; you can't miss it." Mrs. Chin smiled with her lips pressed together, then went back to her paperwork.

Eve placed the box on her table and unfolded the four flaps of cardboard that latticed to make its top. Sitting inside were about a dozen soft-backed notebooks, all identical, with marbleized brown covers, black spines, and white labels containing dates. Before opening any of them, she put them in order. They spanned 1960 to 1969. She opened the first one: 1960, April–November. Inside the cover there was a label: PROPERTY OF.

Mike McGuire was the name scripted on the line provided.

Eve scooted her chair in closer to the table. Mike McGuire. Donald's disciple.

It was a thrilling moment until she realized with a thud that the man she'd hoped to locate—somehow—and interview, was dead. Nothing was going right anymore. She sighed, rubbed her forehead, and pulled out a pad to take notes.

The first notebook told the story of a young man deciding to move to Manhattan from upstate New York, the Finger Lakes region. He wrote about his well-meaning but stifling parents, the factory work he was expected to take on, just like his older brother, the friend who proposed they hitchhike down to the city for a wild weekend the summer after high school. A weekend that turned into a lifetime.

He started in a rented room on MacDougal Street. Apparently, he'd first seen Donald at the San Remo on Bleecker.

We go for the dollar salads and all the bread you can eat. The writers are there and their conversations are spontaneous art, like jazz, meant for public consumption. I don't know how they put themselves on display like that. I find myself looking at one more than the others. He has a short beard and a face that's alert. His eyes miss nothing, not even me in the corner.

And he seems to Get The Joke. You know? I hear he's a short story man. Experimental. A toothbrush as a symbol for the universe. What would Pa and his factory buddies say?

Mike McGuire had hoarded literary journals, looking for inspiration. It took him almost a year to work up the courage to write something himself, and when he did, it was like a gasket had sprung a leak. He couldn't stop. He even began to speak up at the San Remo.

Outside, the blue sky began to darken, and Eve hastened to cram in as much as she could. She couldn't bear to have to come back and finish another time. She read about Mike's invention of the "stoem": a combination of a short story and a poem. It was a somewhat unwieldy enterprise, with some lines rhyming and others not. He'd included several in his diaries and many of them resembled Donald's work at the time, but with heart. More like Donald was writing now. He wasn't as talented as Donald, of course, but his work was passionate.

Mike had died just a few months ago, more than thirty-five years after the final writings in the box. Donald said he'd gone traveling. Did he produce work somewhere else, or had he quit writing? And if so, why? If he'd kept at it, he might have gotten somewhere. Eve kept reading, jotting notes on her pad. She still had one more notebook to go when the library staff began to shuffle around, cleaning up for the night.

She brought back the box. "I'll be back tomorrow. For this last one."

"Not happening," said Hector, the tall and jowly evening manager. "They're going off to be photographed and catalogued in the morning. We should have them back in a couple of weeks, though."

Eve was just about to stammer something when Mrs. Chin came over. "Which one is it, dear?"

"This." She pulled it out of the box.

"I'll keep it for you. As long as you're back tomorrow. Can't hold off the hounds forever." Mrs. Chin gave Hector an elbow to his waist, which was as high as she came on him. He walked off muttering something about the decline of Western civilization.

. . .

As soon as she was done with her bakery shift, at five before seven, Eve was back at the library. Mrs. Chin was helping someone with a rather involved problem and slid the book at her without a word. Moments later, Eve was settled at her table, back in Mike's world.

He fell in love. He didn't write this, but she could tell. Suddenly, his obsession with other writers and his competitiveness with them subsided. They were replaced by a new appreciation for life's small joys. A spring day in Washington Square Park. A Lord & Taylor tie fished out of a bin at the Salvation Army. A marshmallow melting on top of a mug of hot chocolate. He stopped observing everything, and began starring in his own story. There were weeks, even months, when he wrote nothing at all.

Then he was drafted for Vietnam. And everything changed.

They didn't want to send him into battle; they wanted him to write propaganda. The campaign, to be printed on fake Vietnamese banknotes and dropped from aircraft above villages, was to engineer the destruction of the country's economy. He was told little more, other than that he would become part of "a long, noble history" of military psyops.

Even though the assignment would have saved him from combat, Mike refused. He refused because of Donald, because of the long shadow that propaganda writing had cast over Donald's life. Donald had said it was the worst thing a writer could do: to use his ability to deceive, to obfuscate. Mike supposed committing his body to fight in Vietnam was a form of lying, too, since it was not a war he agreed with. But it was more honest than using his God-given writing talent to do the opposite of what words were created to do, which was, he believed, to enlighten.

His girl did not understand. If he took the writing job, he would be in Washington, able to travel to New York often. And he would be safe! How could he abandon her for war when he didn't have to? She implored him to stay. She did his laundry, made him enormous lasagnas that lasted all week, anything to make his life in New York pleasant and comfortable. Unleaveable.

Two hours later, Eve had her elbows on the table, her chin on her fists, just pages from the end. Someone began to dim the lights on the far end of the floor, bringing her back to the present with a start. She wasn't about to give up the notebook for two weeks. She might not even be in New York that long. Eve took a look over her shoulder. An old man was dozing at the table behind her. She slipped the diary into her bag.

Walking with an air of self-assurance, she left the library without speaking to anyone. She hurried along West Tenth Street, under the streetlamps, not looking back.

. . .

Eve hopped onto the last available bar stool at the White Horse. The bourbon tasted rich and warm, like beef. It slid down her throat, all the way to her toes. The men on either side of her offered to buy it for her, offers she politely declined. She opened the journal, skimming hungrily through the last fifteen pages, written while Mike was stationed at Camp Lejeune.

And then, she got to the very end.

I deploy tomorrow.

She leaves, too. Leaves New York.

I've never written her name in these pages. I thought it would jinx everything. It's jinxed anyway.

Am I doing the right thing? Honor versus love. How childish of me to think I'm the first to face this choice, yet that's what it feels like.

Soon I'll be dodging bullets in a jungle.

Why? I ask myself a thousand times a day.

Because the alternative is intolerable.

I'll go east and she'll go west. Opposite directions, literally and figuratively. To that '50s throwback of a man who's crazy about her.

I could ask her to wait for me, but that wouldn't be fair. I might never come back.

Here's the kicker: After me begging all this time, she finally shows me something she's written. Written it just for me, isn't that swell?

A stoem of her own. The very idea of it breaks my heart.

Funny, isn't it? Even as I prepare to sacrifice everything for the honor of words, they have turned their backs on me.

They are but little fiends.

. . .

These were the last lines Mike had written. The only other thing in the diary was a yellowed piece of paper, tucked behind the last page. It was folded up into sixths and slightly curved, as if it had been wedged for a long time inside a wallet.

My Love,

Did you get the brownies? The gang had a fight at the Gaslight the other night about whether the army allows treats or whether they're considered contraband.

I guess you are about done with basic. Thanks for the picture. The short hair suits you, though the boys here would tease you mercilessly.

I know you're doing what you're doing because you believe it's the right thing. I can even agree.

Your sacrifice is to give up safety. My sacrifice is to give up you. I'm part of your fight, whether you see it that way or not.

Just as you're making the choice you can live with, so must I.

I can't live waiting for word about your fate. And I can't live in New York without you.

So I'm starting over, going back home. Try to think of it as a good thing. I'll be "taken care of," as you put it, and you won't have to worry. You can forget me and devote your energy to surviving.

I won't contact you again. Even if I change my mind. So you don't have to waste time hoping.

Yes, I'm doing the easier thing—and I know how much you hate that word! The least I can do is admit it to you.

I know I'll carry the guilt of this choice all my life. And yet the alternative is, to me, unbearable.

Until the great hereafter, when I pray I'll see you again, I leave you with a "stoem" of my own. I know it's not any good; consider it reflective of my mood.

PE

Untitled
I came upon a house of cards, full of jokers and kings. They made me afraid to gamble.
Till I met a wonderful jack. Named Mack.
You called me the girl with the Strawberry Eye, and plucked me from my fears.
I was through the looking glass—but finally everything was right side up.
Now you're leaving. I don't think you're playing with a full deck.
You're going to war; but aren't we worth fighting for?
You say I'm not brave. But I'm the one that you could save.
Now the house of cards is collapsing. I can't hold it up without you.
So I'm putting down my hand and away will I slink.
Raise a glass to me: I'm marrying a man named for a drink.

Eve read the lines again, this time softly aloud, feeling the weight of them in her mouth. The man next to her turned to look at her, but everything faded until all she heard was her heartbeat in her ears.

The reference to "Mack." The girl with the "Strawberry Eye" who married a man "named for a drink." It could only be Penelope.

Penelope had told her she'd loved someone before her father. It was Donald's disciple.

Mack had been the reason she'd loved New York so much, and the reason she'd left it. Done the easier thing, picked the sure thing—Gin. She'd given up on the city and herself.

Eve took another swallow of bourbon and swiveled in her seat. She wondered if Penelope and Mack had ever seen each other again. She guessed that they hadn't.

Penelope's decision to leave, made right here on this piece of paper, had changed her life. Her guilt over abandoning Mack, even if he had abandoned her first, and her regret over leaving New York, had haunted every single day. Eve and her brothers had suffered as a result. So had Gin, who lived with a woman who was always somewhere else.

Here in New York, Eve lived in the shadow of Donald's guilt. And Klieg's. Louisa had apparently lived a life of remorse, too, a life circumscribed by choices she'd made in her youth.

From each action stemmed collateral damage; who knew how much? If Penelope had stayed in New York, when Mack returned from war, he might have kept writing and might have perpetrated Donald's ideas. Penelope might have become a writer or editor herself, if Aunt Fern was right. And if Klieg had let Louisa make a true choice, what then? If she'd picked him, he could have lived in happiness. If she hadn't, he might have found someone else, someone who truly loved him. And if Donald had fought for Louisa, what kind of man, and artist, might he have become?

Donald, Louisa, Penelope. Each had seen dreams go up in smoke because they had done what was, in some way, easier. And each had died, if not *of* a broken heart, then certainly with one.

Sooner or later, somebody should learn from all these mistakes.

"Another for you?" asked the bartender.

Eve looked at herself in the smoky mirror over the bar. "No thanks," she said. "I'm all right."

. . .

It was March 1 and she had not sent in her rent check. She wondered what form De Fief's boom-lowering would take. A slow buildup of harassment? Or a quick strike of some kind? Her real concern was protecting Donald from any upset during whatever happened.

"I have a little surprise for you."

"Oh—hello." Eve hadn't felt him approach, but his tone indicated he had just arrived and hadn't heard anything. "What is it?"

"I've been keeping secrets from you. While you've been at the bakery, I've been doing a little work myself."

"What do you mean?" she asked, heading for the kitchen. She pulled a brioche from the breadbox.

Nothing happened for several moments. Suddenly, inside her head, she felt Donald's oscillations quicken, then disappear. A beat passed. Then two. Three. She looked around the room, eyes wide. Something in the corner caught her eye. It was one of Highball's toys, the ball that looked like a Christmas ornament, given to her by Günter. Had it just moved? Eve stared intently at the ball. It quivered. Then rolled. Slowly at first, then with purpose as if on an errand. As it passed Highball's nose, she jumped up and gave chase.

"Yes, the empty-headed one and I have had quite a time together these last weeks. I was concerned she'd be fearful but she wasn't. She seemed to sense instinctively that the force was friendly," said Donald. "I thought you'd like to know that when you're out, she's having some fun."

Eve's eyes misted over. Highball dropped the ball at her feet, smiling, but before Eve could reach for it, it sped off toward the bathroom. The dog ran after it.

"Thank you," said Eve.

They took turns throwing the ball until a panting Highball lay down in front of the fireplace with a pleased look on her face and Eve remembered her brioche.

. . .

That had settled it. That afternoon, when Donald disappeared, Eve prepared for one last "Hail Mary" bid to stay in the apartment. She opened the French doors to her closet and stepped inside.

The party dresses were in the best shape. She hadn't ever had much occasion to wear them. Most wouldn't even need to be dry-cleaned. She pulled a folded garment bag from the shelf over her shoeboxes and unzipped it in one quick motion, like removing a Band-Aid. She knew if she ruminated on every piece—the delicacy of this bodice, the reassuring volume of that tulle, or the memory of her mother wearing a particular cocktail dress as she sat in their garden gazebo deadheading the roses—she wouldn't be able to part with them. So, very swiftly, she ladled the silks, satins, feathers, and beads into the bag and zipped it up. She did this with three more bags, a total of twelve dresses in all.

"Wowsa," said Gwendolyn. She was wearing a sixties pop-art shift, yellow and green, which, along with her expression of exaggerated surprise, gave her the spirited air of a cartoon character. "This is stunning. Your mother really was amazing." She pulled the dresses out carefully and hung them on a series of hooks behind the counter, clucking and whistling all the way. Immediately, she began to check the important things: the labels, hems and seams, whether there was any discoloration of the fabric or loose sequins that needed to be resewn. "They're beautifully preserved. You really want to sell?"

"Yes."

"Wait a minute." Gwendolyn stopped what she was doing and turned to look at Eve. "Do you need money? Because I can lend you some. You *will* get another job eventually and you shouldn't have to sell off your birthright."

"I know that. And thank you. But I don't want help." This she meant. "Anyway, I need to free up some closet space."

"If you say so." Gwendolyn gave Eve a sideways look as she rubbed the fabric of a blue silk sundress. "Let me go through them and I'll give you a price as quick as I can. Okay?"

"Great. And thank you."

"Want to grab some lunch?" asked Gwendolyn, looking outside at the rain splattering against the front window. "With this weather, I've only had one customer today."

They left the *Back Soon* sign on the door and walked through the gale, umbrellas bumping, over to Greenwich Avenue. They sat in the window at Tea & Sympathy and tucked into a plate of little sandwiches.

"So," said Gwendolyn. "I passed."

"Passed what?"

"My last test. I'm done with all my business courses."

"That's marvelous! Why didn't you tell me when you went to take it? I would have wished you luck."

"Don't take it personally. I didn't tell anyone. I'm superstitious about that stuff."

"Really?" Eve leaned forward, chin in hand. "I wouldn't think superstition would stand a chance with someone as practical as you."

"It's kind of weird," said Gwendolyn, choosing a cucumber and cream cheese triangle. "But the older I get, the more sense I find in the nonsensical. I feel like the first half of life is about mastering the natural world. You know. Skills. Office politics. Trial and error. Blah, blah, blah. But the second half is about letting go, I think. Trusting that you've done the preparation but also that no amount of preparation can ever be enough. At some point, events will overtake whatever you've planned for and you just gotta deal."

They finished their lunch, and as they drank the last of the Darjeeling in the pot, an arrow of sunlight plunged through the clouds, illuminating their faces. Gwendolyn closed her eyes and basked in the sudden warmth. She looked so beatific that Eve followed suit.

"Guess I should get back to the store," said Gwendolyn, opening her eyes.

The rain had stopped and the streets appeared rinsed clean.

The sunshine seemed washed, too, and now shone clearer and brighter. Every window and puddle glinted.

"Aren't we two lucky girls?" said Gwendolyn as they strolled arm in arm. She drew Eve close, their upper arms pressed together. "To be young and healthy and living in Greenwich Village? What could be better?"

"Nothing," said Eve. A rush of feeling moved through her, momentarily taking her breath away. "Absolutely nothing."

. . .

De Fief's men knocked harder. They weren't buying that she wasn't home. Eve wondered if they'd been watching her, tracking her movements, and was grateful that at least Donald wasn't around, because this might get ugly.

Eve picked up the registered letter lying on her nightstand. It had arrived yesterday, March 4, not as quickly as she'd anticipated, but no less serious for that. The landlord was demanding immediate payment of March's rent, plus a five-hundred-dollar penalty for using the fireplace. How did he even know about that? She didn't remember seeing anything about that in the lease, not that she'd read it very carefully. So naïve was she a year ago. Failure to pay at once would result in eviction and/or legal action, De Fief warned.

The banging continued and Highball decided she'd had it. She rose from her spot at Eve's feet and made for the front door, barking.

"*Coming,*" shouted Eve, over the din. She picked up the check from Full Circle. It was signed by Gwendolyn and made out for twelve hundred dollars. Though she was paying a hundred dollars a dress, an extremely generous amount, it was still far from what the men were after. It was something, though. So why was it so difficult to part with? Eve guessed because it would mean her mother's dresses were really, truly gone. Taking them to the store had been only a step. Spending the money she'd gotten for them made it seem final. She tried to shake off these thoughts. The dresses were just yards of fabric; they were not Penelope.

She pulled the dressing gown around her tightly and tucked her hair behind her ears. With all the banging and the barking, she almost didn't hear the phone.

"Hello?"

"Eve?"

Eve pressed a hand to the ear without the phone. "I'm sorry, I'm having a hard time hearing you." The person spoke but again, Eve couldn't understand a word. "Who?"

"*Orla.*"

"Hang on, please." She took the phone into the bathroom, away from the banging and yelling, and closed the door. She perched on the edge of the tub. "Yes?"

"I've been thinking about your proposal," said Orla. "I have some problems with it."

"Uh-huh," said Eve, running her toe along the lines between the tiny black and white floor tiles.

"I have some concerns about its workability. And potential legal issues."

"Mmmm."

"However. They're concerns we should talk about here at the office."

"The office?"

"Well, if you're working for me, that would be the most convenient place."

"You're hiring me?"

"On a trial basis. To see if we can make this thing work."

"But I thought—I mean—"

"I wasn't going to. But I gave it some thought and realized your proposal has possibilities. I also came to the conclusion that between your exploits as a crime-stopper and your takedown of that prima donna Bliss Jones, you've shown gumption I didn't give you credit for. Now you're delivering baked goods, which shows humility and flexibility. Those are qualities I favor in an employee."

"I see."

"Then, as you suggested, I called Mark." Eve wrinkled her nose. That hadn't been a real suggestion. "He is not your biggest fan. And I got the feeling there was something he wasn't telling me. But he did admit that no one has a stronger work ethic. And he says you are skilled at both writing and interviewing. Extremely skilled, in fact." Orla paused. "He said, and I quote, 'Tell Toulouse I wish her well.' Mean anything to you?"

Eve felt a wave of gratitude for her former boss sitting in his little gray box uptown. "That was kind."

"So—when can you come in?" asked Orla.

It took about two minutes from when she hung up the phone until she had endorsed the Full Circle check over to De Fief. She slipped it under the door, though it took at least ten seconds before the goons even noticed. At last they stopped banging and she called out to them in a loud, clear voice. "I know it's not the full amount. But take it to show my good faith. And tell your boss he'll have the rest within the week." After several moments, she heard sounds of surprise and resignation before they shuffled off down the hall and Highball ran circles around the apartment, a victory lap celebrating her show of force.

Chapter 19

It had been a start-and-stop early spring, but finally the weather turned warm, as if someone important had snapped his fingers. Coats came off and cherry blossoms exploded on the Village's narrow streets.

Eve stood in the center of her closet, her brow furrowed in concentration. After the big sell-off, she didn't have many dressy dresses left. She slipped on a tea-length plum sheath and turned this way and that. Highball, lying on the bed, shook her head. No, it wasn't right. Too severe. She was just reaching for a pearl-bedecked cardigan to try to cheer the thing up when the buzzer rang.

"Messenger," came a crackly voice over the intercom.

"Be right there." Eve dashed downstairs, Highball at her heels. The messenger handed her a large, flat box and she signed for it. Back in the apartment, she placed it on her bed and opened the card.

> *Dear Miss Eve,*
> *Thank you for inviting me to celebrate your birthday this evening. I look forward to seeing you.*

Will you please accept this last-minute gift? I only now completed it.

Yours,

MK

Eve opened the box. Inside layers of tissue embossed with the "double K" Klieg logo reposed a little black dress. Simple, flapper-style, with a detachable rosette, it fit her exquisitely. Her very own Klieg original, the most elegant hug in the world.

She hoped this meant he was working again.

"What do you think?" Highball nodded approvingly while Eve slid into a pair of kitten heels.

She looked down at her watch and realized she was late. She threw a wrap around her shoulders and stopped for a long moment in the doorway. She took a last look around before closing the door quietly behind her.

. . .

It was Saturday night at El Faro. The restaurant fizzed like a scene in a Dawn Powell book, with pairs of women in red lipstick threading their way to the ladies' room, eyes glinting with gossip; men telling tall tales, eliciting hoots of laughter; and waiters kissing their favorite customers at the door while carrying dozens of drinks on trays high overhead.

Klieg caught sight of Eve making her way across the room and stood. "There she is," he said, waving. Eve made her way to the table and lost herself inside his bear hug. The wool of his jacket felt like silk against her cheek, his arms surprisingly strong as they encircled her. She felt his chin rest lightly atop her head. "Hello, my dear," he said.

"Hello," she whispered into his tie. Eve's eyes were closed, and when she opened them, she saw the rather startled expressions of everyone at the table: Gwendolyn, Quirine and Victor, Russell and Susan, and . . . Günter.

"He wanted to come," whispered Klieg. "And I thought he could meet some people his own age. I hope it is all right?"

"Of course it is. And thank you for the dress. It's lovely. And so comfortable," she said, winking at him.

It was the first time that she'd assembled a group of New Yorkers, and as Eve introduced everyone she crossed her fingers that they would enjoy one another. She was tickled to see Gwendolyn and Quirine stammer slightly as they leaned across the table to shake Klieg's hand. *"Enchanté,"* said Quirine with feeling.

The waiter arrived to inquire about their orders. Heads tipped over menus and polite conferring ensued. Günter consulted with Quirine in what sounded like perfect French. In the end, they decided on paella for eight.

As she handed her menu in with the others, Eve turned to her former colleagues. "When we talked, you guys weren't sure yet if you'd be safe from the layoffs. How did things shake out? Are you both okay?"

"We are," said Russell. "Cassandra and Steve have less seniority. They're staying, though. It's Quirine who's leaving."

"What?" said Eve, incredulous.

"I'm sick of working nights," said Quirine. "And asking people if they would mind wearing blue contact lenses or covering a birthmark with makeup. So I'm going to follow my dream of being even more overworked and underpaid: I start at Pratt in the fall." She turned to Victor. "This one and I are going to get very sick of each other," she said, kissing him.

"Studying what?" asked Eve.

"Fashion design," said Quirine. "They have a new Eco program. Only sustainable fabrics."

"I have heard about this," said Klieg. "Does the quality approximate traditional textiles?"

"From what I've seen, yes. But I'd be happy to update you once I get started."

"Thank you. And please let me know if I can be of any assistance," said Klieg. "I know some of the faculty."

Quirine looked like she'd just found a thousand dollars in the couch cushions. "Thank you," she said.

"And you?" asked Eve, turning to Russell. "What will you do without Quirine there?"

"Kill myself," he said good-naturedly.

"You must tell me how on earth creative people make a living today," said Klieg. Eve was surprised to see him so open to new people. When she'd first met him, he was almost sullen around strangers. Now he was practically chatty. "When I was young, one could be a painter, a writer, anything—even if one was poor. So many cafés and other businesses took pride in helping out young artists, extending them various courtesies. But from what I've seen of today's New York, you are all very much on your own."

The others agreed, lamenting the difficulties of being young and artistically minded in the big city.

"Would you mind telling us something about your Paris days?" asked Gwendolyn as she took a piece of warm bread from the wire basket being handed around. "I hear from Eve you've known some extraordinary people."

"Oh yes, please," said Susan.

"If you like." Klieg took a sip of water and began. "I thought I knew what I would find in the City of Light, but it outpaced all my expectations. I remember the moment I disembarked the train. . . ." He paused every few minutes as if to see whether he was retaining the table's attention, but everyone only nodded encouragingly.

Once or twice, Eve noticed, Günter prompted his uncle with details he'd forgotten or otherwise amplified on Klieg's tales. Apparently, he knew them now. Eve watched Günter closely for a moment. When he was happy, his face completely changed. His deep blue eyes appeared lit from within and there was a charming guilelessness in his expression she hadn't seen before.

The paella arrived, an enormous pan of gold in the middle of the table. As Eve helped herself to clams and mussels, she smiled to herself, thinking of bouillabaisse.

"You've been so evasive lately. What have you been up to?" asked Quirine as she sliced some chorizo.

"I wanted to wait until we were face-to-face to tell you this," said Eve. She took a sip of rioja. "I'm working for Orla Knock."

Quirine's and Russell's heads jerked back in surprise and Eve filled them in on the documentary, which Orla had agreed to produce. Eve was doing interviews, writing, and research, including tracking down as many hidden masterpieces as she could. Not all of the homeowners she approached could be called enthusiastic. Some wouldn't even take the time to listen; they were simply, like all New Yorkers, too busy. Others had no idea they shared a home with someone famous. "Didn't you notice the plaque outside your front door?" Eve would ask. Of course, they hadn't. A few were skeptical about the proposed hunt for lost material. "I'd love to, dear, but we just had the floors done. . . ."

But others were more accommodating. One family allowed her to poke through Willa Cather's basement, and another, Ted Joans's attic.

Even better, next week Eve was to visit the tenant at the East Tenth Street apartment where Dawn Powell had written *The Happy Island*. She could never tell anyone what that experience would mean to her. Nor could she tell them about a silly but irresistible fantasy she harbored: that if she lingered in the home long enough, if she was very quiet and listened very closely, maybe, just maybe, Dawn would speak to her. What she would want to tell her! And what questions she'd love to ask!

"Very cool," said Russell. "A little more interesting than 'how to exercise your goldfish,' eh?"

"If only you didn't have to work for the dragon lady," said Quirine.

"She's not so bad." Eve lifted a shrimp to her mouth and

chewed it thoughtfully. "I mean, she doesn't exactly hand out gold stars, but she's teaching me a lot. And . . ."

"What?" asked Quirine.

"She gave me an advance on my salary before I even started. Otherwise, I would have had to give up my apartment."

"Wonders . . . ceasing . . . apparently never," said Russell.

Eve answered the rest of their questions, but hugged one secret to herself. She was going to share it with only one person, and not until later. She had sent Donald's now-completed manuscript out to several publishers, explaining that the memoir was to form the backbone of a nationally televised documentary. Today she had gotten letters back from two university presses, expressing interest in publishing it. Who knew? There might even be a bidding war.

· · ·

The candles on the table burned down, the flames faltering as they consumed the last specks of wick. Günter was telling Eve about the arthropods of Capri, speaking in yards and yards of full sentences. His manner was limber, his gestures fluid. He even made a joke about tarantulas, which eluded Eve completely. She laughed anyway, though, because he was so funny as he told it.

"Have you ever been to the Sorrentine Peninsula?" he asked.

"No. I haven't traveled much. Just one trip to France as a child," said Eve. "I'd like to go back, very much."

"Then I am sure that you will," said Günter.

"And you?" asked Eve. "Won't you be leaving soon? I thought your uncle said your year at Plum Island is almost up."

"Yes. I am not sure what I shall do next. I have an offer back in Germany, but also the opportunity to join a practice here in Manhattan."

"You have a big decision to make," said Eve.

"I do," Günter said quietly.

Busboys shuffled by with stacks of plates while bartenders

dried wineglasses before sliding them onto overhead racks, where they clinked rhythmically.

"Think they want to get rid of us?" asked Susan, reaching for her purse under the table. "Where next?"

"I know," said Eve.

. . .

"What are you doing, my dear? Are we breaking into someone's home?" asked Klieg as Eve pushed open the unmarked door of Chumley's. She enjoyed watching the comprehension dawn on his face as he took in the hive of drinking and debate.

They slid into the same booth as the first night Eve had spent in New York, still carrying on their conversations from the walk over. Russell and Victor invited Günter to go fishing somewhere in the Bronx, while Quirine tried to explain her "look" to Klieg. The two of them asked for extra napkins so they could draw silhouettes with Klieg's fountain pen. Gwendolyn and Susan, it turned out, had gone to the same high school. Sitting directly across from Eve, they reminisced about their dreadful biology teacher.

"Did you see that piece in the *Times*?" Eve asked. "About the latest school board battle between biology and creationism in the Bible Belt? Sounds like they're going to have to call in the National Guard."

"I saw that," said Susan. "I'm sure, with Quirine gone, Russell will be on that any day now."

Later, the room began to empty and they didn't have to raise their voices quite so much. "Have any of the dresses sold?" Eve asked Gwendolyn, not sure she wanted to hear the answer.

"I was wondering when you were going to ask that." The room was warm and Gwendolyn's cheeks were flushed. She pushed up the sleeves of her cardigan.

"Well?"

"Nope."

Eve raised an eyebrow. "None of them?"

"Uh-uh."

"Not even the gold sheath? With the lace bolero?"

Gwendolyn shook her head.

"How strange." Eve swirled the bourbon around the glass, listening to the ice cubes clink. It was the last thing she'd expected to hear.

"Not that strange."

"Why not?"

"Because I never put them out."

"What?"

"They've been in the vault downstairs since you brought them in."

"Why?"

"Those dresses belong with you. It's their happy ending. You can buy them back anytime you want. All at once, one sleeve at a time, whatever you can manage."

Eve laid her arm along the table, palm up. "Thank you," she said.

Gwendolyn slid her own palm along it lightly. "No problem."

    • • •

As she sat listening to everyone, Eve's gaze fell to the table and the jumbled pattern of carved initials, the very ones that had helped trigger her déjà vu the previous year. They covered the surface so completely it was difficult to separate them. Some were beautifully done, almost like calligraphy, others quite crude.

RS

ML

JR ♥ *DB*

And then she saw a pair of initials, right next to her highball glass, half an inch high, filled in with black ink: *PE*

P for Penelope . . . *E* for Easton. Could the initials belong to her mother? Could she have carved them herself? Or perhaps

Mack had done it, since Penelope herself had not exactly been the penknife type.

They probably weren't hers at all. So many years later, with so many who'd sat at these tables in the interim, what were the odds?

Still, Eve ran her index finger lightly over the letters. Then she pressed hard so that her skin sank deep into the grooves.

. . .

The bartender announced last call.

During the round robin of goodbye hugs, Quirine and Victor invited everyone to a housewarming party at their new apartment on West Ninth Street the following weekend. They'd be only four blocks from Eve.

Shyly, Quirine looked up at Klieg. "I don't suppose you would like to come, too? I would be most honored."

"If you don't mind an old man's company," he said, and Quirine responded with some soothing-sounding French, which resulted in Klieg bending down to kiss her lightly on the cheek.

Everyone melted away until the bar stood empty except for Eve, Klieg, and Günter and a waitress wiping down tables. They sipped the last of their brandy, speaking in low voices, husky from a long evening's use.

"If you'll excuse me . . ." Klieg departed toward the men's room, shoulders sagging slightly.

Eve's chin rested on her palm and she swayed to the music although the jukebox had long since stopped playing.

Günter leaned in and softly cleared his throat. "This party next weekend. Perhaps we could attend together?"

Eve looked at him in surprise. "Yes," she said, finding that she was smiling. "We could do that."

. . .

The sky was just beginning to shed its black for violet as they hailed a taxi to take Günter to Penn Station and the first train of the day out to Long Island, where he had an early meeting at the lab. It pulled to a stop in front of them and the three stood looking at one another. Günter gave Eve an awkward but sincere hug and, behind him, she noticed Klieg's look of surprise give way to pleasure. Günter hastily shook his uncle's hand and got into the cab. They watched him pull away.

"I could use some fresh air. Would you mind walking a little?" asked Eve.

"Please," said Klieg.

They headed out to the Hudson, and then north along the water, not speaking. The streets were empty and the city hovered over them, ancient and silent.

"Did you enjoy the evening?" asked Eve. "You seemed preoccupied at times."

Klieg's gaze fell to his feet as they crunched over some gravel. He sighed. "It was delightful, my dear. But also a little painful."

"Why?" she asked, looking up at his profile silhouetted against the weak light of the stars.

"It reminded me of so many nights, so long ago. When I, too, was young." The purple light around them faded to pale silver. The surface of the river stirred gently as if waking.

"Paris," Eve said.

"Yes." Klieg ran his eyes over the water. "Tonight it came back to me in the most visceral fashion. In the faces of your friends, I saw my own. In their voices, I heard echoes of my comrades. In their laughter, I heard my very youth. It was like seeing a cherished photo in a different frame. Still beautiful, but the context is somehow all wrong."

The water rose higher now and fell, sending waves onto the shore. Droplets danced on their skin, turning it blue-green.

Eve tucked her arm through his. The moon dipped below the western horizon and they turned inland, toward the first glow of the sunrise, across the cobblestones and past the keening old buildings.

"Knowing you all these months, talking as we have, has been

so good for me. Because of you, I have my family back, and they are a great comfort." He gave her arm a squeeze. "Yet the pangs for my youth do not die. I am still pained by the knowledge of what I had and what I lost. The sin for which I can never atone." One by one, the streetlamps that stretched before them went out, like candles extinguished by an unseen hand. "In the end, we are all alone," he mused. "Donald said that once and I didn't believe it. Now I do."

The wind sighed. Around them the cherry trees began a languid dance. They continued past the wrought-iron gates and the bursting flower boxes. Her front stoop rose up before them. Eve took Klieg's hand just as the sun peeked over the nearest tenement and threw their shadows long over the slate sidewalk.

"This is where I live," said Eve. She pointed to the red brick, glowing yellow in the new light. "You see that spot?" Klieg nodded. "Next month the city's going to put a plaque there, next to the front door, commemorating Donald's life and work."

"Really? How is that?"

"I applied for it and the Landmarks Preservation Foundation approved." Klieg looked at her. "You thought that because of what you did, the world lost Donald. But Donald isn't lost. Not really," said Eve.

"He would have been so pleased," Klieg whispered.

"Yes, he will be," said Eve.

The wind picked up and the trees began to laugh. They shook merrily, letting go the blossoms in their hair and turning the sidewalk into a flower girl's trail.

"*It is as if the world mirrors their happiness; nature herself celebrates the improbability and purity of their friendship,*" murmured Eve. She climbed two steps and turned to face Klieg, eye to eye.

"What, my dear?"

Her heart beat fast. "Would you like to come in? For some coffee?"

He looked at her in surprise. "Are you sure that's a good idea?"

"Why wouldn't it be?"

"Because of the damage."

"What damage?"

"Why, from the fire you suffered recently."

Ah. Eve pushed some blossoms off Klieg's shoulder. "That's all fixed now."

"You know," he said, coming up a step. "The next time one of these accidents befalls your flat, you really must stay with me."

Eve shaded her eyes from the sun. "Actually, I don't think I'll be having so many accidents in the future."

"That is good news. May I assume things are going better for you these days?"

"Yes. Much."

"You've had some difficulties this past year. Perhaps your time has come at last."

Eve exhaled. "Maybe it has."

"Perhaps you will tell me about it? I do feel as if we've spent an inordinate amount of time discussing me. Perhaps I can learn a little more about you sometime? I seem to remember you once saying your mother admired my work. I would very much like to hear about her as well."

Eve smiled. "I would love that." Pink and orange flames licked the sky overhead. "So," she said, nodding toward the door. "What about it?"

Klieg glanced down the street. "I am not sure. I am an old man, tired. I should find a taxi."

"But it's dawn. Time for *le café pour trois.*"

Klieg nodded wistfully. "Ah yes. A shame there are only two of us."

Around them, sound drained. Colors deepened. A bird cried and flew out of a tree.

"Actually, there's someone who wants to see you," said Eve.

Klieg's brow creased, soft bewilderment playing across his features. "At this hour? Whatever can you be talking about?"

Eve took his hand in both of hers. "Remember Christmas Eve?"

"Yes . . ."

"When I told you that everything was going to be all right?"

"Yes."

"Well, it is. You'll see."

"If you say so, my dear." Then he shook his head and straightened his back. "In fact, it is a fine idea. I could use some coffee. And I am curious to see where you live." He looked up, tipping his head back slightly, taking in the building once more. "So, this is your home."

"Yes," said Eve, with a small shrug. "This is me."

Acknowledgments

To the many who held a flashlight as I embarked on the some-times murky path of writing fiction for the first time:

First, to Jessie Sholl, peerless leader, and the rest of my won-derful workshop: Paulina Porizkova, Shizuka Otake, Rashmi Dalai, Melissa Johnson, David Simonetti, Chelsea Ferrette, and Angie Mangiano. I am grateful for your friendship and insight, and the fact that you all live "in town."

To my incomparable agent, Susan Golomb, for crucial guid-ance and for being such fun.

To my delightful editor, Jen Smith, for her keen eye and kind ways.

Also to Jane von Mehren for her support, and to the incredi-ble team at Ballantine, including Melissa Possick, Sharon Prop-son, and Leigh Marchant.

To Pat Mulcahy for her expertise.

Special mention to my remarkable colleagues in television news over the years—especially the writers—for making the dream job of my childhood a dream job in actuality.

To Don B., who once called my apartment home and who, from beyond the grave, provided delicious inspiration, if no ac-tual bumps in the night.

And to Charley McKenna, who gave me more words of en-couragement than are in this book, and whom I love more than words could ever say.

PHOTO © LISA CASE

LORNA GRAHAM was born in the San Francisco Bay Area and graduated from Barnard College. She has written for *Good Morning America* and *Dateline NBC*. She also wrote a short film, *A Timeless Call,* honoring America's military veterans, that was directed by Steven Spielberg. She lives in Greenwich Village.